Student Activities Manual

Interacciones

FOURTH EDITION

Student Activities Manual

Cuaderno de ejercicios / Manual de laboratorio

to accompany

Interacciones

FOURTH EDITION

Emily Spinelli
University of Michigan-Dearborn

Carmen García
Arizona State University

Carol E. Galvin Flood
Bloomfield Hills (Michigan) Schools

THOMSON

HEINLE

Australia Canada Mexico Singapore Spain United Kingdom United States

Interacciones, Fourth Edition, Student Activities Manual
Emily Spinelli, Carmen García, Carol E. Galvin Flood

Printed in the United States of America
   5 6 7 8 9 10   06 05 04

For more information contact Heinle, 25 Thomson Place, Boston, MA 02210 USA,
or you can visit our Internet site at http://www.heinle.com

For permission to use material from this text or product contact us:
Tel   1-800-730-2214
Fax   1-800-730-2215
Web   www.thomsonrights.com

ISBN: 0-03-033974-X

Contents

Manual de laboratorio

Preface

The **Student Activities Manual** containing the **Cuaderno de ejercicios** and **Manual de laboratorio** is an integral part of the **Interacciones** program. Both the workbook and the laboratory manual provide exercises that parallel the sections of the student textbook as well as provide additional sections for skill development and improvement of accuracy. An answer key is provided for the exercises of the **Cuaderno de ejercicios** and **Manual de laboratorio.**

The **Cuaderno de ejercicios** is designed to develop the writing skill. To that end there are exercises and activities for three types of writing. The mechanical exercises or drills teach spelling and the formation of verb forms and tenses, adjective and noun endings as well as word order and syntax. There are numerous exercises and activities that simulate writing tasks performed by native speakers. Filling out forms, writing e-mail messages, notes and letters, composing ads and brochures, taking messages, and making lists are a few of the activities that would be performed by persons living, traveling, or working in the target culture. Lastly, there are exercises that prepare students for writing for academic purposes. Combined with the writing strategies and composition topics of the student textbook, the workbook exercises and activities provide a well-rounded and varied writing component.

Every two-chapter unit in the student textbook begins with a section entitled *Bienvenidos,* which presents geographical and cultural background knowledge pertaining to the Hispanic region covered within the next two chapters. Students practice using this information in the **Cuaderno de ejercicios.** Each chapter of the **Cuaderno de ejercicios** is divided into three sections: *Primera situación, Segunda situación,* and *Expansión de vocabulario.* The first two sections provide written practice for the vocabulary, functional phrases, and grammar taught in the student textbook. The *Expansión de vocabulario* consists of two parts: *Dudas de vocabulario* and *Ampliación.* The *Dudas de vocabulario* section provides definitions and examples of vocabulary items that are similar in meaning or spelling and cause particular problems for students. The words chosen are related to the overall chapter situation or topic. Contextualized cloze exercises provide practice with these vocabulary items. The *Ampliación* section consists of a strategy and exercises devoted to the acquisition of new vocabulary. Information on cognate recognition, prefixes and suffixes, word families, and word building is presented to help students guess the meaning of vocabulary items never before seen and to increase their vocabulary for written production. Exercises for learning the material follow each strategy. The **Clave de respuestas** for the writing exercises of the workbook is placed near the end of the **Student Activities Manual.**

The **Manual de laboratorio** and its accompanying audio cassette or CD program are designed to develop the listening skill and improve pronunciation and accuracy in speaking. Each chapter is divided into a *Primera* and *Segunda situación* with exercises that practice the vocabulary, functional phrases, and grammar of the corresponding textbook chapter and *Situación.* Both listening and speaking exercises are provided.

The many listening passages of the **Manual de laboratorio** contain authentic language and are based on the material taught in the textbook chapter. Students carry out listening tasks similar to those performed by native speakers in a variety of passages: telephone conversations, weather reports, commercials, public announcements such as those heard in stores, airports, and train stations, and so on. Exercises to check comprehension follow.

Each chapter of the textbook includes a listening strategy that provides the student with techniques to help improve listening comprehension in the target language. These strategies are practiced in the student textbook and reinforced in the **Manual de laboratorio** through listening exercises based on monologues, dialogues, or narratives. A section on pronunciation is also provided in each *Situación*. Explanation and practice of the production of individual Spanish sounds as well as intonation and accentuation are given.

The **Clave de respuestas** for the listening and speaking exercises is placed near the end of the **Student Activities Manual** following the **Clave de respuestas** for the workbook. The **Vocabulario inglés-español** for the **Interacciones** program concludes the **Student Activities Manual.**

E. S.
C. G.
C. G. F.

Student Activities Manual

Interacciones

FOURTH EDITION

Cuaderno de ejercicios

To the student

The following suggestions will help you use the *Cuaderno de ejercicios* most effectively.

1. In order to write effectively, you must have a good vocabulary base. It is not enough just to be able to recognize vocabulary items when you see or read them. You must know the vocabulary for each chapter so that you can recall and write the words.

2. Complete the *Primera situación* in your *Cuaderno de ejercicios* after completing the corresponding *situación* in your student textbook. Then, complete the *Segunda situación* after completing that *situación* in your textbook.

3. The *Expansión de vocabulario* can be done at any point after completing the *Primera situación* and *Segunda situación*. This section will provide you with vocabulary help for completing the readings, compositions, and activities in the *Tercera situación* of each chapter in your student textbook and is best done prior to completing that *Tercera situación*.

4. Writing frequently for short periods of time is the ideal way to improve the writing skill. Likewise, completing the writing exercises in the workbook soon after doing the speaking exercises in your textbook is the ideal way to reinforce the expressions and grammar taught.

Capítulo preliminar

Un autorretrato

A.   Un autorretrato. *Para trabajar en la Compañía Excélsior, los trabajadores necesitan describirse a sí mismos. Escriba un autorretrato para las tres personas del siguiente dibujo. Incluya información sobre sus pasatiempos favoritos.*

El señor Galván

La señorita Hernández

El señor Ruiz

El Sr. Galván ——
——
——
——

La Srta. Hernández ——
——
——
——

El Sr. Ruiz _____

_____

_____

_____

B.   Un(-a) estudiante de intercambio. *Ud. es un(-a) estudiante de intercambio (exchange) en Madrid. Antes de recibir su carnet estudiantil, Ud. tiene que llenar (to fill out) el siguiente formulario para la universidad.*

Apellido(s) _____   Nombre(s) _____

Dirección _____

Ciudad _____   Estado _____

Teléfono _____

Lugar de nacimiento _____

Nacionalidad _____

Fecha de nacimiento _____   Edad _____

Estado civil _____

Profesión _____

Descripción física _____

Talla _____

Ojos _____

Pelo _____

Señas personales _____

Especialización _____

Pasatiempos favoritos _____

C.   La primera fiesta. *Es su primera fiesta en la Universidad de Madrid. Ud. decide hablar con otro estudiante nuevo. Complete esta conversación con las frases o preguntas necesarias.*

1. USTED: Me llamo (su nombre).

¿ _____ ?

ÁLVARO: Soy Álvaro Guzmán.

Nombre _____ **Fecha** _____ **Clase** _____

2. USTED: ¿ _____ ?

ÁLVARO: Soy de Ávila.

3. USTED: _____ , ¿dónde está Ávila?

ÁLVARO: Es una ciudad cerca de aquí.

4. USTED: ¿ _____ ?

ÁLVARO: Estudio ingeniería.

USTED: ¡Qué bien! Yo estudio _____ .

5. USTED: ¿ _____ ?

ÁLVARO: En un apartamento cerca de la universidad.

6. USTED: ¿ _____ ?

ÁLVARO: Me gusta ir al cine y también juego mucho al tenis. ¿Y tú?

USTED: _____

_____

_____

D.   Unos números. *Escriba los siguientes números en español usando la forma de una palabra cuando sea posible.*

> ➢ *MODELO*   18
>   **dieciocho**

1.   9 _____   **7.**   22 _____

2.   14 _____   **8.**   36 _____

3.   7 _____   **9.**   23 _____

4.   12 _____   **10.**   46 _____

5.   20 _____   **11.**   75 _____

6.   18 _____   **12.**   61 _____

E.   El inventario. *Ud. trabaja en la residencia para estudiantes de intercambio en la Universidad de Madrid. Ud. tiene que preparar el inventario (inventory) para el fin del año. Escriba el número de artículos en los espacios dados.*

1.   14 _____ camas

2.   81 _____ escritorios

3.   173 _____ sillas

4.   68 _____ alfombras

5.   26 _____ teléfonos

6.   121 _____ almohadas

F.   ¿Qué hora es? *Ud. trabaja en una estación de televisión que siempre anuncia la hora en forma escrita. Ud. tiene que programar la computadora para que dé las horas. Escriba las siguientes horas en español.*

1.   3:20 A.M. _____

2.   10:45 P.M. _____

3.   4:30 P.M. _____

4.   1:05 A.M. _____

5.   8:23 P.M. _____

G.   Verbos regulares. *Usando el tiempo presente de los infinitivos, escriba las formas que corresponden a los sujetos.*

➤ **MODELO**   llegar: él
                              él llega

llegar

tú _____   yo _____

Felipe y yo _____   Ud. _____

ellas _____   el profesor _____

comprender

Enrique _____   Uds. _____

yo _____   nosotras _____

Carlota y Francisco _____   tú _____

Nombre _____ **Fecha** _____ **Clase** _____

vivir

tú _____   los estudiantes _____

la Sra. Ruiz _____   tú y yo _____

yo _____   él _____

H.   Unos pasatiempos. *Explique a qué hora las siguientes personas hacen varias cosas.*

➤ *MODELO*   Mariana / tocar el piano / 9:00
Mariana toca el piano a las nueve.

1. Anita y Jorge / comer en el café / 12:30

_____

2. tú / escribir cartas / 1:00

_____

3. Miguel y yo / charlar / 3:00

_____

4. yo / leer el periódico / 7:30

_____

5. Uds. / bailar en la discoteca / 10:00

_____

6. Gloria / regresar a casa / 11:15

_____

I.   Mis pasatiempos favoritos. *Julio(-a) Villarreal, un(-a) amigo(-a) suyo(-a), vive en Lima, Perú. Escríbale una carta de 9–10 oraciones explicándole sus pasatiempos y cuándo los hace. Incluya por lo menos los siguientes verbos.*

asistir   celebrar   leer   participar
bailar   charlar   mirar   viajar

_____ :

_____

_____

_____

_____

_____

_____

_____

_____

_____

_____ ,

A recordar

Review the following situations and tasks that have been presented and practiced in this chapter.

- Describe yourself and others.
- Find out basic information about others.
- Provide basic information about yourself.
- Count from 0–100; provide addresses, telephone numbers, ages.
- Give the time of day; explain at what time activities take place.
- Address other people in the Spanish-speaking world.

Expansión de vocabulario

Ampliación

The suffix *-dad*

This section is designed to help you expand your vocabulary through knowledge of common Spanish prefixes and suffixes. It will help you learn to identify cognates when reading and listening as well as increase the vocabulary you need to speak and write effectively.

> **SUFFIX**   *-ty*   = **-dad**
> *university* = **universidad**

Nouns ending in **-dad** are feminine.

Práctica

A. *Dé la forma inglesa de las siguientes palabras.*

1. la variedad _____

2. la realidad _____

3. la sociedad _____

4. la responsabilidad _____

5. la formalidad _____

6. la productividad _____

B. *Dé la forma española de las siguientes palabras.*

1. university _____

2. city _____

3. activity _____

4. identity _____

5. nationality _____

6. variety _____

C. *Complete las siguientes oraciones con una palabra que termina en* **-dad** *o* **-dades.**

1. Barcelona y Sevilla son dos _____ grandes e interesantes.

2. Hay muchas estudiantes en la _____ de Madrid.

3. —¿Cuál es la _____ de esa chica?

   —Creo que es argentina.

4. En el mundo hispano hay una gran _____ de gente, países y culturas.

5. Al final de cada capítulo de *Interacciones* hay una serie de _____.

6. Para entrar en un país extranjero es necesario tener un documento de

   _____ como un pasaporte.

Bienvenidos a España

A. Adivinanza. *Para descubrir la palabra en la caja vertical, escriba en las líneas horizontales las palabras que corresponden a las definiciones de cada número.*

1. __ __ __ | __ __ __ __ __
2. __ __ __ | __ __ __ __ __
3. __ __ __ __ __ __ __ | __
4. __ | __ __ __
5. __ __ __ | __
6. __ __ __ __ | __ __ __ __ __ __
7. __ __ __ __ | __
8. __ __ __ __ | __

1. La cuarta ciudad más grande de España
2. El océano al oeste de la península ibérica
3. El otro país que también ocupa la península ibérica
4. La moneda principal de España
5. Las montañas que separan a España de Francia
6. El rey actual de España
7. La capital de España
8. Una importante industria española que se asocia con el mar

B. El mapa. *Usando oraciones completas conteste las siguientes preguntas sobre España.*

1. Nombre tres ciudades importantes de España. _____

_____

_____

2. Nombre tres ríos importantes de España. _____

_____

_____

3. Nombre tres cordilleras importantes de España. _____

_____

_____

4. ¿Cuáles son las industrias importantes? _____

_____

_____

5. ¿Qué tipo de gobierno tiene la nación? _____

_____

_____

6. ¿Cuántos habitantes tiene? _____

_____

_____

7. ¿Cómo son la geografía y el clima? _____

_____

_____

Capítulo 1
La vida de todos los días

Primera situación

A. Acciones y lugares. *Haga una lista de las actividades típicas para los siguientes lugares. (Use infinitivos para hacer listas de actividades.)*

1. La oficina _____

_____

_____

2. La tintorería _____

_____

_____

3. La estación de servicio _____

_____

_____

4. El correo _____

_____

_____

5. La biblioteca de la universidad _____

_____

_____

B. Las diligencias. *Escriba una lista de lo que Ud. tiene que hacer esta semana.*

_____   _____

_____   _____

_____   _____

_____   _____

C. Verbos irregulares. *Escriba la forma para la primera persona singular (yo) de los siguientes infinitivos.*

1. decir _____   **8.** traer _____

2. ver _____   **9.** saber _____

3. oír _____   **10.** hacer _____

4. ir _____   **11.** estar _____

5. dar _____   **12.** salir _____

6. conocer _____   **13.** poner _____

7. tener _____   **14.** destruir _____

D. ¿Con qué frecuencia...? *Explique con qué frecuencia Ud. hace las siguientes cosas.*

> ➤ *MODELO*   ir a la estación de servicio
> **Voy a la estación de servicio una vez a la semana.**

1. reunirse con amigos

_____

2. usar una computadora

_____

3. ir al correo

_____

4. tomar apuntes

_____

5. hacer compras en un centro comercial

_____

6. trabajar horas extras

_____

7. echar una siesta

_____

Nombre _____ **Fecha** _____ **Clase** _____

E. Unas actividades. *Usando una frase de cada columna, forme oraciones explicando lo que hacen las personas.*

a menudo	mi mejor amigo(-a)	decir la verdad
nunca	yo	venir a clase
dos veces a la semana	mis padres	hacer diligencias
siempre	mi compañero(-a) y yo	salir a tiempo
a veces	tú	poner la televisión
todos los días	mi profesor(-a) de español	ir al cine
		conducir rápidamente
		oír música clásica

1. _____

2. _____

3. _____

4. _____

5. _____

6. _____

7. _____

8. _____

F. Más verbos. *Escriba la forma para la primera persona singular (yo) y plural (nosotros) de los siguientes infinitivos.*

	YO	NOSOTROS
1. cerrar	_____	_____
2. repetir	_____	_____
3. querer	_____	_____
4. volver	_____	_____
5. preferir	_____	_____
6. almorzar	_____	_____
7. pedir	_____	_____
8. poder	_____	_____

G. Las actividades de Felipe. *Describa lo que Felipe hace en un día típico.*

➤ *MODELO*   comenzar su tarea a las ocho
                    Felipe comienza su tarea a las ocho.

1. almorzar con amigos

   _____

2. volver a casa a las diez

   _____

3. no perder tiempo

   _____

4. dormir ocho horas

   _____

5. soñar con su futuro

   _____

6. pedirles dinero a sus padres

   _____

H. Las actividades de Ud. y sus amigos. *Usando las actividades de Práctica G, explique si Ud. y sus amigos hacen lo que hace Felipe.*

➤ *MODELO*   comenzar la tarea a las ocho
                    Mis amigos y yo también comenzamos la tarea a las ocho.
                    Mis amigos y yo no comenzamos la tarea a las ocho.

1. _____

2. _____

3. _____

4. _____

5. _____

6. _____

Nombre _____ **Fecha** _____ **Clase** _____

I. **La rutina.** *Escríbales un mensaje por correo electrónico a sus padres describiéndoles sus actividades y diligencias en la universidad este semestre. Explique lo que Ud. hace durante una semana típica.*

_____ :

_____

_____

_____

_____

_____

_____

_____

_____

_____ ,

Segunda situación

A. **La rutina matinal.** *Explique lo que hace cada estudiante en el dibujo. (Los números de las personas en el dibujo corresponden a los números de la práctica.)*

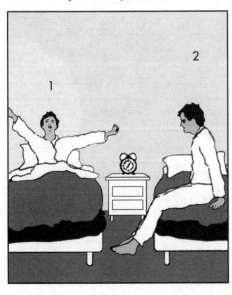 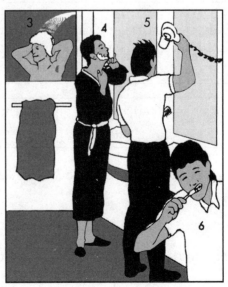

1. _____

2. _____

3. _____

4. _____

5. _____

6. _____

B.   Los artículos personales. *¿Qué cosas o artículos usan los estudiantes en el dibujo durante su rutina matinal?*

1. _____

2. _____

3. _____

4. _____

5. _____

6. _____

C.   Falta de comprensión. *Escriba lo que Ud. diría en las siguientes situaciones.*

1. Ud. habla por teléfono con su madre pero Ud. no oye bien lo que ella dice.

_____

2. Su profesor(-a) de español le hace una pregunta que Ud. no entiende.

_____

3. Ud. estudió horas y horas para su examen de química pero no comprende nada.
Su compañero(-a) le pregunta si está preparado(-a) para el examen.

_____

4. Su mejor amigo(-a) le explica un problema de física pero Ud. no comprende nada.

_____

5. Un(-a) amigo(-a) le da direcciones para llegar a su casa y Ud. quiere confirmar y repetir lo que su amigo(-a) ha dicho.

_____

6. Su novio(-a) le hace una pregunta pero Ud. no estaba prestando atención *(paying attention).*

_____

Nombre _____ **Fecha** _____ **Clase** _____

D. Pronombres reflexivos. *Escriba el pronombre reflexivo que corresponde a los siguientes sujetos.*

1. Manolo _____

2. Uds. _____

3. yo _____

4. ella _____

5. tú _____

6. mis padres _____

7. nosotras _____

8. Ud. _____

E. Verbos reflexivos. *Escriba la conjugación para los siguientes verbos reflexivos.*

secarse

yo _____

tú _____

él / ella / Ud. _____

nosotros(-as) _____

ellos / ellas / Uds. _____

despertarse (ie)

yo _____

tú _____

él / ella / Ud. _____

nosotros(-as) _____

ellos / ellas / Uds. _____

F. Su rutina diaria. *Explique en orden cronológico lo que Ud. hace cada mañana para arreglarse. Incluya las cosas o artículos personales que Ud. usa.*

_____

_____

_____

_____

_____

_____

_____

_____

G.   **En la universidad.** *Explique lo que estas personas hacen en la universidad.*

1. yo / preocuparse por los exámenes

_____

2. Eduardo / dedicarse a sus estudios

_____

3. unos alumnos / quejarse de sus profesores

_____

4. tú / irse los fines de semana

_____

5. mis amigos y yo / divertirse mucho

_____

H.   **La conversación incompleta.** *Ud. está escuchando una conversación telefónica entre su compañero(-a) de cuarto y su madre. Como Ud. sólo oye las respuestas, Ud. tiene que imaginar las preguntas que hace la madre. Escriba las preguntas en los espacios.*

1. _____

Me siento muy bien, mamá.

2. _____

Siempre me levanto a las siete y media.

3. _____

Siempre como dos huevos, pan tostado y bebo un vaso de leche.

4. _____

En el comedor de mi residencia.

5. _____

Siempre como con mi compañero(-a) de cuarto.

6. _____

Mi compañero(-a) es el (la) chico(-a) alto(-a) con el pelo rubio.

7. _____

No te escribo, porque no tengo mucho tiempo.
Adiós, mamá. Hasta luego.

I.   Un(-a) compañero(-a) raro(-a). *Ud. vive en la residencia estudiantil con un(-a) compañero(-a) de cuarto muy raro(-a) que tiene una rutina diaria loca. Escríbale un mensaje de correo electrónico a un(-a) amigo(-a) describiéndole la rutina diaria y las actividades de su compañero(-a). Use su imaginación.*

_____ :

_____

_____

_____

_____

_____

_____

_____

_____ ,

A recordar

Review the following situations and tasks that have been presented and practiced in this chapter.

- Discuss daily activities.
- Discuss and describe daily routine.
- Express the sequence and frequency of actions and events.
- Express lack of comprehension and ask for clarification about what has been said.
- Ask questions about activities and events.
- Prepare an appropriate daily schedule of activities in a Spanish-speaking country.

Expansión de vocabulario

Dudas de vocabulario

to know: conocer / saber

conocer: *to know, to meet, to be acquainted with, to recognize*

Lo conocí en la fiesta de María.	*I met him at María's party.*
Conozco Madrid pero no Sevilla.	*I know Madrid but not Sevilla.*
Lo conozco por su manera de caminar.	*I recognize him by the way he walks.*

saber: *to have knowledge of, to have the ability to do something*

Sé que José Manuel va a venir a la fiesta pero no sé cuándo.	*I know José Manuel is coming to the party, but I don't know when.*
Sé usar la computadora.	*I know how to use the computer.*

to ask: pedir / preguntar / preguntar por

pedir: *to request, to ask for something*

Ella me pidió un dólar pero yo no tenía dinero.	*She asked me for a dollar, but I didn't have any money.*

preguntar: *to ask a question*

Ella me preguntó si yo descansaba los fines de semana.	*She asked me if I rested on weekends.*

preguntar por: *to ask about (inquire about) somebody*

Mis padres me preguntaron por mi novio.	*My parents asked me about my boyfriend.*

movie: el cine / la película / de película

el cine: *the movie theater*

—Vamos al cine.	*Let's go to the movies.*
—¿A cuál?	*Which one?*
—Al Orrantia.	*To the Orrantia.*
—No, al Orrantia no. El cine Orrantia es muy viejo.	*No, not to the Orrantia. The Orrantia movie theater is very old.*

la película: *the film, the motion picture*

Él siempre va a ver las películas españolas.	*He always goes to see Spanish movies.*

de película: *out of the ordinary, incredible.*

No te imaginas lo que me pasó. ¡Es de película!	*You can't imagine what happened to me! It's incredible!*

Práctica

Explique si Ud. sabe o conoce las siguientes cosas.

> ***MODELO***   España
>   (No) Conozco España.

1. a. _____ usar una computadora.

   b. _____ al presidente de los EE.UU.

   c. _____ dónde vive mi mejor amigo(-a).

   d. _____ las obras de Picasso.

   e. _____ a todos mis primos.

Explique lo que el niño Carlos pide o pregunta en casa.

2. a. Carlos _____ helado y dulces.

   b. Carlos _____ dónde está su pelota.

   c. Carlos _____ su papá.

   d. Carlos _____ un abrazo.

*Complete la oración con una forma de **el cine / la película / de película** para explicar lo que van a hacer Federico y Antonia este fin de semana.*

3. Federico y Antonia van _____ para ver

   _____ de Saura.

Ampliación

The suffix *-dor, -dora*

SUFFIX $\left.\begin{array}{l} -er \\ -or \end{array}\right\}$ = -dor, -dora

computer = **la computadora**

razor = **la afeitadora**

The suffixes **-dor** or **-dora** form nouns from verbs and indicate an appliance, piece of equipment, or place that will help carry out the action suggested by the verb: **secar** = *to dry;* **el secador** = *(hair) dryer.* Note that the English word will not always end in *-or, -er:* **el despertador** = *alarm clock.*

Práctica

A. *Dé la forma inglesa de las siguientes palabras.*

1. el procesador _____

2. la fotocopiadora _____

3. la computadora _____

4. la afeitadora _____

5. el despertador _____

6. el secador _____

B. *Dé los infinitivos que se asocian con las siguientes palabras y después escriba la forma inglesa de los sustantivos.*

	Infinitivo	Sustantivo inglés
1. la lavadora	_____	_____
2. el cortador	_____	_____
3. el comedor	_____	_____
4. el mostrador	_____	_____
5. el mirador	_____	_____
6. la calculadora	_____	_____

C. *Complete las oraciones con un sustantivo que termina en* **-dor** *o* **-dora.**

1. Para copiar unos papeles importantes se usa una _____.

2. Para despertarse a una hora fija se usa un _____.

3. Para resolver problemas de matemáticas o estadísticas se usa una _____.

4. Es más fácil escribir informes, cartas o documentos largos con un _____ de textos.

5. Para afeitarse se usa una _____.

6. En muchas casas la familia come en el _____.

5. Ah. Pues yo fui a cenar a la casa de mis abuelos. Fue bastante aburrido.
   (Sympathize with him. Explain you need to end the conversation and go study.)

   _____

   _____

6. Entonces nos vemos mañana a las once y media. Adiós.
   (Say O.K. and good-bye.)

   _____

E. **El pretérito.** *Escriba las formas del pretérito que corresponden a los sujetos.*

nadar	correr
Ana _____	Raúl _____
yo _____	tú y yo _____
mis amigos _____	los García _____
nosotras _____	yo _____
tú _____	tú _____

F. **Formas irregulares.** *Escriba las formas de la tercera persona plural del pretérito para los siguientes verbos.*

1. dar _____
2. andar _____
3. venir _____
4. leer _____
5. poder _____
6. saber _____

7. tener _____
8. construir _____
9. poner _____
10. oír _____
11. estar _____
12. decir _____

G. Las actividades en la playa. *Explique si Ud. hizo o no hizo las siguientes actividades la última vez que fue a la playa.*

> **MODELO**　　practicar el windsurf
> 　　　　　　　(No) **Practiqué el windsurf.**

1. pescar

_____

2. jugar al vólibol

_____

3. gozar del mar

_____

4. buscar conchas

_____

5. navegar en un velero

_____

H. Las vacaciones de los Ayala. *Explique lo que los Ayala hicieron durante sus vacaciones en la Costa Brava. Complete las oraciones con la forma adecuada de uno de los verbos de la lista.*

andar	jugar	pasar
construir	leer	poner
decidir	nadar	tomar
hacer		

Los Ayala _____ las vacaciones en un complejo turístico en la Costa

Brava. Allá los niños _____ esquí acuático. _____ en

el mar y _____ castillos de arena. Nunca _____ la

televisión. La Sra. de Ayala _____ por la playa, _____

el sol y _____ novelas románticas. El padre _____ al

golf. La familia _____ volver al complejo el verano próximo.

Nombre _____ **Fecha** _____ **Clase** _____

Escoja un lugar adónde ir y también un medio de transporte para volver al hotel o a casa para las siguientes personas que están de vacaciones en Madrid.

1. Una pareja que celebra su aniversario de quince años. Quieren oír música contemporánea pero no les gusta la música rock. Van a quedarse allí hasta las dos.

    LUGAR: _____

    MEDIO DE TRANSPORTE: _____

2. Una familia norteamericana con tres jóvenes entre once y catorce años. Quieren probar tapas y volver al hotel a las diez.

    LUGAR: _____

    MEDIO DE TRANSPORTE: _____

3. Un estudiante alemán que tiene mucha hambre. Necesita comer rápidamente porque su tren sale a las nueve de la noche.

    LUGAR: _____

    MEDIO DE TRANSPORTE: _____

4. Cuatro hombres de negocios que están en Madrid para una conferencia. Quieren ver un espectáculo en algún cabaret y después quieren tomar una copa. Van a divertirse hasta las tres.

    LUGAR: _____

    MEDIO DE TRANSPORTE: _____

5. Dos señoritas de veinte años a quienes les encanta bailar y estar con otros jóvenes hasta las tres de la mañana. Les gusta la música rock.

    LUGAR: _____

    MEDIO DE TRANSPORTE: _____

6. Una joven actriz y su novio que es abogado. Quieren tomar una copa con otros amigos y volver a casa a las diez y media.

    LUGAR: _____

    MEDIO DE TRANSPORTE: _____

B.   Sus diversiones. *Ud. tiene tres noches en Madrid. Usando la información de Práctica A, explique lo que va a hacer cada noche y por qué va a hacerlo. Incluya sus medios de transporte.*

_____

_____

_____

_____

_____

C.   Circunlocuciones. *Ud. tiene un(-a) amigo(-a) español(-a) que lee novelas y revistas norteamericanas. Cuando no comprende una frase o palabra, le escribe a Ud. pidiendo una explicación. Escríbale una definición de las siguientes cosas.*

1. time-share condo _____

    _____

    _____

2. barbecue _____

    _____

    _____

3. bingo _____

    _____

    _____

4. get-away weekend _____

    _____

    _____

5. SUV (sports utility vehicle) _____

    _____

    _____

Nombre _____ **Fecha** _____ **Clase** _____

H.   Unas vacaciones fantásticas. *Escríbale una carta breve a un(-a) amigo(-a) describiendo unas vacaciones buenas. Dígale adónde fue y lo que hizo de día y de noche.*

_____ :

_____

_____

_____

_____

_____

_____

_____

_____

_____

_____

_____

_____

_____

_____ ,

A recordar

Review the following situations and tasks that have been presented and practiced in this chapter.

- Make a personal phone call.
- Circumlocute when you cannot recall or do not know the exact vocabulary word.
- Discuss a great variety of past activities.
- Avoid the repetition of nouns by using the appropriate pronoun.
- Sequence events.
- Discuss leisure time and vacation activities in your own culture and in Hispanic culture.

Expansión de vocabulario

Dudas de vocabulario

time: el tiempo / la vez / la hora

el tiempo: *time, period of time; weather*

Ese vestido se usaba en los tiempos de mi abuela.	*That dress was worn in my grandmother's time.*
¡Qué tiempo tan feo!	*What awful weather!*

la vez: *a specific occurrence of time*

La última vez que nadé fue el verano pasado.	*The last time I went swimming was last summer.*

la hora: *time of day*

¿Qué hora es? Son las nueve.	*What time is it? It's nine o'clock.*

to have a good time: divertirse / pasarlo bien

divertirse: *to enjoy oneself, to have fun*

Yo me divierto mucho en las fiestas.	*I have a lot of fun at parties.*

pasarlo bien: *to have a good time*

Este verano fue estupendo. ¡Lo pasé de lo mejor en Madrid!	*This summer was fantastic. I had a great time in Madrid!*

Práctica

1. Complete las oraciones con la forma adecuada de **la hora / el tiempo / la vez.**

    —¿Sabes qué _____ es?

    —Son las tres y media.

    —Entonces, tengo _____ para llamar a la oficina. Es la tercera

    _____ que tengo que llamar al jefe hoy.

2. Complete las oraciones con la forma adecuada de **divertirse / pasarlo bien.**

    Generalmente yo _____ en España, en la Costa del Sol. Gozo del mar y

    del sol. Por la noche voy a una discoteca y _____ muchísimo.

Bienvenidos a México

A. **Adivinanza.** *Para descubrir la palabra en la caja vertical, escriba en las líneas horizontales las palabras que corresponden a las definiciones de cada número.*

1. __ __ | __ __ __ __ __ __
2. __ __ | __ __ __
3. | __ __ __ __ __ __ __ __
4. | __ __ __ __
5. __ | __ __ __
6. | __ __
7. __ __ | __ __ __ __
8. __ | __ __ __ __ __ __ __

1. La santa patrona de México es la Virgen de _____ .
2. El océano al oeste de México
3. Tierras altas entre las montañas
4. La moneda de México
5. La industria principal de México
6. Una ciudad grande en el norte del país
7. La plaza principal de México, D.F.
8. La tercera ciudad más grande de México

B. **El mapa.** *Usando oraciones completas, conteste las siguientes preguntas sobre México.*

1. Nombre cuatro ciudades grandes e importantes. _____

_____

_____

2. Nombre unas playas famosas de México. _____

_____

_____

3. ¿Cuáles son las industrias importantes? _____

_____

_____

4. ¿Dónde vive la mayoría de la población? _____

_____

_____

5. ¿Qué tipo de gobierno tiene México? _____

_____

_____

6. ¿Cómo son la geografía y el clima? _____

_____

_____

Nombre _____ **Fecha** _____ **Clase** _____

B. **Una fiesta.** *¿Qué preguntarían o contestarían las personas en las siguientes situaciones?*

1. Ud. invita a un(-a) amigo(-a) a una fiesta en su casa el viernes que viene.

_____

2. Su amigo(-a) no puede venir porque tiene que trabajar.

_____

3. Ud. siente *(regret)* que su amigo(-a) no pueda venir.

_____

4. Ud. invita a otro(-a) amigo(-a) a la fiesta.

_____

5. El (La) otro(-a) amigo(-a) acepta.

_____

C. **Una invitación.** *Ud. va a dar una fiesta en su apartamento el sábado que viene. Escríbale a un(-a) amigo(-a) invitándolo(-la) a la fiesta. Explíquele cuándo y dónde es, quiénes asistirán, qué tipo de fiesta es, etc.*

_____

_____

_____

_____

_____

_____

_____

_____

_____

_____

D. **¡Qué sorpresa!** *Un amigo ha oído noticias sorprendentes acerca de la boda de Gustavo y Eva. Confirme lo que él ha oído usando la forma adecuada de* **ser** *o* **estar.**

> ➤ *MODELO*   ¿Gustavo y Eva? ¿Novios?
>   **Sí, son novios.**

1. ¿La boda? ¿El sábado a las dos?

Sí, _____

2. ¿La cena? ¿En el Hotel Cozumel?

Sí, _____

3. ¿Gustavo? ¿Del Ecuador?

Sí, _____

4. ¿Eva? ¿Linda y coqueta?

Sí, _____

5. ¿La madre? ¿Contenta?

Sí, _____

6. ¿Los novios? ¿Nerviosos?

Sí, _____

E. **Puerto Vallarta.** *Complete las siguientes oraciones con la forma adecuada de* **ser,** **estar** *o* **haber (hay)** *para describir a Fernando y sus vacaciones.*

_____ el lunes, tres de agosto. _____ las tres de la tarde.

Fernando _____ de vacaciones en Puerto Vallarta con toda su familia. Puerto Vallarta

_____ una de las playas famosas de la costa del Pacífico. Fernando y su esposa

Carmen, que _____ de Guanajuato, _____ tomando el sol en la

playa. Los dos _____ de muy buen humor porque no _____

mucha gente allí y pueden gozar del lugar. Carmen _____ rubia y

_____ un poco preocupada porque hace muchísimo sol y no quiere quemarse.

A recordar

Review the following situations and tasks that have been presented and practiced in this chapter.

- Describe your family and individual members of your family including information about their physical and emotional characteristics, ages, nationalities, and activities.
- Initiate a conversation by using the proper greetings and close the conversation with the proper leave-takings.
- Extend, accept, and decline an invitation in oral and written form.
- Describe what life used to be like.
- Describe conditions and characteristics of people; provide information about the location of persons and things; tell time; indicate origin, nationality, and ownership.
- Express endearment, smallness, or cuteness when referring to people or things.
- Discuss family life, activities, and events in your own and Hispanic culture.

Expansión de vocabulario

Dudas de vocabulario

close: cerca / cercano / unido / íntimo

cerca: *next to, near, close*

Los Méndez no viven cerca de la universidad.   *The Mendezes do not live close to the university.*

cercano: *physical closeness of people or objects. It can also be used to refer to close family relationships.*

Los Gómez, sin embargo, viven
en un pueblo cercano.

*The Gomezes, however, live
in a nearby town.*

Él es hijo de mi hermano;
por lo tanto es un pariente muy cercano.

*He is my brother's son;
consequently, he is a close relative.*

unido: *close-knit ties between friends or relatives*

Todos los miembros de mi familia
somos muy unidos.

*All of the members of my family
are very close to each other.*

íntimo: *close relationship between friends*

Irma es mi amiga íntima.   *Irma is my close friend.*

because: porque / puesto que / como / a causa de

porque: *because.* **Porque** *is followed by a clause that includes a conjugated verb.* **Porque** *cannot begin a sentence.*

Él no vino porque estaba enfermo.	*He didn't come because he was sick.*

puesto que / como: *because, since. Both* **puesto que** *and* **como** *can be used at the beginning of a sentence.*

Como/Puesto que no has terminado de hacer tu tarea, hoy no sales.	*Since you haven't finished your homework, you're not going out today.*

a causa de: *because of; as a consequence of.* **A causa de** *can be used at the beginning of a sentence or in the middle position. It is followed by a noun or an infinitive.*

A causa de trabajar sin parar nunca, se enfermó.	*Because he/she worked without ever stopping, he/she got sick.*

small / little: poco / pequeño / joven / menor

poco: *a small amount; a little*

¿Quiere comer un pedazo de torta?	*Do you want to eat some cake?*
Sólo un poco. No quiero engordar.	*Just a little. I don't want to gain weight.*

pequeño: *small in size*

José Luis es muy pequeño. Él apenas mide 1,40 m.	*José Luis is very small. He is barely 1,40 m. (4'6").*

joven: *young in age*

Él es muy joven. Todavía no maneja.	*He is very young. He doesn't drive yet.*

menor: *younger*

Mi hermano menor tiene 12 años.	*My younger (little) brother is 12.*

Práctica

Complete las oraciones con la forma adecuada de una de las palabras de la lista.

cerca	cercano	unido	íntimo
porque	puesto que	como	a causa de
poco	pequeño	joven	menor

Práctica

Complete la carta de Mercedes en la cual describe una comida en un nuevo restaurante. Use la forma apropiada de las palabras de la siguiente lista.

calor   caliente   picante
probar(se)   tratar (de)

Querida Amelia:

Anoche Manolo y yo fuimos a cenar a un nuevo restaurante mexicano aquí en Los Ángeles. Hacía

mucho _____ todo el día y como el aire acondicionado no funcionaba bien,

toda la casa estaba muy _____ . Por supuesto, yo no quería cocinar.

La comida estuvo riquísima. Yo _____ las enchiladas; estaban sabrosas y

no muy _____ como en muchos restaurantes. A Manolo le gustó muchísimo el

pollo en mole. Cuando yo tenga más tiempo voy a _____ prepararlo en casa.

Pero lo mejor de todo es que no es un restaurante caro y el servicio también es muy bueno; el mesero

nos _____ muy bien.

Bueno, Amelia, tengo que irme. Abrazos de tu amiga,

Mercedes

Ampliación

Describing food

The following observations on word formation will help you understand vocabulary related to food and menu items.

1. In English, nouns are frequently used as adjectives.

   NOUN: I like *chicken*.

   NOUN USED AS ADJECTIVE: I like *chicken* soup.

   In Spanish, nouns cannot be converted into adjectives in the same way as in English. Instead, the phrase **de + noun** is used as an adjective to describe other nouns.

   NOUN: Me gusta el *pollo*.

   DE + NOUN: Me gusta el caldo de *pollo*.

2. Dishes prepared in a certain style or manner are often described with the phrase **a la + feminine adjective** which means "in the style of": **Huachinango a la veracruzana** = *Red Snapper Veracruz Style.*

3. Adjectives denoting a country, city, or region are often used to describe food: **las enchiladas suizas** = *Swiss (cheese) enchiladas.*

Práctica

A. *Dé el equivalente inglés para los siguientes platos.*

1. paella valenciana _____

2. gazpacho andaluz _____

3. tortilla a la española _____

4. enchiladas suizas _____

5. pizza a la italiana _____

B. *Dé el equivalente español para los siguientes platos.*

1. chicken soup _____

2. shrimp cocktail _____

3. beef tacos _____

4. ham sandwich _____

5. cheese enchiladas _____

6. chocolate cake _____

7. tomato salad _____

8. orange juice _____

C. *Complete las oraciones con el nombre de un plato.*

1. Una sopa fría de Andalucía preparada con tomates, pimientos, pepinos, cebollas y ajo es el

   _____ _____ .

2. Las enchiladas preparadas con crema y queso de suiza son las _____ .

3. Un plato de Valencia preparado con arroz, pollo, pescado y mariscos es la _____ .

4. El huachinango preparado según una receta de Veracruz, México, es el _____ .

Bienvenidos a Centroamérica, a Venezuela y a Colombia

A.   Adivinanza. *Para descubrir la palabra en la caja vertical, escriba en las líneas horizontales las palabras que corresponden a las definiciones de cada número.*

1. __ __ __ __ __ __ __ __
2. __ __ __ __ __ __ __
3. __ __ __ __ __ __ __ __
4. __ __ __ __ __
5. __ __ __ __ __
6. __ __ __ __ __ __
7. __ __ __ __ __ __
8. __ __ __ __ __ __
9. __ __ __ __

1. El país más grande de Centroamérica
2. Un país entre Guatemala y Nicaragua
3. El país de Centroamérica cuya capital es San José
4. La capital de Colombia
5. Las montañas de Sudamérica
6. El país dividido por un canal
7. La capital de Venezuela
8. La industria principal de Venezuela
9. Un producto agrícola importante para la economía de varios países de la América Central y del Sur

B.   El mapa. *Usando oraciones completas, conteste las siguientes preguntas sobre Centroamérica, Colombia y Venezuela.*

1. Nombre los seis países hispanos de Centroamérica con sus capitales. _____

_____

_____

2. Nombre las ciudades importantes de Colombia y Venezuela. _____

_____

3. ¿Cuántos habitantes tiene Centroamérica?

_____

¿Colombia? _____

¿Venezuela? _____

4. ¿Qué tipo de gobierno tiene Colombia? _____

_____

¿Venezuela? _____

¿Los países de Centroamérica? _____

_____

5. ¿En qué se basa la economía de estos países? _____

_____

_____

6. ¿Cómo son la geografía y el clima de esta región? _____

_____

Nombre ————————————————————— Fecha —————————— Clase ——————————

XXXII CURSO DE LENGUA Y CULTURA ESPAÑOLAS PARA EXTRANJEROS

PROGRAMA

— **Clases.** Las enseñanzas se impartirán por la mañana de lunes a viernes, incluyendo clases de lengua española (30 horas) y actividades complementarias (20 horas), con el siguiente horario:

HORARIO	De lunes a viernes	N.º de horas
De 9 a 10	Lengua Española	15
De 10 a 11	Prácticas de español	15
Desde 11,30	Actividades complementarias	20
	TOTAL	50

— El primer día del Curso se realizará una prueba escrita para distribuir a los alumnos, según su conocimiento de la lengua española, en los siguientes niveles:

1. Principiante
2. Elemental
3. Medio
4. Superior

— **Actividades complementarias.**

Conferencias, coloquios, seminarios, audiciones y proyecciones sobre los temas objeto de estudio en las clases y sobre aspectos generales de la cultura española.

— **Actos culturales y recreativos.**

1. Visitas a museos y monumentos.
2. Actuaciones teatrales y musicales en la ciudad.
3. Excursiones a lugares de particular interés.

RECEPCIÓN

El día 2 de agosto tendrá lugar la recepción en el Edificio de la Universidad de Barcelona, realizándose de 10 a 12 de la mañana la prueba para evaluar los conocimientos de español de los alumnos y clasificarlos según los niveles previstos.

continúa en la próxima página

CERTIFICADOS

El día 25 de agosto se clausurará el Curso y se entregarán los Certificados Académicos Personales a los alumnos que hayan asistido con asiduidad.

OTROS SERVICIOS

— **Alojamiento.** Los alumnos interesados podrán disponer de alojamiento y desayuno en el Colegio Mayor "Sant Jordi", situado en la calle Maestro Nicolau, 13 - 08021 Barcelona.

Esta Residencia ofrece además:
- Servicio de comedor.
- Servicio médico ordinario.
- Horario flexible de entradas y salidas, respetando la convivencia.

— **Deportes.** el alumno del Curso podrá acceder a las Instalaciones Deportivas de la Universidad de Barcelona.

— **Biblioteca y otros servicios.** Igualmente tendrán acceso a la Biblioteca General de la Universidad, así como a los demás Servicios Universitarios.

— **Seguro de Accidentes.** Los alumnos tendrán cubierto el riesgo de accidentes mediante póliza con una Compañía Internacional de Seguros.

Lea la información sobre el curso para extranjeros y conteste las preguntas.

1. ¿Cuántas horas de clase de lengua española hay por semana? _____

_____

¿Qué días hay clase? _____

_____

¿A qué hora son las clases? _____

_____

2. ¿Cuántos niveles de cursos hay? _____

¿Cuáles son? _____

En su opinión, ¿cuál es su nivel de conocimiento? _____

Nombre _____ **Fecha** _____ **Clase** _____

3. los cursos obligatorios / los cursos electivos (divertido)

_____

4. los cursos de este semestre / los cursos del semestre pasado (difícil)

_____

5. las actividades universitarias / las actividades de la escuela secundaria (bueno)

_____

I. **Mi familia y yo.** *Compárese con miembros de su familia en varias categorías.*

> ➤ *MODELO*   la estatura *(height)*
> **Soy más alto(-a) que mi hermana, pero soy menos alto(-a) que mi padre.**

1. la inteligencia _____

_____

2. el peso *(weight)* _____

_____

3. la estatura _____

_____

4. el estado físico _____

_____

5. la simpatía *(congeniality)* _____

_____

A recordar

Review the following situations and tasks that have been presented and practiced in this chapter.

- Describe the university, its courses, classes, and structure in your own and Hispanic culture.
- Describe university life in your own and Hispanic culture.
- Function within the classroom by asking questions of your instructor and responding to his/her commands.
- Talk about the weather.
- Indicate the location of persons and objects.
- Indicate purpose and time.
- Indicate the recipient of something.
- Express hopes, desires, and requests.
- Make comparisons.

Expansión de vocabulario

Dudas de vocabulario

school: la escuela primaria / el colegio / el liceo / la universidad

la escuela primaria: *a grammar or elementary school*

Jorge tiene seis años y va a la escuela primaria.   *Jorge is six years old and goes to elementary school.*

el colegio: *a private educational institution that offers an elementary and high school education. In some countries,* **el colegio** *refers just to a high school.*

¿A qué colegio vas?   *What school do you go to?*
A San Jorge de Miraflores.   *Saint George's School in Miraflores.*

el liceo: *a public high school in most countries*

Cuando termine el sexto grado, iré   *When I finish sixth grade, I'll go*
al liceo Andrés Bello.   *to Andrés Bello High School.*

la universidad: *a college or university*

Yo quiero ir a la Universidad Nacional   *I want to go to the Universidad Nacional*
Autónoma de México para estudiar economía.   *Autónoma de México to study economics.*

dormitory / residence / bedroom: la residencia (estudiantil) / el dormitorio

la residencia: *used in the phrase* **lugar de residencia** *it means city or area of residence.*

—¿Cuál es tu lugar de residencia?   *Where do you live?*
—Guadalajara, México.   *Guadalajara, Mexico.*

la residencia *can also be used as a synonym of* home, *but it has the connotation of a big and luxurious house.*

La fiesta se llevó a cabo   *The party took place*
en la residencia de los López.   *at the López residence.*

la residencia estudiantil: *student dormitory or residence hall*

—¿En qué residencia estudiantil vives tú?   *What dorm do you live in?*
—En Bishop Hall.   *In Bishop Hall.*

el dormitorio: *bedroom*

Aquella casa tiene cuatro dormitorios   *That house has four bedrooms*
y tres baños.   *and three bathrooms.*

Nombre _____ **Fecha** _____ **Clase** _____

faculty / school / college: **el profesorado / la facultad**

la facultad: *a college or school within a university*

Susana trabaja en la Facultad de Filosofía y Letras y su hermana estudia en la Facultad de Ciencias.	*Susana works in the College of Liberal Arts, and her sister studies in the College of Sciences.*

el profesorado: *the teaching staff of an educational institution*

El Dr. Álvarez forma parte del profesorado de la Universidad Nacional Autónoma de México.	Dr. Álvarez is a faculty member of the Universidad Nacional Autónoma de México.

Práctica

Combine la oración de la columna a la izquierda con una frase de la derecha.

1. _____ Mi hijo Jorge tiene seis años y asiste a _____.

2. _____ A los Gómez no les gusta la idea de una educación privada. Por eso, su hijo de dieciséis años asiste a _____.

3. _____ Los Mendoza creen que la enseñanza en las escuelas públicas es inferior. Por eso sus niños asisten a _____.

4. _____ Diego quiere hacerse médico; ahora estudia en _____ de Medicina en la Universidad de Texas.

5. _____ Ángela asiste a la Universidad de California. Vive en _____ porque la universidad está lejos de su casa.

6. _____ El hermano de Ángela vive en un apartamento porque prefiere _____ privado.

7. _____ _____ de la universidad está de huelga y nadie va a enseñar. Dicen que la universidad no les paga bien.

a. el profesorado

b. la escuela

c. un liceo

d. un dormitorio

e. una escuela primaria

f. una residencia estudiantil

g. un colegio

h. la Facultad

i. la universidad

Ampliación

Courses of study

Many vocabulary words pertaining to courses of study and university activities can be grouped into the following categories based on word formation.

1. -y   = -ía
   anatomy = **la anatomía**

Other words of this type include **la astronomía, la economía, la filosofía, la geografía, la geometría, la trigonometría.**

2. *-ology*   = **-ología**
   sociology = **la sociología**

Other words of this type include **la biología, la fisiología, la geología, la sicología.**

3. **-ar** verb → noun ending in **-ción**
   investigar → **la investigación**

Práctica

A. *Dé la forma inglesa de las siguientes palabras.*

1. la filosofía _____

2. la astronomía _____

3. la trigonometría _____

4. la geología _____

5. la sicología _____

6. la fisiología _____

B. *Dé el sustantivo español basado en el infinitivo. Luego dé el sustantivo inglés.*

	Sustantivo español	Sustantivo inglés
1. comunicar		
2. educar		
3. especializarse		
4. organizar		
5. administrar		
6. recomendar		
7. programar		
8. interpretar		

Nombre _____ **Fecha** _____ **Clase** _____

C.   *Complete las oraciones con el sustantivo apropiado.*

1. El estudio de las estrellas y el cielo es la _____.

2. El estudio del cuerpo humano es la _____.

3. El estudio de la personalidad es la _____.

4. El estudio de las obras de personas como Sócrates y Platón es la _____.

5. El estudio de las sociedades y las culturas es la _____.

6. El estudio de las computadoras es la _____.

7. Para trabajar en la radio o la televisión es necesario estudiar las _____.

8. Para hacerse hombre o mujer de negocios es necesario estudiar la _____ de empresas.

Capítulo 6

En casa

Primera situación

A.   Mi primer apartamento. *Después de una semana en su primer apartamento, Ud. se da cuenta de que hay mucho desorden. Escriba una lista de todos los quehaceres domésticos que Ud. necesita hacer para tener un apartamento bien arreglado. Al lado del quehacer escriba el nombre del (de los) aparato(-s) (equipment) que necesita para hacer el trabajo. Recuerde: Use el infinitivo para preparar una lista de actividades.*

_____

_____

_____

_____

_____

_____

_____

_____

_____

B.   Un(-a) compañero(-a) perezoso(-a). *Su compañero(-a) de cuarto es bastante perezoso(-a), pero Ud. necesita su ayuda para arreglar el apartamento. Usando su lista de Práctica A, decida cuáles de los quehaceres él (ella) puede hacer. Como Ud. tiene que ir a clase, escríbale una nota diciéndole qué hacer. Ud. tiene que ser muy amable porque Ud. necesita su cooperación.*

_____ :

_____

_____

_____

_____

_____

_____

_____

_____ ,

C.   Los mandatos familiares. *Complete la siguiente tabla con el mandato familiar afirmativo y negativo para los infinitivos dados.*

		MANDATO FAMILIAR AFIRMATIVO	**MANDATO FAMILIAR NEGATIVO**
1.	lavar	_____	_____
2.	barrer	_____	_____
3.	sacudir	_____	_____
4.	cerrar	_____	_____
5.	volver	_____	_____
6.	repetir	_____	_____
7.	decir	_____	_____
8.	venir	_____	_____
9.	hacer	_____	_____
10.	poner	_____	_____
11.	salir	_____	_____
12.	ser	_____	_____

Nombre _____ **Fecha** _____ **Clase** _____

D. Su hijo(-a). *Su hijo(-a) de cinco años necesita aprender a ayudarlo(-la) con los quehaceres. Déle consejos según el modelo.*

> ➤ *MODELO* no lavar la pared / lavar los platos
> **No laves la pared. Lava los platos.**

1. no poner la televisión / poner la mesa

_____

2. no hacer un sándwich / hacer la cama

_____

3. no regar la alfombra / regar las plantas

_____

4. no tener prisa / tener paciencia

_____

5. no ser tonto(-a) / ser amable

_____

6. no jugar ahora / colgar la ropa

_____

E. ¡Qué desorden! *Su hijo vive en el apartamento de Práctica A. Ud. acaba de recibir una foto de su apartamento. Escríbale un mensaje de correo electrónico diciéndole lo que debe hacer para arreglarlo todo antes de su visita. Use mandatos familiares.*

_____ :

_____

_____

_____

_____

_____

_____

_____

_____ ,

F.　Las Torres. *Maribel vive en el edificio de apartamentos Las Torres I; Clara vive en Las Torres II. Todos los apartamentos son iguales. Compare el apartamento de Maribel con el de Clara.*

> ➢ *MODELO*　　　El apartamento de Maribel es grande.
> **El apartamento de Clara es tan grande como el apartamento de Maribel.**

1. El apartamento de Maribel es muy lindo.

_____

_____

2. Maribel limpia su apartamento regularmente.

_____

_____

3. El apartamento de Maribel tiene mucha luz.

_____

_____

4. El apartamento de Maribel tiene dos dormitorios.

_____

_____

5. El apartamento de Maribel tiene ocho ventanas.

_____

_____

6. El apartamento de Maribel tiene mucho espacio.

_____

_____

G.　En la tienda de muebles. *Complete la siguiente conversación entre el dependiente y un cliente en una tienda.*

> ➢ *MODELO*　　　DEPENDIENTE:　¿Quisiera ver esta mesa? (allí)
> CLIENTE:　　　　**No, prefiero aquélla.**

1. ¿Quisiera Ud. ver esa cama? (allí)

_____

Nombre _____ **Fecha** _____ **Clase** _____

2. ¿Quisiera Ud. ver aquellas sillas? (aquí)

_____

3. ¿Quisiera Ud. ver esta alfombra? (ahí)

_____

4. ¿Quisiera Ud. ver ese sofá? (allí)

_____

5. ¿Quisiera Ud. ver estos sillones? (ahí)

_____

Segunda situación

A. **Asociaciones.** *Escoja la palabra que no pertenece al grupo y explique por qué.*

1. anunciar   rescatar   informar   entrevistar

_____

_____

2. un terremoto   una inundación   un asesinato   un incendio

_____

_____

3. el asesinato   el delito   el crimen   la cárcel

_____

_____

4. el reportero   el abogado   el testigo   el juez

_____

_____

5. las elecciones   la campaña   la manifestación elegir

_____

_____

B. Un pueblo rural. *Silvia Rivas vive en un pueblo rural en Colombia. Ella ha visto una guía de televisión de los EE.UU. pero hay muchas cosas que no comprende. Por eso ella le pide a Ud. que le escriba una definición de estas cosas.*

1. Who Wants to Be a Millionaire _____

_____

_____

2. Saturday Night Live _____

_____

_____

3. Jeopardy _____

_____

_____

4. a mini-series _____

_____

_____

5. a talk show _____

_____

_____

C. Eres muy amable. *¿Qué les escribiría a las siguientes personas?*

1. Un(-a) amigo(-a) le da una botella de champán para celebrar su cumpleaños.

_____

_____

2. Su compañero(-a) de cuarto insiste en ayudarlo(-la) con su tarea de química pero Ud. no quiere que lo haga.

_____

_____

3. Su madre le envía una caja de sus galletas (*cookies*) favoritas.

_____

_____

4. Su compañero(-a) de cuarto ofrece limpiar todo el apartamento porque Ud. no se siente bien.

_____

_____

5. Su mamá piensa que Ud. trabaja demasiado y ofrece lavar y planchar su ropa.

_____

_____

D. Usos del subjuntivo. *Trace un círculo alrededor de las expresiones que requieren el uso del subjuntivo en la cláusula que sigue.*

es necesario	es terrible	creer	sentarse
es verdad	tal vez	sin embargo	es bueno
es importante	no pensar	es posible	dudar
tener miedo de	es ridículo	alegrarse de	tener calor
es mejor	es frecuente	negar	es imposible

E. Opiniones. *Usando una frase de negación, emoción, duda o juicio, exprese su opinión acerca de las ideas escritas a continuación.*

> **MODELO**   Todos los programas de la televisión son buenos.
> **Dudo / No creo / Es dudoso que todos los programas de la televisión sean buenos.**

1. Los políticos gastan demasiado dinero en sus campañas electorales.

_____

_____

2. Siempre elegimos al mejor candidato.

_____

_____

3. Las guerras no resuelven nada.

_____

_____

4. Hay mucho crimen en los EE.UU.

_____

_____

5. Podemos eliminar el crimen con más cárceles.

_____

_____

6. Las leyes ayudan más a los criminales que a las víctimas.

_____

_____

7. En algunos países arrestan a los participantes de una manifestación.

_____

_____

F.   Opiniones. *Complete las siguientes oraciones para expresar sus opiniones sobre las actividades de compañeros, amigos o miembros de su familia.*

1. Me alegro que _____

_____

2. Tengo miedo que _____

_____

3. Dudo que _____

_____

4. Es bueno que _____

_____

5. Es ridículo que _____

_____

Nombre _____ **Fecha** _____ **Clase** _____

G. Los artículos definidos. *Escriba el artículo definido que corresponde al sustantivo.*

1. _____ padre

2. _____ niñas

3. _____ situación

4. _____ universidades

5. _____ clase

6. _____ mapa

7. _____ madre

8. _____ hombres

9. _____ problema

10. _____ mano

11. _____ día

12. _____ viernes

H. Un servicio de limpieza. *Ud. es el (la) dueño(-a) de un servicio de limpieza doméstico. Complete las instrucciones para su nueva empleada con* **el, la, los, las.**

Mañana Ud. necesita salir temprano para ir a _____ casa de la familia Gómez para limpiarla. Como Ud. no conoce bien _____ ciudad, debe usar _____ mapa que está encima de su escritorio. Al llegar a _____ casa de los Gómez, sacuda _____ muebles de _____ sala. Después, pase _____ aspiradora en _____ primer piso y en _____ dormitorios de _____ segundo piso. Luego, limpie todos _____ baños, haga _____ camas y lave _____ platos y _____ ropa. En esta familia hay cinco hijos; así que _____ cocina siempre está muy sucia. Primero, limpie _____ refrigerador y _____ fregadero. _____ esponjas y _____ trapos están debajo de _____ fregadero. Barra _____ piso y no se olvide de sacar _____ basura.

I.   Una vida mejor. *Explique lo que es necesario e importante que hagan sus amigos o los miembros de su familia para que su vida sea mejor. Incluya sus opiniones sobre su vida actual* (current).

_____

_____

_____

_____

_____

_____

_____

_____

_____

_____

_____

_____

A recordar

Review the following situations and tasks that have been presented and practiced in this chapter.

- Describe a house or apartment; list the rooms and the furniture and appliances in each room.
- Enlist the help of others.
- Tell family members and friends what to do.
- Compare people and things with equal qualities.
- Point out people and things.
- Discuss television programs.
- Express polite dismissal.
- Express judgment, doubt, and uncertainty.
- Talk about people and things.

Expansión de vocabulario

Dudas de vocabulario

to take: tomar / sacar / llevar / coger

tomar: *to take, to drink*

Vamos a tomar el autobús de las tres.	*We're going to take the three o'clock bus.*
Si quieres mejorarte, tienes que tomar este remedio.	*If you want to get better, you have to take this medicine.*
Tengo mucha sed. Tengo que tomar un poco de agua.	*I'm very thirsty. I have to drink some water.*

sacar: *to take out*

Por favor, saca la basura.	*Please take out the garbage.*

llevar: *to take something or somebody from one place to another*

¿Qué vas a llevar a la fiesta de Rosalía?	*What are you going to take to Rosalía's party?*

coger: *to take, to seize*

En la oficina del médico cogí una revista y esperé pacientemente.	*At the doctor's office, I took a magazine and waited patiently.*

television: la televisión / la tele / el televisor

la televisión: *television*

¿Vas a mirar la televisión?	*Are you going to watch television?*

la tele: *TV*

Ella se pasa toda la tarde mirando la tele.	*She spends all afternoon watching TV.*

poner la tele: *to turn on the TV*

Por favor, pon la tele. Ahora dan mi programa favorito.	*Please turn on the TV. They are showing my favorite program now.*

el televisor: *TV set*

¡Ay! ¿Qué voy a hacer? Mi televisor no funciona.	*Oh! What am I going to do? My TV set doesn't work.*

to raise: levantar / alzar / criar / cultivar / crecer

levantar / alzar: *to raise, to lift*

¿Puedes levantar / alzar esa caja, por favor? Pesa mucho para mí.	*Could you please lift that box? It's very heavy for me.*

criar: *to raise, bring up children; to raise animals*

Ellos adoptaron a los hijos de su hermana y los criaron.	*They adopted his sister's children and raised them.*
Ellos crían toda clase de animales en su casa.	*They raise all kinds of animals at their house.*

cultivar: *to grow plants*

Quisiera tener una huerta en mi casa y cultivar tomates y lechugas.	*I'd like to have a garden at my house and grow tomatoes and lettuce.*

crecer: *to grow*

Los niños crecen rápidamente. Antes que uno se dé cuenta ya son más altos que sus padres.	*Children grow up very fast. Before you know it, they are taller than their parents.*

Práctica

Complete el siguiente párrafo con la forma adecuada de una palabra de la lista para aprender más de la telenovela favorita de Bárbara.

poner la tele(visión)	la tele(visión)	el televisor	levantar
crecer	criar	cultivar	

Todas las tardes a las tres en punto _____ para mirar mi

telenovela favorita. Es la historia de una mujer que adoptó a los hijos de sus vecinos muertos y los

_____ . Ella es muy pobre y no puede comprar comida. Por eso

_____ animales, como ovejas y cerdos, y también

_____ legumbres y frutas en su jardín. Sus hijos siempre necesitan

ropa nueva porque _____ rápidamente. Es muy triste. Mi

compañera de cuarto también mira _____ por la tarde pero

prefiere otro programa. Creo que necesitamos comprar otro _____ .

Nombre _____   **Fecha** _____   **Clase** _____

Ampliación

The adjective endings *-al, -ario, -ista*

1. **SUFFIX**   -al   = *-al*
   nacional = *national*

   Adjectives ending in **-al** add **-es** to become plural: **un desastre local; las noticias locales.**

2. **SUFFIX**   -ario   = *-ary*
   ordinario = *ordinary*

   Adjectives ending in **-ario** have four forms to agree in number and gender with the noun modified.

3. **SUFFIX**   -ista   = *-istic, -ist*
   optimista = *optimistic, optimist*

   The suffix **-ista** is both masculine and feminine; the plural form ends in **-s: el hombre optimista, la mujer optimista.** In certain cases the **-ista** ending is used for both nouns and adjectives.

   Tienen un gobierno **socialista.**   *They have a socialist government.*
   Su presidente es **socialista.**   *Their president is a socialist.*

Práctica

A.   *Dé la forma inglesa de las siguientes palabras.*

1. internacional _____

2. local _____

3. comercial _____

4. extraordinario _____

5. primario _____

6. pesimista _____

7. realista _____

8. comunista _____

B. *Dé la forma española de las siguientes palabras.*

1. national _____

2. electoral _____

3. commercial _____

4. contrary _____

5. secondary _____

6. idealistic _____

7. optimistic _____

8. capitalistic _____

C. *Complete las oraciones con la forma adecuada de un adjetivo terminando en **-al**, **-ario** o **-ista**.*

1. Cada cuatro años hay una campaña _____ en los EE.UU.

2. En el periódico *USA Today* nos cuentan las noticias _____ e

   _____. Pero hay pocas noticias _____.

3. China es un país _____.

4. Paco es un hombre como todos; es muy _____.

5. El Sr. Gómez siempre está deprimido y triste; nunca tiene esperanza de mejorarse. Es muy

   _____.

6. Pero la Sra. Gómez es alegre y divertida; siempre cree que la vida es buena. Es

   _____.

Bienvenidos a Bolivia, al Ecuador y al Perú

A.   Adivinanza. *Para descubrir la palabra en la caja vertical, escriba en las líneas horizontales las palabras que corresponden a las definiciones.*

1.
2.
3.
4.
5.
6.
7.
8.

1. La línea que pasa al norte de Quito
2. La capital del Perú
3. El lago navegable más alto del mundo
4. La capital de Bolivia
5. La moneda del Perú
6. La región árida y alta en los Andes de Bolivia
7. Una ciudad grande en el Ecuador
8. Un producto importante de Bolivia

B.   El mapa. *Usando oraciones completas conteste las siguientes preguntas sobre Bolivia, el Ecuador, y el Perú.*

1. Describa la geografía de Bolivia. _____

_____

_____

2. Describa la geografía del Ecuador. _____

_____

_____

3. Describa la geografía del Perú. _____

_____

_____

4. ¿Cuántos habitantes hay en cada uno de los tres países? _____

_____

_____

5. ¿Cuál es la moneda de cada uno de los tres países? _____

_____

_____

6. ¿Cuáles son los productos principales de Bolivia? ¿del Ecuador? ¿del Perú? _____

_____

_____

_____

_____

Capítulo 7

De compras

Primera situación

A.   Algunas tiendas. *Ud. trabaja en la Oficina de Estudiantes Extranjeros de la universidad. Muchos alumnos le escriben a Ud. por correo electrónico pidiendo los nombres de lugares donde pueden comprar varios artículos. Déles el nombre de un lugar donde pueden encontrar los artículos deseados.*

> ➤ **MODELO**   Necesito zapatos para el invierno.
>   **Ve a la Zapatería Carmen.**

Necesito comprar…

1. un regalo para la boda de mi primo.

   _____

2. un par de botas.

   _____

3. una mesa y dos sillas para mi apartamento.

   _____

4. un regalo para el cumpleaños de mi hermanita.

   _____

5. mucha ropa pero tengo poco dinero.

   _____

6. una blusa elegante para mi mamá.

   _____

7. algunos aretes nuevos.

   _____

B. **De compras.** *Ud. está de compras en una boutique. Complete la conversación con la dependienta.*

1. DEPENDIENTA: Buenas tardes, señor / señora / señorita.
¿En qué puedo servirle?

USTED: (Explain that you're looking for a birthday gift for your brother / sister.)

_____

2. DEPENDIENTA: Acabo de recibir unas lindas chaquetas de Italia.

USTED: (Say that they are not appropriate. Ask to see the sweater in the window.)

_____

3. DEPENDIENTA: Sí, cómo no. Aquí lo tiene.

USTED: (Ask the price.)

_____

4. DEPENDIENTA: Es ochenta dólares americanos.

USTED: (Explain that you think the sweater is of good quality, but you'd like something less expensive.)

_____

5. DEPENDIENTA: Bueno, ¿qué le parece este suéter aquí?

USTED: (Say that you like it. Ask the price.)

_____

6. DEPENDIENTA: Es mucho menos que el otro. Cuesta sólo cuarenta dólares americanos. Está en oferta.

USTED: (Say that's fine. You'll take it.)

_____

7. DEPENDIENTA: ¿Desearía Ud. alguna otra cosa?

USTED: (Say no, that's all.)

_____

8. DEPENDIENTA: Aquí lo tiene. Pase por la caja, por favor.

USTED: (Say thank you and take leave.)

_____

Nombre _____ **Fecha** _____ **Clase** _____

C.   Los gerundios (present participles). *Escriba el gerundio que corresponde al infinitivo.*

1. comprar _____

2. decidir _____

3. pedir _____

4. probarse _____

5. divertirse _____

6. escoger _____

7. leer _____

8. dormir _____

9. oír _____

10. traer _____

D.   En Quito. *Explique lo que los miembros de la familia Tamayo están haciendo durante su visita al Ecuador.*

> ➤ *MODELO*   Carlos / caminar por un parque
> **Carlos está caminando por un parque.**

1. el abuelo / leer una guía sobre Quito.

   _____

2. Magdalena / escribirles tarjetas postales a sus amigos

   _____

3. Héctor / visitar la catedral

   _____

4. los padres / comer en un restaurante de lujo

   _____

5. la abuela / quejarse del calor

   _____

6. todos / divertirse

   _____

E.   ¿Qué estaban haciendo? *Explique lo que las siguientes personas estaban haciendo ayer a las tres de la tarde en el centro comercial.*

> ➤ *MODELO*   Ricardo / trabajar
> **Ricardo estaba trabajando.**

1. Teresa / oír música rock

_____

2. tú / escoger un regalo para tu amigo

_____

3. yo / hacer compras

_____

4. Manuel y yo / devolver un suéter

_____

5. Uds. / sentarse a comer

_____

6. Elena / probarse un vestido

_____

F. **Marilisa, la niña mimada.** *Marilisa tiene once años y es una niña mimada (spoiled). Sólo pide lo mejor. Ayúdela a escribir su lista de Navidad.*

➤ **MODELO**   vestido / elegante / almacén
   Quiero el vestido más elegante del almacén.

1. regalos / caro / ciudad

_____

2. pulsera / lindo / joyería

_____

3. botas / bueno / zapatería

_____

4. collar de oro / grande / boutique

_____

5. aretes / fino / tienda

_____

Nombre _____ **Fecha** _____ **Clase** _____

G.   Querida Julia. *Mariana es una estudiante de intercambio en La Paz, Bolivia, y le escribe una carta a su amiga Julia describiéndole una fiesta. Complete la carta con la forma adecuada del artículo definido. Si el artículo no es obligatorio, escriba 0 en el espacio.*

Querida Julia:

¡Qué cansada estoy! Anoche fui a _____ fiesta en casa de _____ Soto.

Viven en _____ casa de enfrente. _____ señor Soto es alto y moreno; es de

_____ Argentina. Su esposa es francesa pero habla _____ español bien. Soy

_____ amiga de su hija Dolores.

Fue una fiesta estupenda. Empezó a _____ ocho y no salimos hasta

_____ tres. Sabes que me encanta _____ música latina. Pues, como ellos

tienen muchos discos, escuchamos _____ música y nos quitamos _____

zapatos y bailamos toda _____ noche. ¡Fue tan lindo!

Bueno, tengo que irme. Espero recibir una carta de ti _____ viernes como siempre.

Abrazos,

Mariana

H.   Mis opiniones. *Explique sus opiniones acerca de los centros comerciales. Comente los aspectos positivos y negativos.*

1. Lo mejor de un centro comercial _____

_____.

2. Lo más divertido _____

_____.

3. Lo más desagradable _____

_____.

4. Lo más interesante _____

_____.

5. Lo peor _____

_____.

I.   En el centro comercial. *Escríbale una carta a su amigo(-a) Juan(-a) Herrera que vive en un pueblo en Bolivia. Explíquele lo que Ud. hizo la última vez que Ud. fue a un centro comercial.*

_____ :

_____

_____

_____

_____

_____

_____

_____

_____

_____

_____

_____

_____ ,

Segunda situación

A.   El catálogo. *Ud. trabaja en Lo Último, una tienda que se especializa en ropa para estudiantes universitarios. Ud. tiene que escribir los anuncios (advertisements) en el catálogo para los clientes hispanos. Describa la ropa de los dibujos en la siguiente página. Incluya información acerca de la tela, el diseño, los colores, el uso y el precio de cada prenda de vestir.*

A. _____

_____

B. _____

_____ /

_____

Nombre _____ **Fecha** _____ **Clase** _____

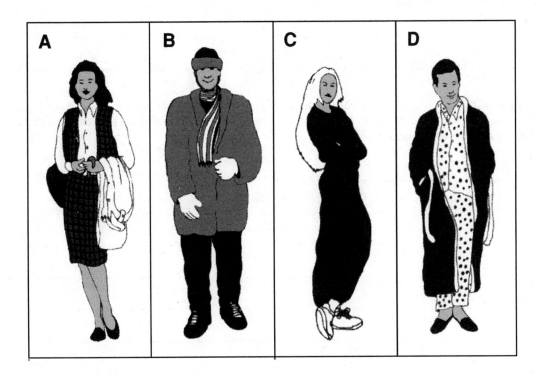

C. _____

_____

_____

_____

D. _____

_____

_____

B.   Un día horrible. *Ud. está en Guayaquil, Ecuador, y va de compras pero tiene muchos problemas. ¿Qué diría Ud. en las siguientes situaciones?*

1. Ud. compra pantalones que cuestan 75.000 sucres pero la cajera le cobra 95.000 sucres.

_____

2. Ud. hace cola desde hace quince minutos. Tiene que pagar, pero no quiere esperar más.

_____

3. Le falta un botón al impermeable que Ud. quiere comprar. El dependiente no quiere arreglarlo.

_____

4. La dependienta es descortés y sarcástica con todos los clientes.

_____

5. Ud. quiere devolver un traje descosido (*unsewn*), pero el gerente le dice que no aceptan devoluciones ni cambios.

_____

_____

C. **La ropa nueva.** *Sus padres le mandaron las siguientes cosas: un par de zapatos de tenis, una chaqueta y un impermeable. Nada le queda bien o no le gusta. Escríbales una carta a sus padres explicándoles el problema; pida otra ropa.*

_____ :

_____

_____

_____

_____

_____

_____

_____

_____

_____

_____

_____ ,

D. **Palabras indefinidas y negativas.** *Complete la siguiente tabla con una palabra indefinida o negativa según lo que falta.*

PALABRAS INDEFINIDAS	PALABRAS NEGATIVAS
1. _____	nadie
2. siempre	_____
3. también	_____
4. _____	de ningún modo
5. algo	_____
6. _____	ni…ni
7. alguno	_____

E. La dependienta perezosa. *Según una carta de recomendación, Consuelo López es la dependienta perfecta. Pero en realidad es lo contrario. Ud. escribe su primera evaluación y tiene que contradecir (contradict) la carta de recomendación.*

1. Consuelo López es muy trabajadora. Siempre hace algo.

_____

2. Se viste bien. Lleva un vestido o un traje todos los días.

_____

3. Es muy popular con sus clientes. Algunos clientes le mandan flores.

_____

4. También le dan regalos.

_____

5. De alguna manera vende más ropa que todas las otras dependientas.

_____

6. Alguien dijo que Consuelo es la dependienta perfecta.

_____

F. Algunos regalos. *Ud. estuvo de vacaciones. Explique a quién le compró los siguientes regalos.*

> **MODELO**   ¿Le compraste los guantes a Felipe?
> **Sí, se los compré a él.**

1. ¿Les compraste las camisetas a tus primas?

_____

2. ¿Le compraste el suéter a David?

_____

3. ¿Le compraste la blusa a Elena?

_____

4. ¿Les compraste los zapatos a Mario y Antonio?

_____

5. ¿Le compraste la bufanda a tu padre?

_____

G.   Unas vacaciones en el Ecuador. *Usando la forma adecuada de **y/o**, complete la tarjeta postal que Roberto piensa mandar a sus padres que viven en Colombia. (+ = y/e; ¿? = o/u)*

Queridos padres:

Estoy muy contento aquí en Quito. Todo está bien excepto el tiempo. Llueve mucho y

afortunadamente tengo mi paraguas (+) _____ impermeable. Nuestro grupo es grande

(+) _____ agradable. Nuestro guía es muy bueno—se llama Óscar (¿?) _____

Octavio; no recuerdo bien, pero es muy simpático. Nos lleva a sitios muy hermosos (+) _____

interesantes. Mañana por la tarde vamos a visitar siete (¿?) _____ ocho sitios

(+) _____ por la noche podemos ir a una discoteca (¿?) _____ a un concierto.

Abrazos,

Roberto

A recordar

Review the following situations and tasks that have been presented and practiced in this chapter.

- Discuss activities and the merchandise available in various shopping areas such as a large department store, a shopping mall, a boutique, a market.
- Make a routine purchase.
- Describe and discuss actions in progress.
- Make comparisons.
- Talk to and about people and things using definite articles.
- Make a complaint about an item of clothing and resolve the problem.
- Deny and contradict what others say.
- Avoid the repetition of previously mentioned people and things by using direct and indirect object pronouns.

Expansión de vocabulario

Dudas de vocabulario

to return: regresar / volver / devolver

regresar / volver: *to return, go back*

¿Cuándo vas a regresar / volver a Bolivia?   *When are you going back to Bolivia?*

volver a +infinitive: *to start to do something again*

Después de recuperarse de su bronquitis, él volvió a fumar.	*After recovering from bronchitis, he started to smoke again.*

devolver: *to return something, to give something back*

Ud. tiene que devolver los libros la próxima semana.	*You have to return the books next week.*

window: **la ventana / la ventanilla / la vitrina / el escaparate**

la ventana: *window*

¡Qué cuarto tan oscuro! ¡No hay ni una sola ventana!	*What a dark room! There is not one single window!*

la ventanilla: *small window; window where tickets are sold*

Los carros modernos ya no tienen una ventanilla en la puerta delantera.	*Modern cars don't have a small window in the front door anymore.*
Pase por la ventanilla para recoger las entradas.	*Go by the window to pick up the tickets.*

la vitrina: *store window (A); display case (E)*

Me encanta ver las decoraciones de Navidad en las vitrinas de Macy's.	*I love to see the Christmas decorations in the store windows at Macy's.*

el escaparate: *cabinet used to display crystal or china; store window (E); display case (A)*

Mi madre guarda los platos finos en el escaparate para que mi hermanito no los agarre.	*My mother puts the fine china in the china cabinet so that my little brother doesn't grab it.*

light: **claro / ligero / débil / la luz / la lámpara**

claro: *light, referring to color*

Ese vestido es azul claro.	*That dress is light blue.*

ligero: *light, referring to weight*

Tú puedes cargar eso porque es muy ligero; no es pesado.	*You can carry that because it's light; it's not heavy.*

débil: *light, referring to sound*

Me asusté cuando oí un suspiro débil en la noche oscura.	*I got scared when I heard a light whisper in the dark night.*

la luz: *light; electricity*

¡Aquí no hay luz! Todo está oscuro.   *There is no light here! It's all dark.*

la lámpara: *light, lamp*

¿Dónde está la lámpara? Prende   *Where's the lamp? Turn*
la luz, por favor.   *the light on, please.*

Práctica

Complete el párrafo con la forma adecuada de las siguientes palabras.

regresar	volver	volver a + inf.	devolver
la ventana	la ventanilla	el escaparate	la vitrina
claro	ligero	débil	
la luz	la lámpara		

Mariana estudia en una universidad en Quito, Ecuador. Esta tarde fue de compras al centro.

Primero miró la ropa nueva en _____ de su almacén favorito. Después entró y

se probó muchos vestidos; compró un vestido azul _____ y una chaqueta

_____ para el verano.

En la residencia Mariana tiene un cuarto con dos _____ grandes desde las

cuales puede ver las montañas. Pero a pesar de eso nunca hay bastante _____

para leer. Por eso compró una _____ nueva para su escritorio.

Mariana _____ a la residencia a las cuatro y _____

estudiar. Pero cuando empezó a leer descubrió que su _____ no funcionaba

bien. Fue al centro otra vez y _____ la lámpara.

Ampliación

The suffix *-ería*

SUFFIX   -ería   = *shop, store*
           la zapatería = *shoe store*

The suffix **-ería** is often added to the name of a product to indicate the shop or store where the product is sold, repaired, or taken care of. In most cases these feminine nouns are formed by adding **-ería** to words ending in a consonant or by dropping the final vowel from the product and adding **-ería: el zapato → zapat- → la zapatería.**

Nombre _____ **Fecha** _____ **Clase** _____

Práctica

A. *Dé la forma inglesa de los siguientes sustantivos.*

1. la joyería _____

2. la perfumería _____

3. la lavandería _____

4. la guantería _____

5. la carnicería _____

6. la heladería _____

7. la panadería _____

8. la papelería _____

B. *Dé el sustantivo español para las siguientes tiendas.*

1. fruit store _____

2. watch repair shop _____

3. fish store _____

4. shoe store _____

5. pastry shop _____

6. bookstore _____

C. *Complete las oraciones con un sustantivo terminando en* **-ería.**

1. Se venden anillos, aretes y pulseras en una _____.

2. Se venden botas, sandalias y pantuflas en una _____.

3. Se venden bolígrafos, lápices, tarjetas y papel en una _____.

4. Se venden libros en una _____.

5. Se venden manzanas, naranjas y melones en una _____.

6. Se venden jabón, maquillaje y perfume en una _____.

Capítulo 8
En la ciudad

Primera situación

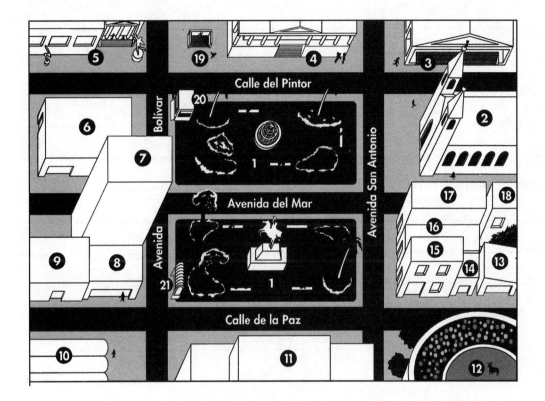

CLAVE

1. Plaza Bolívar
2. Catedral Metropolitana
3. Palacio Presidencial
4. Ayuntamiento
5. Museo de Bellas Artes
6. Almacenes Suárez
7. Hotel Bolívar
8. Supermercado Precios Únicos
9. Apartamentos Don Carlos
10. Estación de Tren
11. Hospital Santa Clara
12. Plaza de Toros
13. Boutique Álvarez
14. Farmacia de la Paz
15. Cine Bolívar
16. Oficina de Turismo
17. Banco Nacional
18. Restaurante del Mar
19. Metro
20. Quiosco
21. Parada de Autobús

A. **La Oficina de Turismo.** *Ud. trabaja en la Oficina de Turismo. Puesto que la mayoría de los turistas le hacen las mismas preguntas, escriba una lista de información indicando dónde los turistas pueden obtener varios objetos o servicios y dónde se encuentra el lugar.*

> ➤ *MODELO*   tomar el tren
> **La estación de trenes está en la esquina de la Avenida Bolívar y la Calle de la Paz, enfrente del Hospital Santa Clara.**

1. tomar el metro _____

_____

_____

2. comprar ropa nueva _____

_____

_____

3. cambiar cheques de viajero _____

_____

_____

4. comprar comida para un picnic _____

_____

_____

5. tomar un autobús _____

_____

_____

6. comprar una revista _____

_____

_____

B. **Un folleto turístico.** *Ud. tiene que escribir un folleto para los turistas. Usando el mapa, describa los sitios de interés.*

_____

_____

_____

_____

Nombre _____ **Fecha** _____ **Clase** _____

_____

_____

_____

_____

_____

_____

_____

_____

_____

_____

C.   **¿Me podría decir...?** _Escríbales direcciones a las siguientes personas que vienen a la Oficina de Turismo para obtener información._

1. Una señorita quiere tomar el metro para visitar a una amiga que vive fuera de la ciudad. _____

_____

_____

2. Un joven quiere visitar a sus tíos que viven en los Apartamentos Don Carlos. _____

_____

_____

3. Un hombre quiere ir a la Plaza de Toros y después al Hotel Bolívar. _____

_____

_____

4. Dos señoras quieren ir al Museo de Bellas Artes. _____

_____

_____

5. Una familia quiere visitar el Palacio Presidencial y después necesitan tomar el tren. _____

_____

_____

D. Mandatos formales. *Escriba el mandato formal singular (Ud.) que corresponde al infinitivo.*

1. pasar _____   8. buscar _____

2. comer _____   9. cruzar _____

3. abrir _____   10. dirigir _____

4. ir _____   11. llegar _____

5. dar _____   12. hacer _____

6. salir _____   13. saber _____

7. ser _____   14. estar _____

E. Consejos turísticos. *Un grupo de turistas le mandó una serie de preguntas relacionadas con su viaje. Escríbale al grupo contestando sus preguntas según el modelo.*

> ➤ *MODELO*   ¿Cuándo debemos visitar su país? (en el verano)
> **Visítenlo en el verano.**

1. ¿Cuándo debemos conseguir el pasaporte? (lo más pronto posible)

   _____

2. ¿Debemos leer algo antes de salir? (sí, una buena guía turística)

   _____

3. ¿Qué sitios históricos debemos ver? (el Palacio Presidencial)

   _____

4. ¿Debemos sacar fotos? (sí, de los sitios de interés)

   _____

5. ¿Dónde debemos almorzar? (en un restaurante típico)

   _____

6. ¿Por cuánto tiempo debemos quedarnos? (por una semana)

   _____

7. ¿Qué debemos hacer el primer día? (darse un paseo por el centro)

   _____

8. ¿Qué podemos hacer por la noche? (ir a una discoteca)

   _____

Nombre _____ **Fecha** _____ **Clase** _____

F. ¿Dónde se hace? *Usando el mapa de la ciudad, escriba respuestas a las preguntas de los turistas explicándoles dónde se puede hacer varias cosas.*

> **MODELO**   ¿Adónde se va para comprar fruta?
> **Se compra fruta en el Supermercado Precios Únicos.**

1. ¿Adónde se va para comprar un periódico?

_____

2. ¿Adónde se va para comer bien?

_____

3. ¿Adónde se va para ver una película?

_____

4. ¿Adónde se va para comprar regalos?

_____

5. ¿Adónde se va para tomar el autobús?

_____

6. ¿Adónde se va para ver una exposición de arte?

_____

G. La familia Quintana. *Complete el párrafo con la forma adecuada del artículo indefinido. Ponga 0 en el espacio si el artículo no es obligatorio.*

Rafael Quintana y su familia viven en el Perú en _____ pueblo pequeño cerca

de Lima. Rafael es _____ dentista y su esposa Teresa es _____

recepcionista en _____ oficina comercial. Teresa es _____ boliviana

pero vive en el Perú desde hace quince años. Rafael y Teresa tienen dos hijos. _____

de sus hijos estudia en la universidad para hacerse _____ abogado y

_____ otro hijo quiere ser _____ profesor de química en

_____ escuela secundaria. Actualmente la familia busca _____ casa

en _____ barrio residencial de su pueblo. Quieren vivir en _____

lugar más tranquilo con _____ jardín.

Segunda situación

A. **¿Qué se puede ver?** *Haga una lista de las cosas que se puede ver en los siguientes lugares.*

1. El museo de arte _____

_____

_____

2. La plaza de toros _____

_____

_____

B. **El parque de atracciones.** *Un parque de atracciones dirige un concurso (contest); el primer premio consiste en veinticinco entradas para Ud., su familia y / o sus amigos. Para ganar el primer premio hay que escribir una composición explicando por qué quiere visitar el parque, con quiénes prefiere ir y lo que todos harán.*

_____

_____

_____

_____

_____

_____

_____

_____

_____

_____

_____

_____

C. **Un(-a) compañero(-a) flojo(-a).** *Su compañero(-a) de cuarto es muy flojo(-a). Ud. necesita animarlo(-la) para hacer sus deberes. ¿Qué le diría para que haga las siguientes actividades?*

1. salir pronto para estudiar en la biblioteca

_____

Nombre _____ **Fecha** _____ **Clase** _____

2. escribir su composición para la clase de inglés

_____

3. lavar la ropa

_____

4. no mirar tanto la televisión

_____

5. empezar la tarea de química

_____

D. **El tiempo futuro.** *Escriba las formas del futuro que corresponden a los sujetos dados.*

	viajar	**volver**
1. Ud.	_____	_____
2. los García	_____	_____
3. yo	_____	_____
4. Julia	_____	_____
5. tú	_____	_____
6. nosotros	_____	_____

E. **Unas formas irregulares.** *Escriba las formas del futuro de la primera persona singular (yo) y plural (nosotros) para los siguientes infinitivos.*

	PRIMERA PERSONA SINGULAR	**PRIMERA PERSONA PLURAL**
1. tener	_____	_____
2. querer	_____	_____
3. decir	_____	_____
4. hacer	_____	_____
5. poder	_____	_____
6. salir	_____	_____
7. poner	_____	_____
8. venir	_____	_____

F.   **Un viaje al Perú.** *Describa lo que las siguientes personas harán durante sus vacaciones en el Perú.*

> ➤ *MODELO*   Mario / visitar Machu Picchu
>   **Mario visitará Machu Picchu.**

1. tú / hacer una excursión a Cuzco

_____

2. los Pereda / levantarse tarde todos los días

_____

3. Carlos del Valle / salir a bailar todas las noches

_____

4. Uds. / ir de compras en el Jirón de la Unión

_____

5. mi novio(-a) y yo / conducir a la playa

_____

6. la Srta. Robles / comer muchos mariscos

_____

7. yo / ¿?

_____

G.   **Algunas probabilidades.** *Para cada dibujo hay una pregunta que expresa una probabilidad acerca de la situación. Forme otras dos preguntas apropiadas y luego conteste todas las preguntas.*

Nombre _____ **Fecha** _____ **Clase** _____

1. ¿De quién será el paquete?

_____

¿_____?

_____

¿_____?

_____

2. ¿Quién me llamará?

_____

¿_____?

_____

¿_____?

_____

3. ¿Qué querrá el jefe?

_____

¿_____?

_____

¿_____?

_____

H. **Dentro de diez años.** *Describa su vida futura dentro de diez años.*

_____

_____

_____

_____

_____

_____

_____

_____

_____

_____

_____

I.   Un día libre. *Ud. y sus amigos tienen un día libre. Usando los mandatos de primera persona plural (nosotros), haga sugerencias sobre lo que Ud. y sus amigos pueden hacer.*

1. asistir a un concierto rock

_____

2. ir al parque de atracciones

_____

3. almorzar en un restaurante

_____

4. salir a bailar

_____

5. tener una fiesta

_____

6. jugar al vólibol

_____

7. ¿?

_____

A recordar

Review the following situations and tasks that have been presented and practiced in this chapter.

- Describe the various buildings and services found in cities.
- Discuss the various activities that can be done in U.S. and Hispanic cities.
- Ask for, understand, and give directions.
- Tell other people what to do.
- Ask for and provide information.
- Talk about other people.
- Persuade others to do what you want them to do.
- Discuss future activities.
- Express probability.
- Suggest group activities.

Nombre _____ **Fecha** _____ **Clase** _____

Expansión de vocabulario

Dudas de vocabulario

date: la cita / la fecha

la cita: *date, as in having a date*

Gregorio está nerviosísimo porque
tiene una cita con Debra.

*Gregorio is very nervous because
he has a date with Debra.*

la fecha: *date, as in the day and month of the year*

¿Qué fecha es hoy?

What is today's date?

to look: buscar / cuidar / mirar / parecer / ver

buscar: *to look for, to seek*

Antonio busca un nuevo apartamento.

Antonio is looking for a new apartment.

cuidar: *to look after, to take care of*

Yo siempre cuido a mi hermanito.

I always take care of my little brother.

mirar: *to look at*

Él se quedó mirando a Rita una hora
sin decir una sola palabra.

*He stayed there looking at Rita for an hour
without saying a single word.*

parecer: *to look, seem*

Sin embargo, él parece ser inteligente, ¿no?

However, he seems to be intelligent, doesn't he?

ver: *to look, see*

Quiero ver qué dice Myrna
después de todo esto.

*I want to see what Myrna says
after all this.*

real: real / verdadero

real / verdadero(-a): *real, actual, true*

La verdadera razón es que él no quiere
ir a tu fiesta.

*The real reason is that he does not want
to go to your party.*

El valor real de sus propiedades es mínimo.

The actual value of their properties is minimal.

actually: en realidad

en realidad: *actually, as a matter of fact*

En realidad, lo único que tienen es una gran fuerza de voluntad.	*Actually/As a matter of fact, the only thing they have is great willpower.*

nowadays: actualmente, hoy (en) día

actualmente / hoy (en) día: *at the present time, nowadays*

Actualmente / hoy (en) día el problema de las drogas está más difundido que hace unos veinte años.	*Nowadays, the drug problem is more widespread than twenty years ago.*

Práctica

Complete el párrafo con el equivalente español de las palabras entre paréntesis.

Rogelio *(looks)* _____ nervioso. Dice que está nervioso a causa de un examen

de física mañana, pero yo sé que la *(real)* _____ razón es que tiene una *(date)*

_____ con Teresa. Como Teresa tiene que *(look after)* _____

a su hermanita, Rogelio y ella van a *(watch)* _____ la televisión o *(see)*

_____ una película en su casa. Ahora mismo Rogelio *(is looking for)*

_____ una película buena de su colección. *(Actually)* _____ es

mejor quedarse en casa porque *(nowadays)* _____ la entrada al cine cuesta demasiado.

Ampliación

Compound nouns

Spanish frequently forms nouns from the combination of a verb and a noun. These compound nouns generally indicate a building, gadget, piece of equipment, furniture, or clothing. The noun is formed by joining the third-person singular of the present tense verb form followed by a noun; these compound nouns are usually masculine: **el rascacielos** = *skyscraper,* **rascar** = *to scrape, scratch;* **el cielo** = *sky.* Note that the English translation generally begins with the equivalent of the Spanish noun.

Nombre _____ **Fecha** _____ **Clase** _____

Práctica

A. *Dé la forma inglesa de los sustantivos.* (**parar** = to stop; **guardar** = to keep, guard; **quitar, sacar** = to remove)

1. el paraguas _____

2. el quitanieve _____

3. el lavaplatos _____

4. el guardarropa _____

5. el pasatiempo _____

6. el limpiacristales _____

7. el paracaídas _____

8. el pararrayos _____

B. *Forme una palabra que corresponda al inglés usando los siguientes infinitivos y sustantivos.*

abrir	**la brisa**
guardar	**los corchos**
limpiar	**los dientes**
parar	**los golpes**
sacar	**las latas**
salvar	**la puerta**
	el sol
	las vidas

1. storm door   la _____

2. can opener   el _____

3. corkscrew   el _____

4. windshield   el _____

5. toothpick   el _____

6. life preserver   el _____

7. sunshade   el _____

8. (automobile) bumper   el _____

C. *Complete las oraciones usando un sustantivo compuesto.*

1. Un edificio muy alto de muchos pisos es un _____ .

2. Cuando llueve usamos un _____ .

3. Después de comer ponemos los platos en el _____ para limpiarlos.

4. Para abrir una botella de vino usamos un _____ .

5. En las casas viejas usan un _____ para la ropa y los zapatos.

6. En un barco siempre hay muchos _____ en caso de emergencia.

Bienvenidos a la comunidad hispana en los EE.UU.

A.   Adivinanza. *Para descubrir la palabra de la caja vertical, escriba en las líneas horizontales las palabras que corresponden a las definiciones de cada número.*

1. __ __ | __ | __ __ __ __ __
2. __ | __ | __ __ __
3. __ | __ | __ __ __
4. __ __ | __ | __
5. __ __ | __ |
6. __ __ __ __ __ | __ | __
7. __ __ __ __ __ | __ | __
8. __ __ __ __ | __ |

1. Personas de origen mexicano que viven en los EE.UU.
2. Una ciudad en la Florida con gran concentración de cubanos
3. El apellido de una cantante popular
4. El apellido de una golfista hispana
5. Una isla en el Caribe
6. Una famosa personalidad de la televisión en lengua española
7. Una ciudad en el noreste de los EE.UU. con gran concentración de puertorriqueños
8. El apellido de un famoso actor de la televisión y del cine

B.   El mapa. *Usando oraciones completas conteste las siguientes preguntas sobre la comunidad hispana en los EE.UU.*

1. ¿Cuántos habitantes hispanos hay actualmente en los EE.UU.?

_____

_____

2. ¿De dónde son los hispanos en los EE.UU.? _____

_____

_____

3. ¿Dónde se encuentran la mayoría de los chicanos? _____

_____

¿Los cubanos? _____

_____

¿Los puertorriqueños? _____

_____

4. Nombre dos hispanos famosos en las siguientes categorías.

Cine y televisión _____

_____

Deportes _____

_____

Literatura _____

_____

Moda _____

_____

Música _____

_____

Política _____

_____

Capítulo 9

En la agencia de empleos

Primera situación

A. Una solicitud de empleo. *Ud. solicita un puesto en una compañía grande e importante. Llene las siguientes secciones de la solicitud.*

APELLIDO(-S) _____ NOMBRE _____

DIRECCIÓN _____

_____

_____

EDUCACIÓN _____

_____

_____

_____

EXPERIENCIA _____

_____

_____

_____

APTITUDES PERSONALES _____

_____

_____

_____

PUESTO DESEADO _____

_____

_____

_____

B.   El empleo ideal. *Escriba un anuncio para el empleo ideal. Mencione por lo menos cinco características.*

_____

_____

_____

_____

_____

_____

_____

_____

_____

C.   Posibilidades de empleo. *Ud. y unos(-as) amigos(-as) están hablando del futuro y las posibilidades de empleo. ¿Qué dicen Uds. en las siguientes situaciones?*

1. Ud. tiene una idea magnífica para obtener un buen empleo.

    _____

2. Ud. quiere proponer la idea de buscar trabajo juntos.

    _____

3. Un(-a) amigo(-a) piensa que su idea no es muy buena y recomienda otra posibilidad.

    _____

4. Otro(-a) amigo(-a) interrumpe y presenta una idea nueva.

    _____

5. Ud. quiere volver al tema original.

    _____

Nombre _____ **Fecha** _____ **Clase** _____

D. **El condicional.** *Escriba las formas del condicional que corresponden a los sujetos dados.*

	trabajar	**escribir**
Carlos y yo	_____	_____
tú	_____	_____
el dueño	_____	_____
Uds.	_____	_____
yo	_____	_____
Julio y Raúl	_____	_____

E. **Unas formas irregulares.** *Escriba las formas del condicional de la tercera persona singular (él, ella, Ud.) y plural (ellos, ellas, Uds.) para los siguientes infinitivos.*

	TERCERA PERSONA SINGULAR	**TERCERA PERSONA PLURAL**
1. poder	_____	_____
2. hacer	_____	_____
3. salir	_____	_____
4. decir	_____	_____
5. saber	_____	_____
6. querer	_____	_____
7. venir	_____	_____
8. tener	_____	_____

F. **Bajo condiciones ideales.** *Describa lo que harían las siguientes personas bajo condiciones ideales.*

> ➤ **MODELO**   Mario / trabajar en una compañía española
> **Mario trabajaría en una compañía española.**

1. tú / construir una casa grande

_____

2. los Fernández / hacerse muy ricos

_____

3. Carlos Morales / encargarse de una compañía grande

_____

4. Uds. / tener su propia compañía

_____

5. mi novio(-a) y yo / poder casarse

_____

6. la Srta. García / salir para México

_____

G.   En otra situación. *Explique lo que Ud. haría con su vida bajo otras condiciones y en otra situación. ¿Dónde viviría Ud. / qué y dónde estudiaría / dónde trabajaría / quiénes serían sus amigos / qué compraría?*

_____

_____

_____

_____

_____

_____

_____

_____

_____

_____

H.   En la Compañía Domínguez. *Describa cómo trabajan los empleados en la Compañía Domínguez.*

> ➤ **MODELO**   el Sr. Suárez / rápido
>   **El Sr. Suárez trabaja rápidamente.**

1. el jefe / eficaz

_____

Nombre _____ **Fecha** _____ **Clase** _____

2. la secretaria / cuidadoso

_____

3. la Sra. Pereda / paciente

_____

4. los gerentes / atento

_____

5. Marcos Duarte / perezoso

_____

6. todos los vendedores / responsable

_____

I. **En la agencia de empleos.** *Explique lo que las siguientes personas hicieron ayer en la Agencia de Empleos Suárez.*

> ***MODELO***   Rafael Cárdenas escribió cartas. (mucho)
>   **Rafael Cárdenas escribió muchas cartas.**

1. El Sr. Cáceres escribió anuncios. (numeroso)

_____

2. Pablo leyó cartas de recomendación. (todo)

_____

3. La Srta. Acosta llenó solicitudes. (demasiado)

_____

4. La Sra. Ocampo despidió a un empleado. (otro)

_____

5. Los Núñez consiguieron entrevistas. (poco)

_____

6. El Dr. Lado describió los beneficios sociales. (alguno)

_____

Segunda situación

A. Los materiales para la oficina. *Ud. es el (la) dueño(-a) de una tienda que alquila todos los materiales (supplies) necesarios para una oficina comercial. Prepare una lista de todos los artículos y muebles que se puede alquilar en su tienda.*

_____

_____

_____

_____

_____

_____

_____

_____

B. El (la) telefonista. *Ud. es el (la) telefonista de una compañía grande que recibe muchas llamadas de clientes que piden información. Para facilitar su trabajo, prepare una lista indicando qué sección de la compañía tiene las siguientes responsabilidades.*

1. Se prepara la propaganda y los anuncios para los periódicos, las revistas, la radio y la televisión.

_____

2. Se preocupa por los problemas con los clientes.

_____

3. Se decide dónde y cómo se venden los productos.

_____

4. Se preocupa de los pedidos, los vendedores y las zonas de ventas.

_____

5. Se maneja (*manages*) la planificación y la coordinación de toda la compañía.

_____

6. Se maneja las responsabilidades financieras.

_____

Nombre _____ Fecha _____ Clase _____

C. **¿Comprende Ud.?** *Explique lo que Ud. diría en las siguientes situaciones.*

1. Ud. habla por teléfono con un(-a) compañero(-a) que no contesta una de sus preguntas.

   _____

2. Ud. le da instrucciones difíciles a su hermanita que no parece entender.

   _____

3. Ud. le sugiere a su novio(-a) que vayan al cine mañana por la noche.

   _____

4. Un(-a) amigo(-a) le da a Ud. noticias increíbles acerca de otro(-a) amigo(-a).

   _____

5. Ud. expresa una opinión política y quiere saber lo que su amigo(-a) piensa de su idea.

   _____

D. **Los nuevos empleados.** *Ud. es el (la) dueño(-a) de una compañía grande que necesita mucho personal nuevo. Explique las calificaciones deseadas de los nuevos empleados.*

> ➤ **MODELO**   una secretaria / hablar español
> **Buscamos una secretaria que hable español.**

Buscamos...

1. una secretaria / saber usar la nueva computadora

   _____

2. un contador / ser inteligente

   _____

3. una gerente / resolver problemas eficazmente

   _____

4. un jefe de ventas / llevarse bien con los clientes

   _____

No queremos nadie que...

5. perder tiempo

_____

6. fumar en la oficina

_____

7. quejarse mucho

_____

8. decir mentiras

_____

E. **El nuevo personal.** *Ud. es el (la) gerente de una compañía que importa muebles de la América del Sur. Ud. necesita una nueva secretaria y un jefe de ventas. Escriba dos anuncios explicando cada puesto y las calificaciones deseadas.*

_____

_____

_____

_____

_____

_____

_____

_____

_____

F. **En la Oficina de Personal.** *Ud. es el (la) supervisor(-a) de una oficina de personal. Cuando sus empleados le preguntan a Ud. quién debe hacer varias cosas, dígales lo que Ud. quiere que hagan sus empleados.*

➤ **MODELO**   ¿Debe escribir las cartas Adela? (Gloria)
                             No. Que las escriba Gloria.

1. ¿Debe empezar el informe Pedro? (el Sr. Robles)

_____

2. ¿Debe resolver los problemas legales Teresa? (Graciela y Mariana)

_____

3. ¿Debe llenar la solicitud la Sra. Marín? (la Sra. González)

_____

4. ¿Debe escribir los anuncios el Sr. Fuentes? (el Sr. Almazán)

_____

5. ¿Debe despedir al nuevo empleado el Sr. Gómez? (el Sr. Ruiz)

_____

6. ¿Debe hacer las llamadas la secretaria? (todos los empleados)

_____

G. Un trabajo ideal. *Para describir el trabajo ideal, complete las oraciones utilizando el superlativo absoluto de las palabras entre paréntesis.*

1. (alto) Tengo un trabajo ideal y recibo un sueldo _____.

2. (bueno / malo) Los supervisores son _____ y no hay

ningún empleado _____.

3. (grande / lindo) Mi oficina es _____ con una vista

_____.

4. (simpático / mucho) Mis compañeros de trabajo son _____

y me tratan con _____ respeto.

5. (poco / largo) Paso _____ tiempo en la oficina y tengo

_____ vacaciones.

H.   Mi trabajo ideal. *Describa su trabajo ideal incluyendo información sobre el tipo de trabajo, los supervisores, los compañeros de trabajo, el sueldo, la oficina o el lugar donde Ud. trabaja y otros detalles. No se olvide de usar el subjuntivo cuando la oración subordinada se refiere a una persona o cosa que no existe o no se conoce.*

_____

_____

_____

_____

_____

_____

_____

_____

_____

A recordar

Review the following situations and tasks that have been presented and practiced in this chapter.

- Discuss and describe various jobs and careers.
- Change directions in a conversation.
- Explain what you would do under certain conditions.
- Describe how actions are done.
- Indicate quantities.
- Double-check comprehension.
- Talk about unknown or nonexistent people and things.
- Explain what you want others to do.
- Express exceptional qualities.

Expansión de vocabulario

Dudas de vocabulario

job / work: el puesto / el trabajo / el empleo / la tarea / la obra

el puesto: *job, position*

Vilma consiguió un buen puesto con la IBM.   *Vilma got a good job with IBM.*

el trabajo: *work, job, task*

Tengo tanto trabajo que no lo terminaré nunca.   *I have so much work that I'll never finish it.*

el empleo: *employment, job*

Sí, tú sabes que ella estuvo sin empleo   *Yes, you know she was without a job*
por varios meses.   *for several months.*

la tarea: *homework*

¿Tienes mucha tarea para mañana?   *Do you have a lot of homework for tomorrow?*

la obra: *literary / artistic / charitable work*

Él no ha leído ni una   *He hasn't read even one*
de las obras de Shakespeare.   *of Shakespeare's works.*

Las obras de la Madre Teresa le ganaron el   *The (charitable) works of Mother Theresa*
amor y el respeto de todo el mundo.   *earned her everybody's love and respect.*

to work: trabajar / funcionar

trabajar: *to work*

Ella trabaja mucho.   *She works too much.*
Uno de estos días se va a enfermar.   *She is going to get sick one of these days.*

funcionar: *to work, to operate, to function*

Este lavaplatos no funciona.   *This dishwasher doesn't work.*
Vas a tener que lavar los platos a mano.   *You'll have to do the dishes by hand.*

to become: hacerse / llegar a ser / ponerse / volverse

hacerse: *to become. It implies a personal effort and can be followed by either a noun or an adjective.*

Se hizo rico trabajando día y noche.   *He became rich working day and night.*
Se hizo abogado después de muchos años.   *He became a lawyer after many years.*

llegar a ser: *to become. It implies a gradual change, but does not necessarily imply a personal effort. It can also be followed by a noun or an adjective.*

Llegó a ser un buen médico.   *He became a good doctor.*
Contrario a lo que todos pensaban,   *Contrary to what everybody thought,*
llegó a ser muy delgada.   *she became very thin.*

ponerse: *to become. It indicates a change in physical and/or emotional state, and can only be followed by an adjective.*

Se puso nervioso.   *He became nervous.*

volverse: *to become. It implies a sudden physical and/or emotional change, and can only be followed by an adjective.*

Se volvió loco cuando la conoció.   *He went crazy when he met her.*

No comprendo cómo los cantantes de rock   *I don't understand how rock singers*
no se vuelven sordos con el ruido.   *don't become deaf with the noise.*

Práctica

1. Explique qué les pasó a las siguientes personas en la Compañía Ordóñez. Complete las oraciones con la forma adecuada de **hacerse / llegar a ser / ponerse / volverse**.

   a. El Sr. Ordóñez, el presidente de la compañía, _____ gordo por comer mucho y no hacer ejercicios.

   b. El hijo del Sr. Ordóñez _____ el vice presidente aunque no trabajó mucho.

   c. La hija del Sr. Ordóñez _____ abogada estudiando de noche y trabajando de día.

   d. La pobre esposa del Sr. Ordóñez casi _____ loca al saber que su esposo se enamoró de su secretaria.

2. Complete la narración acerca de los problemas de Consuelo usando la forma apropiada de las palabras de la lista.

el empleo	la obra	el puesto
la tarea	el trabajo	
funcionar	trabajar	

   Hace cuatro meses que Consuelo está sin _____. Tiene muchos

   problemas. Su coche no _____ bien y tiene que pagar la matrícula de

   este semestre. Aunque prefiere un _____ en una compañía grande,

   busca _____ en cualquier lugar. Está preocupada porque tiene mucha

   _____ también. En su clase de literatura necesita leer dos

   _____ literarias y escribir un informe cada semana. Si tiene que

   _____ por la noche, no sabe cuándo puede estudiar.

Ampliación

Compound verbs

Spanish often forms compound verbs with prefixes attached to existing verbs, nouns, or adjectives. Knowing what the prefixes mean makes it easier to recognize and use these compound verbs.

1. **PREFIX**   **con-, com-** = *con-, com-*
                 contener   = *contain*

   The prefix **con, com** = *with:* **compadecer** = *to sympathize (to suffer with someone).* The prefix **com** is used before the bilabial sounds **p** and **b**.

2. **PREFIX**   **des-**   = *dis-, de-, un-*
                 desaparecer = *disappear*

   The prefix **des-** = *to take away, remove.*

3. **PREFIX**   **en-, em-**   = *en-, in-*
                 encargarse = *to be in charge of, to be entrusted with*

   The prefix **en-, em-** = *to become, to get* and is frequently combined with an adjective such as **engordar (en + gordo)** = *to get fat, to become fat.* The prefix **em-** is used before the bilabial sounds **p** and **b**.

4. **PREFIX**   **pre-**   = *pre-*
                 predecir   = *predict*

   The prefix **pre-** = *to put before.*

5. Compound verbs composed of a prefix + verb are conjugated like the simple verb; that is, **predecir** is conjugated like **decir**. Likewise, **contener** is conjugated like **tener**.

6. **Tener** in compound verbs = *-tain:* **obtener** = *obtain.* **Poner** in compound verbs = *-pose:* **componer** = *compose.*

Práctica

A. *Dé la forma inglesa de las siguientes palabras.*

1. contener _____

2. componer _____

3. desocupar _____

4. deshacer _____

5. empobrecerse _____

6. emborracharse _____

7. predecir _____

8. prescribir _____

B. *Dé la forma española de las siguientes palabras.*

1. to contain _____

2. to compromise _____

3. to dismiss _____

4. to disappear _____

5. to fall in love _____

6. to get sick _____

7. to bury _____

8. to predict _____

C. *Complete las oraciones con el infinitivo de un verbo compuesto que empieza con el prefijo en paréntesis.*

1. Estela come muchos dulces, pasteles y helado. Ella va a (en-) _____.

2. Al final del año todos tratan de (pre-) _____ lo que va a pasar en el año nuevo.

3. Manolo nunca llega a tiempo a su oficina y no trabaja mucho. El jefe va a (des-)

   _____ a Manolo muy pronto.

4. El Sr. Galván va a escribir una ópera. La va a (com-) _____ inmediatamente.

5. Los González van a salir del hotel pero primero van a hacer las maletas y (des-)

   _____ la habitación.

6. Julio e Isabel están en un crucero romántico en el Mediterráneo y siempre están juntos. Es obvio

   que los dos van a (en-) _____.

Capítulo 10

En la empresa multinacional

Primera situación

A. **Las responsabilidades.** *Como el (la) jefe(-a) de personal, Ud. tiene que preparar una descripción de varios puestos dentro de la empresa multinacional donde Ud. trabaja. Incluya por lo menos dos responsabilidades para cada puesto.*

1. el (la) recepcionista _____

_____

_____

2. el (la) oficinista _____

_____

_____

3. el (la) publicista _____

_____

_____

4. el (la) contador(-a) _____

_____

_____

5. el (la) programador(-a) _____

_____

_____

6. el (la) ejecutivo(-a) _____

_____

_____

B.   Una llamada telefónica. *Ud. trabaja en la empresa Contadores Padilla e Hijos. Hace un mes Ud. pidió diez computadoras nuevas de Montalvo y Compañía pero todavía no las ha recibido. Ud. llama a la compañía para resolver el problema.*

1. RECEPCIONISTA: Montalvo y Compañía. Buenos días.

USTED: (Greet her. Ask to speak with the president of the company, Sr. Montalvo.)

_____

_____

2. RECEPCIONISTA: Ha salido en un viaje de negocios. Regresará dentro de quince días.

USTED: (Ask to talk with someone else.)

_____

3. RECEPCIONISTA: ¿Podría Ud. explicarme lo que necesita para que le dirija a la sección apropiada?

USTED: (Briefly explain who you are and what your problem is.)

_____

_____

4. RECEPCIONISTA: Ud. debe hablar con el Sr. Mendoza. Lo siento pero tampoco lo (la) puede atender ahora.

USTED: (Ask to leave a message.)

_____

5. RECEPCIONISTA: Muy bien.

USTED: (Briefly state your problem again. Ask for an appointment with Sr. Mendoza.)

_____

_____

6. RECEPCIONISTA: ¿Para cuándo quisiera la cita?

USTED: (Name the day and time you would like.)

_____

7. RECEPCIONISTA: Está bien. Se lo haré presente al Sr. Mendoza.

USTED: (Thank her and provide an appropriate closing to the conversation.)

_____

RECEPCIONISTA: Adiós, señor / señora / señorita.

Nombre _____ **Fecha** _____ **Clase** _____

C.   El mensaje. *Ud. es el (la) recepcionista en Montalvo y Compañía. Escríbale el mensaje de Práctica B al Sr. Mendoza. Explique quién hizo la llamada, cuándo llamó, y qué quería. Infórmele de la cita.*

_____

_____

_____

_____

_____

_____

_____

_____

_____

_____

_____

_____

D.   El participio pasado. *Escriba el participio pasado que corresponde al infinitivo.*

1. trabajar _____

2. vender _____

3. cumplir _____

4. hacer _____

5. estar _____

6. decir _____

7. ser _____

8. resolver _____

9. ver _____

10. abrir _____

11. volver _____

12. morir _____

13. escribir _____

14. poner _____

15. romper _____

16. cubrir _____

E. El presente perfecto. *Escriba las formas del presente perfecto que corresponden a los sujetos dados.*

	preocuparse	**hacer**
1. los obreros	_____	_____
2. Ud.	_____	_____
3. nosotras	_____	_____
4. yo	_____	_____
5. Carmen	_____	_____
6. tú	_____	_____

F. Un día ocupado. *Explique lo que los empleados en la empresa Sandovar han hecho hoy.*

➤ *MODELO* el Sr. López / vender lo máximo
El Sr. López ha vendido lo máximo.

1. la secretaria / escribir treinta cartas

_____

2. yo / almorzar con unos clientes nuevos

_____

3. los abogados / resolver el problema con la aduana

_____

4. el publicista y yo / hacer la publicidad

_____

5. tú / volver de tu viaje de negocios

_____

6. el gerente / cumplir muchos pedidos

_____

G. Esta semana. *Explique lo que Ud. ha hecho esta semana. Incluya información sobre su rutina diaria, sus estudios, su trabajo y sus diversiones.*

_____

_____

_____

Nombre _____ **Fecha** _____ **Clase** _____

_____

_____

_____

_____

_____

_____

_____

H. Un viaje de negocios. *Ud. está encargado(-a) de preparar un viaje de negocios a Chile para todos los miembros de su sección de la empresa multinacional. Explique lo que Ud. espera que ya hayan hecho sus colegas.*

> ➤ **MODELO**   todos / comprar un billete de avión
> **Espero que todos ya hayan comprado un billete de avión.**

1. Manolo / cambiar el dinero

_____

2. tú / despedirse de su familia

_____

3. todos nosotros / escribirle a la empresa en Chile

_____

4. Marta y Elena / leer una guía sobre Chile

_____

5. la Sra. Chávez / resolver todos los problemas

_____

6. los García / pagar los billetes

_____

I. Los Gutiérrez. *Hoy Manuel y Teresa Gutiérrez celebran sus bodas de oro. ¿Qué hacen para llevarse bien durante cincuenta años?*

> ➤ **MODELO**   hablar / a menudo
> **Manuel y Teresa se hablan a menudo.**

1. escuchar / siempre

   _____

2. escribir / cuando están separados

   _____

3. dar regalos / a menudo

   _____

4. ayudar / cuando tienen problemas

   _____

5. respetar / siempre

   _____

Segunda situación

A.   Actividades bancarias. *Explique lo que las personas deben hacer en las siguientes situaciones.*

1. Los Higuera desean comprar una casa pero no tienen suficiente dinero.

   _____

2. Matilde Guevara llega a Miami de Buenos Aires y sólo tiene dinero argentino.

   _____

3. La universidad sólo acepta cheques personales para la matrícula y Roberto Díaz tiene dinero
   en efectivo.

   _____

4. Estela Morillo tiene muchas joyas preciosas que deben estar en un lugar seguro.

   _____

5. Ud. piensa que tiene más dinero en su cuenta de ahorros de lo que dice el banco.

   _____

6. Héctor Ocampo necesita dinero en efectivo.

   _____

7. Guillermo Núñez, un chico de doce años, ganó mucho dinero cortando el césped de sus vecinos.
   Sus padres le dicen que no debe guardar el dinero en casa.

   _____

Nombre _____ **Fecha** _____ **Clase** _____

B.   Un retiro y un depósito. *Ud. es un(-a) estudiante de intercambio en Lima, Perú. Quiere retirar el equivalente de 500 dólares americanos en nuevos soles peruanos de su cuenta de ahorros y depositarlos en su cuenta corriente. Antes de hacer cola en el banco, llene los formularios de retiro y depósito. (Información: **I = el importe** = amount; 3,52 nuevos soles = $1.)*

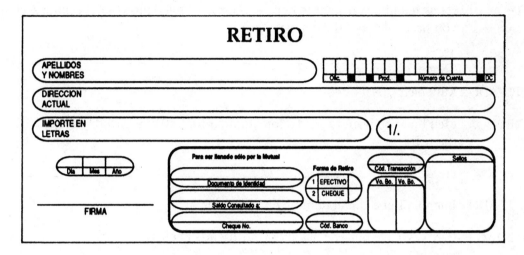

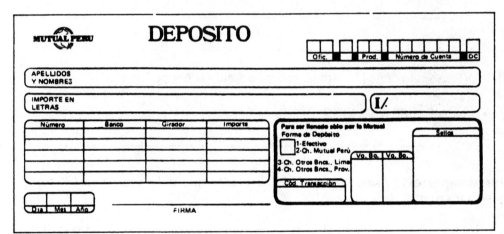

C.   En el banco. *Hable con el empleado en el banco para hacer la transacción de Práctica B.*

1. EMPLEADO: Buenas tardes, señor / señora / señorita. ¿En qué puedo servirle?

     USTED: (Tell him you want to know the balance in your savings account.)

_____

2. EMPLEADO: Un momento. A ver. Hay 2500 nuevos soles.

     USTED: (Say O.K. Tell him you want to withdraw 1760 *nuevos soles.*)

_____

3. EMPLEADO: Llene el formulario de retiro, por favor.

USTED: (Tell him you have already filled it out. Give it to him.)

_____

4. EMPLEADO: Muy bien.

USTED: (Now tell him you want to deposit the *nuevos soles* into your checking account. Say you have filled out the deposit slip.)

_____

5. EMPLEADO: Muy bien. ¿Es todo?

USTED: (Tell him you want to send a foreign draft for $40 as a birthday gift to a friend in the U.S.)

_____

6. EMPLEADO: Bueno. ¿Tiene Ud. el nombre de su banco?

USTED: (Say yes. Give him the name of your friend's bank.)

_____

_____

7. EMPLEADO: Aquí lo tiene Ud. Adiós, señor / señora / señorita.

USTED: (Tell him good-bye and leave.)

_____

D. **El pluscuamperfecto (past perfect).** *Escriba las formas del pluscuamperfecto que corresponden a los sujetos dados.*

	arreglarse	invertir
1. Miguel y yo	_____	_____
2. tú	_____	_____
3. ellas	_____	_____
4. yo	_____	_____
5. la Sra. Ruiz	_____	_____
6. Ud.	_____	_____

Nombre _____ **Fecha** _____ **Clase** _____

E.   Unas actividades. *Explique lo que las siguientes personas habían hecho esta mañana para el mediodía.*

    ➤ *MODELO*   El Dr. Vargas / depositar $1.000
                        El Dr. Vargas había depositado mil dólares.

1. tú / escribir cuatro cheques

   _____

2. mis padres y yo / resolver el problema de la cuenta corriente

   _____

3. Los Estrada / pedir prestado $10.000

   _____

4. La Sra. Rodó / poner unos documentos importantes en la caja de seguridad

   _____

5. Uds. / leer información sobre las hipotecas

   _____

6. yo / hacer el pago inicial del préstamo estudiantil

   _____

F.   Antes de las clases. *Explique lo que Ud. había hecho ayer para la medianoche.*

_____

_____

_____

_____

_____

_____

_____

_____

G. **¿Cuánto tiempo hace...?** *Ud. tiene un problema con el saldo de su cuenta corriente. Conteste las preguntas en el formulario bancario para ayudar al banco a resolver el problema.*

> ➢ *MODELO*   depositar dinero en este banco (5 años)
>   **Hace cinco años que deposito dinero en este banco.**

1. ser cliente del banco (5 años)

_____

2. tener una cuenta corriente (5 años)

_____

3. alquilar una caja de seguridad (1 año)

_____

4. pagar a plazos (3 años)

_____

5. ahorrar dinero en una cuenta (6 meses)

_____

6. no averiguar el saldo de la cuenta (3 meses)

_____

H. **Cheques.** *Ud. es el (la) contador(-a) en una empresa multinacional en Madrid. Complete los cheques para los pedidos escribiendo el importe en letras. Cuidado con la concordancia (agreement) de los números.*

1. (23.486) _____ euros

2. (1.000.000) _____ euros

3. (375.000) _____ euros

4. (57.612) _____ euros

5. (74.531) _____ euros

6. (16.050) _____ euros

Nombre _____ Fecha _____ Clase _____

A recordar

Review the following situations and tasks that have been presented and practiced in this chapter.

- Make a business phone call.
- Discuss completed past actions.
- Explain what you hope has happened.
- Discuss reciprocal actions.
- Complete simple banking tasks.
- Talk about actions completed before other actions.
- Explain the duration of actions.
- Express quantities.
- Write a simple business letter.

Expansión de vocabulario

Dudas de vocabulario

to save: ahorrar / conservar / guardar / salvar

ahorrar: *to save money*

Es importante ahorrar dinero para el futuro.   *It is important to save money for the future.*

conservar: *to keep, preserve*

Mis padres conservaron todas las fotos   *My parents kept all the pictures*
de mi niñez.   *of my childhood.*

Ella conserva su buen humor   *She keeps her good humor*
aun en los momentos más difíciles.   *even in the most difficult moments.*

guardar: *to keep, to put away*

Por favor, guarda todas tus cosas.   *Please put all your things away.*

salvar: *to rescue something or someone*

El perro salvó la vida del niño.   *The dog saved the child's life.*

yet / still: todavía / todavía no

todavía: *still*

Están trabajando todavía.   *They're still working.*

todavía no: *still… not / not yet*

Todavía no han terminado.   *They still have not / They have not yet finished.*

already / anymore: ya / ya no

ya: *already*

Ya han terminado la tarea   *They have already finished their homework*
y ahora van al cine.   *and now they're going to the movies.*

ya no: *not… anymore / no longer*

Alicia ya no vive aquí.   *Alicia doesn't live here anymore / no longer lives here.*

must / have to: deber / tener que / (no) hay que

deber: *must, ought to, should; indicates an obligation*

Debes invertir tu dinero sabiamente.   *You must invest your money wisely.*

tener que + infinitive: *to have to; indicates a strong necessity*

Quisiera ir a bailar pero tengo que estudiar.   *I would like to go dancing, but I have to study.*

hay que: *one must; an impersonal statement of obligation*

Hay que trabajar mucho   *One must work hard*
para triunfar en la vida.   *in order to succeed in life.*

no hay que: *one must not; a strong statement of necessity*

No hay que llegar tarde a la cita   *One must not arrive late for the appointment*
con el jefe.   *with the boss.*

Práctica

A. *Clarifique las obligaciones de Roberto al completar las oraciones con la forma adecuada de* deber / tener que / hay que.

Roberto sabe que para tener éxito en el mundo de los negocios _____

comprender las finanzas. Por eso Roberto estudia la contabilidad. _____

estudiar mucho esta noche porque tiene un examen mañana. Pero antes de salir a la biblioteca

_____ llamar a su novia.

Nombre _____ **Fecha** _____ **Clase** _____

B. *Explique lo que estas personas han hecho en las siguientes situaciones. Complete las oraciones con la forma adecuada de* **ahorrar / conservar / guardar / salvar.**

Hace muchos años que la Sra. Valdés vive en los EE.UU. pero todavía _____

buenos recuerdos de su juventud en Centroamérica. Después de _____

mucho dinero, hizo un viaje a Guatemala para ver a su familia. Mientras estaba allí

_____ su dinero y sus joyas en una caja en su cuarto. Un día hubo un

terremoto (*earthquake*), pero afortunadamente un joven _____ a la señora

y su caja del desastre.

C. *Describa lo que hacen las siguientes personas. Complete las oraciones con* **todavía / ya / ya no.**

Mario tiene sólo diecinueve años y _____ se ha graduado de la

universidad. _____ estudia porque tiene un buen puesto pero

_____ visita a sus amigos universitarios.

Ampliación

Professions

The following suffixes are often used to indicate jobs, careers, and professions.

1. **SUFFIX**   -ista   = *-ist*
                       dentista = *dentist*

   The suffix **-ista** is both masculine and feminine; gender is shown by the article: **el dentista** = *the male dentist;* **la dentista** = *the female dentist.* Plural forms end in **-s: los (las) dentistas.**

2. **SUFFIX**   -ero   = *-er*
                       carpintero = *carpenter*

   The suffix **-ero** has four endings to indicate number and gender: **el (los) carpintero(-s); la(-s) carpintera(-s).**

3. **SUFFIX**   -or   = *-or*
                       doctor = *doctor*

   There are four forms to indicate number and gender. The feminine singular is formed by adding the letter **-a** to the masculine singular ending: **el doctor, los doctores, la doctora, las doctoras.**

Práctica

A. *Dé la forma inglesa para las siguientes profesiones.*

1. el cocinero _____

2. la oficinista _____

3. el zapatero _____

4. el electricista _____

5. la cajera _____

6. la contadora _____

7. el futbolista _____

8. el trabajador _____

B. *Dé la forma española para las siguientes profesiones.*

1. receptionist _____

2. waitress _____

3. carpenter _____

4. stockbroker _____

5. professor _____

6. financier _____

7. artist _____

8. programmer _____

C. *Complete las oraciones con una profesión que termina con la forma adecuada de* **-ista,** **-ero** *u* **-or.**

1. Una _____ enseña en una universidad.

2. Un _____ construye edificios o muebles.

3. Una _____ crea la publicidad para una empresa.

4. Una _____ arregla los dientes.

5. Un _____ hace o vende joyas.

6. Un _____ prepara las comidas en un restaurante.

Bienvenidos a Chile y a la Argentina

A.   Adivinanza. *Para descubrir la palabra en la caja vertical, escriba en las líneas horizontales las palabras que corresponden a las definiciones.*

1. ___ ___ ___ ___ ___ | ___ | ___ ___ ___ ___ ___
2. ___ ___ | ___ | ___ ___ ___
3. ___ ___ | ___ | ___ ___
4. ___ ___ | ___ | ___ ___ ___ ___ ___ ___
5. ___ ___ | ___ | ___ ___ ___ ___
6. ___ ___ | ___ | ___ ___ ___ ___
7. ___ ___ | ___ | ___ ___ ___
8. ___ | ___ | ___ ___ ___ ___

1. La capital de la Argentina

2. La región al norte de la Argentina

3. Un producto importante de la Argentina

4. La región al sur de la Argentina

5. El mar al oeste de Chile

6. El desierto en el norte de Chile

7. Las cataratas en la frontera de la Argentina, el Brasil y Paraguay

8. Un producto importante de Chile

B.   El mapa. *Usando oraciones completas conteste las siguientes preguntas sobre Chile y la Argentina.*

1. Describa la geografía de Chile. _____

_____

_____

2. Describa la geografía de la Argentina. _____

_____

_____

3. ¿Cuál es la población de Chile?¿de la Argentina? _____

_____

_____

4. ¿Cuál es la moneda de Chile?¿de la Argentina? _____

_____

_____

5. ¿Cuáles son los productos principales de Chile? ¿de la Argentina? _____

_____

_____

Capítulo 11

De viaje

Primera situación

A.   En el aeropuerto. *Describa la escena en el aeropuerto. Explique por qué hay tanta gente en la sala de espera.*

_____

_____

_____

_____

_____

_____

_____

_____

B. **Un(-a) pasajero(-a).** *Ud. es un(-a) pasajero(-a) en el aeropuerto de Santiago. Complete la siguiente conversación entre Ud. y una empleada de la aerolínea LanChile.*

1. EMPLEADA: Buenos días, señor / señora / señorita. ¿En qué puedo servirle?

   USTED: (Explain that you need a one-way ticket from Santiago to Caracas and that you need to leave as soon as possible.)

   _____

   _____

2. EMPLEADA: Muy bien. Su pasaporte, por favor.

   USTED: (Hand it to her. Say you'll pay for the ticket with a credit card.)

   _____

   _____

3. EMPLEADA: Está bien. ¿Tiene equipaje?

   USTED: (Answer yes. Ask to have it checked.)

   _____

4. EMPLEADA: Muy bien. ¿Dónde prefiere Ud. sentarse?

   USTED: (Explain you would like an aisle seat in the nonsmoking area.)

   _____

   _____

5. EMPLEADA: Lo siento, señor / señora / señorita, pero no nos queda ningún asiento en el pasillo.

   USTED: (Express your disappointment. Ask at what time the flight leaves.)

   _____

   _____

   _____

6. EMPLEADA: A las once y cuarto. Aquí tiene su pasaporte y su tarjeta de embarque.

   USTED: (Ask what gate you'll leave from.)

   _____

7. EMPLEADA: Por la puerta de embarque número catorce.

   USTED: (Ask what time you'll start boarding.)

   _____

8. EMPLEADA: Dentro de unos veinte minutos. Adiós y buen viaje.

USTED: (Thank her for all she's done and say good-bye.)

_____

C. Unos deseos. *Explique lo que el agente de viajes quería que hicieran sus clientes. Escriba las formas del imperfecto del subjuntivo que corresponden a los sujetos dados.*

> ➤ *MODELO*   viajar y divertirse / Margarita
> **El agente de viajes quería que Margarita viajara y se divirtiera.**

El agente de viajes quería que...

	viajar	**divertirse**
1. Celia y Roberto	_____	_____
2. yo	_____	_____
3. los Sres. Lado	_____	_____
4. Joaquín y yo	_____	_____
5. tú	_____	_____
6. Fernando	_____	_____

D. Unas formas irregulares. *Escriba las formas de la tercera persona plural del pretérito y después la tercera persona plural del imperfecto del subjuntivo para los siguientes infinitivos.*

	EL PRETÉRITO	**EL IMPERFECTO DEL SUBJUNTIVO**
1. hacer	_____	_____
2. tener	_____	_____
3. decir	_____	_____
4. dormir	_____	_____
5. leer	_____	_____
6. estar	_____	_____
7. ir	_____	_____
8. saber	_____	_____
9. poder	_____	_____

	EL PRETÉRITO	**EL IMPERFECTO DEL SUBJUNTIVO**
10. dar	_____	_____
11. traducir	_____	_____
12. ser	_____	_____
13. poner	_____	_____
14. oír	_____	_____

E.   En la terminal. *Explique lo que el empleado de una aerolínea le aconsejó a un pasajero nervioso.*

> ➤ *MODELO*   abordar a tiempo
> **El empleado le aconsejó al pasajero que abordara a tiempo.**

1. facturar el equipaje

_____

2. no perder la tarjeta de embarque

_____

3. tener paciencia

_____

4. poner las etiquetas en las maletas

_____

5. despedirse de la familia en la sala de espera

_____

6. no comer ni beber mucho antes del vuelo

_____

F.   El (La) agente de viajes. *Un grupo de estudiantes de intercambio acaba de salir para Chile. Explique lo que el (la) agente de viajes les recomendó que hicieran antes de salir.*

> ➤ *MODELO*   comprar un billete de ida y vuelta
> **El agente les recomendó que compraran un billete de ida y vuelta.**

1. hacer una reservación

_____

2. conseguir su pasaporte con mucha anticipación

_____

3. sentarse en la sección de no fumar

_____

4. saber el número del vuelo

_____

5. tener cuidado

_____

6. no llevar mucho equipaje

_____

G. **La azafata ofensiva.** *Para ayudar a esta azafata a ser más cortés, escriba de otra manera las siguientes frases.*

1. ¿Qué quiere beber Ud.?

_____

2. ¿Puede Ud. poner su equipaje de mano debajo del asiento?

_____

3. Ud. debe abrocharse el cinturón.

_____

4. Quiero ver su tarjeta de embarque.

_____

5. Siéntese en el asiento del pasillo.

_____

H. **Un viaje a Chile.** *Explique bajo qué circunstancias las siguientes personas irían a Chile.*

> ➤ *MODELO*   el Sr. Valero / tener más tiempo
> **El Sr. Valero iría a Chile si tuviera más tiempo.**

1. yo / no tener que trabajar

_____

2. la Srta. Ocampo / conocer a alguien en Santiago

_____

3. Roberto y Daniel / hablar mejor el español

_____

4. tú / terminar tus cursos

_____

5. mi familia y yo / ganar más dinero

_____

I.   **Los pasajeros cansados.** *Explique lo que harían los pasajeros del dibujo de Práctica A si tuvieran la oportunidad. Varíe sus respuestas.*

1. El piloto _____

_____

2. La madre _____

_____

3. El hijo _____

_____

4. Los hombres de negocios _____

_____

5. La anciana _____

_____

6. El joven _____

_____

J.   **¿Qué haría Ud.?** *Explique lo que Ud. haría si tuviera mucho tiempo y dinero.*

_____

_____

_____

_____

Nombre _____ **Fecha** _____ **Clase** _____

_____

_____

_____

_____

_____

Segunda situación

A. El Hotel Solimar. *Ud. trabaja en una agencia de publicidad y uno de sus clientes es el Hotel Solimar. Los dibujos de arriba van a aparecer en un folleto de publicidad para el hotel. Ud. tiene que escribir el texto de propaganda. Describa el hotel incluyendo información sobre las habitaciones, las facilidades, los servicios y su localidad.*

_____

_____

_____

_____

_____

_____

_____

_____

_____

B.   Los empleados. *El folleto del Hotel Solimar también va a incluir fotos de varios empleados. Al lado de las fotos Ud. tiene que explicar qué hacen estos empleados y cómo son.*

Julio Montoya
Botones

_____

_____

_____

Dolores Rodríguez
Criada

_____

_____

_____

Carlos Ruiz Estrada
Conserje

_____

_____

_____

Juan Díaz
Portero

_____

_____

_____

Nombre _____ **Fecha** _____ **Clase** _____

Silvia López del Río   _____
Recepcionista
                          _____

                          _____

                          _____

C.   En el hotel. *Ud. viaja con dos amigos(-as) en Chile. Uds. llegan a Viña del Mar y de repente deciden quedarse unos días. Complete la siguiente conversación con el recepcionista en el Hotel Las Brisas.*

1. RECEPCIONISTA: Buenas tardes, señor / señora / señorita. ¿En qué puedo servirle?

   USTED: (Explique que necesita una habitación.)

   _____

2. RECEPCIONISTA: ¿Tiene Ud. una reservación?

   USTED: (Conteste negativamente. Explique por qué.)

   _____

3. RECEPCIONISTA: Y ¿qué tipo de habitación necesita Ud.?

   USTED: (Responda.)

   _____

4. RECEPCIONISTA: Muy bien. ¿En qué sección del hotel prefiere su habitación?

   USTED: (Responda.)

   _____

5. RECEPCIONISTA: Bueno.

   USTED: (Ud. quiere saber qué facilidades hay.)

   _____

6. RECEPCIONISTA: La habitación tiene aire acondicionado y un televisor a colores. El hotel tiene una piscina, dos restaurantes y buen servicio de habitación.

   USTED: (Decide quedarse en el hotel por tres días.)

   _____

7. RECEPCIONISTA: Muy bien. Aquí tiene Ud. la llave. Su habitación está en el sexto piso, número 643.

USTED: (Dígale que Uds. tienen mucho equipaje y desean que alguien lo suba.)

_____

_____

RECEPCIONISTA: No hay problema. Que disfruten de su estancia en Viña del Mar.

D.   Un(-a) estudiante de intercambio. *Ud. va a pasar el año que viene en Santiago como estudiante de intercambio. Sus padres tienen muchas preguntas acerca del programa. Escríbales a sus padres contestando sus preguntas.*

> ➤ *MODELO*   ¿Vivirás en la residencia estudiantil? (hasta que / conseguir un apartamento)
> **Sí, viviré en la residencia estudiantil hasta que consiga un apartamento.**

1. ¿Buscarás trabajo? (tan pronto como / poder)

_____

_____

2. ¿Te adaptarás? (con tal que / aprender la lengua)

_____

_____

3. ¿Tendrás muchos problemas? (hasta que / conocer a otros estudiantes)

_____

_____

4. ¿Visitarás otros sitios turísticos? (después que / terminar el primer semestre)

_____

_____

5. ¿Esquiarás en Portillo? (a menos que / no haber nieve)

_____

_____

6. ¿Nos llamarás? (para que / Uds. saber lo que pasa)

_____

_____

Nombre _____ **Fecha** _____ **Clase** _____

E. **El futuro perfecto.** *Escriba las formas del futuro perfecto que corresponden a los sujetos dados.*

	alojarse	**salir**
1. Ud.	_____	_____
2. mis amigos	_____	_____
3. tú	_____	_____
4. nosotros	_____	_____
5. David	_____	_____
6. yo	_____	_____

F. **Un viaje a Chile.** *Ud. está encargado(-a) de un grupo que sale hoy para Chile. Explique lo que los miembros de su grupo habrán hecho antes de salir.*

> ➤ **MODELO** todos / comprar un billete
> **Todos habrán comprado un billete.**

1. Manolo / escribir al hotel

_____

2. tú / despedirse de su familia

_____

3. todos nosotros / conseguir una habitación

_____

4. Felipe y Elena / leer una guía

_____

5. la Sra. Prado / hacer las maletas

_____

6. los Muñoz / pagar los billetes

_____

G.   Sus sueños. *Escríbales una carta a sus padres explicándoles lo que Ud. habrá hecho dentro de los próximos cinco años.*

_____ :

_____

_____

_____

_____

_____

_____

_____

_____

_____

_____

_____ ,

A recordar

Review the following situations and tasks that have been presented and practiced in this chapter.

- Buy a ticket and board a plane.
- Explain previous wants, advice, and doubts.
- Make polite requests.
- Discuss contrary-to-fact situations.
- Explain and hypothesize.
- Obtain a hotel room.
- Explain when actions will occur.
- Describe future actions that will take place before other future actions.

Expansión de vocabulario

Dudas de vocabulario

What is? What are?: ¿Qué es (son)...? ¿Cuál es...? (Cuáles son...?)

¿Qué es (son)...?: *What is (are)...?; asks for a definition.*

—¿Qué es la marinera?	*What's "la marinera"?*
—Es un baile típico del Perú.	*It's a typical Peruvian dance.*
—¿Qué son esos edificios?	*What are those buildings?*
—Son edificios del gobierno.	*They are government buildings.*

¿Cuál es...? (¿Cuáles son...?): *Which one(s)...?, What...?; implies a choice of two or more persons, places, or things.*

—¿Cuál es la capital de Chile?	*What is the capital of Chile?*
—Santiago, por supuesto.	*Santiago, of course.*
—¿Cuáles son las ciudades más importantes de Chile?	*Which are the most important cities in Chile?*
—Son Santiago, Concepción y Valparaíso.	*They are Santiago, Concepción, and Valparaíso.*

to miss: perder / extrañar / echar de menos / faltar a

perder: *to miss, to fail to get something*

Perdí el autobús / tren / avión de las dos. Tendré que esperar una hora más.	*I missed the two o'clock bus / train / plane. I'll have to wait another hour.*
Perdimos la oportunidad de entrevistar a ese famoso autor chileno.	*We missed the chance to interview that famous Chilean writer.*

extrañar / echar de menos: *to miss someone or something that is absent or distant*

Extraño Chile, su gente y su comida.	*I miss Chile, its people, and its food.*

faltar a: *to miss, be absent from*

Él faltó a clases el 70% de las veces y todavía se quejaba de sus notas.	*He was absent from class 70% of the time and still complained about his grades.*

to leave: dejar / irse / salir / partir

dejar: *to leave something behind*

Dejé mis libros en el hotel.   *I left my books at the hotel.*

irse: *to go away, to leave.* **Irse** *is often used when no destination is mentioned.*

Se fueron sin pagar la cuenta.   *They left without paying the bill.*

partir: *to leave, depart; to set off for*

El avión partió a medianoche.   *The plane left / departed at midnight.*

salir (de): *to leave (a place)*

Salí de Santiago en 1995.   *I left Santiago in 1995.*

Práctica

A.   De viaje en Chile.   *Ud. está de vacaciones en Chile y necesita pedir mucha información. Haga preguntas usando ¿Qué es? / ¿Qué son? o ¿Cuál es? / ¿Cuáles son?*

1. ¿_____ la ciudad más grande de Chile?

2. ¿_____ el número de mi habitación?

3. ¿_____ Viña del Mar?

4. ¿_____ unos sitios interesantes para visitar?

5. ¿_____ aquellos edificios?

B.   Enrique, el nervioso.   *Explique lo que le molesta a Enrique cuando viaja. Complete con la forma adecuada de* **echar de menos / extrañar / faltar / perder.**

1. No me gusta viajar. En realidad no me gusta _____ al trabajo por mucho tiempo.

2. Tengo miedo de _____ el avión; por eso nunca llego tarde al aeropuerto.

3. Cuando viajo solo siempre _____ a mi familia.

C.   Una carta de Adolfo.   *Complete esta carta con la forma adecuada de* **dejar / partir / salir.**

Voy a _____ de mi hotel el domingo a las 10. El avión

_____ más tarde a mediodía. Necesito tener mucho cuidado porque la

última vez que vine aquí _____ mi billete dentro de la habitación del hotel.

Nombre _____ **Fecha** _____ **Clase** _____

Ampliación

Spanish equivalent of English words beginning with *sc-, sp-, st-*

Spanish doesn't allow the English consonant pairs **sc-, sp-, st-** at the beginning of a word. The Spanish equivalents generally are preceded by the letter **e-**.

1. **esc-**   = *sc-*
   la escena   = *scene*

2. **esp-**   = *sp-*
   el español   = *Spanish*

3. **est-**   = *st-*
   la estampilla = *stamp*

Práctica

A.   *Dé la forma inglesa de las siguientes palabras.*

1. la escala _____

2. el escándalo _____

3. el escultor _____

4. el espacio _____

5. las espinacas _____

6. la espía _____

7. el estado _____

8. el estilo _____

9. la estatua _____

B.   *Dé la forma española de las siguientes palabras.*

1. scene _____

2. school _____

3. sponge _____

4. specialty _____

5. stomach _____

6. stadium _____

7. student _____

8. stamp _____

C.   *Complete las oraciones con una palabra empezando con **esc-**, **esp-** o **est-**.*

1. Antes de enviar una carta tenemos que poner una _____ en el sobre.

2. La _____ del Restaurante Brisamar es la paella valenciana.

3. Los niños de seis a doce años van a la _____ primaria.

4. Miguel Ángel fue un famoso _____ italiano. Hizo muchas

   _____, incluyendo el David y la Pietá.

5. Hay cincuenta _____ en los EE.UU.

6. En los platos picantes hay muchas _____ como la pimienta, el pimentón, el comino y el orégano.

Capítulo 12

Los deportes

Primera situación

A.   El programa atlético. *El (La) nuevo(-a) director(-a) atlético(-a) de su universidad quiere que Ud. les explique a los estudiantes su programa atlético para el futuro. Prepare un folleto incluyendo información sobre los deportes, los lugares donde se juegan y el equipo deportivo necesario. Incluya por lo menos seis deportes divididos entre deportes para hombres y mujeres y deportes interuniversitarios e intramurales.*

Deportes	Edificios y campos	Equipo deportivo

B.   Su equipo favorito. *¿Qué preguntaría o respondería Ud. en las siguientes situaciones?*

1. Ud. tenía que trabajar y no pudo ir al partido ni escucharlo por la radio.

_____

2. Su equipo favorito ganó el campeonato.

_____

3. Su equipo favorito perdió el último partido.

_____

4. El (La) mejor jugador(-a) se lastimó.

_____

5. Su jugador(-a) favorito(-a) marcó muchos puntos.

_____

C. El condicional perfecto. *Escriba las formas del condicional perfecto que corresponden a los sujetos dados.*

	practicar	**correr**
1. el equipo	_____	_____
2. yo	_____	_____
3. ellas	_____	_____
4. tú	_____	_____
5. Teresa y yo	_____	_____
6. Uds.	_____	_____

D. Con más habilidad. *Las siguientes personas son poco atléticas. ¿Qué habrían hecho en la escuela secundaria si hubieran tenido más habilidad?*

> ➤ **MODELO**   Francisco / jugar al béisbol
> **Francisco habría jugado al béisbol.**

1. Mateo y yo / practicar gimnasia

_____

2. tú / correr

_____

3. Gustavo y Nicolás / ponerse en forma

_____

4. yo / entrenarse más

_____

5. Silvia / hacer ejercicios aeróbicos

_____

Nombre _____ **Fecha** _____ **Clase** _____

6. Uds. / ganar el campeonato

_____

E.　Los deseos del entrenador. _Explique lo que el entrenador quería que hubieran hecho estas personas. Escriba las formas del pluscuamperfecto del subjuntivo que corresponden a los sujetos dados._

　➤ **MODELO**　　el equipo / entrenarse bien
　　　　　　　　El entrenador quería que el equipo se hubiera entrenado bien.

1. tú _____

2. yo _____

3. Tomás y yo _____

4. José Luis _____

5. todos _____

6. Ud. _____

F.　Las necesidades. _Las siguientes personas salieron ayer para jugar en las finales de básquetbol. Explique lo que era necesario que hubieran hecho antes de salir._

　➤ **MODELO**　　todos / practicar
　　　　　　　　Era necesario que todos hubieran practicado mucho.

1. el entrenador / entrenarlos bien

_____

2. yo / hacer ejercicios

_____

3. mi amigo(-a) y yo / ponerse en forma

_____

4. los jugadores / correr cada día

_____

5. tú / ir al gimnasio todos los días

_____

G.   Con más suerte. *Explique lo que no les habría ocurrido a estos atletas si hubieran tenido más suerte.*

> **MODELO**   Rafael Gómez / ganar el partido
> **Si hubiera tenido más suerte, Rafael Gómez habría ganado el partido.**

1. Juanita Sánchez / ganar el campeonato

_____

2. tú / recibir un árbitro justo

_____

3. Uds. / coger todas las pelotas

_____

4. los futbolistas / patear mejor

_____

5. yo / jugar bien

_____

6. el jugador de béisbol y yo / tirar la pelota bien

_____

H.   El campeonato. *Ud. es el (la) entrenador(-a) de un equipo de béisbol que nunca sigue sus consejos. Así que su equipo perdió el campeonato. Dígales a los miembros de su equipo que no habrían perdido el campeonato si hubieran escuchado sus consejos.*

> **MODELO**   comer bien todo el año
> **Uds. no habrían perdido el campeonato si hubieran comido bien todo el año.**

1. jugar bien

_____

2. hacer ejercicios de calentamiento

_____

3. mantenerse en forma

_____

4. escucharme

_____

Nombre _____ **Fecha** _____ **Clase** _____

5. correr rápidamente

_____

6. tener árbitros justos

_____

I. **En la escuela secundaria.** *Ud. está pensando en los días de la escuela secundaria. Explique lo que habría hecho si tuviera más tiempo / dinero / habilidad / oportunidades.*

_____

_____

_____

_____

_____

_____

_____

_____

_____

_____

_____

_____

_____

_____

_____

_____

Segunda situación

A. ¿Qué les duele? *Explique lo que les duele a las personas en el dibujo.*

1. A la señora _____

2. A la muchacha _____

3. Al joven _____

4. Al hombre _____

5. A la anciana _____

6. Al niño _____

B. Los síntomas y los remedios. *Describa los síntomas para las siguientes enfermedades y sugiera un remedio.*

1. la gripe _____

_____

_____

2. el insomnio _____

_____

Nombre _____ **Fecha** _____ **Clase** _____

3. la pulmonía _____

_____

4. un catarro _____

_____

_____

C. **La conmiseración.** *Ud. es el (la) médico(-a) para el consultorio del dibujo de Práctica A. Escríbales una tarjeta a todos los pacientes expresándoles su conmiseración y sus buenos deseos. Varíe sus expresiones.*

1. _____

_____

2. _____

_____

3. _____

_____

4. _____

_____

5. _____

_____

6. _____

_____

D. **¡La mala suerte!** *Explique lo que les pasó a las personas del dibujo de Práctica A. Use frases de la siguiente lista.*

caer un libro	olvidar las píldoras
dañar el dedo	perder las gafas
olvidar el impermeable	romper el tobillo

➤ **MODELO**   El niño estaba en la biblioteca leyendo un libro muy grande.
   Se le cayó un libro grande.

1. La señora caminaba por el parque. Estaba lloviendo y no llevaba ni impermeable ni paraguas.

_____

2. La muchacha se quemó en la cocina porque no podía ver bien.

_____

3. El joven estaba jugando al fútbol.

_____

4. El hombre estaba trabajando muchas horas en el jardín y no recordó tomar sus píldoras.

_____

5. La anciana estaba cortando vegetales con mucha prisa.

_____

E. **En el consultorio.** *Explique quiénes son las personas en el dibujo de Práctica A. Siga el modelo.*

➤ **MODELO**   La Srta. Morelos es enfermera. La Srta. Morelos ayuda a los pacientes.
   La Srta. Morelos es la enfermera que ayuda a los pacientes.

1. La señora tiene catarro. La señora caminó por el parque sin impermeable.

_____

2. La muchacha ayudó a su madre en la cocina. La muchacha se quemó.

_____

3. Ayer el joven jugó al fútbol norteamericano. El joven se fracturó el tobillo.

_____

4. El hombre trabajó en su jardín ayer. El hombre se lastimó el hombro.

_____

Nombre _____ **Fecha** _____ **Clase** _____

5. La mujer anciana cocinó una cena especial anoche. La mujer se cortó el dedo.

_____

6. El niño jugó al béisbol en el parque. El niño se rompió la pierna.

_____

F. **¿Qué es esto?** *Explique qué son las siguientes cosas. Combine las dos oraciones en una nueva oración usando una preposición y una forma de* **el que** *o* **el cual.**

> ➤ *MODELO*　　　Éste es el consultorio. El médico ayuda a los pacientes en el consultorio.
> **Éste es el consultorio en el cual el médico ayuda a los pacientes.**

1. Éstos son los antibióticos. Los médicos no curan muchas enfermedades sin los antibióticos.

_____

_____

2. Ésta es la farmacia. Preparan recetas dentro de la farmacia.

_____

_____

3. Éstas son las pastillas. Pagué cien dólares por estas pastillas.

_____

_____

4. Éste es el jarabe. Caminé a la farmacia para este jarabe.

_____

_____

5. Éstas son mis vitaminas. Nunca viajo sin las vitaminas.

_____

_____

G.   Para evitar un accidente. *Su amigo(-a) se ha lastimado jugando al tenis. Escríbale una carta expresando su conmiseración y sus deseos para el futuro. También explíquele que habría evitado el problema si hubiera escuchado sus consejos.*

_____ :

_____

_____

_____

_____

_____

_____

_____

_____

_____ ,

A recordar

Review the following situations and tasks that have been presented and practiced in this chapter.

- Discuss sports and games.
- Explain what you would have done under certain conditions.
- Discuss what you hoped would have happened.
- Discuss contrary-to-fact situations.
- Describe illnesses and medical problems.
- Express sympathy and good wishes.
- Discuss unexpected events.
- Link ideas.

Nombre _____ Fecha _____ Clase _____

Expansión de vocabulario

Dudas de vocabulario

game: el juego / el deporte / el partido

el juego: *game*

A mí no me gustan los juegos de mesa.   *I don't like board games.*

el deporte: *sport*

Nuestro deporte favorito es el vólibol,   *Our favorite sport is volleyball,*
pero también practicamos el tenis.   *but we also play tennis.*

el partido: *game, match*

¿A qué hora empieza el partido de fútbol?   *At what time does the soccer match / game start?*

to play: jugar / tocar

jugar: *to play a game*

Él jugaba al fútbol cuando estaba en secundaria.   *He played soccer when he was in high school.*

tocar: *to play an instrument*

Siempre quería aprender a tocar el piano.   *I always wanted to learn how to play the piano.*

to hurt: doler / lastimar / hacer daño / ofender

doler: *to ache, feel pain; either physical or emotional*

¿Te duele la rodilla?   *Does your knee hurt?*
Su indiferencia me dolió mucho.   *His (Her) indifference hurt me a lot.*

lastimar: *to injure, hurt*

Carlos se lastimó durante el partido de fútbol.   *Carlos injured himself during the soccer game.*

hacer daño: *to harm*

El fumar hace daño.   *Smoking is harmful.*

ofender: *to offend*

Como él no le agradeció su regalo,   *Since he did not thank her for her gift,*
ella se ofendió.   *she got offended.*

Práctica

A. Los gemelos. *Complete la descripción de Emilio y Alberto con una forma adecuada de* **el juego / el deporte / el partido / jugar / tocar.**

Emilio y Alberto son gemelos pero no les interesan las mismas cosas. Emilio es muy atlético;

_____ al fútbol y al béisbol, pero su deporte favorito es el básquetbol. Todos

los fines de semana participa en un _____ de básquetbol o mira uno en la

televisión. Por otra parte Alberto es más intelectual. _____ el violín y el

piano. Para divertirse prefiere el _____ de ajedrez.

B. El doctor Ruiz. *Complete este relato del Dr. Ruiz acerca de Manuel Álvarez. Use la forma adecuada de* **doler / lastimar / hacer daño / ofender.**

Manuel Álvarez se _____ jugando al fútbol norteamericano.

Aunque está mucho mejor todavía le _____ mucho las rodillas. No quiero

_____ a nadie, pero tengo que decirles que muchas veces los deportes son

violentos y _____.

Ampliación

Words borrowed from English

Just as English vocabulary is often composed of words borrowed from other languages, such as **plaza, taco,** or **sierra,** the Spanish language often borrows words from English. These borrowed words sometimes are admitted into Spanish without change, but often are modified to conform to Spanish rules for grammar and spelling. In order to recognize and use these English borrowings, keep in mind the following spelling changes.

1. The English consonant clusters with *h* are generally single consonants in Spanish.

ph   **photography**   = f   **la fotografía**

th   **theater**   = t   **el teatro**

ch   **mechanic**   = c   **el mecánico**

Nombre _____ **Fecha** _____ **Clase** _____

2. English double letters are generally single letters in Spanish.

    commercial = **el anuncio comercial**

    volleyball = **el vólibol**

    tennis = **el tenis**

3. The prefixes **super-** *(big),* **hiper-** *(very large),* and **mini-** *(small)* are frequently used in Spanish; they precede nouns: **el supermercado** *(supermarket);* **el hipermercado, el hiper** *(a very large supermarket and department store under one roof);* **la minifalda** *(miniskirt).*

Práctica

A. *Dé la forma inglesa de las siguientes palabras.*

1. el vólibol _____

2. el champú _____

3. la hamburguesa _____

4. el sándwich _____

5. el esquí _____

6. la videocasetera _____

7. el detergente _____

8. los jeans _____

B. *Dé la forma española de las siguientes palabras.*

1. penicillin _____

2. tennis _____

3. photograph _____

4. television _____

5. computer _____

6. baseball _____

7. basketball _____

8. aerobics _____

C.   *Defina o describa las siguientes palabras.*

1.   el ketchup _____

_____

_____

2.   el antibiótico _____

_____

_____

3.   el golf _____

_____

_____

4.   la minifalda _____

_____

_____

5.   la margarina _____

_____

_____

6.   el jogging _____

_____

_____

Manual de laboratorio

To the student

The following suggestions will help you use the ***Manual de laboratorio*** most effectively.

1. Be patient with yourself as you acquire proficiency in listening comprehension. Time and practice are essential to developing your ability to understand spoken Spanish.

2. Know the vocabulary thoroughly. Trying to complete the listening exercises without first mastering the vocabulary is a waste of time. For this reason, complete the *Primera situación* in your ***Manual de laboratorio*** after completing the corresponding *situación* in your student textbook. Complete the *Segunda situación* after completing that *situación* in your textbook.

3. Practice listening selectively. Do not try to understand every word you hear. At first, focus on the main idea. As your listening skill improves, you will understand more details that you will be able to associate with the main idea.

4. Be alert and ready to concentrate on what is being said in each exercise. Any distraction will hurt your ability to comprehend. Listen to the exercise several times if necessary.

Capítulo preliminar

Un autorretrato

Presentación

A. Estudiantes de intercambio. *You are helping to find roommates for the following exchange students who are coming to study at your university. Listen as each student gives a personal description and make notes on the chart. If you need to listen again, replay the recording.*

Nombre	Edad	Nacionalidad	Pasatiempos
Amalia			
Tomás			
Maricarmen			
Carlos			
Beatriz			

B. En el aeropuerto. *You have volunteered to meet the exchange students at the airport. Listen as they describe themselves and take notes so you will be able to recognize each student. If you need to listen again, replay the recording.*

1. Amalia: _____

2. Tomás: _____

3. Maricarmen: _____

4. Carlos: _____

5. Beatriz: _____

Para escuchar bien

In this chapter you have learned to anticipate and predict what you are going to hear based on previous experiences you have had in similar situations. Now practice anticipating what will be said in the following exercises.

A.   En el aeropuerto de Barajas.   *Imagine that you have just arrived in Spain and are going through customs. Listen to the following conversations, and circle* **SÍ** *if what you hear matches your expectations. Circle* **NO** *if what you hear does not match your expectations.*

1. SÍ   NO   4. SÍ   NO

2. SÍ   NO   5. SÍ   NO

3. SÍ   NO

B.   En el centro estudiantil.   *You will hear a series of short conversations in which students exchange personal information. As you listen, circle the letter of the phrase that best completes each statement. If you need to listen again, replay the recording.*

1. Los estudiantes hablan de
    a.   sus trabajos.
    b.   la ciudad donde nacieron.
    c.   sus familias.
    d.   sus pasatiempos.

2. Los pasatiempos de Joaquín son
    a.   hacer ejercicios y leer periódicos.
    b.   escribir cartas y tocar el piano.
    c.   ver televisión y leer novelas.
    d.   jugar al tenis y hacer ejercicios.

3. Claudia vive
    a.   sola en una residencia estudiantil.
    b.   con su esposo en un apartamento.
    c.   con sus amigos en una casa.
    d.   sola en un apartamento.

4. Las dos muchachas
    a.   trabajan en la cafetería y estudian en la universidad.
    b.   trabajan de las tres a las seis de la tarde y estudian por la noche.
    c.   estudian de las ocho a las diez de la noche y trabajan por el día.
    d.   necesitan dinero y trabajan poco.

Nombre _____ **Fecha** _____ **Clase** _____

Así se dice

The letters **a**, **e**, **i**, **o**, **u**, and sometimes **y** are used to represent vowel sounds in both English and Spanish, but their pronunciation in the two languages is very different. Note the following.

1. Spanish has fewer vowel sounds than English. It is generally said that Spanish has five basic sounds while English has many more.

2. Spanish vowel sounds are generally shorter than English vowel sounds. In addition, English vowel sounds often glide into or merge with other vowels to produce combination sounds. These combination sounds are called diphthongs. As a general rule, you should pronounce Spanish vowels with a short, precise sound. Listen to the difference in the pronunciation of the following two words: **me** (Spanish), *may* (English).

3. In English, vowels in unstressed positions are reduced to a neutral sound similar to *uh*; this neutral sound is called a *schwa*. The letter **i** in the English word *president* is pronounced in this fashion. Compare the pronunciation of the letter **i** in the Spanish and English words: **presidente**, *president*.

Práctica

A. *Now listen to the following pairs of words and decide if the first word of each pair is a Spanish or an English word. Circle your answer. Each pair of words will be repeated.*

1. español	inglés		**4.** español	inglés
2. español	inglés		**5.** español	inglés
3. español	inglés		**6.** español	inglés

B. *Now listen to the following pairs of words and decide if the first word of each pair is a Spanish or an English word. Circle your answer. Each pair of words will be repeated.*

1. español	inglés		**4.** español	inglés
2. español	inglés		**5.** español	inglés
3. español	inglés		**6.** español	inglés

Now concentrate on the Spanish vowel sound /a/. In a stressed or unstressed position the Spanish /a/ is pronounced similarly to the /a/ sound of the English word *father;* it is spelled **a** or **ha**.

Práctica

A. *Listen to the following sentences and mark how many times you hear the sound /a/. Each sentence will be repeated.*

1. _____   **2.** _____   **3.** _____   **4.** _____

B. *Listen to the following Spanish words with the /a/ sound and repeat each after the speaker.*

1. a	**6.** mano	**11.** identidad	**16.** Madrid
2. ala	**7.** estado	**12.** pasaporte	**17.** Sevilla
3. ama	**8.** pasea	**13.** Caracas	**18.** ciudad
4. ésa	**9.** moza	**14.** Barajas	
5. bala	**10.** tarjeta	**15.** Granada	

C. *Listen and repeat each sentence of the following minidialogues after the speaker.*

1. —Estoy muy preocupada.   **2.** —Estoy exhausta.   **3.** —¿Cuándo descansas?
    —Yo también.   —A mí me pasa lo mismo.   —Los fines de semana.

Estructuras

A. Números de identidad. *You are talking on the telephone to a secretary in the Registrar's Office of your university. She is reading the exchange students' identification numbers to you. Repeat each number and then match the student with his or her identification number. Each number will be repeated.*

1. _____ Amalia Lázaro	**a.** 66-76-35
2. _____ Tomás Fernández	**b.** 53-13-07
3. _____ Maricarmen Tizón	**c.** 03-58-96
4. _____ Carlos Carranza	**d.** 42-17-29
5. _____ Beatriz González	**e.** 21-49-87

B. ¿A qué hora? *You have called the airport for information about the following flights which are arriving tomorrow. Listen to the flight numbers and arrival times and write the information below. The flight information will be repeated.*

1. Guadalajara, México   Vuelo _____ _____

2. Santiago de Chile   Vuelo _____ _____

3. Sevilla, España   Vuelo _____ _____

4. Arequipa, Perú   Vuelo· _____ _____

5. Caracas, Venezuela   Vuelo _____ _____

C. Los pasatiempos. *Using the cues, tell what the following people do when they have some free time. Repeat the correct answer after the speaker.*

> ➤ *MODELO*   María / practicar los deportes
>   **María practica los deportes.**

Capítulo 1
La vida de todos los días

Primera situación

Presentación

Las actividades. *Listen to the following people describe their daily activities. After each monologue you will hear three questions. Answer each question from the response given below. If you need to listen again, replay the recording.*

Monólogo 1

1. **a.** todos los días   **b.** de vez en cuando   **c.** nunca

2. **a.** dos veces al día   **b.** nunca   **c.** a veces

3. **a.** todas las noches   **b.** una vez a la semana   **c.** frecuentemente

Monólogo 2

1. **a.** después   **b.** por último   **c.** primero

2. **a.** cada lunes   **b.** de vez en cuando   **c.** todos los días

3. **a.** finalmente   **b.** primero   **c.** nunca

Monólogo 3

1. **a.** todos los días   **b.** tres veces a la semana   **c.** cada dos días

2. **a.** a menudo   **b.** todas las noches   **c.** de vez en cuando

3. **a.** frecuentemente   **b.** cada fin de semana   **c.** del amanecer al anochecer

Para escuchar bien

In this chapter you have learned that intonation, gestures, the topic being discussed, and the situation in which it is being given can help you understand the gist or the general idea of what the speaker is saying. Now practice getting the gist of a conversation and anticipating what the speakers will say in the following exercises.

A.   La publicidad.   *You are in a Spanish-speaking country and have the radio on. When the music stops, a series of commercials begins. Listen to each and write the number of the commercial before the product or place that is being advertised. Read the possibilities before you listen to the commercials.*

_____ clases de computación   _____ alfombras   _____ restaurante

_____ supermercado   _____ programa deportivo _____ libros

                                      _____ artículos para el hogar   _____ agencia de empleos

B.   Unos estudiantes hablan.   *You will hear a conversation between two university students, José and Maribel. They are talking about what they have to do for their different classes. Before listening to their conversation, mark an **X** next to the topics you think they will discuss. Then listen to their conversation and mark the appropriate topics.*

Temas	Antes de escuchar	Después de escuchar
1. hora de levantarse y acostarse		
2. exámenes y trabajos escritos		
3. cursos que toman		
4. diversiones		
5. amigos comunes		
6. planes de verano		

Now choose the sentence that best summarizes what you heard.

1. José and Maribel are very happy, and although they have a lot of work, they enjoy their classes.

2. Maribel is good in Spanish and José is good in math so they agree to help each other.

3. José and Maribel are worried because they have a lot of work to do for their different classes.

4. José and Maribel think their professors are too demanding and they have no time left for fun.

C.   La vida de mi vecina.   *You will hear a homemaker describing her daily routine. But before listening to her description, mark an **X** next to the topics you think she will talk about. Then listen to her description and mark the topics she mentions.*

Nombre _____ **Fecha** _____ **Clase** _____

Temas	Antes de escuchar	Después de escuchar
1. hora de levantarse y acostarse		
2. quehaceres domésticos (*domestic tasks*)		
3. exámenes y trabajos escritos		
4. diversiones		
5. problemas		
6. posibles soluciones		

Now choose the sentence that best summarizes what you heard.

1. This woman seems to be very content with her life, but she occasionally gets bored and so she calls her friends on the phone.

2. Although she is satisfied with the present state of affairs, this woman is worried about her children's future and is planning to go back to work.

3. This woman's days are very busy and she does not have any time for herself. However, she is planning to go back to school.

4. This woman wakes up early in the morning and goes to bed late at night. She does all the household chores and works in an office to pay for her children's education.

Así se dice

In a stressed or unstressed position the Spanish /e/ is pronounced similarly to the /e/ sound of the English word *mess*; it is spelled **e** or **he**. Remember that Spanish vowel sounds are short and precise. They do not glide like some English vowel sounds.

Práctica

A. *Listen to the following pairs of words and decide if the first word of each pair is a Spanish word or an English word. Circle your answer. Each pair of words will be repeated.*

1. español   inglés

2. español   inglés

3. español   inglés

4. español   inglés

5. español   inglés

6. español   inglés

B.   *Listen to the following sentences and mark how many times you hear the sound /e/. Each sentence will be repeated.*

1. _____   **2.** _____   **3.** _____   **4.** _____

C.   *Listen to the following Spanish words with the /e/ sound and repeat each after the speaker.*

1. el   **5.** tele   **9.** estudie   **13.** aceite

2. en   **6.** este   **10.** cesta   **14.** almacén

3. espejo   **7.** lee   **11.** España   **15.** siesta

4. me   **8.** escribe   **12.** Barcelona

D.   *Listen and repeat each sentence of the following minidialogues after the speaker.*

1. —Este libro es interesante.   **2.** —Tiene siete hermanos   **3.** —¿Cuándo vienes?
       —Préstemelo, por favor.   muy inteligentes.   —El viernes. ¿Te parece?
                                              —¡Qué bien!

Estructuras

A.   **Yo también.**   *A friend is commenting on the activities of various people. Say that you do the same things. Then repeat the correct answer after the speaker.*

> **MODELO**   Enrique estudia en la biblioteca.
>   **Yo también estudio en la biblioteca.**

B.   **Las noticias.**   *Your friends have some news to share with you. Listen to what they have to say and write the missing words. Each news item will be repeated.*

1. ¿_____ a Tomás Fernández? _____ uno de los

estudiantes de intercambio. Pues, él _____ a mi casa esta noche.

_____ con María y Paco. _____ un poco nerviosa

pero _____ que _____ a divertirnos.

2. ¿_____ la noticia? Van a _____ el viejo edificio que

_____ al lado del almacén. _____ que van a

_____ una estación de servicio. _____ que esta ciudad

cambia demasiado. No la _____ .

Nombre _____ **Fecha** _____ **Clase** _____

C.   **¿Quién?** *Mark an* **X** *in the chart under the subject of the verb you hear. Each sentence will be repeated.*

	yo	tú	él	nosotros	ellos
1.					
2.					
3.					
4.					
5.					
6.					
7.					

Segunda situación

Presentación

A.   **El arreglo personal.**   *Listen to the following definitions. Then write the number of the definition under the picture of the object or objects being defined. Each sentence will be repeated.*

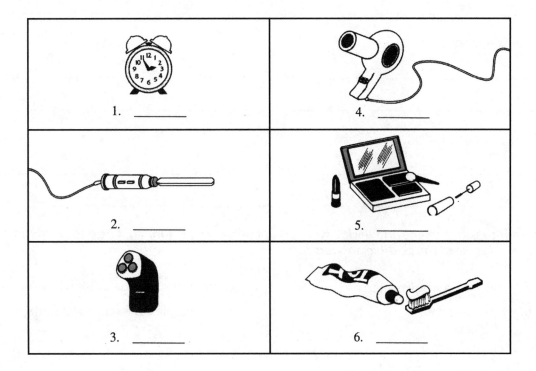

1. _____   4. _____

2. _____   5. _____

3. _____   6. _____

B. ¿Qué quieres decir? *Listen to the following statements and possible responses. Write the letter of the response you would give to show that you do not understand what is being said. The statements and responses will be repeated.*

1. _____ 2. _____ 3. _____ 4. _____

Para escuchar bien

In this chapter you have learned to understand the gist or general idea of what the speaker is saying. Now practice getting the gist of a conversation when you do the following exercises.

A. ¡Dímelo! *You will hear a series of people talk about their daily activities. Before you listen to their descriptions, make a list of routine activities for each of the following persons.*

1. a doctor of medicine

   _____

   _____

2. a university professor

   _____

   _____

3. a salesperson at a department store

   _____

   _____

4. a homemaker

   _____

   _____

5. a high-school student

   _____

   _____

Now listen to each passage and decide what occupation each person has. Circle the letter of the correct answer. Read the possible answers first.

1. **a.** un profesor universitario   **c.** un estudiante de la escuela secundaria

    b. un arquitecto   **d.** un empleado en un restaurante

Nombre _____ **Fecha** _____ **Clase** _____

2. a. una recepcionista   **c.** una vendedora

 b. un ama de casa   **d.** una secretaria

3. a. un estudiante universitario   **c.** un médico

 b. un investigador   **d.** un profesor

B.   Ay, por favor...   *Listen to the following conversation between Gladys and Marisela, two roommates at the University of Madrid. But before you listen to their conversation, make a list of the things you think they will talk about.*

_____

_____

_____

_____

Now listen to the conversation and circle the sentence that best describes what you heard. Read the possible answers first.

1. Marisela y Gladys se están maquillando.

2. Marisela se toma mucho tiempo en el baño.

3. Gladys no puso el despertador y se quedó dormida.

4. Gladys va a llegar tarde a clase porque durmió mucho.

Así se dice

The Spanish /i/ is a shorter and tenser sound than the English /i/. Be careful not to confuse the Spanish /i/ sound with the English /iy/ sound of *sea*, the /i/ sound of *tip*, or the schwa of *president*. The closest approximation to the Spanish /i/ sound is the letter **i** in the English word *machine*. In Spanish, the /i/ sound is spelled **i**, **hi**, or **y**.

Práctica

A.   *Listen to the following pairs of words and decide if the first word of each pair is a Spanish word or an English word. Circle your answer. Each pair of words will be repeated.*

1. español   inglés   **4.** español   inglés

2. español   inglés   **5.** español   inglés

3. español   inglés   **6.** español   inglés

B.   *Listen to the following sentences and mark how many times you hear the sound /i/. Each sentence will be repeated.*

1. _____   2. _____   3. _____   4. _____

C.   *Listen to the following Spanish words with the /i/ sound and repeat each after the speaker.*

1. tipo	**5.** peine	**9.** pintura	**13.** Chile
2. hiciste	**6.** pie	**10.** caliente	**14.** México
3. lápiz	**7.** presidente	**11.** fría	**15.** Lima
4. sin	**8.** cepillo	**12.** cambiar	

D.   *Listen and repeat each sentence of the following minidialogues after the speaker.*

1. —¿Has visto mi peine?
     —Está al lado de tu cepillo de dientes.

2. —¿Vas a afeitarte?
     —Sí, pero primero voy a terminar este libro.

3. —El miércoles tienes una cita con el dentista.
     —¡Qué pesadilla!

Estructuras

A.   Por la mañana.   *Using the cues you hear, explain what the following people do every morning. Repeat the correct answer after the speaker.*

> **MODELO**   Silvia / vestirse
              Silvia se viste.

B.   Preguntas.   *You were not paying attention to what your friend was saying to you. Ask questions so that you can understand what was being said. Use **qué, quién, cuándo, adónde, por qué,** and **cuánto** in your questions. Repeat the correct answer after the speaker.*

> **MODELO**   Maricarmen se levanta tarde.
              ¿Quién se levanta tarde?

Capítulo 2

De vacaciones

Primera situación

Presentación

A.   Las vacaciones.   *You are trying to decide where to spend your vacation. Listen to the following ads for vacation spots and then list the activities available at each one. If you need to listen again, replay the recording.*

Complejo la Playita	Hotel Serenidad	Hotel Cosmopolita
_____	_____	_____
_____	_____	_____
_____	_____	_____
_____	_____	_____
_____	_____	_____

B.   El teléfono.   *The telephone is ringing. Complete the following conversation by responding with what you would say or what would be said to you according to the cues. Repeat the correct answer after the speaker.*

Para escuchar bien

In this chapter you have learned to use visual aids to help you understand what is being said. Now practice using visual aids in the following exercises.

A.   Descripciones.   *Look at the drawing in your textbook on page 47. You will hear four statements. Determine if each is accurate or not based on the information you see in the picture. If it is accurate, circle* **SÍ**, *and if not, circle* **NO**.

1. SÍ   NO   **3.** SÍ   NO

2. SÍ   NO   **4.** SÍ   NO

B.   ¿Qué dices tú?   *You will hear four statements for each drawing below. Look at each drawing and circle* **CIERTO** *if the statement is true and* **FALSO** *if the statement is false.*

1.	**a.**	CIERTO	FALSO	**3.**	**a.**	CIERTO	FALSO
	b.	CIERTO	FALSO		**b.**	CIERTO	FALSO
	c.	CIERTO	FALSO		**c.**	CIERTO	FALSO
	d.	CIERTO	FALSO		**d.**	CIERTO	FALSO

1. a.   CIERTO   FALSO   **3. a.**   CIERTO   FALSO

    b.   CIERTO   FALSO   **b.**   CIERTO   FALSO

    c.   CIERTO   FALSO   **c.**   CIERTO   FALSO

    d.   CIERTO   FALSO   **d.**   CIERTO   FALSO

2. a.   CIERTO   FALSO   **4. a.**   CIERTO   FALSO

    b.   CIERTO   FALSO   **b.**   CIERTO   FALSO

    c.   CIERTO   FALSO   **c.**   CIERTO   FALSO

    d.   CIERTO   FALSO   **d.**   CIERTO   FALSO

C.   ¿Quién dice esto?   *Look again at the drawings above and then listen to the following passages. Mark the number of the passage that best illustrates what the person in the drawing would most likely be thinking. If you need to listen again, replay the recording.*

Drawing 1 _____   Drawing 2 _____   Drawing 3 _____   Drawing 4 _____

Nombre _____ Fecha _____ Clase _____

Así se dice

The Spanish /o/ sound is pronounced by rounding the lips. As with the other vowels, make sure you pronounce the Spanish /o/ without a glide. The /o/ sound of the English word *hotel* is similar to the Spanish /o/ sound; it is spelled **o** or **ho**.

Práctica

A. *Listen to the following pairs of words and decide if the first word of each pair is a Spanish word or an English word. Circle the answer. Each pair of words will be repeated.*

1. español   inglés
2. español   inglés
3. español   inglés

4. español   inglés
5. español   inglés
6. español   inglés

B. *Listen to the following sentences and mark how many times you hear the sound /o/. Each sentence will be repeated.*

1. _____   2. _____   3. _____   4. _____

C. *Listen to the following Spanish words with the /o/ sound and repeat each after the speaker.*

1. lo
2. ola
3. como
4. sol

5. corro
6. polo
7. complejo
8. toldo

9. forma
10. loción
11. castillo
12. pongo

13. Colombia
14. Puerto Rico
15. Toledo

D. *Listen and repeat each sentence of the following minidialogues after the speaker.*

1. —¿Lo viste?
   —No, no lo vi.

2. —¿Dónde está mi sombrero?
   —No lo sé.

3. —¿No quiso tomar el sol?
   —No, no trajo su loción.

Estructuras

A. ¿Hoy o ayer? *Are these people telling you about activities that happened yesterday or that are happening now? Listen carefully and check* **PRETERITE** *or* **PRESENT,** *according to the verbs you hear. Each sentence will be repeated.*

➤ **MODELO**   You hear: Julio pesca.
              You check: **PRESENT**

	1	2	3	4	5	6	7	8
PRESENT								
PRETERITE								

B.   Ayer.   *A friend is telling you what certain people are doing today. Explain that you did the same things yesterday. Repeat the correct answer after the speaker.*

> **MODELO**   Maricarmen y Amalia van a la playa.
> **Yo fui a la playa ayer.**

C.   En la playa.   *Explain what the following people did at the beach yesterday. Repeat the correct answer after the speaker.*

> **MODELO**   Maricarmen / ir a la playa
> **Maricarmen fue a la playa.**

D.   Más historia.   *What do you know about the history of Spanish literature? Listen to the following facts. Write the number of the sentence you hear next to the date mentioned. Each sentence will be repeated.*

1. _____ 1681   **5.** _____ 1605

2. _____ 1140   **6.** _____ 1562

3. _____ 1989   **7.** _____ 1936

4. _____ 1554

Segunda situación

Presentación

A.   Recomendaciones.   *Your friends would like to do one of the following activities tonight. Where would you tell them to go? Repeat the correct answer after the speaker.*

> **MODELO**   Queremos bailar.
> **Deben ir a una discoteca.**

B.   ¿Cuál es la palabra?   *Name the object or place that is being described. Then repeat the correct answer after the speaker.*

> **MODELO**   Es una cosa que la gente puede leer cada día para saber las noticias.
> **Es el periódico.**

Nombre _____ Fecha _____ Clase _____

C. **A Ud. le toca.** *Now it is your turn. Imagine that you do not know the names of the following objects. How would you make yourself understood? Use the expressions* **Es un lugar donde...** *and* **Es una cosa que se pone...** *in your answers. Repeat the correct answer after the speaker.*

> *MODELO* el traje de baño
>   **Es una cosa que se pone cuando uno quiere nadar.**

1. el bar

2. las gafas de sol

3. el cine

4. el sombrero

5. el gimnasio

Para escuchar bien

Practice the strategy of forming mental images when listening in the following exercises.

A. **¿Adónde fuiste tú?** *You will hear a conversation between two university students who are talking about what they did during their summer vacation. But before you listen to their conversation, make a list of the activities you think they may say they did.*

_____

_____

_____

_____

Now listen to their conversation. As you listen, circle the sentences that reflect the content of their conversation. First read the possible answers.

1. Susana y Marisabel son muy buenas amigas y posiblemente van a ir de vacaciones juntas el próximo año.

2. Marisabel trabajó todo el verano en la oficina de su padre y se aburrió muchísimo.

3. Evidentemente la familia de Marisabel tiene mucho dinero.

4. Susana vio a sus amigos de la escuela secundaria y fue al cine con ellos.

5. En la Costa del Sol Marisabel se enfermó y tuvo que regresar a su casa.

6. Una de las muchachas sacó muchas fotos y se las va a enseñar a su amiga.

7. Las dos muchachas fueron de vacaciones al mismo lugar pero no se vieron.

8. Según lo que dicen, en la Costa del Sol sólo se puede ir a nadar y a esquiar.

B. ¿Qué hay? *You are listening to the radio and hear the following announcement. Listen to it and mark an X before the items mentioned. If you need to listen again, replay the recording.*

_____ bailes   _____ fuegos artificiales

_____ corridas de toros   _____ ropa deportiva

_____ loción de broncearse   _____ partidos de fútbol

_____ competencias de natación   _____ películas de terror

_____ exposición de arte   _____ maratón

_____ conciertos   _____ obras teatrales

Así se dice

The Spanish /u/ sound is pronounced with the tongue arched high towards the back of the mouth and with a rounding of the lips. It is tenser and shorter than the English /u/ sound. As with the other vowels, make sure you pronounce the Spanish /u/ without a glide. The Spanish /u/ sound is similar to the /u/ sound in the English word *fool*. The Spanish sound /u/ is spelled **u** or **hu**.

Práctica

A. *Listen to the following pairs of words and decide if the first word of each pair is a Spanish word or an English word. Circle the answer. Each pair of words will be repeated.*

1. español   inglés   **4.** español   inglés

2. español   inglés   **5.** español   inglés

3. español   inglés   **6.** español   inglés

B. *Listen to the following sentences and mark how many times you hear the sound /u/. Each sentence will be repeated.*

1. _____   **2.** _____   **3.** _____   **4.** _____

C. *Listen to the following Spanish words with the /u/ sound and repeat each after the speaker.*

1. una   **5.** película   **9.** música   **13.** Perú

2. luna   **6.** pudo   **10.** futuro   **14.** Cuba

3. usted   **7.** incluyo   **11.** mula   **15.** Uruguay

4. durmió   **8.** universidad   **12.** deuda

Nombre _____ **Fecha** _____ **Clase** _____

D. *Listen and repeat each sentence of the following minidialogues.*

1. —¿Fumas? **2.** —¿Fuiste a Cuba? **3.** —Tú eres Raúl, ¿no?
—No, no fumo. —No, fui a Venezuela. —No, yo soy Luis. Él es Raúl.

Estructuras

A. **¿Cuándo?** *Are you hearing about activities that happened yesterday or that are happening now? Listen carefully and check* **PRETERITE** *or* **PRESENT,** *according to the verbs you hear. Each sentence will be repeated.*

> **MODELO** You hear: Yo preferí ir a la playa.
> You check: **PRETERITE**

	1	**2**	**3**	**4**	**5**	**6**	**7**	**8**
PRESENT								
PRETERITE								

B. **Anoche.** *Describe what the following people did last night or how they felt. Repeat the correct answer after the speaker.*

> **MODELO** Roberto / sentirse muy contento
> **Roberto se sintió muy contento.**

C. **En la playa.** *Tell what or whom Susana saw at the beach yesterday. Repeat the correct answer after the speaker.*

> **MODELO** un castillo de arena
> **Vio un castillo de arena.**

D. **¿Lo trajo Miguel?** *Tell whether or not Miguel brought the following things to the beach. Use direct object pronouns and the cue you hear to answer each question. Repeat the correct answer after the speaker.*

> **MODELO** ¿Trajo Miguel la sombrilla? (Sí)
> **Sí, la trajo.**

Capítulo 3

En familia

Primera situación

Presentación

A. La familia de Alicia. *Alicia's grandmother is telling you about her family. Listen to what she says. Then describe Alicia's family by completing the following sentences. If you need to listen again, replay the recording.*

1. Juan Luis y Amalia son los _____ de Alicia.

2. Fernando es su _____.

3. Isabel y Julieta son sus _____.

4. Luis es su _____.

5. Alberto, Enrique y Carlota son sus _____.

6. Juan y Mariana son sus _____.

7. Felipe es su _____.

B. Los saludos. *How would you greet the following people? Listen to a description of the person and three possible choices. Then write the letter of the most appropriate greeting. The descriptions and choices will be repeated.*

1. _____   2. _____   3. _____   4. _____   5. _____

Para escuchar bien

In this chapter, you have learned that when you listen to a passage you don't need to understand every single word that is being said, but that instead you can focus on certain details or specific information. Now practice focusing on certain details or specific information in the following exercises.

A. Recuerdo que... *You are going to hear two men in their fifties reminiscing about their youth and comparing their lifestyles in the past with their present situations. But before you listen to their conversation, make a list of the things you think they may reminisce about.*

_____   _____

_____   _____

Now listen to their conversation. As you listen, fill in the chart with their names and the activities they mention.

Nombres	Actividades de antes	Actividades de ahora
1. _____	_____	_____
	_____	_____
	_____	_____
	_____	_____
2. _____	_____	_____
	_____	_____
	_____	_____
	_____	_____

B.   Cuando era niño.   *You will hear a series of people describe what they used to do on weekends when they were young. Listen to their descriptions and fill in the chart with their names, the relatives they mention, and the activities they say they used to do.*

Nombres	Parientes	Actividades
1. _____	_____	_____
_____	_____	_____
2. _____	_____	_____
_____	_____	_____
3. _____	_____	_____
_____	_____	_____
4. _____	_____	_____
_____	_____	_____

Nombre _____ **Fecha** _____ **Clase** _____

Así se dice

In Spanish there are two types of diphthongs with the sound /i/: (1) the /i/ sound occurs in first position in front of another vowel as in **Diana**, **Diego**, and **Dios**; (2) the /i/ sound occurs in second position after the vowel as in **caimán**, **peine**, and **hoy**. If the /i/ sound has an accent, then each letter is pronounced. For example, /ia/ in **hacia** is pronounced as a diphthong, but not in **hacía**.

Práctica

A. *Listen to the following Spanish words and repeat each after the speaker.*

1. Diana	**4.** bien	**7.** dio	**10.** pariente
2. piano	**5.** fiesta	**8.** julio	**11.** estudia
3. familia	**6.** tiene	**9.** Amalia	**12.** Antonio

B. *Listen to the following Spanish words and repeat each after the speaker.*

1. caigo	**4.** Jaime	**7.** hoy	**10.** reinado
2. traiga	**5.** rey	**8.** doy	**11.** peinado
3. baila	**6.** peine	**9.** voy	**12.** ley

C. *Listen to the following words and decide if each contains a diphthong or not. Circle* **SÍ** *or* **NO**. *Each word will be repeated.*

1. SÍ   NO   **4.** SÍ   NO

2. SÍ   NO   **5.** SÍ   NO

3. SÍ   NO   **6.** SÍ   NO

D. *Listen to each of the following sentences and mark how many times you hear a diphthong. Each sentence will be repeated.*

1. _____   **2.** _____   **3.** _____   **4.** _____

E. *Listen and repeat each sentence of the following minidialogues after the speaker.*

1. —Tía Emilia, ¿vienes a comer con nosotros este viernes?
    —¿El viernes? No, voy el miércoles.

2. —¿Quieres algo de comer?
    —¿Qué tienes?

3. —Mi familia vive en Viena.
    —La mía también vive en Austria.

Estructuras

A. ¿Cuándo? *Are you hearing about activities that used to happen or that are happening now? Listen carefully and check* **IMPERFECT** *or* **PRESENT** *according to the verb you hear. Each sentence will be repeated.*

> ➤ **MODELO**   Yo estudiaba en la biblioteca.
>   You check: **IMPERFECT**

	1	2	3	4	5	6	7	8
IMPERFECT								
PRESENT								

B. Cada semana. *Tell what the following people used to do every week last year. Repeat the correct answer after the speaker.*

> ➤ **MODELO**   José / lavar el coche
>   **Cada semana José lavaba el coche.**

C. Cada domingo. *Listen as Alicia's grandmother describes what her family used to do every Sunday and write the missing verbs. The description will be repeated.*

Cada domingo toda la familia _____ después de ir a misa. Los niños

_____ al fútbol mientras Julieta o Mariana _____ la cena.

Martín y Juan _____ al dominó. Después de almorzar,

_____ la sobremesa y _____ de todo lo que había

pasado durante la semana. A veces _____ de excursión al parque o al museo.

¡Cuánto me _____ aquellos domingos en familia!

D. ¿Cómo era? *Describe the following people according to the cues. Repeat the correct answer after the speaker.*

> ➤ **MODELO**   Isabel / cariñoso
>   **Isabel era cariñosa.**

E. Diminutivos. *Provide the diminutive form of the words you hear. Repeat the correct answer after the speaker.*

> ➤ **MODELO**   regalo
>   **regalito**

Nombre _____ Fecha _____ Clase _____

Segunda situación

Presentación

A. **¿Qué pasa?** *Look at the following drawings. You will hear two statements for each drawing. Write the correct sentence under the corresponding picture. Each pair of sentences will be repeated.*

1. _____

2. _____

3. _____

4. _____

B.   Las invitaciones.   *Listen to the following statements. Under what conditions would you hear each one? Check **A** if an invitation is being extended, **B** if it is being accepted, or **C** if it is being declined. Each statement will be repeated.*

	1	2	3	4	5	6	7
A							
B							
C							

C. ¿Quién es quién?   *Luisa María is explaining to her young cousin how her new husband's family is related to her. Listen to what she says. In each sentence you will hear a beep in place of a word. Write the missing word. Each sentence will be repeated.*

1. _____   4. _____

2. _____   5. _____

3. _____

Para escuchar bien

Practice listening for details and specific information in the following exercise.

¿Cuál es el mensaje?   *In each of the following telephone conversations you will hear a person extending an invitation for a social gathering. Before you listen to the conversation, though, make a list of some phrases that are used to extend, accept, and decline invitations.*

_____

_____

_____

_____

Nombre _____ Fecha _____ Clase _____

Now listen to each conversation and fill in the chart with the name of the person calling, the nature of the social gathering, the date and time; also mark if the invitation was accepted or declined.

Nombre de la persona que llamó	Reunión social	Fecha	Hora	Aceptada	Rechazada
1. _____	_____	_____	_____	_____	_____
2. _____	_____	_____	_____	_____	_____
3. _____	_____	_____	_____	_____	_____

Así se dice

In Spanish there are two types of diphthongs with the vowel sound /u/: (1) the /u/ sound occurs in first position in front of another vowel as in **agua, hueso, muy,** and **cuota;** (2) the /u/ sound occurs in second position after the vowel as in **auto** and **deuda.**

Práctica

A. *Listen to the following Spanish words and repeat each after the speaker.*

1. guapo
2. cuatro
3. cuanto
4. abuelo
5. muerde
6. puerto
7. Luis
8. juicio
9. ruido
10. cuota
11. cauta
12. deuda

B. *Listen to each of the following sentences and mark how many times you hear a diphthong with /u/. Each sentence will be repeated.*

1. _____
2. _____
3. _____
4. _____

Estructuras

A. La boda. *Listen as your friend describes the wedding of her sister. You will hear a beep in place of the verb. Repeat each sentence using the appropriate form of* **ser, estar,** *or* **haber** *to complete the sentence. Then repeat the correct answer after the speaker.*

> ➤ **MODELO**   Mi hermana *BEEP* muy feliz.
>   **Mi hermana es muy feliz.**

B.   ¿Dónde está?   *The following people have misplaced their belongings. Tell what they are looking for. Repeat the correct answer after the speaker.*

> ➤ *MODELO*   Tomás / libros
> **Tomás busca sus libros.**

C.   Está perdido.   *Explain that the following people have lost their belongings. Repeat the correct answer after the speaker.*

> ➤ *MODELO*   ¿Dónde están los libros de Tomás?
> **Los suyos están perdidos.**

D.   Aquí está.   *Your friend Esteban thinks that he has found the missing items. Tell him that he is wrong. Repeat the correct answer after the speaker.*

> ➤ *MODELO*   Aquí están los libros de Tomás.
> **No, no son suyos.**

Capítulo 4

En el restaurante

Primera situación

Presentación

A.   ¿Qué le puedo ofrecer?   *You are working in the Restaurante Casa Lupita. Listen as the following customers give you their orders. Write what they want. If you need to listen again, replay the recording.*

1. _____

   _____

   _____

2. _____

   _____

   _____

3. _____

   _____

   _____

B.   En el restaurante.   *Who is probably making the following statements? Check the most logical answer. Each statement will be repeated.*

	1	2	3	4	5	6	7	8
MESERO								
CLIENTE								

Para escuchar bien

In this chapter you have learned that you don't need to remember the exact words that were used to convey the message, but that instead you can paraphrase, that is, use different words or phrases to convey the same message. Now practice paraphrasing in the following exercises.

A. **En El Quince Letras.** *Listen to the following conversation. Circle* **SÍ** *if the statements accurately paraphrase what you heard and* **NO** *if they do not.*

SÍ   NO   **1.** Es mediodía.

SÍ   NO   **2.** La comida en este restaurante no es muy buena.

SÍ   NO   **3.** Por lo menos dos personas han estado en ese restaurante anteriormente.

SÍ   NO   **4.** Nadie quiere tomar sopa.

SÍ   NO   **5.** Es tarde y tienen que apurarse.

B. **¿Quién dice qué?** *Look at the drawing and imagine what the people there are saying to each other. For each of the four minidialogues you will hear, circle the letter of the statement that best paraphrases each one. Then write the number of the minidialogue under the appropriate group of people.*

1. **a.** La madre le da un refresco al niño.

   b. El niño quiere un refresco.

   c. El niño quiere toda su comida.

2. **a.** Las dos personas disfrutan de su comida.

   b. A una de las personas no le gusta la sopa.

   c. El gazpacho es más sabroso que el ceviche.

3. **a.** No han terminado de almorzar.

   b. Es tarde y no hay mucho tiempo.

   c. Es necesario que todos tomen un café.

Nombre _____ **Fecha** _____ **Clase** _____

4. **a.** Los dos no se ponen de acuerdo.

   b. A los dos les gustan cosas similares.

   c. Uno de ellos prefiere café.

Así se dice

The Spanish /g/ sound is almost identical to the English /g/ sound. It occurs after the /n/ sound as in **angosto** or **un garaje**, and at the beginning of a phrase or sentence as in **Gloria, gracias por tu ayuda**. It is spelled **g** before **a, o,** or **u** as in **gato, goma,** and **gusto**. However, the sound is spelled **gu** before the letters **e** and **i**, as in **Guevara** and **Guillermo**. The [g̶] variant of this sound occurs within a word or phrase, except after the letter **n**. This sound is spelled **g** before **a, o,** or **u**, and **gu** before **e** and **i**.

Práctica

A. *Listen to the following Spanish words with the [g] sound and repeat each after the speaker.*

1. gallo
2. golpe
3. ganga
4. ponga
5. grande

6. guerra
7. guitarra
8. Galicia
9. Guevara
10. Guillermo

B. *Listen to the following Spanish words with the [g̶] sound and repeat each after the speaker.*

1. amigo
2. agua
3. luego
4. lago
5. paraguas

6. algodón
7. dígame
8. Bogotá
9. Tegucigalpa
10. Santiago

C. *Listen to the following minidialogues containing the [g] and [g̶] sounds and repeat each sentence after the speaker.*

1. —¿Cómo se llama tu amigo?
   —Gustavo Esteban González.

2. —Guillermo, ¿quieres un vaso de agua?
   —Ahora no. Luego.

3. —Gloria, ¿vives en el barrio San Gabriel?
   —Sí, en la calle angosta cerca del Restaurante Angola.

Estructuras

A. La cena de Susana. *You are helping Susana serve her guests. Tell her what you have served to whom. Repeat the correct answer after the speaker.*

> **MODELO**   el café / Juan
>   **Le serví el café a Juan.**

B. ¿Le gusta el flan? *You have been asked to participate in a survey about food preferences. Listen to the following items and say that you like or dislike each one according to the cue you hear. Repeat the correct answer after the speaker.*

> **MODELO**   ¿el flan? (no)
>   **No, no me gusta el flan.**

C. Los intereses. *Explain what interests the following people, using the cues you hear. Repeat the correct answer after the speaker.*

> **MODELO**   Marisa / la ópera
>   **A Marisa le interesa la ópera.**

D. Las molestias. *Explain what bothers the following people. Repeat the correct answer after the speaker.*

> **MODELO**   Miguel / el trabajo
>   **A Miguel le molesta el trabajo.**

Segunda situación

Presentación

A. De compras. *You have offered to do the grocery shopping. Listen as Susana explains to you what she needs to prepare dinner. Make a list of things that Susana tells you to buy. If you need to listen again, replay the recording.*

_____

_____

_____

_____

_____

_____

Nombre _____ **Fecha** _____ **Clase** _____

B.   Poner la mesa. *You are teaching your young cousins how to set the table. However, they are not sure what certain items of the place setting are called. Listen to their questions and identify the object. Repeat the correct answer after the speaker.*

> **MODELO**   ¿En qué se sirve el café?
>   **La taza.**

C.   En la mesa. *Listen to the following statements and possible responses. Write the letter of the most appropriate response. The statements and responses will be repeated.*

1. _____   2. _____   3. _____   4. _____   5. _____

Para escuchar bien

Practice paraphrasing in the following exercises.

A.   Una cena. *You will hear a description of a meal Ignacio had with his friends in a restaurant. Before you listen to him though, make a list of the items you think Ignacio and his friends would order.*

_____

_____

_____

_____

Now listen to the description and mark **CIERTO** *next to the statements that best paraphrase either part or all of what you heard and* **FALSO** *next to those that do not.*

CIERTO	FALSO	**1.**	Gerardo invitó al narrador y a sus amigos a cenar al «Todo Fresco».
CIERTO	FALSO	**2.**	El narrador estaba muy contento con sus amigos porque lo invitaron a cenar.
CIERTO	FALSO	**3.**	Uno de los jóvenes no quiso pagar.
CIERTO	FALSO	**4.**	Cuando llegaron al «Todo Fresco», se dieron cuenta de que había mucha gente y no tenían dónde sentarse.
CIERTO	FALSO	**5.**	Todos los muchachos comieron lo mismo.
CIERTO	FALSO	**6.**	Al final de la cena hubo problemas para pagar la cuenta.
CIERTO	FALSO	**7.**	Desafortunadamente, todos se fueron muy disgustados porque no querían pagar.
CIERTO	FALSO	**8.**	El narrador fue a buscar su carro porque se molestó al ver a sus amigos discutir.

B. **¿Cómo son estos muchachos?** *You are going to hear a description of four students: Gerardo, Armando, Roberto, and Pepe. As you listen, take notes. At the end of the passage, you will hear some statements that paraphrase what you have heard. Mark* **CIERTO** *if the statement is a good paraphrase and* **FALSO** *if it is not. If you need to listen again, replay the recording.*

_____

_____

_____

_____

_____

_____

_____

_____

1. CIERTO   FALSO   **4.** CIERTO   FALSO

2. CIERTO   FALSO   **5.** CIERTO   FALSO

3. CIERTO   FALSO   **6.** CIERTO   FALSO

Así se dice

The Spanish /p/ sound is produced without aspiration, or the puff of air, that the English /p/ sound has. The unaspirated Spanish /p/ sound is equivalent to the /p/ sound of the English words *special* and *speak*. It generally appears at the beginning of a word as in **pato, perro, para,** and **por,** but it can also appear within a word preceding the /t/ sound as in **captar.**

Práctica

A. *Listen to the following pairs of words and decide if the first word of each pair is a Spanish word or an English word. Circle the answer. Each pair of words will be repeated.*

1. español   inglés   **4.** español   inglés

2. español   inglés   **5.** español   inglés

3. español   inglés   **6.** español   inglés

Nombre _____ **Fecha** _____ **Clase** _____

B. *Listen to the following Spanish words with the /p/ sound and repeat each after the speaker.*

1. pez
2. papa
3. Pedro
4. Perú

5. papel
6. Pamplona
7. comprar
8. golpear

9. sopa
10. copa
11. séptimo
12. inscripción

13. Paraguay
14. capturar
15. Pepe

C. *Listen and repeat each sentence of the following minidialogues after the speaker.*

1. —¿En qué te especializas, Pepita?
   —En ciencias políticas.

2. —¿Estudias periodismo?
   —No, me especializo en pintura.

3. —¿Qué deporte practicas?
   —Prefiero el polo.

Estructuras

A. Una comida fantástica. *Listen as Paco tells you what happened last night. Check IMPERFECT or PRETERITE according to the verb you hear in each sentence.*

➤ *MODELO*   You hear: Ayer después de las clases, fui directamente a casa.
                You check: **PRETERITE**

	1	2	3	4	5	6	7
IMPERFECT							
PRETERITE							

B. En el restaurante. *Listen as Paco finishes his story. You will hear a beep in place of the verb in each sentence. Decide which form of the verb should complete the sentence and circle it. Each sentence will be repeated.*

1. entrábamos   entramos
2. saludaba   saludó
3. daba   dio
4. Pedía   Pedí

5. era   fue
6. era   fue
7. regresábamos   regresamos

C.   En el parque.   *What happened in the park on the day of that terrible storm? Listen and complete the following sentences. If you need to listen again, replay the recording.*

_____ un día bonito de mayo. _____

mucho sol. Los pájaros _____. Cerca de nosotros algunos chicos

_____ al vólibol. Todo el mundo _____ de

buen humor.

De repente Paco _____ de que _____ de traer

las bebidas. Y Susana no _____ bastante comida para todos. Y con eso,

_____ el picnic.

D.   La carrera.   *Using the cues you hear, explain in what order the following people finished in the bicycle race. Repeat the correct answer after the speaker.*

➥ **MODELO**   Paco / seis
Paco fue el sexto.

Capítulo 5

En la universidad

Primera situación

Presentación

A. Definiciones. *Listen to the following phrases and then write the word being defined. Each phrase will be repeated.*

1. _____

2. _____

3. _____

4. _____

5. _____

6. _____

7. _____

B. En la clase. *Who is probably making the following statements? Check the most logical answer. Each statement will be repeated.*

	1	2	3	4	5	6	7
ESTUDIANTE							
PROFESOR							

Para escuchar bien

In this chapter you have learned that knowing where and when a given conversation or an announcement takes place helps you to understand the message more accurately. Now practice focusing on the setting of the following exercises.

A. ¿Dónde? *Listen to the following announcements and decide where you would probably hear each. Then mark the number of the announcement next to the place where you would most likely hear it. But before you listen to the announcements, read the list of possible settings.*

_____ el centro

_____ el campo deportivo

_____ el aeropuerto

_____ la residencia estudiantil

_____ la biblioteca

_____ la sala de clase

B.   En la cafetería estudiantil.   *Imagine that you are sitting in the student cafeteria of a university in Costa Rica and overhear a group of students who are talking about their majors and their plans for the future. Make a list of the majors you think they may mention in their conversation.*

_____

_____

_____

_____

_____

Now listen to their conversation and write in the chart the students' majors and their plans for the future.

Estudiantes	Especialidad	Planes futuros
Carmen		
Manuel		
Ana		
Rosa		

Así se dice

The Spanish /b/ sound can be spelled with the letters **b** or **v** and is similar to the English /b/ of *boy*. The /b/ sound has two variants: [b] and [ƀ]. The sound [b] occurs when the letters **b** or **v** follow the letters **m** or **n** as in **un viaje, un barco,** or **Colombia** and when the letters **b** or **v** begin a phrase or sentence, as in **Vicente es mi amigo** and **Ven acá, Bernardo.** However, when the letters **b** or **v** occur within a word or phrase, except after the letters **m** or **n**, then the sound [ƀ] occurs. The sound [ƀ] is similar to the [b] sound, but your lips barely touch, as in **lobo, el beso,** and **lavo.** This [ƀ] sound has no English equivalent.

Nombre _____ **Fecha** _____ **Clase** _____

Práctica

A. *Listen to the following Spanish words with the [b] sound and repeat each after the speaker.*

1.	bola	**6.**	banco
2.	beso	**7.**	veinte
3.	bien	**8.**	vino
4.	vaca	**9.**	cambiar
5.	vaso	**10.**	símbolo

B. *Listen to the following Spanish words and phrases with the [ƀ] sound and repeat each after the speaker.*

1.	lavo	**6.**	abuela
2.	robo	**7.**	el vino
3.	Cuba	**8.**	mi vestido
4.	cerveza	**9.**	no voy
5.	probar	**10.**	¡Qué bien!

C. *Listen to the following words and phrases with the [b] and [ƀ] sounds and repeat each after the speaker.*

1.	voy	yo voy	**4.**	vestido	mi vestido
2.	beso	el beso	**5.**	banco	voy al banco
3.	vaca	la vaca	**6.**	baila	no baila

D. *Listen to the following minidialogues containing the [b] and [ƀ] sounds and repeat each sentence after the speaker.*

1. —Violeta, ¿vas a Colombia?
   —Sí, voy con Víctor.

2. —Habla Gabriela.
   —Hola. ¿Cómo está el bebé?

3. —¿Sabes si él viene el viernes?
   —No, viene el sábado.

Estructuras

A.   Opuestos.   *Say the opposite of the words you hear. Repeat the correct answer after the speaker.*

> *MODELO*   You hear: debajo de
>   You say: **sobre**

B.   La cena.   *You are making arrangements for a dinner party. Listen to the following sentences and write the names of the guests according to where they are to sit. Each sentence will be repeated.*

Pablo		

C.   Pobre Ricardo.   *Listen as Ricardo explains why he cannot go to the movies tonight. In each of his sentences, you will hear a beep in place of a preposition. Decide if the missing preposition should be **por** or **para**. Check the correct answer. Each sentence will be repeated.*

> *MODELO*   You hear: *BEEP* supuesto, me gustaría ir al cine.
>   You check **por** because the answer is **Por supuesto, me gustaría ir al cine.**

	1	2	3	4	5	6	7
POR							
PARA							

D.   ¿Para quién?   *Who will receive the following gifts? Use prepositional pronouns and the cues you hear to answer this question. Repeat the correct answer after the speaker.*

> *MODELO*   las flores / María
>   **Las flores son para ella.**

E.   En la biblioteca.   *Using the cues you hear, explain what happened yesterday in the library. Repeat the correct answer after the speaker.*

> *MODELO*   Miguel / poder terminar el trabajo
>   **Miguel pudo terminar el trabajo.**

Nombre _____ **Fecha** _____ **Clase** _____

Segunda situación

Presentación

A. Una buena amiga. *Your friend Adela called to tell you what classes everyone you know is taking this semester, but you weren't home so she left the following message on your answering machine. After listening to her message, make a list of each person's classes so you can remember them. If you need to listen again, replay the recording.*

Paco

_____

_____

_____

Adela

_____

_____

_____

Susana

_____

_____

_____

Enrique

_____

_____

_____

B.   ¿Qué tiempo hace? *You are planning to travel to Central America and you need to know what the weather is like. Listen to the following weather report, and make notes about the climate of the cities listed. If you need to listen again, replay the recording.*

1. Guatemala: _____

_____

2. la costa del Pacífico: _____

_____

3. San José: _____

_____

4. Panamá: _____

_____

Para escuchar bien

Practice focusing on the setting and listening for specific information in the following exercises.

A.   ¿Dónde y cuándo?   *You will hear three conversations between two university students. As you listen, decide when and where the conversations are taking place. Circle the word or phrase that best completes each sentence.*

Conversación 1

1. Estas estudiantes están conversando en

   a. la biblioteca.

   b. la cafetería.

   c. su cuarto.

2. La conversación se lleva a cabo por

   a. la mañana.

   b. la noche.

   c. la tarde.

Conversación 2

1. Estos estudiantes están conversando en

   a. la oficina de un profesor.

   b. una reunión social.

   c. el salón de clase.

2. La conversación se lleva a cabo

   a. muy temprano por la mañana.

   b. muy tarde por la noche.

   c. por la tarde.

Conversación 3

1. Estos estudiantes están conversando en

   a. el laboratorio de idiomas.

   b. el salón de computadoras.

   c. el laboratorio de ciencias.

2. La conversación se lleva a cabo

   a. antes de clase.

   b. después de clase.

   c. durante la clase.

B.   ¿Quién, cuándo y dónde?   *You will hear a series of instructions. As you listen, decide who is giving them and the setting. Circle the letter of the phrase with the appropriate information. But before you listen to the instructions, read the different possibilities.*

1. a. una profesora, antes de un examen, en el salón

  b. una madre, antes de una fiesta, en su casa

  c. una estudiante, después de clase, en su cuarto

2. a. una secretaria, la primera semana de clases, en su oficina

  b. una compañera, después de una clase aburrida, en el carro

  c. una profesora, el primer día de clase, en su oficina

3. a. un empleado, en la biblioteca, a las doce de la noche

  b. un vendedor, en la librería, a las ocho de la mañana

  c. un instructor, en el laboratorio, a las seis de la tarde

Así se dice

The Spanish /d/ is pronounced very differently from the English /d/ sound. It is produced by pressing the tip of your tongue against the back of your upper teeth; this sound is always spelled with the letter **d**. The /d/ sound has three variants: [d], [đ], and [ø]. The Spanish [d] sound occurs at the beginning of a phrase or sentence as in **Diego, ¿cómo estás?**, after a pause within a phrase as in **Ángela, dame tu libro**, or after the letters **n** or **l** as in **ando** and **falda**. The variant [đ] is pronounced like the *th* in the English word *either*. It occurs within a word or phrase, except after **n** or **l**, as in **todo, cada,** or **Adiós, Adela.** The variant [ø] is no sound at all. When the letter **d** occurs at the end of a word, it is often not pronounced although it appears in writing, as in **usted** and **verdad.**

Práctica

A. *Listen to the following Spanish words with the [d] sound and repeat each after the speaker.*

1.	debe	**6.**	anda
2.	dame	**7.**	cuando
3.	delicioso	**8.**	Honduras
4.	Delia	**9.**	caldo
5.	Díaz	**10.**	molde

B. *Listen to the following Spanish words and phrases with the /đ/ variant sounds and repeat each after the speaker.*

1.	cada	**6.**	Estados Unidos
2.	todo	**7.**	usted
3.	helado	**8.**	ciudad
4.	adiós	**9.**	¿Verdad?
5.	ensalada	**10.**	Madrid

C. *Listen to the following minidialogues containing the /d/ sound and its variants and repeat each sentence after the speaker.*

1. —¿Vive Diego en El Salvador?
　　—No, ahora vive en Honduras.

2. —¿Adónde va usted?
　　—A la Tienda Novedades.

3. —Ustedes deben venir a mi oficina esta tarde.
　　—Como usted diga.

Estructuras

A.   Sé que... Ojalá que.   *You hear only the end of the following statements. How does each sentence begin? Listen carefully to the verb and check* **SÉ QUE** *if the sentence you hear is in the indicative. Check* **OJALÁ QUE** *if the sentence you hear is in the subjunctive. Each phrase will be repeated.*

> ➤ *MODELO*   You hear: ...Paco cumple veintiún años.
> You check: **SÉ QUE**

	1	**2**	**3**	**4**	**5**	**6**	**7**	**8**
SÉ QUE								
OJALÁ QUE								

B.   Consejos.   *What advice do you have for Paco as he starts a new semester at the university? Repeat the correct answer after the speaker.*

> ➤ *MODELO*   llegar a tiempo a sus clases
> **Le aconsejo que llegue a tiempo a sus clases.**

C.   Es necesario que...   *Give advice about doing well in your studies. Repeat the correct answer after the speaker.*

> ➤ *MODELO*   Uds. / elegir las clases con cuidado
> **Es necesario que Uds. elijan las clases con cuidado.**

D.   ¿Mejor o peor?   *Describe the following activities. Then repeat the correct answer after the speaker.*

> ➤ *MODELO*   divertirse de vez en cuando / estudiar todo el tiempo
> **Divertirse de vez en cuando es mejor que estudiar todo el tiempo.**

Capítulo 6

En casa

Primera situación

Presentación

A. Antes de la visita.   *Your family is expecting weekend guests. While you are out, your mother calls with instructions about what needs to be done around the house before the guests arrive. Listen to the message she left on the telephone answering machine and make a list of chores for each person. If you need to listen again, replay the recording.*

Paco: _____

_____

Juan: _____

_____

María: _____

_____

Isabel: _____

_____

Carlota: _____

_____

B. Si fueras tan amable...   *Listen to the following statements. Under what conditions would you hear each one? Check **A** if someone is making a request, **B** if the request is being accepted, or **C** if the request is being refused. Each statement will be repeated.*

	1	2	3	4	5	6	7	8
A								
B								
C								

Para escuchar bien

In this chapter you have learned to listen for the main idea of what is being said and the supporting details. Now practice identifying the main ideas and supporting details in the following exercises.

A.   Anuncios radiales.   *You will hear three radio announcements asking for people to perform different services. As you listen, write the main ideas and supporting details. But before you listen to the announcements, make a list of the different kinds of services or chores that can be performed in a house.*

_____

_____

_____

_____

Now listen to each announcement and take notes of the main ideas and supporting details.

1. **Main idea:** _____

    Supporting details: _____

    _____

    _____

2. **Main idea:** _____

    Supporting details: _____

    _____

    _____

3. **Main idea:** _____

    Supporting details: _____

    _____

    _____

B.   Con los empleados.   *You will hear three conversations between the employers who paid for the previous radio announcements and the people they hired. As you listen, write the main ideas and the supporting details. But before you listen to the conversations, mentally review the formation of the affirmative and negative forms of the familiar and formal commands. Now listen and write down the main ideas and supporting details for each conversation.*

Nombre _____ **Fecha** _____ **Clase** _____

1. Main idea: _____

   Supporting details: _____

   _____

   _____

2. Main idea: _____

   Supporting details: _____

   _____

   _____

3. Main idea: _____

   Supporting details: _____

   _____

   _____

   _____

Así se dice

The Spanish /t/ sound is pronounced with the tip of your tongue against the back of your front teeth. Like the /p/ sound, the /t/ is pronounced without aspiration, or the puff of air, that the English sound has. For example, **tú**, **estudia**, **matemáticas**, and **texto**.

Práctica

A. *Listen to the following pairs of words and decide if the first word of each pair is a Spanish word or an English word. Circle the answer. Each pair of words will be repeated.*

1. español   inglés   **4.** español   inglés

2. español   inglés   **5.** español   inglés

3. español   inglés   **6.** español   inglés

B. *Now listen to the following Spanish words with the /t/ sound and repeat each after the speaker.*

1. tú	**5.** deporte	**9.** tres	**13.** Toledo
2. tengo	**6.** quita	**10.** tabú	**14.** Argentina
3. teatro	**7.** meta	**11.** Alberto	**15.** Guatemala
4. todo	**8.** tuna	**12.** matemáticas	

C.   *Listen and repeat each sentence of the following minidialogues after the speaker.*

1.   —Espero que no me quiten mi beca.
—¿Quién te la va a quitar?

2.   —¿Dónde está el estadio?
—Detrás de las oficinas administrativas.

3.   —¿Te gustan las matemáticas?
—Sí. Este semestre me inscribí en tres cursos de matemáticas.

Estructuras

A.   ¿Mandatos?   *Listen to the following sentences. Are they commands directed to someone addressed as* **tú** *or are they statements explaining what someone addressed as* **tú** *is doing? Listen carefully and check* **COMMAND** *or* **STATEMENT** *according to the verb you hear. Each sentence will be repeated.*

> ➤ *MODELO*   You hear: Barre el piso.
>   You check: **COMMAND**

	1	2	3	4	5	6	7	8
COMMAND								
STATEMENT								

B.   Los quehaceres domésticos.   *Explain to your roommate what he must do to get ready for tonight's party. Repeat the correct answer after the speaker.*

> ➤ *MODELO*   lavar los platos
>   **Lava los platos.**

C.   No lo hagas.   *You are willing to help your roommate with the chores. Tell him not to do certain things because you will do them. Repeat the correct answer after the speaker.*

> ➤ *MODELO*   limpiar la cocina
>   **No limpies la cocina. Yo lo hago.**

D.   Las hermanas.   *Margarita and Carlota are sisters who look and act alike. Describe Margarita by comparing her to Carlota. Repeat the correct answer after the speaker.*

> ➤ *MODELO*   bonito
>   **Margarita es tan bonita como Carlota.**

E. Así es la vida. *Your friend is complaining about all the obligations she has. Tell her that you have as many obligations as she does. Repeat the correct answer after the speaker.*

> **MODELO** exámenes
> Yo tengo tantos exámenes como tú.

F. Tanto como tú. *Your brother accuses you of not doing as many chores around the house as he does. Tell him that you do as much as he does. Repeat the correct answer after the speaker.*

> **MODELO** preparar la cena
> Yo preparo la cena tanto como tú.

G. Un cliente difícil. *A salesman is helping you select items you need to purchase. As he points out various items, you tell him that you would like a different one. Repeat the correct answer after the speaker.*

> **MODELO** ¿trapo?
> No quiero este trapo. Prefiero ése.

Segunda situación

Presentación

Un desastre. *You are a journalism student working in Bogotá for the summer. Your job is to report details of important stories to your home newspaper. Listen to the following news broadcast and then answer the questions. If you need to listen again, replay the recording.*

1. ¿Cuál fue el desastre? _____

2. ¿Dónde ocurrió? _____

3. ¿Cuándo ocurrió? _____

4. ¿Cuántas personas murieron? _____

5. ¿Por qué se han arrestado a unas veinte personas? _____

6. ¿Qué hicieron los políticos? _____

7. ¿Qué ocurrió en las regiones costeras? _____

Para escuchar bien

Practice listening for the main ideas and supporting details in the following exercises.

A.   Noticiero.   *You will hear three news reports. As you listen, write the main ideas and supporting details of each news item.*

1. **Main idea:** _____

    Supporting details: _____

    _____

    _____

2. **Main idea:** _____

    Supporting details: _____

    _____

    _____

3. **Main idea:** _____

    Supporting details: _____

    _____

    _____

B.   Programas de televisión.   *You will hear two conversations that take place on a Latin American TV show. As you listen, write the main ideas and supporting details.*

1. **Main idea:** _____

    Supporting details: _____

    _____

    _____

2. **Main idea:** _____

    Supporting details: _____

    _____

    _____

Nombre _____ Fecha _____ Clase _____

Así se dice

The Spanish /k/ sound is pronounced without the aspiration, or puff of air, that the English /k/ sound has at the beginning of a word. That is, it follows the same patterns as the Spanish /p/ and /t/ sounds. The /k/ sound is spelled **c** before **a, o,** or **u** as in **casa, cosa,** and **cura.** It is also spelled **c** at the end of a syllable in words such as **rector** and **tractor.** However, before **e** or **i** the /k/ sound is spelled **qu** as in **queso** and **quisieron.** Only words of foreign origin and words that refer to the metric system are spelled with a **k.** This is the case in words like **kilo** and **Alaska.**

Práctica

A. *Listen to the following pairs of words and decide if the first word in each pair is a Spanish word or an English word. Circle the answer. Each pair of words will be repeated.*

1. español   inglés
2. español   inglés
3. español   inglés

4. español   inglés
5. español   inglés
6. español   inglés

B. *Listen to the following Spanish words with the /k/ sound and repeat each after the speaker.*

1. casa	5. kilómetro	9. escoba	13. Caracas
2. que	6. curso	10. banco	14. Colombia
3. come	7. parque	11. histórico	15. Barranquilla
4. quiso	8. esquina	12. rector	

C. *Listen and repeat each sentence of the following minidialogues after the speaker.*

1. —¿Quieres que compre alguna cosa?
   —Sólo queso y mantequilla, por favor.

2. —No pude comprar el periódico en el quiosco.
   —¿Por qué?

3. —Este cruce es muy peligroso.
   —Y aquél también.

Estructuras

A.   Dudo que...   *Your friend suggests that you vote for his favorite candidate. However, you don't think it is a good idea. Express your doubts. Repeat the correct answer after the speaker.*

> ➤ *MODELO*   Dice la verdad siempre.
> **Dudo que diga la verdad siempre.**

B.   Tengo que limpiar la casa.   *Your friend is cleaning her house. Explain what she must do. Repeat the correct answer after the speaker.*

> ➤ **MODELO**   sacar la basura
>   **Es importante que saques la basura.**

C.   Los quehaceres.   *Your little sister is helping you with the chores. Tell her you need the following items. Repeat the correct answer after the speaker.*

> ➤ **MODELO**   esponjas
>   **Necesito las esponjas.**

Capítulo 7

De compras

Primera situación

Presentación

A.   En el Centro Comercial Mariposa.   *Listen to the following advertisement for a new shopping center. What kinds of stores are being described? Next to the name of the store, indicate what kind of store it is. If you need to listen again, replay the recording.*

1. Hermanos Gómez _____

2. Tienda Felicidades _____

3. Boutique Elegancia _____

4. Tienda Ortiz _____

B.   En la tienda.   *Who is probably making the following statements? Check the most logical answer. Each statement will be repeated.*

	1	2	3	4	5	6	7	8
COMPRADOR								
DEPENDIENTE								

Para escuchar bien

In this chapter you have learned that when participating in a conversation either you or the person you are talking to might not say exactly what you mean. Consequently, you have to infer the real meaning of a question or an answer. Now practice making inferences from what you hear in the following exercises.

A.   ¿Qué quiere decir?   *You will hear three short conversations between a salesperson and a customer. After you listen to each conversation, write what the customer meant by his or her reply. But before you listen to these conversations, write some of the phrases that the customer would use to make a purchase and the phrases that the salesperson would use to reply.*

_____

_____

_____

Now listen to the conversations and write what each customer meant.

1. _____

2. _____

3. _____

B.   ¡Pero, mamá!   *Now you are going to hear a series of comments made by a mother to her teenage daughter who is going out on a date. After you listen to each comment, write what the mother really meant by her comment. But before you listen, write some of the things you think the mother might say or ask.*

_____

_____

_____

_____

Now listen and write the meaning of each statement.

1. _____

2. _____

3. _____

4. _____

5. _____

6. _____

Así se dice

The Spanish /x/ sound is pronounced with friction. It is similar to the initial sound of the English words *house* and *home,* but the Spanish sound is harsher. In some Spanish dialects, it is similar to the sound made when breathing on a pair of glasses to clean them. It is spelled **j** before **a, o,** and **u** as in **jamón, joven,** and **juego; g** or **j** before **e** and **i** as in **gente, gitano, jefe,** and **jinete.** In some cases it can be spelled **x** as in **México** and **Xavier.**

Práctica

A.   *Listen to the following Spanish words with the /x/ sound and repeat each after the speaker.*

1. jefe	**5.** jabón	**9.** cruje	**13.** mujer
2. José	**6.** juega	**10.** déjame	**14.** México
3. Javier	**7.** dibujo	**11.** traje	**15.** Texas
4. gente	**8.** queja	**12.** maneja	

Nombre _____ **Fecha** _____ **Clase** _____

B. *Listen and repeat each sentence of the following minidialogues after the speaker.*

1. —Mujer, ¿has visto a Xavier?
   —Está en el jardín con José.

2. —No quiero jugar a las cartas.
   —Pero Josefa, no seas mala gente.

3. —Jorge, te dije que dejaras el jamón.
   —Mamá, pero tengo hambre. Déjame probarlo.

Estructuras

A. **¿Cuándo?** *Are these activities currently in progress or will they take place soon? Check* **PROGRESSIVE** *or* **PRESENT** *according to the verb you hear. Each sentence will be repeated.*

➤ **MODELO**   You hear: Lupe está bailando.
              You check: **PROGRESSIVE**

	1	2	3	4	5	6	7	8
PROGRESSIVE								
PRESENT								

B. **Ahora mismo.** *Explain what the following people are doing right now. Repeat the correct answer after the speaker.*

➤ **MODELO**   María / comprar un regalo
              María está comprando un regalo.

C. **Anoche.** *Explain what the following people were doing last night at eight o'clock. Repeat the correct answer after the speaker.*

➤ **MODELO**   nosotros / descansar
              Nosotros estábamos descansando.

D. **La Boutique Elegancia.** *Enrique Morales, a shopping consultant, has described many of the stores in the Centro Comercial Mariposa. What does he say about Boutique Elegancia? Repeat the correct answer after the speaker.*

➤ **MODELO**   mercancía / caro
              Tiene la mercancía más cara del centro comercial.

Segunda situación

Presentación

Las devoluciones.   *You are working as a salesclerk in the department store Hermanos Gómez. Each day you must make a list of the purchases returned and the reasons why they were returned. Listen to the following customers. Then list the items returned and the reasons for their return. If you need to listen again, replay the recording.*

1. _____

2. _____

3. _____

4. _____

5. _____

6. _____

Para escuchar bien

Practice making inferences and using visual cues in the following exercises.

A.   ¿En qué piensan?   *Look at the drawings and try to imagine what the people are thinking. Then listen to the sentences. Write the letter of each sentence next to the number of the drawing it matches. Each sentence will be repeated.*

1. _____

2. _____

3. _____

4. _____

B. **Me parece...** *Look at the drawings again and try to imagine a possible monologue or dialogue for each drawing. As you listen to the recording, write the letter of each monologue or dialogue next to the number of the drawing it matches. If·you need to listen again, replay the recording.*

1. _____ **2.** _____ **3.** _____ **4.** _____

Así se dice

The Spanish /s/ has many regional variations. In Spanish America, the /s/ sound is usually similar to the English /s/ of *sent* or *summer.* The /s/ sound is spelled differently depending on where it occurs in a word. For example, it is spelled **s** and **z** before vowels and at the end of a word as in **sopa, zapato,** and **paz**; **s** and **x** before /p/ and /t/ as in **espero, estudio, explorar,** and **extensión**; and **c** before /e/ and /i/ as in **dice** and **cinta.**

In contrast, in most parts of Spain the **c** before **e** and **i** and the **z** are pronounced like the /th/ sound in the English word *thing*: **pobreza, dice,** and **prejuicio.** In the following exercises, you will practice the Spanish American pronunciation of the /s/ sound.

Práctica

A. *Listen to the following Spanish words with the /s/ sound and repeat each after the speaker.*

1. señor	**5.** prejuicio	**9.** dice	**13.** necesita
2. sembrar	**6.** así	**10.** cerveza	**14.** pobreza
3. soy	**7.** vaso	**11.** basura	**15.** explotar
4. ese	**8.** regreso	**12.** serie	

B. *Listen and repeat each sentence of the following minidialogues after the speaker.*

1. —¿Qué dices, Josefa, conseguiremos trabajo?
   —Yo creo que sí, Sergio.

2. —El problema de la emigración es bastante serio.
   —Más serio es el problema de la inflación.

3. —¿Quiénes son esas personas?
   —No sé. No las conozco.
   —¿Serán extranjeros?
   —Seguramente sí.

Estructuras

A.   Los regalos.   *Tell which gifts you are giving to the following people. Repeat the correct answer after the speaker.*

> ➢ **MODELO**   a Joaquín / una guitarra
>   Se la regalo a Joaquín.

B.   Las compras.   *You and your friend are going shopping today. However, you are in a bad mood and contradict whatever your friend says. Repeat the correct answer after the speaker.*

> ➢ **MODELO**   Siempre estoy lista para ir de compras.
>   Nunca estoy lista para ir de compras.

Capítulo 8

En la ciudad

Primera situación

Presentación

A.   Un paseo.   *Look at the map below as you listen to Enrique. He will tell you about some places he visited in the city. When he pauses, write the name of the place he is identifying. If you need to listen again, replay the recording.*

1. _____

2. _____

3. _____

4. _____

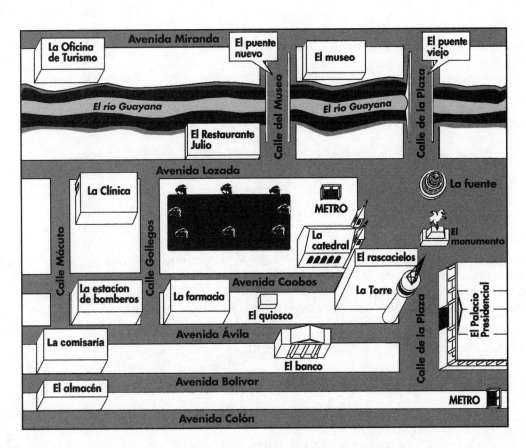

B.   ¿Dónde queda?   *Look at the map again. Someone is asking you where the following places are located. Answer by naming the street or avenue. Repeat the correct answer after the speaker.*

> *MODELO*   ¿Dónde queda el Restaurante Julio?
> **El Restaurante Julio está en la Avenida Lozada.**

Para escuchar bien

In this chapter you have learned to take notes on what you hear. Taking notes helps you to remember what was said and improves your writing skills in Spanish. Now practice taking notes in the following exercises.

A.   ¿Cómo se va al parque?   *You will hear a short dialogue in which a young woman asks for directions to a park. But before you hear the dialogue, make a list of phrases that can be used to ask for and give directions.*

_____

_____

_____

_____

_____

_____

Now listen to the dialogue and write the missing words.

SEÑORITA: _____, señora, pero ¿ _____ cómo se

va al Parque las Leyendas?

SEÑORA: Cómo no. Camine derecho _____ y luego doble

_____. El parque está _____.

SEÑORITA: _____ gracias.

B.   Se perdió María.   *You are going to hear a conversation between Zoila and a police officer. Zoila is reporting that her friend María got lost. A transcript of the information that Zoila provides is given on the following pages, but there is some information missing. You will have to supply that information. But before you listen to the conversation, read the transcript.*

POLICÍA: Bueno, señorita, dígame, ¿cuándo se perdió su amiga?

ZOILA: La última vez que la vi fue a las nueve de la mañana de hoy,

_____. Íbamos al _____ pero nos

dimos cuenta de que no se abría sino hasta las once del día. Decidimos ir a dar una vuelta

por los alrededores y cuando me di cuenta, María había desaparecido.

POLICÍA: ¿Cuál es su nombre completo?

ZOILA: ¿El mío? _____.

Nombre _____ **Fecha** _____ **Clase** _____

POLICÍA: ¿Y el de su amiga?

ZOILA: _____.

POLICÍA: ¿Cómo es su amiga María?

ZOILA: Ella es alta y _____. Mide _____.

Es delgada y tiene el pelo _____, bien corto. Tiene los ojos

_____ y un lunar en la _____.

POLICÍA: ¿Y cuántos años tiene?

ZOILA: _____ años.

POLICÍA: ¿Y es soltera o casada?

ZOILA: _____. Nosotras estamos de vacaciones. Vinimos a Lima

pero no sé cómo María desapareció. La busqué por todas partes pero no la encontré.

POLICÍA: ¿Y cómo llegaron Uds. al país?

ZOILA: Vinimos en avión de Bogotá. Apenas llegamos ayer.

POLICÍA: ¿En qué hotel están alojadas?

ZOILA: En el hotel «Las Américas». El teléfono de nuestra habitación es

_____.

POLICÍA: Mire, señorita, muchos turistas se separan de sus compañeros pero no se pierden. Estoy

seguro de que su amiga debe estar buscándola a Ud. o esperándola en su hotel. De todas

maneras nosotros vamos a empezar la búsqueda. En cuanto sepamos cualquier cosa le

avisamos.

ZOILA: ¿Y qué hago yo ahora?

POLICÍA: Vaya a su hotel. Uno de nuestros oficiales la llevará. Si sabe algo de su amiga, por favor,

háganos saber.

ZOILA: Por supuesto y muchas gracias.

Now complete the following form.

PARTE POLICIAL

Nombre de la persona desaparecida: _____

Nombre de la persona que reporta la desaparición: _____

Lugar de residencia de la persona que reporta la desaparición:

_____   Teléfono: _____

Lugar donde fue vista la persona la última vez:

_____

Fecha cuando fue vista la persona la última vez:

_____

Descripción de la persona desaparecida:

Estatura: _____   Color de ojos: _____

Color de piel: _____   Marcas o cicatrices: _____

Color del cabello: _____   Estado civil: _____

Edad: _____

Así se dice

The Spanish /l/ sound is pronounced similarly to the English /l/ sound in *Lee*. It is always spelled l.

Práctica

A.   *Listen to the following pairs of words and decide if the first word in each pair is a Spanish word or an English word. Circle the answer in your lab manual. Each pair of words will be repeated.*

1. español   inglés   4. español   inglés

2. español   inglés   5. español   inglés

3. español   inglés   6. español   inglés

B.   *Listen to the following Spanish words with the /l/ sound and repeat each after the speaker.*

1. lo   5. plan   9. papel   13. mal

2. ley   6. caldo   10. lavandería   14. problema

3. la   7. claro   11. papelería   15. Lima

4. alma   8. plancha   12. al

Nombre _____ Fecha _____ Clase _____

C. *Listen and repeat each sentence of the following minidialogues after the speaker.*

1. —Pásame la sal, Celia.
—Está a tu lado.

2. —Leo, tienes que cortar el césped.
—Pero si lo corté la semana pasada.

3. —¿Le diste de comer al perro?
—No. Creí que lo había hecho Laura.

Estructuras

A. ¿Cómo se llega? *Señora Santana has asked you for directions to the Oficina de Turismo. Give her directions according to the cues you hear. Repeat the correct answer after the speaker.*

> ***MODELO***   bajar del metro en la Avenida Bolívar
>   **Baje Ud. del metro en la Avenida Bolívar.**

B. Una excursión a la ciudad. *Your friends ask you what points of interest they should see while visiting your city. Give them some suggestions according to the cues you hear. Repeat the correct answer after the speaker.*

> ***MODELO***   visitar el Ayuntamiento
>   **Visiten Uds. el Ayuntamiento.**

C. Se pintan letreros. *You have volunteered to paint signs for your friends. Listen to the following situations and tell what your sign will say. Repeat the correct answer after the speaker.*

> ***MODELO***   Alquilo mi apartamento.
>   **Se alquila apartamento.**

Segunda situación

Presentación

¿No crees que sería mejor si...? *Where are the following people trying to persuade their friends to spend the afternoon? In the spaces provided, indicate whether the speaker would like to go to* **la corrida, el centro cultural,** *or* **el parque de atracciones.** *If you need to listen again, replay the recording.*

1. _____   **5.** _____

2. _____   **6.** _____

3. _____   **7.** _____

4. _____

Para escuchar bien

Practice taking dictation in the following exercises.

A.   Aquí tienen...   *You will hear a museum guide informing some tourists about the different works of art they can see at the museum. But before you listen to the passage, make a list of the things you think he is going to mention.*

_____

_____

_____

_____

Now listen to the passage and write what he says in the pauses provided. If you need to listen again, replay the recording.

_____

_____

_____

_____

_____

_____

_____

_____

_____

_____

_____

_____

_____

_____

_____

_____

Nombre _____ Fecha _____ Clase _____

B. Cuéntame. *You will hear a conversation between two friends who are sightseeing in Lima. But before you listen to their conversation, make a list of the places you think they visited.*

_____

_____

_____

_____

_____

Now listen to their conversation and write the names of all the places you hear them mention.

Mujer 1

_____

_____

_____

Mujer 2

_____

_____

_____

Así se dice

In most of the Spanish-speaking world the /y/ sound before **a, e, o**, and **u** at the beginning of a word or beginning of a syllable is similar to the English /y/ sound in *yes* and *yarn*. It is spelled **hi, y,** or **ll.**

Práctica

A. *Listen to the following Spanish words with the /y/ sound and repeat each after the speaker.*

1. llama	**5.** bella	**9.** talla	**13.** llave
2. lleno	**6.** sello	**10.** platillo	**14.** llano
3. lluvia	**7.** Castilla	**11.** grillo	**15.** silla
4. millón	**8.** rollo	**12.** ella	

B. *Listen to the following Spanish words with the /y/ sound and repeat each after the speaker.*

1. yema	**5.** yeso	**9.** reyes	**13.** hierba
2. Yolanda	**6.** hiena	**10.** yelmo	**14.** hielo
3. yarda	**7.** raya	**11.** leyes	**15.** yerno
4. yuca	**8.** hiato	**12.** yo-yo	

C. *Listen and repeat each sentence of the following minidialogues after the speaker.*

1. —¿Tienes la llave?　　**2.** —Llama a Yolanda.　　**3.** —Quiero un poco de hielo.
　　—No, la tiene ella.　　　　　—Ya la llamé.　　　　　　—Está allí.

Estructuras

A. **¿Cuándo?** *Are these people telling you about activities that are happening now or that will happen in the future? Listen carefully and check* **PRESENT** *or* **FUTURE** *according to the verb you hear. Each sentence will be repeated.*

> ➤ **MODELO**　　　You hear:　　Llamaré a los invitados.
> 　　　　　　　　　You check:　**FUTURE**

	1	2	3	4	5	6	7	8
PRESENT								
FUTURE								

B. **El viaje.** *Tomorrow you are leaving on an important trip. Describe what you will do. Repeat the correct answer after the speaker.*

> ➤ **MODELO**　　　levantarse temprano
> 　　　　　　　　　**Me levantaré temprano.**

C. **En el futuro.** *What will the following people probably be doing in the future? Make a guess. Repeat the correct answer after the speaker.*

> ➤ **MODELO**　　　Tomás / ganar la lotería
> 　　　　　　　　　**Tomás ganará la lotería.**

D. **En el parque de atracciones.** *You are taking your nephew to an amusement park. He asks about some of the things he will see and do. Answer his questions by saying* Let's *do what he would like to do there. Repeat the correct answer after the speaker.*

> ➤ **MODELO**　　　¿Vamos a visitar la casa de espejos?
> 　　　　　　　　　**Sí, visitemos la casa de espejos.**

Capítulo 9

En la agencia de empleos

Primera situación

Presentación

A. Conseguir un empleo. *Listen as an employment counselor gives you advice about finding a job. Then list the things you should do to be successful. If you need to listen again, replay the recording.*

1. _____

2. _____

3. _____

4. _____

5. _____

6. _____

7. _____

B. Hablando de... *Listen to the following statements. Under what conditions would you hear each one? Check **A** if someone is expressing an idea, **B** if someone is changing the subject, or **C** if someone is interrupting. Each statement will be repeated.*

	1	2	3	4	5	6	7	8
A								
B								
C								

Para escuchar bien

In this chapter you have learned to summarize what you hear. To do this you have to recall factual information and categorize it logically in the proper format. Now practice summarizing what you hear in the following exercises.

A.   Sus obligaciones.   *You will hear a short conversation between an employer and a prospective secretary. As you listen, fill in the following outline with the corresponding information. But before you listen, write a list of possible tasks the employer might mention.*

_____

_____

_____

_____

_____

Now listen to the conversation and fill in the outline.

AGENCIA DE EMPLEOS

A.   **Obligaciones de la secretaria**

1.   _____

2.   _____

3.   _____

4.   _____

5.   _____

B.   **Obligaciones de la señorita Méndez**

1.   _____

2.   _____

B.   ¿Qué harás tú?   *You will hear a group of recent college graduates discuss the results of their job search. As you listen, fill in the following outline. But before you do this, write what you plan to do after you graduate.*

_____

_____

_____

_____

_____

_____

Nombre _____ **Fecha** _____ **Clase** _____

Now listen and fill in the following outline.

Mujer 1

Periódico: _____

Departamento: _____

Responsabilidades: _____

Mujer 2

Periódico: _____

Departamento: _____

Responsabilidades: _____

Hombre 1

Situación presente: _____

Expectativas: _____

C. Noticias del futuro. *You will hear a short lecture given by a futurologist, who is describing the workplace and working conditions in twenty years. As you listen, fill in the following outline with the information provided. But before you listen, make five predictions about what the workplace will be like in twenty years.*

1. _____

2. _____

3. _____

4. _____

5. _____

Now listen to the lecture and fill in the outline.

EFECTOS DE LOS AVANCES TECNOLÓGICOS

Mayor número de personas trabajarán en sus casas

Consecuencias positivas

1. En la ciudad

    a. _____

    b. _____

2. En la familia

    a. _____

    b. _____

3. En la tecnología y economía

    a. _____

Consecuencia negativa

1. _____

Así se dice

The Spanish /n/ sound is generally similar to the English /n/ sound in the word *not,* although it varies slightly according to the sound that follows it. For example, the tip of your tongue touches the back of your upper front teeth when /n/ precedes /t/, /d/, and /s/ as in **pinto, donde,** and **mensual.** When the /n/ precedes a vowel, /l/, /r/, /rr/, or when it occurs at the end of a word or sentence, the tip of your tongue touches the gum ridge as in **nada, ponla, honrado,** and **con.** When /n/ occurs in front of **ch** as in **concha** and **ancho,** the tip of your tongue touches the back part of your palate.

Práctica

A. *Listen to the following Spanish words with the /n/ sound and repeat each after the speaker.*

1. no	**5.** mensual	**9.** honrado	**13.** poncho
2. nada	**6.** pinto	**10.** con	**14.** rancho
3. nadie	**7.** nunca	**11.** concha	**15.** Enrique
4. donde	**8.** ponla	**12.** ancha	

B. *Listen to the following sentences and mark how many times you hear the sound /n/. Each sentence will be repeated.*

1. _____   **2.** _____   **3.** _____   **4.** _____

Nombre _____ Fecha _____ Clase _____

C. *Listen and repeat each sentence of the following minidialogues after the speaker.*

1. —¿Ud. es la señorita Méndez?
—Sí, señor.

2. —Estoy muy contenta con mi trabajo.
—Cuánto me alegro.

3. —Pronto conseguirás una entrevista.
—Ojalá, porque todavía no he oído nada.

Estructuras

A. **¿Cuándo?** *Are these people telling you about activities that will happen in the future or that would happen when certain conditions are present? Listen carefully and check* **FUTURE** *or* **CONDITIONAL** *according to the verb you hear. Each sentence will be repeated.*

> **MODELO**   You hear: Lo ayudaré.
>   You check: **FUTURE**

	1	**2**	**3**	**4**	**5**	**6**	**7**	**8**
FUTURE								
CONDITIONAL								

B. **La entrevista.** *Explain what you would do if you were preparing for a job interview. Repeat the correct answer after the speaker.*

> **MODELO**   enterarme de las condiciones del trabajo
>   **Me enteraría de las condiciones del trabajo.**

C. **Un trabajo nuevo.** *What would the following people do if they had to work in a new job? Repeat the correct answer after the speaker.*

> **MODELO**   José / hacer bien el trabajo
>   **José haría bien el trabajo.**

D. **Los clientes.** *Explain to a co-worker how he should treat the clients who come into your office. Repeat the correct answer after the speaker.*

> **MODELO**   cortés
>   **Trata a los clientes cortésmente.**

E.   El aspirante.   *You are being asked your opinion about an applicant for a job in your department. Answer the questions according to the cues you hear. Repeat the correct answer after the speaker.*

> ➤ *MODELO*   ¿Tiene conocimientos técnicos? (poco)
> **Tiene pocos conocimientos técnicos.**

Segunda situación

Presentación

¡Grandes rebajas!   *The Papelería Comercial is having a sale on office furniture, machines, office supplies and computer ware. Listen to their radio ad and list the office supplies that are on sale. If you need to listen again, replay the recording.*

_____

_____

_____

Para escuchar bien

Practice summarizing what you hear in the following exercises. Remember that a summary can be in the form of a chart, outline, or paragraph.

A.   Nuestra empresa.   *You will hear a short presentation by a business manager who is explaining the corporate structure of the company to the new personnel. As you listen, complete the paragraphs with the information provided. But before you listen, make a list of the different departments you think a company might have and the functions each performs within the corporate structure.*

_____

_____

_____

_____

Now listen to the presentation and complete the following paragraphs.

1. El Presidente de la Compañía tiene tres asesores. Éstos son el Asesor de Asuntos

    _____, el Asesor de Asuntos de _____ y el

    Asesor de _____ .

Nombre _____ **Fecha** _____ **Clase** _____

2. El Asesor de _____ trabaja con el _____ y con

el Jefe de _____ . Él _____ se encarga de la

_____ , _____ y _____

de nuestros productos. Él está a cargo de los diferentes _____ regionales.

3. El Asesor de _____ trabaja directamente con el Jefe de Personal. El Jefe

de Personal contrata al _____ y éste contrata a cada una de las dos

_____ y a los dos _____ de la empresa.

4. El Asesor de _____ está a cargo de la coordinación de todos los aspectos

de la _____ de nuestra empresa. Trabaja directamente con un

_____ y dos dibujantes.

B. **Tengo que hacer un pedido.** *You will hear a short conversation between a secretary and the office manager. The secretary is placing an order for office equipment. As you listen, complete the following chart with the information provided. But before you listen, make a list of the items you think she might order.*

_____

_____

_____

_____

Now listen and complete the chart.

PEDIDO

1. Para la oficina de la secretaria

a. _____   **c.** _____

b. _____   **d.** _____

2. Para la oficina del Supervisor de Ventas

a. _____   **c.** _____

b. _____

3. Para la Oficina de Relaciones Públicas

a. _____   **c.** _____

b. _____

Así se dice

The Spanish /ñ/ sound is pronounced similarly to the English sound /ny/ in *union* and *canyon*. It always occurs in word or syllable initial position and is spelled **ñ**.

Práctica

A. *Listen to the following Spanish words with the /ñ/ sound and repeat each after the speaker.*

1. ñato	**5.** español	**9.** niño	**13.** enseñar
2. mañana	**6.** señal	**10.** uña	**14.** daño
3. año	**7.** paño	**11.** caña	**15.** peña
4. cuñada	**8.** señor	**12.** baño	

B. *Listen to the following sentences and mark how many times you hear the sound /ñ/. Each sentence will be repeated.*

1. _____   **2.** _____   **3.** _____   **4.** _____

C. *Listen and repeat each sentence of the following minidialogues after the speaker.*

1. —No me arañes con   **2.** —Enséñame tu carro nuevo.   **3.** —Hola, cuñada. ¿Qué buscas?
      tus uñas.   —No es nuevo. Es del   —Busco la caña de pescar
      —Disculpa, Toño.   año pasado.   de mi niño.

Estructuras

A.   El trabajo ideal.   *You are looking for the perfect job. Describe this job according to the cues you hear. Repeat the correct answer after the speaker.*

> ***MODELO***   ofrecer vacaciones largas
> **Quiero un trabajo que ofrezca vacaciones largas.**

B.   Las compras.   *The manager of the Purchasing Department is ordering supplies. You hope he accomplishes certain objectives. What do you say to your colleague? Repeat the correct answer after the speaker.*

> ***MODELO***   comprar bastantes teléfonos celulares
> **Que compre bastantes teléfonos celulares.**

C.   El aspirante ideal.   *Listen as the speaker asks about the characteristics of the ideal job applicant. Answer the questions in the affirmative using the absolute superlative. Repeat the correct answer after the speaker.*

> ***MODELO***   ¿Es bueno que sea maduro?
> **Sí, es buenísimo.**

Capítulo 10

En la empresa multinacional

Primera situación

Presentación

A.   En la agencia de empleos.   *You are working as a personnel consultant for an employment agency. You are listening to a client who has a wonderful product to sell and enough capital to start a small business. Listen to what he tells you and make a list of the people he needs to hire.*

_____

_____

_____

B.   Por teléfono.   *Who is probably making the following statements? Check* **A** *if it is the person calling and* **B** *if it is the person answering the call. Each statement will be repeated.*

	1	2	3	4	5	6	7
A							
B							

Para escuchar bien

In this chapter you have learned to report to others what you have heard. You do this by retelling the story of what happened or reporting what was said. Now practice reporting messages and orders in the following exercises.

A.   Tomando apuntes.   *You will hear a series of messages left on the answering machine of Mr. Robles. As you listen, take notes using indirect commands so you can report the messages to him later.*

1. _____

_____

2. _____

_____

3. _____

_____

4. _____

_____

B.   El jefe.   *You will hear a short conversation between two secretaries; one is reporting the manager's orders to the other one. As you listen, make a list of the orders given using indirect commands. But before you do this, write five orders you think the manager of an import-export firm might give to a secretary.*

1. _____

2. _____

3. _____

4. _____

5. _____

Now listen to the conversation and write the orders as you would report them.

1. _____

2. _____

3. _____

4. _____

5. _____

Así se dice

When the Spanish /r/ does not begin a word, it is pronounced by a single flap of the tip of the tongue on the ridge behind the upper front teeth. The Spanish /r/ sound is similar to the English sounds of /tt/ in *batter* or /dd/ in *ladder*; it is always spelled **r.**

Práctica

A.   *Listen to the following Spanish words with the /r/ sound and repeat each after the speaker.*

1. febrero	**5.** pero	**9.** mar	**13.** Caracas
2. cargar	**6.** cara	**10.** gordo	**14.** Perú
3. partir	**7.** Toronto	**11.** pronto	**15.** Uruguay
4. tarde	**8.** comer	**12.** ir	

Nombre _____ **Fecha** _____ **Clase** _____

B. *Listen to the following sentences and mark how many times you hear the sound /r/. Each sentence will be repeated.*

1. _____ 2. _____ 3. _____ 4. _____

C. *Listen and repeat each sentence of the following minidialogues after the speaker.*

1. —Mira, Teresa, ¿te gusta esta pulsera de oro?
   —Me encanta. ¿Me la vas a regalar, hermano?

2. —¿Trabajas en el Banco Hipotecario?
   —Sí, ¿por qué? ¿Quieres pedir un préstamo?

3. —Señor Martínez, averigüe cuál es la tasa de interés para préstamos a corto plazo, por favor.
   —Es el diez por ciento.

Estructuras

A. **¿Cuándo?** *Are these people telling you about completed activities or about activities that are happening now? Listen carefully and check* **PRESENT** *or* **PRESENT PERFECT** *according to the verb you hear. Each sentence will be repeated.*

> ***MODELO***   You hear: José ha ejecutado todos los pedidos.
>   You check: **PRESENT PERFECT**

	1	**2**	**3**	**4**	**5**	**6**	**7**	**8**
PRESENT								
PRESENT PERFECT								

B. **¿Has terminado...?** *You are working as an account executive. Today you would like to leave the office before the end of the work day. However, your boss wants to know if you have finished certain tasks. Repeat the correct answer after the speaker.*

> ***MODELO***   terminar el informe para mañana
>   **Sí, he terminado el informe para mañana.**

C. **¿Cuándo?** *Are these people telling you about activities that they hope are completed or about activities that they hope are happening now? Listen carefully and check* **PRESENT SUBJUNCTIVE** *or* **PRESENT PERFECT SUBJUNCTIVE** *according to the verb you hear. Each sentence will be repeated.*

> ***MODELO***   You hear: Espero que la publicista haya creado los anuncios.
>   You check: **PRESENT PERFECT SUBJUNCTIVE**

	1	2	3	4	5	6	7	8
PRESENT SUBJUNCTIVE								
PRESENT PERFECT SUBJUNCTIVE								

D. Un buen gerente. *Everyone in the office is happy that the manager has made all the arrangements for the project. Tell what they are glad that he has done. Repeat the correct answer after the speaker.*

> ➤ *MODELO*   hablar con el ejecutivo
> **Se alegran de que haya hablado con el ejecutivo.**

E. Los amigos. *Explain what you and your friends do. Repeat the correct answer after the speaker.*

> ➤ *MODELO*   Paco le escribe a Marilú. Marilú le escribe a Paco.
> **Paco y Marilú se escriben.**

Segunda situación

Presentación

A. Un desastre fiscal. *Listen to the following news bulletin and then answer the questions. If you need to listen again, replay the recording.*

1. ¿Qué sube cada mes?

_____

2. ¿Cómo es el presupuesto nacional?

_____

3. ¿Cuál es el otro problema que le preocupa al gobierno?

_____

4. ¿Qué quiere empezar la administración?

_____

5. ¿En qué va a insistir el gobierno?

_____

Nombre _____ **Fecha** _____ **Clase** _____

B. **Definiciones.** *Listen to the following phrases and then write the word or expression being defined. Each phrase will be repeated.*

1. _____   5. _____

2. _____   6. _____

3. _____   7. _____

4. _____

Para escuchar bien

Using the strategies you have learned, practice reporting what you hear and retelling a story in the following exercises.

A. **¡Qué situación!** *Two friends are discussing their banking activities. Listen to their conversation and from the options presented, circle the four options that best retell the story you heard. But before you listen, read the options and write a list of six words or phrases related to banking that you would expect to hear in this conversation.*

_____   _____

_____   _____

_____   _____

Now listen to the conversation and make your choices.

1. Elena está muy contenta porque va a comprarse una casa.
2. Elena había ido al Banco Hipotecario a pedir consejo financiero.
3. Elena y Jorge habían ahorrado por muchos años.
4. La tasa de interés no ha bajado.
5. Elena y Jorge no habían vivido en una casa alquilada por mucho tiempo.
6. Elena y Jorge no van a tener que hacer ningún cambio en sus vidas para poder pagar su nueva casa.
7. Elena y Jorge ya han reunido bastante dinero.
8. El esposo de Elena se acaba de comprar un carro nuevo; por eso van a tener problemas para pagar las cuotas mensuales.

B. **El banco.** *You will hear an advertisement for El Banco Latino. As you listen, take notes on the important information. Then stop the recording and write a short paragraph summarizing the advertisement.*

Now listen and take notes.

_____

_____

_____

_____

Now write your summary.

_____

_____

_____

_____

Así se dice

The Spanish /rr/ sound is pronounced by flapping the tip of the tongue on the ridge behind the upper teeth in rapid succession. This sound is called trilling; it occurs between vowels, at the beginning of a word, and after /n/, /l/, or /s/. The trilled /rr/ is spelled **rr** between vowels as in **perro** and **carro**. In other positions, it is spelled **r** as in **ropa** and **honrado**.

Práctica

A.   *Listen to the following Spanish words with the /rr/ sound and repeat each after the speaker.*

1. carro	**5.** roto	**9.** enrejado	**13.** Israel
2. perro	**6.** rubia	**10.** alrededor	**14.** rasgar
3. barro	**7.** honrado	**11.** ropa	**15.** rascar
4. raro	**8.** enredo	**12.** repaso	

B.   *Listen to the following sentences and mark how many times you hear the sound /rr/. Each sentence will be repeated.*

1. _____   **2.** _____   **3.** _____   **4.** _____

C.   *Listen and repeat each sentence of the following minidialogues after the speaker.*

1.   —¿Ya compraste el carro?
       —Sí, es rojo.

2.   —Mi perro me rasgó la ropa.
       —¡Qué raro!

3.   —Voy a Roma pronto.
       —¡Cómo me encantaría ir también!

Nombre _____ Fecha _____ Clase _____

Estructuras

A. ¿Cuándo? *The following people are describing past activities. Some of these activities were completed before today; others were not. Listen carefully and check* **PRESENT PERFECT** *or* **PAST PERFECT** *according to the verb you hear. Each sentence will be repeated.*

> ➤ *MODELO*   You hear: Había pedido consejo financiero.
>   You check: **PAST PERFECT**

	1	2	3	4	5	6	7	8
PRESENT PERFECT								
PAST PERFECT								

B. Antes de las tres. *What did you accomplish by three o'clock yesterday afternoon? Repeat the correct answer after the speaker.*

> ➤ *MODELO*   archivar los documentos
>   **Había archivado los documentos.**

C. En el banco. *What did the following people do in the bank before it closed today? Repeat the correct answer after the speaker.*

> ➤ *MODELO*   Marta / cerrar su cuenta corriente
>   **Marta había cerrado su cuenta corriente.**

D. ¿Cuánto tiempo hace? *How long has the Empresa Multinac been providing the following services? Repeat the correct answer after the speaker.*

> ➤ *MODELO*   10 años / exportar productos
>   **Hace 10 años que exporta productos.**

E. Llevo mucho tiempo... *Explain how long you have been assuming the following responsibilities. Repeat the correct answer after the speaker.*

> ➤ *MODELO*   5 años / trabajar en esta empresa
>   **Llevo 5 años trabajando en esta empresa.**

F.   Las cuentas.   *You are verifying account numbers for new clients. Listen as a co-worker reads the client's name and account number. Match the client with his or her account number. Each name and account number will be repeated.*

1. _____ Juan Luis Domínguez   **a.** 7.747

2. _____ María Herrera   **b.** 10.834

3. _____ Pablo Ortiz   **c.** 1.683

4. _____ Carlos Santana   **d.** 8.528

5. _____ Jaime Velásquez   **e.** 3.951

6. _____ Lucía López   **f.** 6.475

7. _____ Isabel Ochoa   **g.** 9.362

Capítulo 11

De viaje

Primera situación

Presentación

A.   Una excursión.   *While listening to the radio program «El viajero feliz», you hear about an interesting excursion. You decide to organize a weekend trip for your friends. Listen carefully and make notes about the trip. If you need to listen again, replay the recording.*

¿Dónde? _____

¿Cuándo? _____

¿Cómo? _____

¿Por qué? _____

_____

B.   A bordo.   *Who is probably making the following statements? Check the most logical answer. Each statement will be repeated.*

	1	2	3	4	5	6	7	8
AZAFATA								
PASAJERO								

Para escuchar bien

In this chapter you have learned to answer questions about a conversation or passage and to give your personal interpretation of the situation. Now practice answering content-related questions and making personal interpretations in the following exercises.

A.   ¿Qué hago?   *You will hear a short conversation between a customs official and a traveler at an airport. As you listen, identify the main problem and be ready to give your personal reaction to it. But before you listen, read the following questions.*

Now listen and write the answers to the questions.

1.   ¿Qué problema se presentó en la aduana?

_____

2. ¿Por qué se presentó este problema?

_____

3. ¿Qué le parece la actitud del empleado? ¿Y la de la viajera?

_____

4. En su opinión, ¿quién tenía razón? ¿Por qué?

_____

_____

5. ¿Qué haría Ud. en una situación semejante?

_____

_____

6. ¿Cómo cree Ud. que es el empleado físicamente? ¿Y cómo cree Ud. que es su personalidad?

_____

_____

7. Describa Ud. a la viajera física y sicológicamente.

_____

_____

B. **En el avión.** *You will hear a conversation between a passenger and a flight attendant on a plane. As you listen, identify the main problem and be ready to give your personal reaction to it. But before you listen, read the following questions.*

Now listen to the conversation and write the answers to the questions.

1. ¿Qué problema surgió antes del despegue?

_____

2. ¿Qué solución ofreció la aeromoza?

_____

3. ¿Fue esta solución del agrado de la viajera? Explique.

_____

_____

Nombre _____ **Fecha** _____ **Clase** _____

4. ¿Cuál fue la actitud de la viajera? ¿Qué frases usó que le hacen pensar así?

_____

_____

5. ¿Y la aeromoza? ¿Cuál fue su actitud con la viajera?

_____

6. Si Ud. fuera la viajera, ¿qué habría hecho?

_____

_____

7. Si Ud. fuera la aeromoza, ¿qué habría hecho?

_____

8. Describa a la viajera física y sicológicamente.

_____

_____

_____

Así se dice

Spanish words have two kinds of syllables: stressed and unstressed. In addition, Spanish words tend to have only one stressed syllable, for example, **Ni-ca-ra-gua** (unstressed-unstressed-stressed-unstressed), **li-te-ra-tu-ra** (unstressed-unstressed-unstressed-stressed-unstressed). English words, on the other hand, have three types of syllables: those with primary stress, secondary stress, or unstressed, for example *Nic-a-ra-gua* (secondary stress-unstressed-primary stress-unstressed), *lit-er-a-ture* (primary stress-unstressed-unstressed-secondary stress). When pronouncing a Spanish word for the first time, you need to learn to identify the stressed syllable so that you say the word correctly.

Práctica

A. *Listen to the following words and decide which syllable the stress falls on. Underline the stressed syllable. Each word will be repeated.*

1. bie-nes-tar

2. com-pa-ñe-ro

3. in-mi-gran-tes

4. vo-lun-ta-ria-men-te

5. de-ma-sia-do

6. i-dio-mas

7. a-dop-ti-va

8. tra-ba-ja-ran

9. as-cen-den-cia

10. be-ne-fi-ciar

B.   *Listen and repeat each of the following Spanish words after the speaker.*

1. jefatura	**5.** ciudadano	**9.** legalmente
2. autonomía	**6.** hispano	**10.** herencia
3. bienestar	**7.** celebración	**11.** universidades
4. mayoría	**8.** ascendencia	**12.** bilingüismo

C.   *Listen and repeat each sentence of the following minidialogues after the speaker.*

1.   —¿Qué opinas tú del bilingüismo?
        —Me parece estupendo. Ojalá todo el mundo hablara más de un idioma.

2.   —Nosotros queremos mucho nuestra patria adoptiva.
        —Claro, vinimos aquí voluntariamente.

3.   —Mis compañeros trabajarán en la celebración de la independencia nacional.
        —¿La que habrá en el consulado?

Estructuras

A.   Sabía que... o Dudaba que...   *You hear only the end of the following sentences. How does each sentence begin? Listen carefully to the verb and check* **SABÍA QUE** *if the verb you hear is in the indicative. Check* **DUDABA QUE** *if the verb you hear is in the subjunctive. Each phrase will be repeated.*

> ➤ **MODELO**   You hear: … Paco hiciera una reservación.
>   You check: **DUDABA QUE**

	1	**2**	**3**	**4**	**5**	**6**	**7**	**8**
SABÍA QUE								
DUDABA QUE								

B.   Antes del viaje.   *Explain what was necessary for you to do before your last trip. Repeat the correct answer after the speaker.*

> ➤ **MODELO**   hacer una reservación
>   **Era necesario que hiciera una reservación.**

C.   Los consejos.   *What advice did you give the following people before they left on a tour of Chile and Argentina? Repeat the correct answer after the speaker.*

> ➤ **MODELO**   Isabel / escuchar el programa «El viajero feliz»
>   **Le aconsejé a Isabel que escuchara el programa «El viajero feliz».**

Nombre _____ Fecha _____ Clase _____

D. Iría a Viña del Mar. *Tell under what conditions you would go to Viña del Mar. Repeat the correct answer after the speaker.*

> ➤ *MODELO* tener más tiempo
> Si tuviera más tiempo, iría a Viña del Mar.

Segunda situación

Presentación

A. En la recepción. *You are working as a desk clerk at the Hotel Miraflores. The phone has been ringing constantly. Listen carefully and make a list of the room numbers and the services requested by each guest. If you need to listen again, replay the recording.*

Habitación	Servicio

B. En el hotel. *Who is probably making the following statements? Check **A** if it is the guest and **B** if it is the hotel desk clerk. Each statement will be repeated.*

	1	2	3	4	5	6	7	8
A								
B								

Para escuchar bien

In this chapter you have learned to answer questions about a conversation or passage and to give your personal interpretation of the situation. Now practice answering content-related questions and making personal interpretations in the following exercises.

A. ¡Qué barbaridad!   *You will hear a conversation between a couple. As you listen, identify the main problem and be ready to give your personal reaction to it. But before you listen, read the following questions.*

Now listen and write the answers to the questions.

1. ¿Qué problemas hay en la habitación?

_____

2. ¿Cuál es la actitud de la mujer? ¿Y la del hombre?

_____

3. ¿Qué ha pasado con el equipaje de los viajeros? ¿Qué consecuencias tiene esto?

_____

4. ¿Comó cree Ud. que se va a resolver la situación?

_____

5. Describa a los empleados del hotel. ¿Cómo cree Ud. que son?

_____

B. El Hotel Crillón.   *You will hear a telephone conversation between a desk clerk and a prospective guest. Listen for the verb tenses. Are the speakers talking about future actions that will take place before other future actions, using the future perfect tense, or discussing contrary-to-fact situations or polite requests, using the imperfect subjunctive? As you listen for these verb tenses, write in column A the verbs you hear in the future perfect tense and in column B the verbs you hear in the imperfect subjunctive. But before you listen, mentally review the forms of the future perfect tense and imperfect subjunctive of the following verbs:* **hacer, cerrar, llegar, querer, venir, tener.** *Now listen and write the verbs in the appropriate columns.*

Nombre _____ **Fecha** _____ **Clase** _____

A: Future Perfect	**B: Imperfect Subjunctive**
_____	_____
_____	_____
_____	_____
_____	_____

Así se dice

Linking, or the running together of words, occurs in Spanish and English. However, the two languages differ in how they run their words together. English tends to run two consonants together as in *hot tea*, whereas Spanish runs a final consonant and a beginning vowel together as in **un árbol** or two vowels together as in **eso es**. Proper linking of words will make you sound more like a native speaker.

Práctica

A. *Listen to the following Spanish sentences and mark how many words you hear in each sentence. Each sentence will be repeated.*

1. _____   3. _____   5. _____

2. _____   4. _____   6. _____

B. *Listen to the sentences from Exercise A again and write each one. Each sentence will be repeated.*

1. _____

2. _____

3. _____

4. _____

5. _____

6. _____

C. *Listen and repeat each sentence of the following minidialogues after the speaker.*

1. —Mi estancia en ese hotel fue un desastre.
   —¿Por qué dices eso?

2. —Necesito otra almohada. Así no puedo dormir.
   —Ten la mía.

3. —Los empleados de este hotel son muy amables.
   —¿Verdad que sí? Yo estoy encantada.

Estructuras

A.   Hotel Colonial. *Explain why we would stay at the Hotel Colonial. Repeat the correct answer after the speaker.*

> ➤ *MODELO*   a menos que / el hotel no tener una habitación
> **Nos quedamos en el Hotel Colonial a menos que el hotel no tenga una habitación.**

B.   ¿Cuándo? *Are the following people describing activities that have been completed or that will be completed by some future time? Listen carefully and check **PRESENT PERFECT** or **FUTURE PERFECT** according to the verb you hear. Each sentence will be repeated.*

> ➤ *MODELO*   You hear: Ha viajado a Chile.
>   You check: **PRESENT PERFECT**

	1	2	3	4	5	6	7	8
PRESENT PERFECT								
FUTURE PERFECT								

C.   Para las cinco. *Tell what you will have done by five o'clock this afternoon. Repeat the correct answer after the speaker.*

> ➤ *MODELO*   preparar la cena
> **Habré preparado la cena.**

D.   Para el próximo año. *Tell what the following people will have done by next year. Repeat the correct answer after the speaker.*

> ➤ *MODELO*   José / aprender a hablar español
> **José habrá aprendido a hablar español.**

Capítulo 12

Los deportes

Primera situación

Presentación

El partido de ayer. *Listen to the following statements. Under what conditions would you hear each one? Check **A** if the speaker is asking for information about the game, **B** if the speaker is making a positive comment, and **C** if the speaker is making a negative comment. Each statement will be repeated.*

	1	2	3	4	5	6	7	8
A								
B								
C								

Para escuchar bien

In this chapter you have learned to identify the different levels of politeness used in a conversation. You know that these vary from the least polite to the most polite. Now practice identifying the different levels of speech or politeness in the following exercises.

A.   ¡A jugar!   *You will hear a series of statements and requests. As you listen to each, write the number of the sentence in column **A** if you think it illustrates a polite style of speech; column **B** if it illustrates a friendly style; and column **C** if it illustrates a rude or abrupt style. But before you listen, mentally review the singular affirmative and negative formal and informal commands of the following verbs: **ir, hacer, jugar, correr, ganar, entrenarse.** Now listen to the different statements and write the number of the statement in the appropriate column.*

A: POLITE STYLE	B: FRIENDLY STYLE	C: RUDE/ABRUPT STYLE
_____	_____	_____
_____	_____	_____
_____	_____	_____
_____	_____	_____

B.   El partido de fútbol.   *You will hear two short dialogues. As you listen to each, write your impression of the speaker's tone (formal, friendly, rude).*

1. **Hombre:** _____

    Mujer: _____

2. **Hombre:** _____

    Mujer: _____

C.   Tengo unas entradas.   *You will hear a conversation between two men about some tickets for a soccer game. As you listen, write your impression of each speaker's tone (formal, friendly, rude) and the words or phrases that influenced your decision.*

Hombre 1: _____

Expresiones: _____

_____

_____

Hombre 2: _____

Expresiones: _____

_____

_____

Así se dice

Pitch refers to the level of force with which words are produced within a sentence; it is used for emphasis and contrast. For example, there is a difference between **La niña está *enferma*** (emphasis on the condition) and **La *niña* está enferma** (emphasis on who is ill). In Spanish there are three levels of pitch. Based on these pitch levels, simple statements in Spanish follow the intonation pattern (1 2 1 1 ↓) and emphatic statements (1 2 3 1 ↓).

Práctica

A.   *Listen to the following simple statements and repeat each after the speaker.*

1. José Emilio se rompió la pierna la semana pasada.

2. A Juan le faltan vitaminas. Siempre anda muy cansado.

3. Al pobre se le torció el tobillo mientras jugaba al fútbol.

4. Si me hubiera puesto una inyección a tiempo, ahorita no me sentiría tan mal.

5. Emilio está muy deprimido porque se rompió el brazo.

Nombre _____ Fecha _____ Clase _____

B.   *Listen to the following emphatic statements and repeat each after the speaker.*

1. Se rompió el brazo, no la rodilla.

2. Tuvo una contusión.

3. No tengo escalofríos; tengo náuseas y mareos.

4. Padecía de alergias.

5. Está muy mal.

C.   *Listen to the following statements and decide if each is* **SIMPLE** *or* **EMPHATIC**. *Circle the answer. Each statement will be repeated.*

1. Simple   Emphatic   **4.** Simple   Emphatic

2. Simple   Emphatic   **5.** Simple   Emphatic

3. Simple   Emphatic   **6.** Simple   Emphatic

Estructuras

A.   **¿Cuándo?**   *Listen to the following statements. Are these people telling you about activities they would do or that they would have done under certain conditions? Listen carefully and check* **CONDITIONAL** *or* **CONDITIONAL PERFECT** *according to the verb you hear. Each sentence will be repeated.*

> ➤ ***MODELO***   You hear: Ganaríamos el partido.
>   You check: **CONDITIONAL**

	1	2	3	4	5	6	7	8
CONDITIONAL								
CONDITIONAL PERFECT								

B.   **Con un poco más de talento.**   *Tell what you would have done if you had had a little more talent. Repeat the correct answer after the speaker.*

> ➤ ***MODELO***   entrenarse más
>   **Me habría entrenado más.**

C.   ¡Qué mala suerte!   *Explain what the following people would have done in order to win the championship. Repeat the correct answer after the speaker.*

> **MODELO**   el pueblo / construir un nuevo estadio
>   **El pueblo habría construido un nuevo estadio.**

D.   Dudo que... o Dudaba que...   *You hear only the end of the following sentences. How does each one begin? Listen carefully to the verb and check* **DUDO QUE** *if the verb you hear is in the present perfect subjunctive. Check* **DUDABA QUE** *if the verb you hear is in the past perfect subjunctive. Each phrase will be repeated.*

> **MODELO**   You hear: ... el equipo hubiera practicado bastante.
>   You check: **DUDABA QUE**

	1	**2**	**3**	**4**	**5**	**6**	**7**	**8**
DUDO QUE								
DUDABA QUE								

E.   Era necesario.   *What was it necessary for the following people to have done if they wanted to be successful playing a sport? Repeat the correct answer after the speaker.*

> **MODELO**   Isabel / hacer ejercicios
>   **Era necesario que Isabel hubiera hecho ejercicios.**

F.   Si hubiera tenido más cuidado...   *Explain what would not have happened if you had been more careful. Repeat the correct answer after the speaker.*

> **MODELO**   fracturarse el brazo
>   **Si hubiera tenido más cuidado, no me habría fracturado el brazo.**

Segunda situación

Presentación

A.   Me siento mal.   *Your friends are not feeling well. What do you suggest that they do? Listen to their complaints and check the most logical answer. If you need to listen again, replay the recording.*

	1	**2**	**3**	**4**	**5**
GUARDAR CAMA					
LLAMAR AL MÉDICO					
IR AL HOSPITAL					

Nombre _____ **Fecha** _____ **Clase** _____

B. Que te vaya bien. *Listen to the following statements. Under what conditions would you hear each one? Check **A** if the speaker is expressing sympathy or **B** if the speaker is expressing good wishes. Each statement will be repeated.*

	1	2	3	4	5	6	7	8
A								
B								

Para escuchar bien

Practice identifying different levels of politeness in the following exercises.

A. En el consultorio. *You will hear a conversation that takes place at the doctor's office. As you listen, write your impression of the style (formal, friendly, rude) of each speaker and identify the words or phrases used that influenced your decision. But before you listen, write three things that a patient might say to his or her doctor.*

_____

_____

_____

_____

_____

Now listen and write your impressions.

Médico: _____

Expresiones: _____

_____

_____

_____

_____

Joven: _____

Expresiones: _____

_____

_____

_____

_____

B.   ¡Qué enferma estoy!   *You will hear a conversation between two friends; one of them is sick. As you listen, write your impression of the tone (formal, friendly, rude) of each speaker and identify the words or phrases used that influenced your classification. But before you listen, write three things a close friend would tell you to do if you were sick.*

_____

_____

_____

_____

Now listen to the conversation and write your impressions.

Mujer 1: _____

Expresiones: _____

_____

_____

_____

Mujer 2: _____

Expresiones: _____

_____

_____

_____

Así se dice

Spanish uses two intonation patterns for questions. The pattern for questions requesting a yes or no answer is similar to the English pattern for yes-no questions (1 2 2 2 ↑): **¿Te duele el estómago?** The pattern for questions requesting information is (1 2 3 1 ↓): **¿Cuándo vas a hablar con el médico?**

Práctica

A. *Listen to the following* yes-no questions *in Spanish and repeat each after the speaker.*

1. ¿Te duele la cabeza?

2. ¿De verdad que te fracturaste la muñeca?

3. ¿Tienes la rodilla hinchada?

4. ¿Le dijiste al médico que se te perdieron las muletas?

5. ¿Crees que si llamara a tu madre te sentirías mejor?

6. ¿Me podrá él recetar un remedio?

B. *Listen to the following Spanish information questions and repeat each after the speaker.*

1. ¿Qué te dijo el médico que hicieras?

2. ¿Cómo crees que te sentirías si tomaras dos aspirinas ahora mismo?

3. ¿Dónde me dijiste que se te cayeron los remedios?

4. ¿Cuándo te dio pulmonía?

5. ¿Cómo te lastimaste el hombro?

6. ¿Quién te recetó esos remedios?

C. *Listen to the following questions and decide if they are* information questions *or* yes-no questions. *Write the answer. Each question will be repeated.*

1. _____

2. _____

3. _____

4. _____

5. _____

6. _____

Estructuras

A.   Se me olvidó.   *Explain what accidentally happened to you. Repeat the correct answer after the speaker.*

➤ **MODELO**   perder las gafas
                    Se me perdieron las gafas.

B.   Se nos perdieron...   *Explain what accidentally happened to the following people. Repeat the correct answer after the speaker.*

➤ **MODELO**   nosotros / acabar la aspirina
                    Se nos acabó la aspirina.

C.   En el consultorio.   *Listen as the nurse tells Dr. Ochoa which patients he will see today. Repeat each sentence, replacing the beep with **que** or **quien**. Then repeat the correct answer after the speaker.*

➤ **MODELO**   Miguel Morales es el paciente *BEEP* sufre de pulmonía.
                    Miguel Morales es el paciente que sufre de pulmonía.

D.   En la clínica.   *You work in the Trauma Center of the Clínica la Paz. Describe to a co-worker some of the patients you have helped today. Repeat each of the following sentences, replacing the beep with an appropriate form of **cuyo**. Then repeat the correct answer after the speaker.*

➤ **MODELO**   Marta Ferrer es la paciente *BEEP* brazo estaba enyesado.
                    Marta Ferrer es la paciente cuyo brazo estaba enyesado.

Clave de respuestas
Cuaderno de ejercicios

Clave de respuestas
Cuaderno de ejercicios

Capítulo preliminar

A. *Answers may vary—especially ages and activities.*

El Sr. Galván. Soy el Sr. Galván. Tengo sesenta años. Soy de talla media, un poco gordo y calvo. Llevo anteojos y tengo bigote. Me gusta mirar la televisión, leer el periódico y jugar al golf.
La Srta. Hernández. Soy la Srta. Hernández. Tengo dieciocho años y soy estudiante. Tengo el pelo negro, largo y rizado. Soy baja y delgada. Me gusta bailar, ir a conciertos, ir de compras y charlar con amigos.
El Sr. Ruiz. Soy el Sr. Ruiz. Tengo treinta años. Soy muy alto y atlético. También soy fuerte. Tengo el pelo corto y rubio. Me gusta practicar todos los deportes, jugar al fútbol y al tenis y hacer ejercicios.

B. *Answers vary.*

C. *Answers may vary.*

1. Me llamo *(your name)*. Y tú, ¿cómo te llamas?
2. ¿De dónde eres?
3. Dime, por favor, …
4. ¿Qué estudias? Yo estudio *(list subjects)*.
5. ¿Quieres decirme, por favor, dónde vives?
6. ¿Cuál es tu pasatiempo favorito? Me gusta(-n) *(list hobbies)*.

D.
1. nueve
2. catorce
3. siete
4. doce
5. veinte
6. dieciocho
7. veintidós
8. treinta y seis
9. veintitrés
10. cuarenta y seis
11. setenta y cinco
12. sesenta y uno

E.
1. catorce
2. ochenta y un
3. ciento setenta y tres
4. sesenta y ocho
5. veintiséis (veinte y seis)
6. ciento veintiuna (veinte y una)

F.
1. Son las tres y veinte de la mañana.
2. Son las once menos cuarto (las diez y cuarenta y cinco) de la noche.
3. Son las cuatro y media de la tarde.

    4. Es la una y cinco de la mañana.

    5. Son las ocho y veintitrés (veinte y tres) de la noche.

G. **llegar**

llegas	llego
llegamos	llega
llegan	llega

    comprender

comprende	comprenden
comprendo	comprendemos
comprenden	comprendes

    vivir

vives	viven
vive	vivimos
vivo	vive

H. **1.** Anita y Jorge comen en el café a las doce y media.

    2. (Tú) Escribes cartas a la una.

    3. Miguel y yo charlamos a las tres.

    4. (Yo) Leo el periódico a las siete y media.

    5. Uds. bailan en la discoteca a las diez.

    6. Gloria regresa a casa a las once y cuarto.

I. *Answers vary.*

Expansión de vocabulario

Ampliación

A. **1.** variety   **4.** responsibility

    2. reality   **5.** formality

    3. society   **6.** productivity

B. **1.** la universidad   **4.** la identidad

    2. la ciudad   **5.** la nacionalidad

    3. la actividad   **6.** la variedad

C. **1.** ciudades   **4.** variedad

    2. Universidad   **5.** actividades

    3. nacionalidad   **6.** identidad

Bienvenidos a España

A.
1. Sevilla
2. Atlántico
3. Portugal
4. euro
5. Pirineos

6. Juan Carlos I
7. Madrid
8. pesca

La caja vertical: VALENCIA

B.
1. Unas ciudades importantes son Madrid, Barcelona, Sevilla y Valencia.
2. Los ríos de España incluyen el Guadalquivir, el Tajo, el Guadiana y el Duero.
3. Las cordilleras importantes son los Pirineos, la Sierra de Guadarrama, la Sierra Nevada y la Cordillera Cantábrica.
4. Las industrias importantes son el turismo, la agricultura, la pesca y la fabricación de acero, barcos, vehículos y artículos de cuero.
5. El gobierno de España es una monarquía constitucional.
6. Hay 40.000.000 de habitantes.
7. España es el tercer país más grande de Europa y el segundo en Europa en altitud media. Es un país marítimo. El clima es muy variado según la región.

Capítulo 1

Primera situación

A.
1. escribir a máquina, usar una computadora / una fotocopiadora / una máquina de escribir eléctrica / un procesador de textos
2. llevar ropa sucia, recoger ropa limpia
3. llenar el tanque, revisar el aceite
4. comprar estampillas / sellos / timbres, enviar una carta / un paquete
5. estudiar, hacer la tarea, leer, prepararse para los exámenes, tomar apuntes

B. *Answers vary.*

C.
1. digo
2. veo
3. oigo
4. voy
5. doy
6. conozco
7. tengo

8. traigo
9. sé
10. hago
11. estoy
12. salgo
13. pongo
14. destruyo

D. *Verb forms are constant; frequency phrases will vary.*

    1. Me reúno con amigos…

    2. Uso una computadora…

    3. Voy al correo…

    4. Tomo apuntes…

    5. Hago compras en un centro comercial…

    6. Trabajo horas extras…

    7. Echo una siesta…

E. *Answers vary.*

F. **1.** cierro / cerramos   **5.** prefiero / preferimos

    2. repito / repetimos   **6.** almuerzo / almorzamos

    3. quiero / queremos   **7.** pido / pedimos

    4. vuelvo / volvemos   **8.** puedo / podemos

G. **1.** (Felipe) Almuerza con amigos.   **4.** Duerme ocho horas.

    2. Vuelve a casa a las diez.   **5.** Sueña con su futuro.

    3. No pierde tiempo.   **6.** Les pide dinero a sus padres.

H. *Affirmative / negative answers vary; verb forms are constant.*

    1. …almorzamos con amigos.   **4.** …dormimos ocho horas.

    2. …volvemos a casa a las diez.   **5.** …soñamos con nuestro futuro.

    3. …perdemos tiempo.   **6.** …les pedimos dinero a nuestros padres.

I. *Answers vary.*

Segunda situación

A. **1.** Se despierta.   **4.** Se afeita; se mira en el espejo.

    2. Se levanta.   **5.** Se seca el pelo; se peina.

    3. Se lava el pelo; se ducha.   **6.** Se lava los dientes.

B. **1.** el despertador, la cama   **4.** la afeitadora, la crema de afeitar, el espejo

    2. el despertador, la cama   **5.** el secador, el peine, el espejo

    3. el champú, el agua caliente; el jabón   **6.** el cepillo de dientes, la pasta de dientes

C. *Answers may vary.*

    1. ¿Quieres decir que…?   **4.** No entiendo (comprendo) nada.

    2. ¿Puede Ud. repetir, por favor?   **5.** A ver si comprendo bien…

    3. ¡Estoy perdido(-a)!   **6.** ¿Cómo dijiste?

D. **1.** se
2. se
3. me
4. se

5. te
6. se
7. nos
8. se

E. me seco
te secas
se seca
nos secamos
se secan

me despierto
te despiertas
se despierta
nos despertamos
se despiertan

F. *Answers vary.*

G. **1.** (Yo) Me preocupo por los exámenes.
2. Eduardo se dedica a sus estudios.
3. Unos alumnos se quejan de sus profesores.
4. (Tú) Te vas los fines de semana.
5. Mis amigos y yo nos divertimos mucho.

H. **1.** Hijo(-a), ¿cómo te sientes?
2. ¿A qué hora te levantas generalmente?
3. ¿Qué comes para el desayuno?
4. ¿Dónde almuerzas?
5. ¿Con quién(-es) comes?
6. ¿Cuál es tu compañero(-a) de cuarto?
7. ¿Por qué no me escribes?

I. *Answers vary.*

Expansión de vocabulario

Dudas de vocabulario

Affirmative/negative answers vary; verb forms are constant.

1. a. Sé **b.** Conozco **c.** Sé **d.** Conozco **e.** Conozco
2. a. pide **b.** pregunta **c.** pregunta por **d.** pide
3. al cine, una película

Ampliación

A. **1.** processor
2. photocopier
3. computer

4. razor
5. alarm clock
6. (hair) dryer

B.
1. lavar / washer
2. cortar / cutter, trimmer
3. comer / dining room
4. mostrar / display area, counter top
5. mirar / look-out point
6. calcular / calculator

C.
1. fotocopiadora
2. despertador
3. calculadora
4. procesador
5. afeitadora
6. comedor

Capítulo 2

Primera situación

A. *Answers vary but should include twelve items similar to those in the following list.*

unas camisetas, un colchón neumático, mucho dinero, las gafas de sol, unos libros, la loción solar, unos pantalones cortos, un radio portátil, la raqueta de tenis, la ropa para ir a bailar, las sandalias, un sombrero, una sombrilla, unas toallas para la playa, el traje de baño, los zapatos de tenis

B. *Answers vary.*

C.
1. Buenas tardes, señora Cela. Quisiera hablar con Julio, por favor.
2. (*Your name.*)
3. Por favor, dígale que me llame.
4. Adiós, señora.

D.
1. Hola, Julio. ¿Cómo estás?
2. Te llamé para invitarte a ir a la playa conmigo y unos compañeros de clase.
3. Pensamos ir mañana a eso de las once y media.
4. (*Answers vary—use preterite tense.*)
5. Lo siento. Disculpa, pero tengo que ir a estudiar.
6. Bueno. Hasta mañana entonces.

E. **nadar:** nadó / nadé / nadaron / nadamos / nadaste
correr: corrió / corrimos / corrieron / corrí / corriste

F.
1. dieron
2. anduvieron
3. vinieron
4. leyeron
5. pudieron
6. supieron
7. tuvieron
8. construyeron
9. pusieron
10. oyeron
11. estuvieron
12. dijeron

G. *Affirmative / negative answers vary; verb forms are constant.*

1. Pesqué.

2. Jugué al vólibol.

3. Gocé del mar.

4. Busqué conchas.

5. Navegué en un velero.

H. pasaron, hicieron, Nadaron, construyeron, pusieron, anduvo, tomó, leyó, jugó, decidió

I. 1. Cristóbal Colón llegó a las Américas en mil cuatrocientos noventa y dos.

2. Felipe II envió la Armada Invencible a Inglaterra en mil quinientos ochenta y ocho.

3. Miguel de Cervantes escribió la primera parte de *Don Quijote* en mil seiscientos cinco.

4. Felipe V mandó construir el Palacio Real en mil setecientos treinta y cuatro.

5. Antonio Gaudí empezó el Templo de la Sagrada Familia en Barcelona en mil ochocientos ochenta y tres.

J. *Answers vary.*

Segunda situación

A. 1. Plaza de Santa Ana y Calle Huertas; un taxi o un automóvil

2. Puerta del Sol y Plaza Mayor; el metro o el autobús

3. Zona de Argüelles; el metro o el autobús

4. Zona de Gran Vía; un taxi

5. Barrio de Malasaña; un taxi o un automóvil

6. Glorietas de Bilbao y Alonso Martínez; el metro o el autobús

B. *Answers vary.*

C. *Answers vary.*

D. 1. pedí / pidió

2. me divertí / se divirtió

3. dormí / durmió

4. me vestí / se vistió

5. seguí / siguió

E. 1. Federico y Yolanda pidieron un whisky en un bar.

2. (Yo) No me divertí nada.

3. Mi novio(-a) y yo nos despedimos temprano.

4. El Sr. Medina se sintió mal.

5. (Tú) Te dormiste tarde.

F. **1.** (Graciela) Vio a su primo Emilio.

2. Vio la Torre de Oro.

3. Vio al cantante Enrique Iglesias en concierto.

4. Vio a un torero famoso.

5. Vio el Alcázar.

6. Vio a algunas bailarinas flamencas.

G. **1.** Sí, lo necesito. Ponlo en la maleta.

2. Sí, las necesito. Ponlas en la maleta.

3. Sí, los necesito. Ponlos en la maleta.

4. No, no la necesito. No la pongas en la maleta.

5. Sí, la necesito. Ponla en la maleta.

6. No, no los necesito. No los pongas en la maleta.

H. *Answers vary.*

Expansión de vocabulario

Dudas de vocabulario

1. hora, tiempo, vez

2. lo paso bien, me divierto

Ampliación

A. **1.** lotion

2. introduction / presentation

3. nation

4. definition

5. situation

6. conversation

B. **1.** la emoción / las emociones

2. la tradición / las tradiciones

3. la definición / las definiciones

4. la sección / las secciones

5. la loción / las lociones

6. la recomendación / las recomendaciones

C. **1.** vacaciones

2. imaginación

3. naciones

4. situaciones

5. tradición

Bienvenidos a México

A.
1. Guadalupe
2. Pacífico
3. altiplano
4. peso
5. turismo

6. León
7. Zócalo
8. Monterrey
La caja vertical: ACAPULCO

B.
1. Las ciudades importantes de México son Guadalajara, León, México, D.F., Monterrey y Puebla.
2. Unas playas famosas son Acapulco, Cancún, Mazatlán y Puerto Vallarta.
3. Las industrias importantes son el turismo, el petróleo, los productos agrícolas, la fabricación de equipo de vehículos, las materias primas y la artesanía.
4. La mayoría de la población vive en el Altiplano.
5. México es una república federal compuesta de treinta y un estados.
6. México es el tercer país más grande de Latinoamérica. Se divide en varias regiones. El clima varía según la altura.

Capítulo 3

Primera situación

A.
1. el padre, el esposo, el abuelo
2. la madre, la esposa, la abuela
3. el hijo, el hermano
4. la hija, la nieta, la sobrina

B. *Answers may vary.*
1. ¿Qué tal? Pues nos vemos.
2. ¡Tanto tiempo sin verla a Ud.! ¿Cómo está Ud.? Muy bien. Que le vaya bien.
3. ¡Encantado(-a) de verte! ¿Qué hay de nuevo? Muy bien. Pues, te llamo. Chau. Hasta luego.

C. **amar:** amaba / amaba / amábamos / amaban / amabas
asistir: asistía / asistía / asistíamos / asistían / asistías

D.
1. vivíamos
2. estábamos
3. veíamos
4. jugábamos
5. hacíamos

6. íbamos
7. podíamos
8. nos levantábamos
9. teníamos
10. éramos

E. **1.** El doctor Gallego les aconsejaba a todos.

 2. Vicente y yo jugábamos al dominó.

 3. Uds. almorzaban con sus tíos.

 4. Mariana veía a sus abuelos a menudo.

 5. (Tú) Te divertías con tus primos.

 6. Carlos y Anita iban a misa.

F. *Answers vary. Verbs must be in the imperfect.*

G. **1.** Los Ruiz viven en una nueva casa grande y cómoda.

 2. Acaban de comprar dos antiguas sillas francesas.

 3. La Sra. Ruiz es española, vieja e inteligente.

 4. Tienen dos hijas que son altas y muy bonitas.

 5. También tienen una nieta de cinco años que es guapa y cariñosa, pero un poco traviesa.

H. **1.** Es rubia y bonita. Es joven y feliz.

 2. Es bajo, gordo y calvo.

 3. Es morena, bonita y de talla media.

 4. Es alto, moreno y guapo.

 5. Es joven, baja y muy mona.

I. *Answers vary.*

J. Adelita   Evita

 Manolito   Luisito

 Rosita   Susanita

 Lolita   Juanito

 Paquito   Pepito

Segunda situación

A. **1.** el esposo   **6.** el yerno

 2. Claudia García de Moreno   **7.** la nuera

 3. el suegro   **8.** los parientes políticos

 4. cuñadas   **9.** María Teresa Vargas Casona de García Muñoz

 5. cuñados

B. *Answers may vary.*

 1. Estoy preparando una fiesta para el viernes y me gustaría que vinieras.

 2. Me encantaría, pero tengo que trabajar.

 3. ¡Qué lástima que no puedas venir!

4. ¿Crees que podrías venir a una fiesta en mi casa este viernes?

5. Con mucho gusto. ¿A qué hora?

C. *Answers vary.*

D. **1.** …la boda es el sábado a las dos.

2. …la cena es en el Hotel Cozumel.

3. …es del Ecuador.

4. …es linda y coqueta.

5. …está contenta.

6. …están nerviosos.

E. Es / Son / está / es / es / están / están / hay / es / está

F.
1. es **6.** es **10.** está **14.** es

2. Es (una) **7.** es **11.** hay **15.** estoy

3. Es **8.** está **12.** está **16.** estar

4. es **9.** es **13.** hay **17.** está

5. ser

G.
1. ¿Es tuyo este paraguas azul?

No, no es mío. El mío es rojo.

2. ¿Son tuyos estos discos viejos?

No, no son míos. Los míos son más nuevos.

3. ¿Es tuya esta bufanda amarilla?

No, no es mía. La mía es más larga.

4. ¿Son tuyas estas gafas rojas?

No, no son mías. Las mías son negras.

5. ¿Son tuyos estos guantes blancos?

No, no son míos. Los míos están más sucios.

H. *Answers vary.*

Expansión de vocabulario

Dudas de vocabulario

unida, cerca, A causa de, porque, pequeña, joven, cercano

Ampliación

A.
1. stepchildren

2. great-great-grandmother

3. brother(s)- and sister(s)-in-law

4. great-great-grandfather

5. great-grandson

6. godfather

7. parents-in-law

8. stepsister

B.   **1.** la madrastra

      2. la hijastra

      3. el hermanastro

      4. el padrastro

C.   **1.** suegros

      2. bisabuelo

      3. hermanastra

      5. el bisabuelo

      6. la bisabuela

      7. la biznieta

      8. el rebisabuelo (tatarabuelo)

      4. rebisabuela (tatarabuela)

      5. compadre, comadre

      6. biznieto

Capítulo 4

Primera situación

A.   **1.** Se mencionan cinco grupos: sopas y cremas, huevos y pastas, mariscos, entradas y postres. Los mariscos son la especialidad de la casa.

      2. Un plato italiano es Spaghettis Napolitana. Dos platos franceses son Consomé gelée y Petite Marmite.

      3. El gazpacho andaluz es la sopa más típica de España. La paella es la entrada más típica de España. El flan es el postre más típico de España.

      4. Se puede elegir un plato de las sopas y cremas, un plato de los Grupos 2: Huevos y pastas, 3: Mariscos o 4: Entradas y un plato de los postres. Se puede beber el vino.

      5. *Answers vary.*

B.   **1.** Todavía no sé qué pedir. ¿Podría Ud. regresar dentro de un momento, por favor?

      2. De entrada (*answers vary*).

      3. ¿Cuál es la especialidad de la casa?

      4. ¿Cómo están preparadas las gambas?

      5. ¿Es picante este plato de gambas?

      6. *Answers vary.*

      7. *Answers vary.*

      8. *Answers vary.*

C.   **1.** Le trajo las enchiladas suizas a la Sra. Montoya.

      2. Les trajo el pollo en mole a los Gómez.

      3. Le trajo la sopa de albóndigas al Sr. González.

      4. Les trajo la ensalada mixta a Uds.

      5. Nos trajo las empanadas a Felipe y a mí.

      6. Le trajo los tacos de pollo a Ud.

D. **1.** Pregúnteles a los Suárez lo que quieren comer.

2. Explíquele al cocinero lo que va a preparar.

3. Escríbale las invitaciones a toda la familia.

4. Tráigale el vino al Sr. Suárez.

5. Envíele la cuenta a la Sra. Suárez.

E. **1.** Al Dr. Higuera le gusta la tortilla Bajamar.

2. A mí me gustan las gambas.

3. A los Ramírez les gusta el flan al caramelo.

4. A ti te gustan las ostras supergigantes.

5. A mi madre y a mí nos gusta la paella especial.

6. A Uds. les gustan los huevos revueltos Bajamar.

7. A Carolina le gusta el gazpacho andaluz.

8. A Ramón y a Carmen Soto les gusta la sopa de pescado.

F. *Answers vary.*

G. **1.** El cocinero supo que recibió el premio "Cocinero del Año."

2. Pablo tuvo buenas noticias de su familia en Veracruz.

3. Mónica pudo trabajar aunque estuvo enferma.

4. Los turistas querían pedir el pollo en mole pero no quedaba más.

5. El dueño no sabía los ingredientes para el plato del día.

H. *Answers vary.*

Segunda situación

A. Mesero, tráiganos…

1. un cuchillo, por favor.

2. una cuchara, por favor.

3. un salero, por favor.

4. un pimentero, por favor.

5. una copa, por favor.

6. un vaso, por favor.

7. una taza, por favor.

8. una servilleta, por favor.

B. *Answers vary.*

C. **1.** Sr. Guzmán, le presento a la Sra. Rodríguez.

2. Anita, te presento a Yolanda.

3. Permítame que me presente. Yo soy (*your name*).

4. Encantado(-a) de conocerla (a Ud.).

5. Mucho gusto, Gloria.

6. El gusto es mío.

D.
1. regresó / preparó / comió / leyó / miró
2. estuvo
3. era / quería
4. entramos / comían
5. preparaban / servían
6. conocía / conocí

E. *Answers vary.*

F. estudiaba / salíamos / fue / tomé / estudié / repasamos / aprendimos / estaba / me sentía / falté / pude / devolvió / saqué

G.
1. el séptimo menú
2. el tercer café
3. la segunda mesa
4. la sexta entrada
5. la novena comida
6. el quinto desayuno
7. el cuarto mesero
8. el octavo postre

H. *Answers vary.*

Expansión de vocabulario

Dudas de vocabulario

calor, caliente, probé, picantes, tratar de, trató

Ampliación

A.
1. Valencian-style paella (seafood casserole)
2. gazpacho (cold vegetable soup) from Andalucía
3. Spanish-style omelette (tortilla)
4. Swiss-style enchiladas
5. Italian-style pizza

B.
1. el caldo de pollo
2. el cóctel de camarones (gambas)
3. los tacos de carne de res
4. el sándwich de jamón
5. las enchiladas de queso
6. la torta de chocolate
7. la ensalada de tomate
8. el jugo (zumo) de naranja

C.
1. gazpacho andaluz
2. enchiladas suizas
3. paella valenciana
4. huachinango a la veracruzana

Bienvenidos a Centroamérica, a Venezuela y a Colombia

A.
1. Nicaragua
2. Honduras
3. Costa Rica
4. Bogotá
5. Andes
6. Panamá
7. Caracas
8. petróleo
9. café

La caja vertical: GUATEMALA

B.
1. Los seis países hispanos de Centroamérica son Guatemala (Ciudad de Guatemala), Honduras (Tegucigalpa), El Salvador (San Salvador), Nicaragua (Managua), Costa Rica (San José), Panamá (Ciudad de Panamá).
2. Las ciudades importantes de Colombia son Bogotá, Cali y Medellín. La ciudad más importante de Venezuela es Caracas.
3. El número de habitantes de Centroamérica es 32.500.000; Colombia tiene 35.100.000 de habitantes y Venezuela tiene 21.800.000.
4. Los gobiernos de Colombia y Venezuela son democráticos. En los países de Centroamérica hay una gran variedad en los gobiernos y la política.
5. La economía de Centroamérica se basa en productos agrícolas y el turismo. La economía de Venezuela se basa en el petróleo y la de Colombia en el café y el turismo.
6. Centroamérica, Colombia y Venezuela tienen una geografía similar con una costa tropical y la región templada de las montañas. Venezuela también tiene llanos. El clima varía según la altura.

Capítulo 5

Primera situación

A. Estudió en la Facultad de
1. Ciencias de la Educación
2. Arquitectura
3. Ingeniería
4. Administración de Empresas
5. Derecho
6. Bellas Artes
7. Filosofía y Letras

B. 1. e 2. d 3. a 4. b 5. f 6. c

C. *Answers may vary.*
1. ¿Podría Ud. explicarlo otra vez?
2. ¿De cuántas líneas?
3. ¿Cómo se dice «to register» en español?
4. ¿Podría Ud. hablar más despacio?
5. No sé.
6. ¿Puede Ud. repetir la pregunta?

D. *Answers vary.*

E.   *Answers vary.*

F.   Por, para, para, para, Por, por, para, por, por, por, Por, para, por

G.   **1.** Sí, son de él.   **3.** Sí, son de ellos.

2. Sí, es de ella.   **4.** Sí, son de ellas.

Segunda situación

A.   El tema central es un curso de lengua y cultura españolas para extranjeros. Los temas secundarios son las clases, las actividades complementarias, la recepción, los certificados y los otros servicios del curso.

1. Hay cinco horas de lengua española por semana. Hay clase de lunes a viernes. La clase de lengua española es de las 9 a las 10; la clase de prácticas de español es de las 10 a las 11.

2. Hay cuatro niveles: el principiante, el elemental, el medio y el superior. *Answer will vary.*

3. Son conferencias, coloquios, seminarios, audiciones y proyecciones sobre los temas de las clases.

4. Hay actos culturales y recreativos incluyendo visitas a museos y monumentos, actuaciones teatrales y musicales y excursiones.

5. La recepción de estudiantes nuevos es el dos de agosto. El examen es el dos de agosto de las 10 a las 12.

6. Cada estudiante recibirá un Certificado Académico Personal.

7. Ofrece alojamiento, servicio de comedor, servicio médico ordinario y un horario flexible.

8. Ofrece deportes, acceso a la biblioteca y seguro de accidentes.

B.   **1.** Hace sol y calor. Hace buen tiempo.   **4.** Hace muchísimo calor.

2. Hace mucho frío.   **5.** *Answer will vary.*

3. Hace mucho viento.

C.   **1.** tome   **6.** haga   **11.** coma   **16.** conozca

2. escriba   **7.** pague   **12.** vaya   **17.** pida

3. sea   **8.** pueda   **13.** dé   **18.** ponga

4. sepa   **9.** duerma   **14.** esté   **19.** tenga

5. salga   **10.** vuelva   **15.** busque   **20.** se divierta

D.   *All answers begin with* **Los profesores quieren que…**

1. (tú) estudies y aprendas.

2. Raquel estudie y aprenda.

3. (yo) estudie y aprenda.

4. Manolo y yo estudiemos y aprendamos.

5. Uds. estudien y aprendan.

6. todos los alumnos estudien y aprendan.

E. *The beginning phrase will vary among* **Quiero que… / Espero que… / Es necesario que…**

1. Claudia asista a sus clases cada día.
2. (Claudia) siga las recomendaciones de sus profesores.
3. (Claudia) tome apuntes en clase.
4. (Claudia) no salga por la noche en vez de estudiar.
5. (Claudia) entregue su tarea a tiempo.
6. (Claudia) preste mucha atención en clase.
7. (Claudia) cumpla con los requisitos.

F. *Each answer begins with* **Le recomiendo (a Claudia) que…**

1. incluya vegetales en su dieta.
2. no escoja pasteles en la cafetería estudiantil siempre.
3. almuerce.
4. no pida papas fritas o pizza siempre.
5. no tome muchas bebidas alcohólicas.
6. sepa mucho de nutrición.

G. *Answers vary.*

H. *Answers may vary.*

1. Mi cuarto en casa es más cómodo que mi cuarto en la residencia estudiantil.
2. Los profesores son mayores que los estudiantes.
3. Los cursos electivos son más divertidos que los cursos obligatorios.
4. Los cursos de este semestre son más difíciles que los cursos del semestre pasado.
5. Las actividades universitarias son mejores que las actividades de la escuela secundaria.

I. *Answers vary.*

Expansión de vocabulario

Dudas de vocabulario

1. e   2. c   3. g   4. h   5. f   6. d   7. a

Ampliación

A.
1. philosophy
2. astronomy
3. trigonometry
4. geology
5. psychology
6. physiology

B. 1. la comunicación / communication
2. la educación / education
3. la especialización / major, specialty
4. la organización / organization
5. la administración / administration
6. la recomendación / recommendation
7. la programación / programming
8. la interpretación / interpretation

C. 1. astronomía
2. anatomía (fisiología)
3. sicología
4. filosofía
5. sociología
6. programación
7. comunicaciones
8. administración

Capítulo 6

Primera situación

A. *Answers may vary.*

barrer el piso—una escoba; colgar la ropa—unas perchas; hacer la cama; lavar y secar los platos—el jabón, una esponja, una toalla; lavar y secar la ropa—la lavadora, el detergente, la secadora; limpiar el fregadero—un trapo; pasar la aspiradora—la aspiradora; planchar la ropa—la tabla de planchar, una plancha; recoger la mesa; sacar la basura; sacudir los muebles—un trapo

B. *Answers vary.*

C. 1. lava / no laves
2. barre / no barras
3. sacude / no sacudas
4. cierra / no cierres
5. vuelve / no vuelvas
6. repite / no repitas
7. di / no digas
8. ven / no vengas
9. haz / no hagas
10. pon / no pongas
11. sal / no salgas
12. sé / no seas

D. 1. No pongas la televisión. Pon la mesa.
2. No hagas un sándwich. Haz la cama.
3. No riegues la alfombra. Riega las plantas.
4. No tengas prisa. Ten paciencia.
5. No seas tonto(-a). Sé amable.
6. No juegues ahora. Cuelga la ropa.

E. *Answers vary.*

F. 1. El apartamento de Clara es tan lindo como el apartamento de Maribel.
2. Clara limpia su apartamento tan regularmente como Maribel.
3. El apartamento de Clara tiene tanta luz como el apartamento de Maribel.

4. El apartamento de Clara tiene tantos dormitorios como el apartamento de Maribel.

5. El apartamento de Clara tiene tantas ventanas como el apartamento de Maribel.

6. El apartamento de Clara tiene tanto espacio como el apartamento de Maribel.

G. **1.** No, prefiero aquélla.   **4.** No, prefiero aquél.

2. No, prefiero éstas.   **5.** No, prefiero ésos.

3. No, prefiero ésa.

Segunda situación

A. **1.** rescatar: las otras palabras describen las acciones de los reporteros.

2. un asesinato: las otras palabras son desastres naturales.

3. la cárcel: las otras palabras son crímenes.

4. el reportero: las otras palabras tienen que ver con el derecho y las leyes.

5. la manifestación: las otras palabras tienen que ver con las elecciones.

B. **1.** Un programa de concursos en el cual los jugadores tienen la oportunidad de ganarse un millón de dólares contestando preguntas.

2. Un programa en vivo de la televisión que empieza el sábado por la noche a las once y media. Es humorístico y divertido y satiriza muchos aspectos de la vida diaria en el mundo.

3. Un programa de concursos en el cual les dan a los jugadores las respuestas y ellos tienen que adivinar las preguntas.

4. Un programa generalmente de tema histórico; se presenta por dos o tres horas durante tres, cuatro o cinco noches.

5. Un programa con un(-a) anfitrión(-ona) que entrevista a personas famosas. Así el público tiene la oportunidad de conocer a personas importantes y célebres.

C. *Answers may vary.*

1. Gracias. No te hubieras molestado.

2. No es necesario, gracias.

3. Muchas gracias. No te hubieras molestado.

4. No te preocupes por eso.

5. Gracias, pero no te molestes.

D. *Las siguientes frases requieren el uso del subjuntivo. Las frases que no requieren el subjuntivo no aparecen en la lista.*

es necesario	es terrible		
	tal vez		es bueno
es importante	no pensar	es posible	dudar
tener miedo de	es ridículo	alegrarse de	
es mejor		negar	es imposible

E. *Opening phrases will vary but the verbs in the second clause will be in the subjunctive.*

    1. …los políticos gasten demasiado dinero en sus campañas electorales.

    2. …siempre elijamos al mejor candidato.

    3. …las guerras no resuelvan nada.

    4. …haya mucho crimen en los EE.UU.

    5. …podamos eliminar el crimen con más cárceles.

    6. …las leyes ayuden más a los criminales que a las víctimas.

    7. …en algunos países arresten a los participantes de una manifestación.

F. *Answers vary.*

G.

1. el	**4.** las	**7.** la	**10.** la
2. las	**5.** la	**8.** los	**11.** el
3. la	**6.** el	**9.** el	**12.** el

H. la, la, el, la, los, la, la, el, los, del, los, las, los, la, la, el, el, Las, los, del, el, la

I. *Answers vary.*

Expansión de vocabulario

Dudas de vocabulario

pongo la televisión, crió, cría, cultiva, crecen, la tele(visión), televisor

Ampliación

A.

1. international	**5.** primary
2. local	**6.** pessimistic
3. commercial	**7.** realistic
4. extraordinary	**8.** communist(ic)

B.

1. nacional	**5.** secundario
2. electoral	**6.** idealista
3. comercial	**7.** optimista
4. contrario	**8.** capitalista

C.

1. electoral	**4.** ordinario
2. nacionales, internacionales, locales	**5.** pesimista
3. comunista	**6.** optimista

Bienvenidos a Bolivia, al Ecuador y al Perú

A.
1. ecuador
2. Lima
3. Titicaca
4. La Paz
5. nuevo sol
6. Altiplano
7. Guayaquil
8. estaño

La caja vertical: AMAZONAS

B.
1. Bolivia es uno de los dos países de la América del Sur sin costa marítima. Es un país montañoso; dentro de los Andes se encuentra el Altiplano, una región muy alta y árida. El lago Titicaca es el lago navegable más alto del mundo.

2. El Ecuador tiene dos regiones distintas. En el oeste se encuentra la costa y en el este se encuentran las montañas. La línea del ecuador pasa al norte de la capital, Quito.

3. El Perú es el tercer país más grande de Sudamérica. Tiene tres regiones distintas. En el oeste se encuentra la costa; en el centro se encuentran las montañas; en el este se encuentra el río Amazonas y la selva que ocupa más de la mitad del territorio.

4. Bolivia: 7.400.000 de habitantes; El Ecuador: 11.500.000 de habitantes; El Perú: 23.800.000 de habitantes.

5. Bolivia: el boliviano; El Ecuador: el sucre; El Perú: el nuevo sol

6. Los productos principales de Bolivia son productos agrícolas, el estaño, la plata, el plomo y otros metales. Los productos principales del Ecuador son el petróleo, la banana, el café, el cacao y el pescado. Los productos principales del Perú son el cobre, la plata, el plomo y otros metales, el pescado y el petróleo.

Capítulo 7

Primera situación

A. *Answers vary, but all begin* **Ve a / al**…

B.
1. Busco un regalo de cumpleaños para mi hermano(-a).
2. No me parecen apropiadas. ¿Podría ver el suéter en el escaparate / la vitrina?
3. ¿Me podría decir cuánto cuesta, por favor?
4. Lo encuentro fino pero quisiera algo menos caro.
5. Oh, me gusta mucho. Y ¿cuánto cuesta, por favor?
6. Está bien. Lo compro.
7. No, es todo.
8. Muchas gracias. Adiós, señora.

C. 1. comprando   6. escogiendo
       2. decidiendo   7. leyendo
       3. pidiendo   8. durmiendo
       4. probándose   9. oyendo
       5. divirtiéndose   10. trayendo

D. 1. El abuelo está leyendo una guía sobre Quito.
       2. Magdalena les está escribiendo / está escribiéndoles tarjetas postales a sus amigos.
       3. Héctor está visitando la catedral.
       4. Los padres están comiendo en un restaurante de lujo.
       5. La abuela se está quejando / está quejándose del calor.
       6. Todos se están divirtiendo / están divirtiéndose.

E. 1. Teresa estaba oyendo música rock.
       2. (Tú) Estabas escogiendo un regalo para tu amigo.
       3. Yo estaba haciendo compras.
       4. Manuel y yo estábamos devolviendo un suéter.
       5. Uds. se estaban sentando / estaban sentándose a comer.
       6. Elena se estaba probando / estaba probándose un vestido.

F. 1. Quiero los regalos más caros de la ciudad.
       2. Quiero la pulsera más linda de la joyería.
       3. Quiero las mejores botas de la zapatería.
       4. Quiero el collar de oro más grande de la boutique.
       5. Quiero los aretes más finos de la tienda.

G. la, los, la, El, la, 0, la, las, las, la, la, los, la, el

H. *Answers vary.*

I. *Answers vary.*

Segunda situación

A. *Prices will vary. Since artwork appears only in black and white, colors may vary.*

   A. Una falda a cuadros que hace juego con el chaleco. Una blusa de un solo color: el blanco. Unos zapatos bajos de cuero negro; medias. Un impermeable de algodón blanco con un paraguas negro. Una bolsa de cuero negro.

   B. Un abrigo gris de lana pura, una bufanda a rayas, un sombrero negro y guantes blancos. Unas botas de lujo de cuero negro. Unos pantalones negros de lana.

   C. Un calentador de algodón de un solo color: el azul marino, el gris, el negro o el rojo. Unos calcetines blancos de algodón y zapatos de tenis de cuero.

   D. Un pijama de seda con lunares en dos colores. Una bata de seda negra y pantuflas negras de cuero.

B. **1.** Creo que Ud. se ha equivocado. Los pantalones cuestan sólo 75.000 sucres.

2. ¡No puedo seguir esperando!

3. ¡Qué falta de responsabilidad! Arrégleme el botón o cóbreme menos.

4. ¡Pero qué se ha creído!

5. ¡Esto no puede ser! Uds. tienen que arreglar este traje descosido.

C. *Answers vary.*

D. **1.** alguien

2. nunca, jamás

3. tampoco

4. de algún modo

5. nada

6. o…o

7. ninguno

E. **1.** Consuelo López no es muy trabajadora. Nunca hace nada.

2. No se viste bien. No lleva ni vestido ni traje.

3. No es muy popular con los clientes. Ningún cliente le manda flores.

4. Tampoco le dan regalos.

5. De ninguna manera vende más ropa que todas las otras dependientas.

6. Nadie dijo que Consuelo es la dependienta perfecta.

F. **1.** Sí, se las compré a ellas. **4.** Sí, se los compré a ellos.

2. Sí, se lo compré a él. **5.** Sí, se la compré a él.

3. Sí, se la compré a ella.

G. e, y, u, e, u, y, o

Expansión de vocabulario

Dudas de vocabulario

la vitrina / el escaparate, claro, ligera, ventanas, luz, lámpara, volvió / regresó, volvió a, lámpara, devolvió

Ampliación

A. **1.** jewelry store **5.** butcher shop

2. cosmetics store **6.** ice cream parlor

3. laundry **7.** bakery

4. glove store **8.** stationery store

B.
1. la frutería
2. la relojería
3. la pescadería
4. la zapatería
5. la pastelería
6. la librería

C.
1. joyería
2. zapatería
3. papelería
4. librería
5. frutería
6. perfumería

Capítulo 8

Primera situación

A.
1. Se puede encontrar una estación de metro en la Avenida Bolívar al lado del Ayuntamiento.

2. Se puede comprar ropa nueva en los Almacenes Suárez en la Avenida Bolívar entre la Calle del Pintor y la Avenida del Mar.

3. Se puede cambiar cheques de viajero en el Banco Nacional que se encuentra en la esquina de la Avenida San Antonio y la Avenida del Mar al lado de la Oficina de Turismo.

4. Se puede comprar comida para un picnic en el Supermercado Precios Únicos en la esquina de la Avenida Bolívar y la Calle de la Paz. Está al lado del Hotel Bolívar.

5. Hay una parada de autobús en la Plaza Bolívar en la esquina de la Avenida Bolívar y la Calle de la Paz.

6. Se puede comprar revistas y periódicos en el quiosco que está en la Plaza Bolívar en la esquina de la Avenida Bolívar y la Calle del Pintor; está enfrente de los Almacenes Suárez.

B. *Answers vary but should include:* el Ayuntamiento, la Catedral Metropolitana, el Museo de Bellas Artes, el Palacio Presidencial y la Plaza Bolívar.

C. *Answers may vary.*
1. Tome el metro. Siga derecho por la Avenida San Antonio hasta llegar a la Calle del Pintor. Doble a la izquierda y siga derecho hasta la Avenida Bolívar. Doble a la derecha. La estación de metro está al lado del Ayuntamiento.

2. Camine por la Avenida San Antonio hasta la Calle de la Paz. Doble a la derecha. Siga derecho cruzando la Avenida Bolívar. El edificio está al lado del Supermercado Precios Únicos.

3. La Plaza de Toros está muy cerca, en la esquina de la Avenida de San Antonio y la Calle de la Paz. Después de la corrida, siga derecho por la Calle de la Paz. Doble a la derecha en la Avenida Bolívar. El hotel está al lado del Supermercado Precios Únicos.

4. Sigan derecho por la Avenida San Antonio hasta la Calle del Pintor. Doblen a la izquierda y sigan derecho hasta la Avenida Bolívar. Está en la esquina.

5. Caminen derecho hasta la esquina de la Calle del Pintor. El Palacio Presidencial está allá enfrente. Después, sigan por la Calle del Pintor. Al llegar a la Avenida Bolívar, doblen a la izquierda y caminen a la esquina de la Calle de la Paz.

D. *The use of* **Ud.** *following each command is optional.*

1. pase	**6.** salga	**11.** llegue
2. coma	**7.** sea	**12.** haga
3. abra	**8.** busque	**13.** sepa
4. vaya	**9.** cruce	**14.** esté
5. dé	**10.** dirija	

E. **1.** Consíganlo lo más pronto posible.

 2. Sí, lean una buena guía turística.

 3. Vean el Palacio Presidencial.

 4. Sí, saquen fotos de los sitios de interés.

 5. Almuercen en un restaurante típico.

 6. Quédense por una semana.

 7. Dense un paseo por el centro el primer día.

 8. Vayan a una discoteca por la noche.

F. **1.** Se compran periódicos en el quiosco.

 2. Se come bien en el Restaurante del Mar.

 3. Se puede ver una película en el Cine Bolívar.

 4. Se compran regalos en la Boutique Álvarez.

 5. Se toma el autobús en la parada de autobús.

 6. Se ve la exposición de arte en el Museo de Bellas Artes.

G. un, 0, 0, una, 0, Uno, 0, 0, 0, una, 0, un, un, 0

Segunda situación

A. **1.** los cuadros, una exposición de arte, las galerías, las pinturas, las obras de arte, los retratos

 2. el desfile, la espada, el matador, la taquilla, el traje de luces, el toro

B. *Answers vary.*

C. *Answers vary.*

D. **1.** viajará, volverá **4.** viajará, volverá

 2. viajarán, volverán **5.** viajarás, volverás

 3. viajaré, volveré **6.** viajaremos, volveremos

E. **1.** tendré, tendremos **5.** podré, podremos

 2. querré, querremos **6.** saldré, saldremos

 3. diré, diremos **7.** pondré, pondremos

 4. haré, haremos **8.** vendré, vendremos

F. **1.** (Tú) Harás una excursión a Cuzco.

2. Los Pereda se levantarán tarde todos los días.

3. Carlos del Valle saldrá a bailar todas las noches.

4. Uds. irán de compras en el Jirón de la Unión.

5. Mi novio(-a) y yo conduciremos a la playa.

6. La Srta. Robles comerá muchos mariscos.

7. *Answers vary.*

G. *Questions may vary; answers will vary.*

1. ¿Qué habrá en esta caja? ¿Será un regalo de cumpleaños?

2. ¿Qué querrá? ¿Ganaré mucho dinero?

3. ¿Qué tendré que hacer? ¿Trabajaré horas extras?

H. *Answers vary.*

I. **1.** Asistamos a un concierto rock.

2. Vamos al parque de atracciones.

3. Almorcemos en un restaurante.

4. Salgamos a bailar.

5. Tengamos una fiesta.

6. Juguemos al vólibol.

7. *Answers vary.*

Expansión de vocabulario

Dudas de vocabulario

parece, verdadera / real, cita, cuidar, mirar, ver, está buscando, En realidad, actualmente / hoy (en) día

Ampliación

A. **1.** umbrella

2. snowplow

3. dishwasher

4. wardrobe

5. pastime

6. window cleaner

7. parachute

8. lightning rod

B. **1.** guardapuerta

2. abrelatas

3. sacacorchos

4. parabrisas

5. limpiadientes

6. salvavidas

7. parasol

8. paragolpes

C. **1.** rascacielos

2. paraguas

3. lavaplatos

4. sacacorchos

5. guardarropa

6. salvavidas

Bienvenidos a la comunidad hispana en los EE.UU

A.
1. chicanos
2. Miami
3. Estefan
4. López
5. Cuba
6. Cristina
7. Nueva York
8. Olmos

La caja vertical: HISPANOS

B.
1. Actualmente hay 35.300.000 de hispanos en los EE.UU.

2. El 64% son de México, el 11% son de Puerto Rico y 5% son de Cuba. El 20% son de los demás países del mundo hispano.

3. Los chicanos se encuentran en el suroeste, de Texas a California. Los cubanos se encuentran en Miami y en el sur de la Florida. Los puertorriqueños se encuentran en la Ciudad de Nueva York y la región cosmopolita.

4. *Answers vary but should include some of the following people:* **Cine y televisión:** Daisy Fuentes, Andy García, Ricardo Montalbán, Rita Moreno, Edward James Olmos, Cristina Saralegui, Jimmy Smits. **Deportes:** Joaquín Andújar, Pedro Guerrero, Willie Hernández, Óscar de la Hoya, Nancy López, Sammy Sosa, Lee Treviño. **Literatura:** Sandra Cisneros, Judith Ortiz Cofer, Esmeralda Santiago, Pedro Juan Soto. **Moda:** Adolfo, Carolina Herrera, Óscar de la Renta. **Música:** Marc Anthony, Celia Cruz, Gloria Estefan, Ricky Martin, Jon Secada. **Política:** Robert Meléndez, Silvestre Reyes, Ileana Ros-Lehtinen.

Capítulo 9

Primera situación

A. *Answers vary.*

B. *Answers vary.*

C.
1. Se me ocurrió esta idea.
2. Yo propongo que busquemos trabajo juntos.
3. No creo que su idea pueda funcionar. En cambio yo propongo…
4. Un momento. Pero yo tengo otra idea.
5. Volviendo al tema original…

D.

trabajaríamos, escribiríamos	trabajarían, escribirían
trabajarías, escribirías	trabajaría, escribiría
trabajaría, escribiría	trabajarían, escribirían

E.
1. podría, podrían
2. haría, harían
3. saldría, saldrían
4. diría, dirían
5. sabría, sabrían
6. querría, querrían
7. vendría, vendrían
8. tendría, tendrían

F.
1. (Tú) Construirías una casa grande.
2. Los Fernández se harían muy ricos.
3. Carlos Morales se encargaría de una compañía grande.
4. Uds. tendrían su propia compañía.
5. Mi novio(-a) y yo podríamos casarnos.
6. La Srta. García saldría para México.

G. *Answers vary.*

H.
1. El jefe trabaja eficazmente.
2. La secretaria trabaja cuidadosamente.
3. La Sra. Pereda trabaja pacientemente.
4. Los gerentes trabajan atentamente.
5. Marcos Duarte trabaja perezosamente.
6. Todos los vendedores trabajan responsablemente.

I.
1. El Sr. Cáceres escribió numerosos anuncios.
2. Pablo leyó todas las cartas de recomendación.
3. La Srta. Acosta llenó demasiadas solicitudes.
4. La Sra. Ocampo despidió a otro empleado.
5. Los Núñez consiguieron pocas entrevistas.
6. El Dr. Lado describió algunos beneficios sociales.

Segunda situación

A. *Answers vary but should include the following:* los archivos; las calculadoras; las carpetas; la cinta adhesiva; las computadoras; las engrapadoras; los escáneres; los escritorios; las impresoras, las máquinas de escribir; los monitores, las pantallas, las papeleras; los programas; los quitagrapas; los sacapuntas; el software multimedia; los teléfonos celulares.

B.
1. la publicidad
2. las relaciones públicas
3. el mercadeo
4. las ventas
5. la administración
6. las finanzas

C.
1. ¿Me has oído bien?
2. ¿Comprendes?
3. ¿Te parece bien?
4. ¿Estás seguro(-a)?
5. ¿Qué te parece?

D. Buscamos…

    1. una secretaria que sepa usar la nueva computadora.

    2. un contador que sea inteligente.

    3. una gerente que resuelva problemas eficazmente.

    4. un jefe de ventas que se lleve bien con los clientes.

No queremos nadie que…

    5. pierda tiempo.

    6. fume en la oficina.

    7. se queje mucho.

    8. diga mentiras.

E. *Answers vary.*

F.   **1.** No. Que lo empiece el Sr. Robles.

    2. No. Que los resuelvan Graciela y Mariana.

    3. No. Que la llene la Sra. González.

    4. No. Que los escriba el Sr. Almazán.

    5. No. Que lo despida el Sr. Ruiz.

    6. No. Que las hagan todos los empleados.

G.   **1.** altísimo

    2. buenísimos, malísimo

    3. grandísima, lindísima

    4. simpatiquísimos, muchísimo

    5. poquísimo, larguísimas

H. *Answers vary.*

Expansión de vocabulario

Dudas de vocabulario

    1. a. se puso   **b.** llegó a ser   **c.** se hizo   **d.** se volvió

    2. empleo, funciona, puesto, trabajo, tarea, obras, trabajar

Ampliación

A.   **1.** to contain

    2. to compose

    3. to vacate

    4. to undo

    5. to become poor

    6. to get drunk

    7. to predict

    8. to prescribe

B. 1. contener   5. enamorarse
        2. comprometer   6. enfermarse
        3. despedir   7. enterrar
        4. desaparecer   8. predecir

C. 1. engordar   4. componer
        2. predecir   5. desocupar
        3. despedir   6. enamorarse

Capítulo 10

Primera situación

A. *Answers may vary.*

1. Atiende al público. Contesta el teléfono.

2. Archiva los documentos. Escribe a máquina.

3. Crea los anuncios comerciales. Hace publicidad.

4. Trabaja con números. Maneja las responsabilidades financieras.

5. Crea los programas nuevos para la computadora. Resuelve problemas con la computadora.

6. Coordina todos los departamentos. Maneja la planificación.

B. 1. Buenos días, señorita. Si fuera tan amable, quisiera hablar con el presidente de su compañía, el Sr. Montalvo.

2. Entonces quisiera hablar con otro ejecutivo.

3. Soy *(your name)* y trabajo en Contadores Padilla e Hijos. Hace un mes pedí diez computadoras nuevas de su compañía pero todavía no las hemos recibido. Quisiera resolver el problema.

4. ¿Podría dejarle un mensaje / recado?

5. (Repeat previous explanation.) ¿Podría hacer una cita con el Sr. Mendoza?

6. *Answers vary.*

7. Se lo agradezco infinitamente. Adiós, señorita.

C. *Answers vary.*

D. 1. trabajado   5. estado   9. visto   13. escrito
        2. vendido   6. dicho   10. abierto   14. puesto
        3. cumplido   7. sido   11. vuelto   15. roto
        4. hecho   8. resuelto   12. muerto   16. cubierto

E. **1.** se han preocupado, han hecho

  2. se ha preocupado, ha hecho

  3. nos hemos preocupado, hemos hecho

  4. me he preocupado, he hecho

  5. se ha preocupado, ha hecho

  6. te has preocupado, has hecho

F. **1.** La secretaria ha escrito treinta cartas.

  2. (Yo) He almorzado con unos clientes nuevos.

  3. Los abogados han resuelto el problema con la aduana.

  4. El publicista y yo hemos hecho la publicidad.

  5. (Tú) Has vuelto de tu viaje de negocios.

  6. El gerente ha cumplido muchos pedidos.

G. *Answers vary.*

H. Espero que…

  1. Manolo ya haya cambiado el dinero.

  2. (tú) te hayas despedido de tu familia.

  3. todos nosotros ya le hayamos escrito a la empresa en Chile.

  4. Marta y Elena ya hayan leído una guía sobre Chile.

  5. la Sra. Chávez ya haya resuelto todos los problemas.

  6. los García ya hayan pagado los billetes.

I. Manuel y Teresa…

  1. se escuchan siempre.

  2. se escriben cuando están separados.

  3. se dan regalos a menudo.

  4. se ayudan cuando tienen problemas.

  5. se respetan siempre.

Segunda situación

A. **1.** Los Higuera deben solicitar una hipoteca.

  2. Matilde Guevara debe averiguar la tasa de cambio y cambiar dinero.

  3. Roberto Díaz debe abrir una cuenta corriente.

  4. Estela Morillo debe alquilar una caja de seguridad.

  5. Debo verificar el saldo.

  6. Héctor Ocampo debe sacar dinero de su cuenta.

  7. Guillermo Núñez debe depositar su dinero en una cuenta de ahorros.

B.   *Personal information varies.*

Importe en letras: mil setecientos sesenta nuevos soles

1/. = 1760 (nuevos soles)

C.   **1.**   Quisiera verificar el saldo de mi cuenta de ahorros.

   2.   Muy bien. Quisiera sacar mil setecientos sesenta nuevos soles.

   3.   Ya lo he llenado. Aquí lo tiene Ud.

   4.   Ahora quisiera depositar los soles en mi cuenta corriente. También he llenado el formulario de depósito.

   5.   También quiero enviarle un giro al extranjero a un amigo en los EE.UU. Es un giro de cuarenta dólares estadounidenses como regalo de cumpleaños.

   6.   Sí. *Answers vary.*

   7.   Muchas gracias por todo y adiós, señor.

D.   **1.**   nos habíamos arreglado, habíamos invertido

   2.   te habías arreglado, habías invertido

   3.   se habían arreglado, habían invertido

   4.   me había arreglado, había invertido

   5.   se había arreglado, había invertido

   6.   se había arreglado, había invertido

E.   **1.**   (Tú) Habías escrito cuatro cheques.

   2.   Mis padres y yo habíamos resuelto el problema de la cuenta corriente.

   3.   Los Estrada habían pedido prestado $10.000.

   4.   La Sra. Rodó había puesto unos documentos importantes en la caja de seguridad.

   5.   Uds. habían leído información sobre las hipotecas.

   6.   (Yo) Había hecho el pago inicial del préstamo estudiantil.

F.   *Answers vary.*

G.   **1.**   Hace cinco años que soy cliente del banco.

   2.   Hace cinco años que tengo una cuenta corriente.

   3.   Hace un año que alquilo una caja de seguridad.

   4.   Hace tres años que pago a plazos.

   5.   Hace seis meses que ahorro dinero en una cuenta.

   6.   Hace tres meses que no averiguo el saldo de la cuenta.

H.   **1.**   Veintitrés mil cuatrocientos ochenta y seis

   2.   Un millón de

   3.   Trescientos setenta y cinco mil

   4.   Cincuenta y siete mil seiscientos doce

5. Setenta y cuatro mil quinientos treinta y un

6. Dieciséis mil cincuenta

Expansión de vocabulario

Dudas de vocabulario

A. hay que, Debe, tiene que

B. conserva, ahorrar, guardó, salvó

C. ya, Ya no, todavía

Ampliación

A.
1. cook, chef
2. office worker
3. shoemaker
4. electrician
5. cashier
6. accountant
7. soccer player
8. worker

B.
1. el (la) recepcionista
2. la camarera/la mesera
3. el (la) carpintero(-a)
4. el (la) accionista
5. el (la) profesor(-a)
6. el (la) financista
7. el (la) artista
8. el (la) programador(-a)

C.
1. profesora
2. carpintero
3. publicista
4. dentista
5. joyero
6. cocinero

Bienvenidos a Chile y a la Argentina

A.
1. Buenos Aires
2. Chaco
3. carne
4. Patagonia
5. Pacífico
6. Atacama
7. Iguazú
8. cobre

La caja vertical: SANTIAGO

B.
1. Chile es un país largo y angosto con casi 3.000 kilómetros de costa. En el norte está el desierto de Atacama; en el centro se encuentran tierras fértiles; al este están las montañas.

2. La Argentina tiene grandes variaciones geográficas. En la parte central está la pampa. En el norte se encuentra el Chaco y al sur está Patagonia, una región fría.

3. Chile tiene 14.200.000 de habitantes. La Argentina tiene 34.600.000 de habitantes.

4. La moneda de Chile es el peso; la moneda de la Argentina es el peso también.

5. Los productos principales de Chile son el cobre, las uvas y el vino. La Argentina produce automóviles, lana y productos agrícolas como la carne y el trigo.

Capítulo 11

Primera situación

A. *Answers vary.*

B.
1. Quiero un pasaje de ida de Santiago a Caracas. Necesito salir tan pronto como (sea) posible.
2. Aquí lo tiene Ud. Voy a pagar con una tarjeta de crédito.
3. Sí. Quisiera facturar el equipaje, por favor.
4. Quiero sentarme al lado del pasillo en la sección de no fumar.
5. ¡Qué lástima! ¿A qué hora sale el vuelo?
6. ¿Por qué puerta de embarque salen los pasajeros?
7. Y, ¿a qué hora empiezan a abordar?
8. Muchas gracias por toda su ayuda. Adiós, señorita.

C.
1. viajaran, se divirtieran
2. viajara, me divirtiera
3. viajaran, se divirtieran
4. viajáramos, nos divirtiéramos
5. viajaras, te divirtieras
6. viajara, se divirtiera

D.
1. hicieron, hicieran
2. tuvieron, tuvieran
3. dijeron, dijeran
4. durmieron, durmieran
5. leyeron, leyeran
6. estuvieron, estuvieran
7. fueron, fueran
8. supieron, supieran
9. pudieron, pudieran
10. dieron, dieran
11. tradujeron, tradujeran
12. fueron, fueran
13. pusieron, pusieran
14. oyeron, oyeran

E. El empleado le aconsejó al pasajero…
1. que facturara el equipaje.
2. que no perdiera la tarjeta de embarque.
3. que tuviera paciencia.
4. que pusiera las etiquetas en las maletas.
5. que se despidiera de la familia en la sala de espera.
6. que no comiera ni bebiera mucho antes del vuelo.

F.　El agente les recomendó que…

　1. hicieran una reservación.

　2. consiguieran su pasaporte con mucha anticipación.

　3. que se sentaran en la sección de no fumar.

　4. que supieran el número del vuelo.

　5. que tuvieran cuidado.

　6. que no llevaran mucho equipaje.

G.　1. ¿Qué quisiera beber Ud.?

　2. ¿Pudiera Ud. poner su equipaje de mano debajo del asiento?

　3. Ud. debiera abrocharse el cinturón.

　4. Quisiera ver su tarjeta de embarque.

　5. ¿Pudiera Ud. sentarse en el asiento del pasillo?

H.　1. (Yo) Iría a Chile si no tuviera que trabajar.

　2. La Srta. Ocampo iría si conociera a alguien en Santiago.

　3. Roberto y Daniel irían si hablaran mejor el español.

　4. (Tú) Irías si terminaras tus cursos.

　5. Mi familia y yo iríamos si ganáramos más dinero.

I.　*Answers vary. Phrases should follow this pattern:* Si tuviera la oportunidad, el piloto + conditional tense.

J.　*Answers vary.*

Segunda situación

A.　*Answers vary.*

B.　*Descriptions of employees will vary; job descriptions may vary.* **El botones:** Carga, sube y baja el equipaje de los clientes. **La criada:** Limpia y arregla las habitaciones; hace las camas. **El conserje:** Atiende a los clientes; los ayuda con billetes de tren o avión, reservaciones para un restaurante, el teatro o la ópera. **El portero:** Ayuda a los clientes cuando llegan al hotel; les abre las puertas o saca su equipaje de su automóvil o taxi. **La recepcionista:** Trabaja en la recepción; saluda a los clientes, llena las tarjetas de recepción, cobra a los clientes, les da la llave de la habitación.

C.　1. Quisiera una habitación, por favor.

　2. No. Acabamos de llegar y decidimos quedarnos unos días.

　3. Necesitamos una habitación con tres camas.

　4. *Answer will vary.*

　5. ¿Qué facilidades o servicios tiene el hotel?

　6. Bueno. Vamos a quedarnos aquí por tres días.

　7. Tenemos mucho equipaje. Necesitamos a alguien que pueda subirlo.

D.   1. Sí, buscaré trabajo tan pronto como pueda.

  2. Sí, me adaptaré con tal que aprenda la lengua.

  3. Sí, tendré muchos problemas hasta que conozca a otros estudiantes.

  4. Sí, visitaré otros sitios turísticos después que termine el primer semestre.

  5. Sí, esquiaré en Portillo a menos que no haya nieve.

  6. Sí, los llamaré (a Uds.) para que Uds. sepan lo que pasa.

E.   1. se habrá alojado, habrá salido

  2. se habrán alojado, habrán salido

  3. te habrás alojado, habrás salido

  4. nos habremos alojado, habremos salido

  5. se habrá alojado, habrá salido

  6. me habré alojado, habré salido

F.   1. Manolo habrá escrito al hotel.

  2. (Tú) Te habrás despedido de tu familia.

  3. Todos nosotros habremos conseguido una habitación.

  4. Felipe y Elena habrán leído una guía.

  5. La Sra. Prado habrá hecho las maletas.

  6. Los Muñoz habrán pagado los billetes.

G.   *Answers vary.*

Expansión de vocabulario

Dudas de vocabulario

A.   1. ¿Cuál es…?

  2. ¿Cuál es…?

  3. ¿Qué es…?

  4. ¿Cuáles son…?

  5. ¿Qué son…?

B.   1. faltar

  2. perder

  3. echo de menos / extraño

C.   salir, partirá, dejé

Ampliación

A. 1. scale   **4.** space   **7.** state
        2. scandal   **5.** spinach   **8.** style
        3. sculptor   **6.** spy   **9.** statue

B. 1. la escena   **5.** el estómago
        2. la escuela   **6.** el estadio
        3. la esponja   **7.** el estudiante
        4. la especialidad   **8.** la estampilla

C. 1. estampilla   **4.** escultor, estatuas
        2. especialidad   **5.** estados
        3. escuela   **6.** especias

Capítulo 12

Primera situación

A. *Answers vary.*

B. *Answers may vary.*
        1. ¿Qué tal el partido?
        2. ¡Increíble!
        3. ¡No me digas!
        4. ¡Qué lástima!
        5. ¡Me alegro!

C. 1. habría practicado, habría corrido
        2. habría practicado, habría corrido
        3. habrían practicado, habrían corrido
        4. habrías practicado, habrías corrido
        5. habríamos practicado, habríamos corrido
        6. habrían practicado, habrían corrido

D. 1. Mateo y yo habríamos practicado gimnasia.
        2. (Tú) Habrías corrido.
        3. Gustavo y Nicolás se habrían puesto en forma.
        4. (Yo) Me habría entrenado más.
        5. Silvia habría hecho ejercicios aeróbicos.
        6. Uds. habrían ganado el campeonato.

E.   *All answers begin with* El entrenador quería que…

    1. te hubieras entrenado bien.

    2. me hubiera entrenado bien.

    3. nos hubiéramos entrenado bien.

    4. se hubiera entrenado bien.

    5. se hubieran entrenado bien.

    6. se hubiera entrenado bien.

F.   *All answers begin with* Era necesario…

    1. que el entrenador los hubiera entrenado bien.

    2. que (yo) hubiera hecho ejercicios.

    3. que mi amigo(-a) y yo nos hubiéramos puesto en forma.

    4. que los jugadores hubieran corrido cada día.

    5. que (tú) hubieras ido al gimnasio todos los días.

G.   **1.** Si hubiera tenido más suerte, Juanita Sánchez habría ganado el campeonato.

    2. Si hubieras tenido más suerte, (tú) habrías recibido un árbitro justo.

    3. Si hubieran tenido más suerte, Uds. habrían cogido todas las pelotas.

    4. Si hubieran tenido más suerte, los futbolistas habrían pateado mejor.

    5. Si hubiera tenido más suerte, (yo) habría jugado bien.

    6. Si hubiéramos tenido más suerte, el jugador de béisbol y yo habríamos tirado la pelota bien.

H.   *Uds. no habrían perdido el campeonato si…*

    1. hubieran jugado bien.

    2. hubieran hecho ejercicios de calentamiento.

    3. se hubieran mantenido en forma.

    4. me hubieran escuchado.

    5. hubieran corrido rápidamente.

    6. hubieran tenido árbitros justos.

I.   *Answers vary.*

Segunda situación

A.   **1.** le duelen la nariz y la garganta.

    2. le duelen las manos.

    3. le duele el tobillo.

    4. le duele el hombro.

    5. le duele el dedo.

    6. le duele la pierna.

B. **1.** El (la) paciente tiene fiebre. También tiene dolor de cabeza y de garganta. Tose y estornuda mucho. También puede padecer de dolores musculares. El (la) paciente debe tomar aspirinas, descansar y beber muchos líquidos.

2. El (la) paciente no puede dormirse fácilmente o no duerme toda la noche. Debe tomar unas píldoras para dormir o preocuparse menos.

3. Un catarro / resfriado muy fuerte. El (la) paciente tose frecuentemente y tiene fiebre. Debe tomar antibióticos y descansar.

4. El (la) paciente se suena la nariz, tose y estornuda. Puede tener dolor de cabeza también. El (la) paciente debe descansar, beber muchos líquidos y tomar aspirinas.

C. *Answers vary.*

D. **1.** Se le olvidó el impermeable a la señora.

2. Se le perdieron las gafas a la muchacha.

3. Se le rompió el tobillo al joven.

4. Se le olvidaron las píldoras al hombre.

5. Se le dañó el dedo a la anciana.

E. *Answers may vary.*

1. La señora que caminó por el parque sin impermeable tiene catarro.

2. La muchacha que se quemó ayudó a su madre en la cocina.

3. El joven que jugó al fútbol norteamericano ayer se fracturó el tobillo.

4. El hombre que trabajó en su jardín ayer se lastimó el hombro.

5. La mujer anciana que cocinó una cena especial anoche se cortó el dedo.

6. El niño que jugó al béisbol en el parque se rompió la pierna.

F. *Answers may vary.*

1. Éstos son los antibióticos sin los cuales los médicos no curan muchas enfermedades.

2. Ésta es la farmacia dentro de la cual preparan recetas.

3. Éstas son las pastillas por las cuales pagué cien dólares.

4. Éste es el jarabe para el cual caminé a la farmacia.

5. Éstas son mis vitaminas sin las cuales nunca viajo.

G. *Answers vary.*

Expansión de vocabulario

Dudas de vocabulario

A. juega, partido, Toca, juego

B. lastimó, duelen, ofender, hacen daño

Ampliación

A.
1. volleyball
2. shampoo
3. hamburger
4. sandwich
5. skiing
6. videocassette player
7. detergent
8. jeans

B.
1. la penicilina
2. el tenis
3. la fotografía
4. la televisión
5. la computadora
6. el béisbol
7. el básquetbol
8. los ejercicios aeróbicos

C.
1. Una salsa de tomates y especias que se usa en las hamburguesas y las papas fritas.
2. Un remedio fuerte contra muchas infecciones y enfermedades.
3. Un deporte al aire libre en el cual el jugador tiene que poner una pequeña pelota blanca en una serie de agujeros a lo largo de una cancha.
4. Una falda corta.
5. Un sustituto más sano para la mantequilla; contiene menos colesterol que la mantequilla.
6. Un ejercicio en el cual el individuo corre o trota bastante rápidamente. Muchas personas lo hacen cada día para mantenerse en buena forma.

Clave de respuestas
Manual de laboratorio

Clave de respuestas
Manual de laboratorio

Capítulo preliminar

Presentación

A. 1. **Amalia:** 18 años, chilena, ir de compras, jugar al tenis, bailar
   2. **Tomás:** 20 años, peruano, reunirse con amigos, charlar, contar chistes, leer novelas, escribir cartas, mirar la televisión
   3. **Maricarmen:** 19 años, española, escuchar música, tocar la guitarra, ir a los conciertos
   4. **Carlos:** 20 años, mexicano, practicar deportes (jugar al fútbol, tenis, golf), ir al cine
   5. **Beatriz:** 18 años, venezolana, jugar al tenis, hacer ejercicios, tocar el piano, leer novelas románticas

B. 1. **Amalia:** delgada, de talla media, ojos verdes, pelo rubio, corto y rizado
   2. **Tomás:** no es gordo, tampoco flaco, muy alto, moreno, ojos negros, anteojos
   3. **Maricarmen:** baja, un poco gorda, pelirroja, ojos azules, pecas
   4. **Carlos:** alto, moreno, atlético, pelo ondulado, ojos negros
   5. **Beatriz:** alta, esbelta, pelo castaño, largo y liso, ojos de color café

Para escuchar bien

A. 1. Sí   2. No   3. Sí   4. No   5. Sí

B. 1. b   2. d   3. d   4. a

Así se dice

A. 1. español   2. español   3. inglés   4. español   5. español   6. español

B. 1. español   2. inglés   3. inglés   4. español   5. español   6. español

A. 1. 3   2. 3   3. 2   4. 1

Estructuras

A. 1. c   2. e   3. a   4. b   5. d

B. 1. Guadalajara, México   Vuelo 37   7:05
   2. Santiago de Chile   Vuelo 85   8:20
   3. Sevilla, España   Vuelo 64   9:30
   4. Arequipa, Perú   Vuelo 99   10:45
   5. Caracas, Venezuela   Vuelo 74   11:15

Capítulo 1

Primera situación

Presentación

Monólogo 1:

    1. a   **2.** c   **3.** b

Monólogo 2:

    1. c   **2.** b   **3.** a

Monólogo 3:

    1. c   **2.** b   **3.** b

Para escuchar bien

A.   **1.** supermercado

      2. agencia de empleos

      3. programa deportivo

      4. clases de computación

B.   *Note:* Answers for pre-listening exercises that involve hypothesizing about what will be discussed in the listening selection are not provided in this *Clave de respuestas* since there is no one correct answer.

      1. hora de levantarse / acostarse

      2. exámenes, trabajos escritos

      3. cursos que toman

   Best summary sentence: 3

C.   **1.** hora de levantarse / acostarse

      2. quehaceres domésticos

      4. diversiones

      5. problemas

      6. posibles soluciones

   Best summary sentence: 2

Así se dice

A. **1.** inglés   **2.** español   **3.** inglés   **4.** español   **5.** español   **6.** inglés

B. **1.** 6   **2.** 5   **3.** 6   **4.** 3

Estructuras

B. **1.** ¿<u>Conoces</u> a Tomás Fernández? <u>Es</u> uno de los estudiantes de intercambio. Pues, él <u>viene</u> a mi casa esta noche. <u>Salimos</u> con María y Paco. <u>Estoy</u> un poco nerviosa pero <u>sé</u> que <u>vamos</u> a divertirnos.

2. ¿<u>Oyes</u> la noticia? Van a <u>destruir</u> el viejo edificio que <u>está</u> al lado del almacén. <u>Dicen</u> que van a <u>construir</u> una estación de servicio. <u>Parece</u> que esta ciudad cambia demasiado. No la <u>reconozco</u>.

C. **1.** yo   **5.** tú

2. nosotros   **6.** yo

3. él   **7.** él

4. ellos

Segunda situación

Presentación

A. **1.** 2   **2.** 1   **3.** 4   **4.** 6   **5.** 5   **6.** 3

B. **1.** b   **2.** a   **3.** c   **4.** b

Para escuchar bien

A. **1.** c   **2.** b   **3.** d

B. Best summary sentence: 2

Así se dice

A. **1.** español   **2.** inglés   **3.** inglés   **4.** inglés   **5.** español   **6.** inglés

B. **1.** 4   **2.** 3   **3.** 6   **4.** 3

Capítulo 2

Primera situación

Presentación

A. **1.** **Complejo la Playita:** broncearse, nadar, practicar el esquí acuático y el windsurf, dar un paseo, recoger conchas

2. **Hotel Serenidad:** jugar al golf, pescar, montar a caballo, montar (en) bicicleta

3. **Hotel Cosmopolita:** hacer ejercicios, nadar, correr, ir de compras, comer en un restaurante elegante

Para escuchar bien

A. **1.** No **2.** No **3.** Sí **4.** No

B. **1.** **a.** Falso **b.** Cierto **c.** Falso **d.** Falso

2. **a.** Falso **b.** Falso **c.** Falso **d.** Cierto

3. **a.** Cierto **b.** Falso **c.** Falso **d.** Cierto

4. **a.** Falso **b.** Cierto **c.** Falso **d.** Falso

C. Drawing 1: 2   Drawing 3: 1

Drawing 2: 4   Drawing 4: 3

Así se dice

A. **1.** español **2.** inglés **3.** español **4.** español **5.** español **6.** español

B. **1.** 4 **2.** 5 **3.** 4 **4.** 4

Estructuras

A. **1.** Preterite   **5.** Preterite

2. Preterite   **6.** Present

3. Present   **7.** Preterite

4. Preterite   **8.** Present

D. **1.** 4 **2.** 1 **3.** 7 **4.** 2 **5.** 5 **6.** 3 **7.** 6

Segunda situación

Para escuchar bien

A. 1, 3, 4, 6

B. bailes, corridas de toros, competencias de natación, conciertos, partidos de fútbol, maratón, obras teatrales

Así se dice

A. **1.** inglés **2.** español **3.** inglés **4.** español **5.** español **6.** inglés

B. **1.** 3 **2.** 3 **3.** 2 **4.** 2

Estructuras

A. **1.** Preterite   **5.** Present

2. Present   **6.** Preterite

3. Preterite   **7.** Present

4. Preterite   **8.** Preterite

Capítulo 3

Primera situación

Presentación

A.
1. bisabuelos
2. abuelo
3. tías
4. tío
5. primos
6. padres
7. hermano

B. **1.** A   **2.** A   **3.** C   **4.** B   **5.** B

Para escuchar bien

A. **Emilio:** antes—jugaba al básquetbol, trabajaba, salía

ahora—juega a las cartas, ve televisión

Alfredo: antes—trabajaba, jugaba al básquetbol, nadaba, jugaba al béisbol

ahora—colecciona estampillas, va al cine, va al teatro

B.

Nombres	Parientes	Actividades
1. José Pérez	abuela, primos, padres	jugaba, se quedaba a dormir
2. Alicia Suárez	hermanos	iba a la playa, nadábamos, esquiábamos, íbamos al campo, pasábamos el día al lado del río
3. Gerardo López	primo, tíos	jugaba al fútbol, iba al club, iba al cine, iba a comer a la calle
4. Miriam Robles	madre, hermanas	limpiábamos, lavábamos la ropa, preparábamos la comida, iba al cine

Así se dice

C. **1.** Sí   **2.** No   **3.** Sí   **4.** Sí   **5.** No   **6.** No

D. **1.** 2   **2.** 1   **3.** 2   **4.** 0

Estructuras

A. **1.** Present   **5.** Imperfect

      2. Imperfect   **6.** Imperfect

      3. Imperfect   **7.** Imperfect

      4. Present   **8.** Present

C. Cada domingo toda la familia <u>se reunía</u> después de ir a misa. Los niños <u>jugaban</u> al fútbol mientras Julieta o Mariana <u>preparaba</u> la cena. Martín y Juan <u>jugaban</u> al dominó. Después de almorzar <u>hacíamos</u> la sobremesa y <u>hablábamos</u> de todo lo que había pasado durante la semana. A veces <u>íbamos</u> de excursión al parque o al museo. ¡Cuánto me <u>gustaban</u> aquellos domingos en familia!

Segunda situación

Presentación

A. **1.** José se compromete con Luisa María.

      2. Hay muchos invitados en la iglesia.

      3. Es el día de la boda.

      4. Los recién casados salen de luna de miel.

B. **1.** A   **2.** C   **3.** A   **4.** B   **5.** C   **6.** A   **7.** B

C. **1.** cuñado   **2.** nuera   **3.** suegros   **4.** yerno   **5.** cuñada

Para escuchar bien

Nombre de la persona que llamó	Reunión social	Fecha	Hora	Aceptada	Rechazada
1. Arturo	esponsales	sábado	8 P.M.	NO	SÍ
2. Elena	fiesta de cumpleaños	próxima semana	7 P.M.	SÍ	NO
3. Armando	boda	21 de junio	7 P.M.	NO	SÍ

Así se dice

B. **1.** 1   **2.** 1   **3.** 2   **4.** 1

Capítulo 4

Primera situación

Presentación

A. 1. guacamole, nachos, enchiladas, sangría, flan
2. ensalada mixta, arroz con pollo, agua mineral, fruta
3. tacos, ceviche, cerveza, empanadas de dulce

B. 1. Mesero
2. Cliente
3. Cliente
4. Mesero
5. Cliente
6. Mesero
7. Cliente
8. Cliente

Para escuchar bien

A. 1. No 2. No 3. Sí 4. No 5. Sí

B. 1. b 2. a 3. b 4. a

Groups of people:

Dialogue 1: Mother and young son
Dialogue 2: Two women near the clock
Dialogue 3: Three people in the right foreground
Dialogue 4: Couple in the left foreground

Segunda situación

Presentación

A. dos pollos, un kilo de camarones, tres tomates, manzanas, queso manchego, agua mineral

C. 1. B 2. A 3. C 4. C 5. A

Para escuchar bien

A. 1. Falso 2. Cierto 3. Falso 4. Falso 5. Falso 6. Cierto 7. Falso 8. Falso

B. 1. Cierto 2. Falso 3. Cierto 4. Cierto 5. Cierto 6. Cierto

Así se dice

A. **1.** inglés   **2.** español   **3.** inglés   **4.** inglés   **5.** inglés   **6.** español

Estructuras

A. **1.** Preterite
2. Imperfect
3. Imperfect
4. Imperfect

5. Preterite
6. Preterite
7. Preterite

B. **1.** entramos
2. saludó
3. dio
4. Pedí

5. era
6. era
7. regresamos

C. Era un día bonito de mayo. Hacía mucho sol. Los pájaros cantaban. Cerca de nosotros algunos chicos jugaban al vólibol. Todo el mundo estaba de buen humor. De repente Paco se dio cuenta de que se le olvidó de traer las bebidas. Y Susana no trajo bastante comida para todos. Y con eso, terminó el partido.

Capítulo 5

Primera situación

Presentación

A. **1.** la matrícula
2. la residencia estudiantil
3. el título
4. el examen de ingreso

5. la librería
6. la beca
7. especializarse

B. **1.** Estudiante
2. Profesor
3. Profesor
4. Estudiante

5. Profesor
6. Estudiante
7. Estudiante

Para escuchar bien

A. **1.** la sala de clase
2. el campo deportivo
3. la residencia estudiantil

B.   **Carmen:**   Economía; maestría

     Manuel: Farmacia

     Ana: Educación; maestría; doctorado

     Rosa: Arquitectura; trabajar

Estructuras

B.   Pablo   Elena   Andrés

     Luis   Clara   Carlos

C.   **1.** para   **5.** por

       2. por   **6.** para

       3. para   **7.** por

       4. para

Segunda situación

Presentación

A.   **Paco:**   matemáticas, química, sociología

     Adela: matemáticas, biología, español

     Susana: física, español, ciencias políticas

     Enrique: matemáticas, económicas, ciencias sociales

B.   **1.** **Guatemala:**   hace fresco, no está nublado

       2. **la costa del Pacífico:**   hace mucho calor y sol

       3. **San José:**   está nublado, hace viento

       4. **Panamá:**   está muy húmedo, hace mucho calor

Para escuchar bien

A.   **Conversación 1:**   **1.** a   **2.** b

     Conversación 2:   **1.** a   **2.** c

     Conversación 3:   **1.** c   **2.** a

B.   **1.** a   **2.** a   **3.** c

Estructuras

A.   **1.** ojalá que   **5.** sé que

       2. sé que   **6.** ojalá que

       3. ojalá que   **7.** ojalá que

       4. ojalá que   **8.** sé que

Capítulo 6

Primera situación

Presentación

A. **Paco:** arregla el garaje, corta el césped, riega las flores

Juan: ayuda a tu hermano, vacía las papeleras, saca la basura

María: haz las camas, cuelga la ropa, pon la ropa sucia en la lavandería

Isabel: arregla la sala, pasa la aspiradora, sacude los muebles

Carlota: limpia la cocina, barre el piso, prepara la ensalada

B. **1.** A **2.** B **3.** C **4.** B **5.** C **6.** A **7.** B **8.** A

Para escuchar bien

A. **1.** **Main idea:** Una familia busca empleada para realizar quehaceres domésticos.

Supporting details: Es necesario que sepa cocinar, lavar y planchar.

2. **Main idea:** Una empresa de construcciones está buscando jardineros con experiencia y excelentes referencias.

Supporting details: El trabajo incluye diseño de jardines y plantar césped, árboles y plantas ornamentales.

3. **Main idea:** La Compañía Lava-seca necesita empleados.

Supporting details: Se necesita experiencia en el manejo de las máquinas de lavar, secar y planchar.

B. **1.** **Main idea:** Esta noche vienen unos amigos del señor y quieren comer comida criolla.

Supporting details: No laves ni planches. Prepara una comida especial: arroz con frijoles negros, pollo asado, una ensalada mixta y flan de coco. Ve a la tienda y compra tres botellas de vino tinto. Pon la mesa.

2. **Main idea:** Deje lo que está haciendo y arregle los jardines de estas casas.

Supporting details: Plante palmeras y ponga unas plantas tropicales.

3. **Main idea:** Trabaje más rápido porque toda la ropa tiene que estar lista.

Supporting details: No barra el piso. Lave y planche todas las camisas. Lave y seque los uniformes; no los planche.

Así se dice

A. **1.** inglés **2.** español **3.** inglés **4.** inglés **5.** inglés **6.** inglés

Estructuras

A.
1. Statement	**5.** Statement
2. Command	**6.** Command
3. Command	**7.** Statement
4. Command	**8.** Statement

Segunda situación

Presentación

1. un terremoto
2. en Cali
3. esta tarde a eso de las tres
4. No se sabe.
5. Robaron las tiendas y las casas desocupadas.
6. Los políticos dejaron su campaña electoral para ir al sitio del desastre.
7. Hubo grandes inundaciones y varias personas se ahogaron.

Para escuchar bien

A.

1. **Main idea:** El presidente expresa duda que el país pueda continuar pagando mensualmente la deuda externa.

   Supporting details: El país disminuirá la suma mensual que paga a los bancos internacionales e invertirá el dinero en programas nacionales.

2. **Main idea:** Terremoto en la zona occidental de Colombia.

   Supporting details: No ha habido muertos ni heridos.

3. **Main idea:** El presidente de Guatemala anunció fuertes medidas económicas.

   Supporting details: Estas medidas consisten en el congelamiento de sueldos, abandono de subsidios y privatización de las empresas del estado.

B.

1. **Main ideas:** José Luis Rodríguez, famoso cantante venezolano, está de regreso en Caracas.

   Supporting details: José Luis ha viajado por América del Sur. Ha estado en Lima, Bogotá, Santiago, Buenos Aires y Montevideo. Ha tenido mucho éxito.

2. **Main ideas:** Reinaldo y Teresa empiezan el programa juntos después del regreso de Reinaldo de sus vacaciones.

   Supporting details: Reinaldo y Teresa tienen invitados de fama internacional. Algunos invitados son: Conchita Alonso, Regina Alcóver y Fernando Larrañaga.

Así se dice

A.   **1.** español   **2.** inglés   **3.** español   **4.** inglés   **5.** español   **6.** español

Capítulo 7

Primera situación

Presentación

A.   **1.** Hermanos Gómez: (grandes) almacenes
    2. Tienda Felicidades: tienda de regalos
    3. Boutique Elegancia: tienda de lujo
    4. Tienda Ortiz: tienda de liquidaciones

B.   **1.** Dependiente   **3.** Dependiente   **5.** Comprador   **7.** Comprador
    2. Comprador   **4.** Dependiente   **6.** Dependiente   **8.** Comprador

Para escuchar bien

A.   **1.** Son muy caras.
    2. Una pulsera de dama / mujer.
    3. Espero que sea un buen precio.

B.   **1.** Te has puesto mucho maquillaje.   **4.** Regresa a casa temprano.
    2. Ponte aretes.   **5.** Ponte un abrigo / chaqueta.
    3. No estás bien vestida.   **6.** Ya es tarde.

Estructuras

A.   **1.** Progressive   **3.** Progressive   **5.** Progressive   **7.** Progressive
    2. Present   **4.** Present   **6.** Present   **8.** Present

Segunda situación

Presentación

    1. un calentador   Es demasiado vistoso.
    2. un traje de baño   Está pasado de moda.
    3. unos guantes   Son feos, de mal gusto.
    4. un chaleco   No hace juego con la ropa que tiene el cliente.
    5. unos calcetines   El cliente usa una talla más grande.
    6. un impermeable   No le queda bien al cliente.

Para escuchar bien

A.   **1.** b   **2.** a   **3.** d   **4.** c

B.   **1.** d   **2.** c   **3.** a   **4.** b

Capítulo 8

Primera situación

Presentación

A. **1.** la catedral **3.** la Oficina de Turismo
2. el rascacielos La Torre **4.** el Restaurante Julio

Para escuchar bien

A. **Señorita:** Disculpe, me podría decir
Señora: tres cuadras, a mano derecha, ahí mismo
Señorita: Muchísimas

B. **Zoila:** viernes 19 de octubre, Museo de Arte
Zoila: Zoila Chávez
Zoila: María Ramos
Zoila: morena, un metro setenta, negro, marrones, mejilla derecha
Zoila: Veinticuatro
Zoila: Soltera
Zoila: 633–9894

PARTE POLICIAL

Nombre de la persona desaparecida: **María Ramos**

Nombre de la persona que reporta la desaparición: **Zoila Chávez**

Lugar de residencia de la persona que reporta la desaparición: **Hotel «Las Américas»**

Teléfono: **633-9894**

Lugar donde fue vista la persona la última vez: **alrededores del Museo de Arte**

Fecha cuando fue vista la persona la última vez: **viernes, 19 de octubre**

Descripción de la persona desaparecida:

Estatura: **1.70 m.** Color de ojos: **marrones**

Color de piel: **morena** Marcas o cicatrices: **lunar en la mejilla derecha**

Color del cabello: **negro** Estado civil: **soltera**

Edad: **24 años**

Así se dice

A. **1.** inglés **2.** español **3.** español **4.** inglés **5.** español **6.** español

Segunda situación

Presentación

1. el centro cultural
2. la corrida
3. el parque de atracciones
4. la corrida
5. el centro cultural / la corrida
6. el parque de atracciones
7. el centro cultural

Para escuchar bien

A.   Buenos días, señoras y señores. Bienvenidos al Museo de Arte. Como Uds. verán, el museo tiene numerosas obras de arte de famosos pintores y escultores venezolanos. En el ala derecha del museo están las obras de arte de famosos pintores y en el ala izquierda, así como también en el patio central, están las esculturas de nuestros artistas más famosos.

    El museo frecuentemente organiza exposiciones de arte con obras especialmente seleccionadas. Para tales exposiciones cada dibujo, cada pintura, cada escultura es cuidadosamente seleccionada por el director del museo en colaboración con el artista mismo. El día de la inauguración de la exposición hay una recepción a la cual asisten numerosos artistas e intelectuales de nuestra comunidad, así como también el público en general.

    Ahora pasemos a la primera sala donde podrán apreciar la obra del maestro Szysslo.

B.   **Mujer 1:** el centro de la ciudad, la Plaza de Armas, la catedral, el Palacio Torre Tagle, un restaurante, el Museo Nacional.

       Mujer 2: Barranco, el Museo Pedro de Osma, el Puente de los Suspiros, la Bajada de los Baños, el Parque Municipal, el café, el Museo de Oro

Estructuras

A.
1. Present
2. Future
3. Future
4. Present
5. Future
6. Future
7. Present
8. Future

Capítulo 9

Primera situación

Presentación

A.
1. Es importante que Ud. se informe de todas las posibilidades de empleo.
2. Debe buscar información más específica.
3. Haga una evaluación honesta de lo que Ud. puede ofrecer.
4. Llame a la oficina de personal para pedir una solicitud y una entrevista.
5. Vaya a la entrevista bien preparado.
6. En la entrevista hable de sus aptitudes y cualidades.
7. Si le ofrece el puesto, esté preparado para tomar una decisión.

B. **1.** C **2.** A **3.** B **4.** B **5.** A **6.** C **7.** A **8.** C

Para escuchar bien

A. **A. Obligaciones de la secretaria**

1. recibir a los aspirantes

2. archivar los documentos

3. contestar el teléfono

4. tomar mensajes

5. trabajar con la señorita Méndez

B. Obligaciones de la señorita Méndez

1. revisar los documentos

2. hacer las citas para los aspirantes

B. **Mujer 1**

Periódico: *El Latino*

Departamento: Noticias internacionales

Responsabilidades: recibir cables y escribir noticias

Mujer 2

Periódico: *El Latino*

Departamento: Noticias nacionales

Responsabilidades: Escribir noticias políticas y económicas

Hombre 1

Situación presente: Esperando respuesta

Expectativas: Conseguir trabajo en un periódico

C. Consecuencias positivas

1. En la ciudad

   a. Descongestión del tráfico en las grandes ciudades

   b. Disminución de la contaminación ambiental

2. En la familia

   a. Mejoramiento de las relaciones familiares

   b. No habrá separación de las familias

3. En la tecnología y economía

   a. Mejora de la calidad y disminución de los precios de los servicios de comunicación y de las computadoras

Consecuencia negativa

1. Disminución de las relaciones de amistad y camaradería entre los empleados

Así se dice

B.   **1.** 3   **2.** 1   **3.** 2   **4.** 1

Estructuras

A.

1. Conditional	**3.** Future	**5.** Future	**7.** Conditional
2. Conditional	**4.** Conditional	**6.** Future	**8.** Future

Segunda situación

Presentación

Answers may vary but should include the following: calculadoras; papel de todo tamaño, color y uso; grapas; engrapadoras; quitagrapas; carpetas; lápices; sacapuntas

Para escuchar bien

A.   **1.** Económicos, Personal, Relaciones Públicas

       2. Asuntos Económicos, economista, Ventas, economista, compra, distribución, venta, supervisores

       3. Asuntos de Personal, supervisor, secretarias, contadores

       4. Relaciones Públicas, publicidad, publicista

B.   **1.** Para la oficina de la secretaria

         a. archivo de metal blanco

         b. papelera

         c. engrapadora eléctrica

         d. carpetas tamaño carta

       2. Para la oficina del Supervisor de Ventas

         a. teléfono

         b. dos cajas de discos para la computadora

         c. una calculadora eléctrica

       3. Para la Oficina de Relaciones Públicas

         a. papel

         b. dos nuevos archivos

         c. un nuevo lector de discos

Así se dice

B.   **1.** 2   **2.** 2   **3.** 1   **4.** 2

Capítulo 10

Primera situación

Presentación

A. abogado, contador, publicista, representante de ventas, oficinista

B. **1.** A **2.** B **3.** B **4.** A **5.** A **6.** B **7.** B

Para escuchar bien

A. **1. El doctor Ortiz:** que lo llame al 385–9432 de las 7 a las 9 de la noche

2. La señora Salazar: que mande un especialista porque la computadora no funciona; su teléfono es el 678–0965

3. Sr. Rodríguez: que llame a la oficina en cuanto llegue

4. La publicista: que les avisen cuándo sería conveniente hacer la demostración; su teléfono es el 447–0014

B. **1.** Que haga los pedidos.

2. Que archive los documentos.

3. Que llame a la oficina de importación Céspedes.

4. Que pague los derechos de aduana.

5. Que resuelva los problemas.

Así se dice

B. **1.** 3 **2.** 2 **3.** 3 **4.** 5

Estructuras

A. **1.** Present

2. Present

3. Present perfect

4. Present perfect

5. Present

6. Present

7. Present perfect

8. Present perfect

C. **1.** Present subjunctive

2. Present perfect subjunctive

3. Present perfect subjunctive

4. Present subjunctive

5. Present perfect subjunctive

6. Present subjunctive

7. Present perfect subjunctive

8. Present subjunctive

Segunda situación

Presentación

A. 1. La renta personal, el costo de vida y la inflación suben cada mes.

2. El presupuesto nacional es un desastre.

3. El problema de la evasión fiscal le preocupa al gobierno.

4. Quiere empezar proyectos de desarrollo.

5. Va a insistir en la reforma fiscal y el reajuste de salarios.

B. 1. ahorrar

2. el pago mensual

3. depositar

4. pagar a plazos

5. el giro al extranjero

6. el saldo

7. la hipoteca

Para escuchar bien

A. 1, 2, 3, 7

B. El Banco Latino ofrece una serie de facilidades. Ofrece cuentas corrientes pagando 6% de interés anual. Además, ofrece una serie de cuentas de ahorro a plazo fijo pagando desde 7,5% hasta 9% dependiendo de la cantidad de dinero depositada. Con mil dólares, por 60 días, 7,5% y por 150 días, 8%. De cinco a diez mil dólares, por un año, 9%.

Así se dice

B. 1. 2   2. 1   3. 2   4. 4

Estructuras

A. 1. Past perfect

2. Past perfect

3. Present perfect

4. Past perfect

5. Present perfect

6. Past perfect

7. Present perfect

8. Past perfect

F. 1. c   2. e   3. g   4. a   5. d   6. f   7. b

Capítulo 11

Primera situación

Presentación

A. **¿Dónde?:** un mercado indígena

¿Cuándo?: el sábado y el domingo

¿Cómo?: por tren o automóvil

¿Por qué?: Es un mercado indígena interesante. El viaje que pasa por la sierra principal de los Andes es magnífico.

B.

1. Pasajero	**3.** Azafata	**5.** Azafata	**7.** Pasajero
2. Azafata	**4.** Pasajero	**6.** Pasajero	**8.** Azafata

Para escuchar bien

A.
1. Una profesora quería ingresar una computadora personal a Chile para hacer su trabajo de investigación.
2. No se permite el ingreso de computadoras en Chile sin el pago de un alto impuesto.
3. Empleado: descortés; Viajera: cortés
4. *Answers vary.*
5. *Answers vary.*
6. *Answers vary.*
7. *Answers vary.*

B.
1. El cinturón de seguridad de una viajera no funcionaba.
2. Cambiar a la pasajera de asiento.
3. No, porque quería estar en la ventana al lado de su nieto y además pensaba que cambiarse de asiento le iba a dar mala suerte.
4. **Actitud:** descortés, impaciente, desconfiada **Expresiones:** No, no y no. / Que arreglen esto y pronto. / ¡Es el colmo! / ¿Qué es esto? / ¡Cambiarme de asiento! / ¡Habráse visto! / Apúrese.
5. **Actitud:** cortés, paciente, confiada
6. *Answers vary.*
7. *Answers vary.*
8. *Answers vary.*

Así se dice

A.
1. bienes<u>tar</u>
2. compa<u>ñe</u>ro
3. inmi<u>gra</u>ntes
4. voluntaria<u>men</u>te
5. dema<u>sia</u>do
6. <u>idio</u>mas
7. adop<u>ti</u>va
8. traba<u>ja</u>ran
9. ascen<u>den</u>cia
10. benefi<u>ciar</u>

Estructuras

A.
1. Dudaba que
2. Dudaba que
3. Sabía que
4. Dudaba que
5. Dudaba que
6. Sabía que
7. Dudaba que
8. Sabía que

Segunda situación

Presentación

A.
514   arreglar la calefacción
318   subir el equipaje
623   llevar más toallas de baño
415   llamar mañana por la mañana a las 6:30 en punto
308   avisarle cuando llegue el mensaje
236   arreglar el aire acondicionado
326   traerle un menú para el servicio de habitación

B.   **1.** A   **2.** A   **3.** B   **4.** A   **5.** A   **6.** B   **7.** A   **8.** B

Para escuchar bien

A.
1. El cuarto es feo, sucio, viejo e incómodo. No hay agua caliente.
2. Ella está furiosa. Él está más calmado.
3. El equipaje no llega y la mujer no se puede cambiar.
4. *Answers vary.*
5. *Answers vary.*

B.
   A. **Future Perfect:** habré hecho, habrá cerrado
   B. **Imperfect Subjunctive:** quisiera, llegaran, quisiera, vinieran

Así se dice

A.   **1.** 5   **2.** 6   **3.** 7   **4.** 8   **5.** 7   **6.** 12

B. **1.** Tú eres estudiante de español.

2. Los amigos de Elena son extranjeros.

3. Los beneficios sociales son importantes para ellos.

4. Hay que llenar una solicitud para ese puesto.

5. Él tiene que encargarse de eso personalmente.

6. Es orgullosísimo y no quiere que nadie sepa que está sin trabajo.

Estructuras

B. **1.** Present perfect **5.** Future perfect

2. Future perfect **6.** Present perfect

3. Future perfect **7.** Future perfect

4. Present perfect **8.** Present perfect

Capítulo 12

Primera situación

Presentación

1. B **2.** A **3.** C **4.** A **5.** B **6.** C **7.** A **8.** C

Para escuchar bien

A. **A:** 2, 3, 7 **B:** 4, 5, 10 **C:** 1, 6, 8, 9

B. **1.** **Hombre:** friendly **Mujer:** friendly

2. **Hombre:** rude **Mujer:** rude

C. **Hombre 1 (Sr. Góngora):** friendly

Expresiones: Joselito; tú; déjame...; si necesitas cualquier cosa...

Hombre 2 (Joselito): formal

Expresiones: Ud.; Sr. Góngora; qué ocurrencia, señor; para mí será un gusto...

Así se dice

C. **1.** Simple **3.** Simple **5.** Emphatic

2. Emphatic **4.** Simple **6.** Emphatic

Estructuras

A.
1. Conditional
2. Conditional
3. Conditional perfect
4. Conditional perfect
5. Conditional
6. Conditional perfect
7. Conditional
8. Conditional perfect

D.
1. Dudo que
2. Dudaba que
3. Dudaba que
4. Dudo que
5. Dudo que
6. Dudaba que
7. Dudo que
8. Dudaba que

Segunda situación

Presentación

A.
1. Llamar al médico / Guardar cama
2. Ir al hospital
3. Guardar cama
4. Llamar al médico
5. Guardar cama

B.   **1.** A   **2.** B   **3.** A   **4.** B   **5.** B   **6.** A   **7.** A   **8.** B

Para escuchar bien

A.   **Médico:** formal but rude

Expresiones: Pase.; Yo se lo advertí.; Si me hubiera hecho caso…; ¿Me entiende?; Le he dicho que se cuide.; Me va a hacer perder la paciencia.

Joven: formal but friendly

Expresiones: Por favor.; Sí, doctor.; Ya, doctor.; No se moleste.

B.   **Mujer 1:** rude

Expresiones: Te lo dije.; Te lo mereces por terca.; Eres insoportablemente malcriada y engreída.; Que te aguante otra.

Mujer 2: rude

Expresiones: Cállate la boca; Vete de mi cuarto.; Déjame en paz.; Vete de aquí.; A mí qué me importa.; Mientras más rápido te vayas, mejor.

Así se dice

C.
1. information question
2. yes–no question
3. information question
4. yes–no question
5. yes–no question
6. information question

Vocabulario inglés-español

A

a, an un(-a)
A.M. de la mañana
able: be able to poder
about acerca de, de, sobre; **be about** tratarse de
abroad en el extranjero
absent ausente; **be absent from** faltar a
absurd absurdo
accent *n* acento; *v* acentuar
accept aceptar
access acceso
accident accidente *(m)*
accommodate acomodar
accomplish llevar a cabo
according to según
account cuenta; **checking account** cuenta corriente; **fixed account** cuenta a plazo fijo; **joint bank account** cuenta mancomunada; **savings account** cuenta de ahorros; **take into account** tener en cuenta
accountant contador(-a)
accounting contabilidad *(f)*
accused acusado
accustomed: be accustomed to doing something soler (ue) + *inf;* **become accustomed** acostumbrarse
ache *n* dolor *(m);* *v* doler (ue); **have a ... ache** tener dolor de...
achieve lograr
acknowledge defeat darse por vencido
acquaintance conocido(-a)
acquainted: be acquainted with conocer
across a través de, enfrente de
act actuar
active activo
activity actividad *(f)*
actual real, verdadero
actually en realidad
add añadir
address dirección *(f)*
adjective adjetivo
adjustment reajuste *(m)*
administration: business administration administración *(f)* de empresas
administrative office oficina administrativa
admire admirar
admission ingreso
adore encantar
adorn adornar
advance *n* adelanto, avance *(m);* *v* avanzar
advanced avanzado
advancement adelanto
advantage ventaja; **take advantage of** aprovechar
adventure *n* aventura; *adj* de aventura
adverb adverbio
advertise hacer publicidad
advertisement anuncio
advertising publicidad *(f);* **advertising person** publicista *(m/f)*
advice consejo; **financial advice** consejo financiero; **give advice** aconsejar, dar consejos

advisable aconsejable
advise aconsejar, avisar
advisor consejero(-a)
aerobic aeróbico
affection cariño
affectionate cariñoso
afraid: be afraid tener miedo de
after *prep* después de; *conj* después que
afternoon tarde *(f);* **in the afternoon** por la tarde; **P.M.** de la tarde
afterwards después, luego
again otra vez
against contra
age edad *(f)*
agency agencia; **employment agency** agencia de empleos; **travel agency** agencia de viajes
agent agente *(m/f)*
aggressive agresivo
ago hace + *unit of time + verb in preterite*
agree convenir; estar de acuerdo
agreement acuerdo; **be in agreement** estar de acuerdo; **I agree** de acuerdo; **reach an agreement** llegar a un acuerdo
agricultural agrícola
air aire *(m);* *adj* aéreo; **air-conditioning** aire acondicionado; **air mattress** colchón *(m)* neumático; **air pollution** contaminación *(f)* del aire
airline línea aérea
airplane avión *(m)*
airport aeropuerto
aisle pasillo
alarm clock despertador *(m);* poner el despertador **to set the alarm clock**
alcoholic alcohólico
alert vivo (with *ser*)
alive vivo (with *estar*)
all todo
all right *adj* regular; *adv* bueno
allergic alérgico; **be allergic to** ser alérgico a
allergy alergia
allow dejar, permitir
almost casi
alone solo
already ya
also también
alternative alternativa
although aunque
altitude altitud *(f)*, altura
always siempre
amazed maravillado
amethyst amatista
among entre
amusement diversión *(f)*
amusement park parque *(m)* de atracciones; **amusement park ride** atracción *(f)*
amusing chistoso, divertido, gracioso
analysis análisis *(m)*
ancient antiguo
and y, e (replaces **y** before words beginning with **i-** or **hi-**)
anecdote anécdota

angel   ángel (m)
anger   enojo
angry   enojado;   **get angry** enfadarse, enojarse
ankle   tobillo
announce   anunciar
announcer   locutor(-a)
annoy   molestar
annoyed   molesto
another   otro
answer   n respuesta;   v contestar
antibiotic   antibiótico
anticipate   anticipar
anxious   ansioso
any   adj algún, alguna, alguno; cualquier;   pron cualquiera
apartment   apartamento
appear   aparecer;   presentarse
appetite   apetito;   **have an appetite for** apetecer
appetizer   aperitivo, entremés (E)
applaud   aplaudir
apple   manzana
appliance   aparato, electrodoméstico
applicant   aspirante (m/f)
application form   solicitud (f)
apply   solicitar
appointment   cita
appraise   valorar
appreciate   agradecer
approach   acercarse a
appropriate   apropiado
April   abril (m)
aptitude   aptitud (f)
arch   arco
architect   arquitecto(-a)
architecture   arquitectura
Argentine   argentino
arm   brazo
aroma   olor (m)
around   alrededor de;   **around here** por aquí;   **around there** por allí;   **turn around** dar vuelta(s)
arrange   arreglar
arrangement   arreglo
arrest   arrestar
arrive   llegar
art   arte (m);   **fine arts** bellas artes (f);   **art gallery** galería
article   artículo;   **article of clothing** prenda de vestir
artist   artista (m/f)
artistic   artístico;   **artistic work** obra
as   como;   **as** + adj or adv + **as** tan +adj or adv + como;   **as if** como si;   **as much** tanto(-a);   **as much as** tanto como;   **as soon as** así que, en cuanto, luego que, tan pronto como
ask a question   hacer preguntas, preguntar;   **ask about** preguntar por;   **ask for** pedir (i)
asparagus   espárragos (m)
aspect   aspecto
aspirin   aspirina
associate   asociarse
assorted   variado

assure   asegurar
astonish   asombrar
at   a, en
athlete   atleta (m/f)
athletic   atlético;   **athletic shoes** zapatos deportivos
atmosphere   ambiente (m)
attack   atacar
attempt   intentar;   tratar de
attend   asistir a;   **attend to** atender (ie)
attendance   asistencia;   **take attendance** pasar lista
attention   atención (f);   **pay attention** prestar atención, fijarse en
attentive   atento
attitude   actitud (f)
attract   atraer
attraction   atracción
attribute to   atribuir
audience   público
audit   ser oyente
August   agosto
aunt   tía;   **great aunt** tía abuela
authority   autoridad (f)
automobile   automóvil (m)
autumn   otoño
available   disponible
avenue   avenida
average   medio
avocado   aguacate (m);   **avocado dip** guacamole
avoid   evitar
aware   consciente;   **become aware of** darse cuenta de
awful   espantoso;   **How awful**! ¡Qué barbaridad!

B

baby   bebé (m/f)
babysit   hacer de niñero(-a)
babysitter   niñero(-a)
bachelor   soltero
bachelor's degree   licenciatura;   **receive a bachelor's degree** licenciarse en
back   n espalda;   adv atrás;   **in back of** detrás de
background   fondo
backpack   mochila
bad   adv mal;   adj mal, malo;   **bad-humored** malhumorado;   **bad-mannered** mal educado;   **That's too bad!** ¡Qué lástima!;   **the bad part** lo malo
baggage   equipaje (m);   **baggage claim area** sala de reclamación de equipaje;   **baggage claim check** talón (m)
balance   balanza;   **balance of payments** balanza de pagos
balcony   balcón (m)
bald   calvo
ball   pelota
balloon   globo
ballpoint pen   bolígrafo
band   conjunto
Band-Aid   curita
bandage   n venda;   v vendar

bank banco; **bank account balance** saldo de la cuenta bancaria; **bank draft** giro; **bank statement** estado de cuenta; **joint bank account** cuenta mancomunada
banker banquero(-a)
banking *adj* bancario
baptism bautismo
bar bar (*m*)
barber shop peluquería
bargain ganga
baseball béisbol (*m*)
basement sótano
basket canasta
basketball básquetbol (*m*) **(A),** baloncesto **(E)**
Basque vasco; **Basque language** vascuence
bat *n* bate (*m*); *v* batear
bath: take a bath bañarse
bathing suit traje de baño (*m*)
bathroom baño; cuarto de baño
bathtub bañera
be estar (*conditions*), haber (*existence*), ser (*characteristics*); **be in style** estar de moda; **be on a diet** estar a dieta; **be on sale** estar en liquidación; **be on strike** estar de huelga; **be on vacation** estar de vacaciones; **be opposed** oponerse; **be well (poorly) brought up** estar bien (mal) educado; **be within reach** estar al alcance
beach playa; **beach umbrella** sombrilla
bean frijol (*m*)
beard barba
beat batir
beautiful hermoso
beauty belleza; **beauty mark** lunar (*m*)
beauty shop peluquería
because a causa de, como, porque, puesto que
become convertirse, hacerse, llegar a ser, ponerse, volverse
bed cama; **go to bed** acostarse (ue); **make the bed** hacer la cama
bedroom dormitorio
beef carne (*f*) de res
beer cerveza
before *prep* ante, antes de; *conj* antes que
beg rogar (ue)
begin comenzar (ie), empezar (ie)
beginning inicio; **beginning of school term** apertura de clases; **in the beginning** al principio
behave comportarse, portarse
behavior comportamiento
behind detrás de, de atrás
believe creer
bellman botones (*ms*)
belong pertenecer
belt cinturón (*m*)
benefit *n* beneficio; *v* beneficiar; **fringe benefit** beneficio social
beside al lado de
besides además
best mejor; **best man** padrino; **make the best**

of something disfrutar de, gozar de; **the best thing** lo mejor
better mejor; **get better** mejorar, mejorarse
between entre
beverage bebida
bicycle bicicleta; **ride a bicycle** montar (en) bicicleta
big grande
biking ciclismo
bill billete (*currency*) (*m*); cuenta, factura
billboard letrero, rótulo
biology biología
bird ave (*m*), pájaro
birth nacimiento; **birthplace** lugar (*m*) de nacimiento
birthday cumpleaños (*ms*)
bitter amargo
black negro
blanket manta
block cuadra **(A),** manzana **(E)**
blocks cubos de letras
blond rubio
blood sangre (*f*)
blouse blusa
blue azul
board *n* tabla; *v* abordar, embarcar; **full board** pensión completa; **ironing board** tabla de planchar; **on board** a bordo; **windsurfing board** tabla de windsurf
boarding house pensión (*f*)
boarding pass tarjeta de embarque
boat barco; **motorboat** lancha
body cuerpo
boil hervir (ie, i)
bond bono
bone hueso
boo chiflar
book libro
bookstore librería
boot bota
booth puesto
border *n* frontera; *v* lindar
bore aburrir; **be boring** ser pesado; **get bored** aburrirse; **bored, boring** aburrido
born: be born nacer
borrow pedir (i, i) prestado
boss jefe(-a)
bother *n* molestia; *v* molestar
bouquet ramo
boutique boutique (*f*)
box *n* caja, estuche (*m*); *v* practicar el boxeo; **safety deposit box** caja de seguridad
boxing boxeo
boy chico, muchacho
boyfriend novio
bracelet pulsera
brand marca
brave valiente
bread pan (*m*)
break romper

breakfast desayuno; **have breakfast** desayunar
brick ladrillo
bride novia
bridesmaid dama de honor
bridge puente (*m*)
briefcase maletín (*m*)
bring traer; **bring up children** criar
broadcast emitir
brochure folleto
broken *pp* roto
broom escoba
broth caldo
brother hermano
brother-in-law cuñado
brown de color café; **pardo**
bruise contusión (*f*); **be bruised** tener una contusión
brunette moreno
brush *n* cepillo; **brush one's teeth** cepillarse, lavarse los dientes; **toothbrush** cepillo de dientes
bucket cubo
budget presupuesto
build construir
building edificio
bull toro
bullfight corrida de toros
bullfighter matador (*m*), torero; **bullfighter's suit** traje (*m*) de luces
bullfighting tauromaquia
bullring plaza de toros
burn quemar, quemarse
bus autobús (*m*), ómnibus (*m*); **bus stop** parada de autobús
business negocios; **business administration** administración (*f*) de empresas; **business and management** administración de empresas; **business office** oficina comercial; **businessman** hombre (*m*) de negocios; **businesswoman** mujer (*f*) de negocios
busy ocupado
but pero, sino; **but rather** *conj* sino que
buy comprar
buyer comprador(-a)
by por, para

C

cafe café (*m*); **outdoor cafe** café al aire libre
cake torta
calculate calcular
calculator calculadora
calculus cálculo
calendar calendario
call *n* llamada; *v* llamar; **be called** llamarse; **telephone call** llamada telefónica; **Who is calling?** ¿De parte de quién?
calm *n* tranquilo; *v* calmar, tranquilizar
campus ciudad (*f*) universitaria
Canadian canadiense (*m/f*)
candy dulces (*m pl*)
capital capital (*city*) (*f*); capital (*money*) (*m*)

car carro, coche (*m*)
caramel caramelo; **caramel custard** flan (*m*)
card tarjeta; **credit card** tarjeta de crédito; **I.D. card** tarjeta de identidad; **playing cards** naipes (*m*), cartas
care arreglo; **care for** cuidar; **take care of** atender (ie); **take care of oneself** cuidarse
career carrera
careful cuidadoso **be careful** ¡Ojo!; tener cuidado
carefully con cuidado
carnation clavel (*m*)
carousel caballitos, tiovivo
carpenter carpintero(-a)
carpet alfombra
carry llevar, traer; cargar; **carry out** cumplir; llevar a cabo
cartoon dibujo animado, tira cómica
case: display case escaparate (*m*) **(A)**, vitrina **(E)**; **in case (that)** *conj* en caso que; **in that case** entonces
cash dinero en efectivo; **cash a check** cobrar un cheque; **cash register** caja
cashier cajero(-a)
cast yeso; **put a cast on** enyesar
castle castillo
cat gato
Catalan catalán(-ana)
catch coger
cathedral catedral (*f*)
catholic católico
cause causar, ocasionar
CD disco compacto
celebration celebración (*f*)
cellular celular
cement cemento
center centro; **cultural center** centro cultural; **shopping center** centro comercial; **student center** centro estudiantil
centigrade centígrado
century siglo
certain cierto, seguro
chain cadena
chair silla; **armchair** sillón (*m*)
chambermaid camarera, criada
champion campeón(-ona)
championship campeonato
chance oportunidad (*f*); **by chance** de casualidad, por casualidad
change *n* cambio; *v* cambiar; **change clothes** cambiarse de ropa; **change money** cambiar dinero; **loose change** sencillo, suelto; **money returned as change** vuelto
channel canal (*m*)
chapter capítulo
character personaje (*m*)
characteristic característica
charge: additional charge recargo; **be in charge** encargarse; **be in charge of** estar encargado; **charge money** cobrar

charm *n* encanto; *v* encantar; **charming** encantador

chart esquema (*m*)

chat charlar

check *n* cheque (*m*), cuenta; *v* chequear, revisar; **cash a check** cobrar un cheque; **check in** registrarse; **check luggage** facturar el equipaje; **check out a book** sacar prestado un libro; **security check** control (*m*) de seguridad; **traveler's check** cheque de viajero

checkbook chequera (**A**), talonario (**E**)

checkered a cuadros

checkers damas

checking account cuenta corriente

cheerful alegre

cheers salud

cheese queso

chemist químico(-a)

chemistry química

chess ajedrez (*m*)

chest pecho

chestnut castaño

chew masticar

chewing gum chicle (*m*)

chicken pollo; **chicken noodle soup** caldo de pollo con fideos; **chicken with rice** arroz (*m*) con pollo

child niño(-a); **children** hijos, niños

chills escalofríos

chimney chimenea

Chinese chino

chocolate chocolate (*m*); **hot chocolate** chocolate (*m*)

choose elegir (i, i), escoger, seleccionar

chore quehacer (*m*) doméstico

Christmas Navidad (*f*); **Christmas Eve** Nochebuena

church iglesia

cider sidra

cigarette cigarrillo

city ciudad (*f*); **city hall** ayuntamiento

claim pretender; **claim luggage** reclamar el equipaje

clam almeja

class clase (*f*); **class notes** apuntes (*m*); **economy class** clase económica; **elective class** curso electivo; **first class** primera clase; **required class** curso obligatorio

classical clásico; **classical music** música clásica

classified ad anuncio clasificado

classmate compañero(-a) de clase

clean *adj* limpio; *v* fregar (ie), limpiar

cleaning limpieza; **cleaning products** productos de limpieza

cleanliness limpieza

clear claro; **clear the table** recoger la mesa; **clear up** aclarar; **clear up** (*weather*) despejarse

clerk: desk clerk recepcionista (*m/f*); **sales clerk** dependiente(-a)

clever listo (*with* ser)

click hacer clic

cliff acantilado

climate clima (*m*)

clinic clínica

clock reloj (*m*); **alarm clock** despertador (*m*)

close *adj* cercano, íntimo; *adv* cerca; *v* cerrar (ie); **be close friends** ser amigos de confianza; **close-knit** unido

clothes ropa; **clothes dryer** secadora; **clothes hanger** gancho de colgar (**A**), percha de colgar (**E**)

clothing ropa; **article of clothing** prenda de vestir; **men's clothing** ropa de caballeros; **women's clothing** ropa femenina

cloudy nublado

club palo; **golf club** palo de golf

coach *n* entrenador(-a); *v* entrenar

coast costa

coat abrigo

cocktail cóctel (*m*); **cocktail lounge** salón (*m*) de cóctel; **seafood cocktail** cóctel de mariscos; **shrimp cocktail** cóctel de camarones

cod bacalao

coffee café (*m*); **black coffee** café solo; **coffee shop** café (*m*); **coffee with warmed milk** café con leche

coin moneda

coincide coincidir

coincidentally justo

cold *adj* frío; *n* catarro, resfriado; **be cold** tener frío; **have a cold** estar resfriado; **It's cold.** Hace frío.

collaborate colaborar

college universidad; **university college** facultad

Colombian colombiano

colonial colonial

color color (*m*); **melon colored** de color melón; **solid color** de un solo color

comb peine (*m*); **comb one's hair** peinarse

combine combinar

come venir; **come in** adelante, pasar adelante; **come out** salir

comedy comedia

comet cometa

comfort comodidad (*f*)

comfortable cómodo

comic strip dibujo animado, tira cómica

comment comentar

commercial anuncio comercial

commitment compromiso

committee comité (*m*)

commotion tumulto

communicate comunicar

community comunidad (*f*)

companion compañero(-a)

company compañía; empresa; **Co.** Cía.

compare comparar

compete competir (i, i)

complain (about) quejarse (de)

complete completo; *v* completar **completely** completamente, por completo

complicated complicado; **become complicated** complicarse

composed *pp* compuesto

computer computadora **(A)**, ordenador *(m)* **(E)**; **computer disk** disco; **computer file** documento; **computer hardware** maquinaria; **computer operator** operador(-a) de computadoras; **computer programming** programación *(f)* de computadoras; **computer science** informática

concerning acerca de

concert concierto

concierge conserje *(m)*

conciliatory conciliatorio

concise conciso

conclude concluir

condiment condimento

condolence pésame *(m)*

confess confesar (ie)

confide in confiar en

confidence confianza

confirm confirmar

conflictive conflictivo

confused confundido; **be confused** confundirse

confusion confusión *(f)*

congratulate felicitar; **congratulations** felicidades *(f)*, felicitaciones *(f)*

connect conectar

conqueror conquistador *(m)*

consent consentir (ie, i)

consider considerar

consist of consistir en

constitute constituir

constitutional constitucional

construct construir

construction construcción *(f)*

consumption consumo

contact lenses lentes *(m)* de contacto

content *n* contenido; *adj* contento

continue continuar

contract contrato; **contracted** contratado

contribute contribuir

control controlar; *n* control *(m)*; **remote control** control remoto, mando a distancia **(E)**

convenient conveniente

conversation conversación *(f)*; **after-dinner conversation** sobremesa; **have after-dinner conversation** hacer la sobremesa

converse conversar

convert convertir (ie, i)

convince convencer

cook *n* cocinero(-a); *v* cocinar

coolness fresco; **It's cool.** Hace fresco.

cooperate cooperar

cooperation cooperación *(f)*

cooperative cooperador(-a)

coordination coordinación *(f)*

copper cobre *(m)*

copying machine fotocopiadora

corner esquina, rincón *(m)*

correct *v* corregir (i, i)

correspond corresponder

cosmopolitan cosmopolita

cost *n* costo; *v* costar (ue); **cost of living** costo de vida

costume disfraz *(m)*; **costume jewelry** joyas de fantasía; **costume party** fiesta de disfraces

cotton algodón *(m)*; **cotton candy** algodón de azúcar

cough *n* tos *(f)*; *v* toser; **cough syrup** jarabe *(m)* para la tos

counselor consejero(-a)

count contar (ue)

counter mostrador *(m)*

country país *(m)*; **country** *(rural area)* campo; **native country** patria

couple pareja *(f)*; **engaged couple** novios; **married couple** matrimonio

courageous valiente

course curso; plato *(food)*; **elective course** curso electivo; **main course** plato principal; **Of course!** ¡Claro! ¡Cómo no! ¡Por supuesto!; **required course** curso obligatorio; **take courses** cursar, seguir un curso, tomar un curso

court corte *(f)*; cancha; **tennis court** cancha de tenis

courteous cortés

courtesy cortesía

cousin primo(-a); **first cousin** primo(-a) hermano(-a); **second cousin** primo(-a) segundo(-a)

cover cubrir; **covered** *pp* cubierto

craftsmanship artesanía

craziness locura; **crazy** loco; **be crazy about** estar loco por

create crear

creation creación *(f)*

credit crédito; **credit card** tarjeta de crédito

crime crimen *(m)*, delito

crisis crisis *(f)*

criticize criticar

cross atravesar (ie), cruzar

crossword puzzle crucigrama *(m)*

cruise crucero

crutches muletas

cry llorar

Cuban cubano

culture cultura; **cultural center** centro cultural

cup taza

cure *n* cura; *v* curar

curl one's hair rizarse el pelo; **curlers** tenacillas de rizar; **curly** rizado

currency moneda; **exchange currency** cambiar dinero

current actual

custom costumbre *(f)*

customer cliente *(m/f)*

customs aduana; **customs agent** aduanero; **go through customs** pasar por la aduana

cut cortar; **cut oneself** cortarse; **cut the grass** cortar el césped

cute mono

cycling ciclismo

D

daily diario
damp húmedo
dance *n* baile *(m)*; *v* bailar
dancer bailarín(-ina)
dangerous peligroso
date fecha, cita; **date of birth** fecha de nacimiento; **date someone** salir con; **due date** fecha de vencimiento; **up to date** al día
daughter hija
daughter-in-law nuera
dawn amanecer *(m)*, madrugada
day día *(m)*; **day after tomorrow** pasado mañana; **day before yesterday** anteayer; **day's work** jornal *(m)*; **every day** todos los días; **every other day** cada dos días; **per day** al día; **present-day** actual
dead *pp* muerto
deal negocio; **deal with** tratarse de
dear querido
debt deuda
December diciembre *(m)*
decide decidir
decision decisión *(f)*; **make a decision** tomar una decisión
declaration declaración *(f)*
decorate adornar, decorar
decoration adorno
defeat derrotar, vencer
defend defender (ie)
definite cierto
degree título; **having a university degree** licenciado
delay *n* demora; *v* demorarse; **delayed** de retraso, retrasado
delicate delicado
delicious delicioso, rico, sabroso
delight encantar
deliver entregar, repartir
deluxe de lujo
demand exigir; **demanding** exigente
demonstrate demostrar (ue)
demonstration manifestación *(f)*
demoralized desmoralizado
dentist dentista *(m/f)*; **dentist's office** consultorio
deny negar (ie)
deodorant desodorante *(m)*
depart partir
department sección *(f)*, departamento; **department store** (grandes) almacenes *(m)*
departure salida
depend depender de
deposit depositar, ingresar
depressed deprimido
depressing deprimente
describe describir
description descripción *(f)*
desert desierto
deserve merecer
design diseño
desire *n* gana; *v* desear
desk clerk recepcionista *(m/f)*

dessert postre *(m)*
destroy destruir
detail detalle *(m)*
detain detener
detergent detergente *(m)*
deteriorate deteriorarse
develop desarrollar
development desarrollo
devote oneself to dedicarse a
dial a telephone discar
dialogue diálogo
diamond brillante *(m)*, diamante *(m)*; **diamond necklace** collar *(m)* de brillantes
die morir (ue, u)
diet dieta; **be on a diet** estar a dieta
different diferente
difficult difícil
difficulty dificultad *(f)*
diminish disminuir
dining room comedor *(m)*
dinner cena; **eat dinner** cenar; **have after-dinner conversation** hacer la sobremesa
direct *v* dirigir; *adj* directo
direction dirección *(f)*
dirty sucio
disadvantage desventaja
disappear desaparecer
disaster desastre *(m)*
discotheque discoteca
discount *n* descuento; *v* descontar (ue); **discount store** tienda de liquidaciones
discourteous descortés
discover descubrir; **discovered** *pp* descubierto
discuss discutir, tratar
discussion discusión *(f)*
disease enfermedad *(f)*
dish plato; **main dish** entrada; **dishwasher** lavaplatos
disk disco; **CD-ROM drive** lector CD-ROM; **computer disk** disco; **disk drive** lector *(m)* de discos; **hard disk** disco duro
dismiss despedir (i, i); **dismissed** despedido
disinfectant desinfectante
disorder desorden *(m)*
display *n* exhibición *(f)*; *v* exhibir
display case escaparate *(m)* **(A)**, vitrina **(E)**
displease disgustar
distinguish distinguir
distracted distraído
distraction distracción *(f)*
distribute distribuir
diverse diverso
divide compartir, dividirse
divorced divorciado
dizziness mareo; **feel dizzy** marearse
do hacer; **do something again** volver a + *inf*; **done** hecho
doctor médico(-a); **doctor's office** consultorio
doctorate doctorado
document documento; **documentary** película documental

dog perro
doll muñeca; **dollhouse** casa de muñecas
dollar dólar (m)
domestic doméstico
dominoes dominó
done pp hecho
door puerta
doorman portero
dormitory residencia estudiantil
doubt n duda; v dudar; **doubtful** dudoso
down payment pago inicial
downpour aguacero
downtown centro
draft v redactar; **foreign draft** giro al extranjero
drama drama (m)
dramatize dramatizar
drawer cajón (m)
drawing dibujo
dream n sueño; v soñar (ue)
dress vestido; **dressing** condimento; **dressy** elegante; **get dressed** vestirse (i, i); **get undressed** desvestirse (i, i)
drink n bebida, copa; v beber, tomar; **soft drink** refresco
drive conducir, manejar; **driver** conductor(-a); **driver's license** permiso de conducir
drop gota; **drop a class** dejar una clase
drown ahogarse
drugstore farmacia
drunk borracho; **get drunk** emborracharse
dry secar; **dry one's hair** secar el pelo; **dry oneself** secarse; **clothes dryer** secadora; **hair dryer** secador (m)
dry cleaner tintorería
due date fecha de vencimiento
during durante
dusk anochecer (m)
dust n polvo v sacudir
Dutch holandés(-esa)
duty free libre de derechos de aduana
duty tax derecho de aduana

E

each cada
early adelantado, temprano; **early riser** madrugador(-a)
earring arete (m)
earthquake terremoto
east este (m)
Easter Pascua
easy fácil
eat comer, tomar; **eat dinner** cenar
economics ciencias económicas
economy economía
education educación (f); **course of study** ciencias de la educación
effect efecto; **personal effects** efectos personales
efficient eficaz
effort esfuerzo; **make an effort** esforzarse (ue)
egg huevo

eight ocho; **eight hundred** ochocientos
eighteen dieciocho
eighth octavo
eighty ochenta
either ... or o ... o
elect elegir (i, i); **election** elecciones (f pl); **elective class** curso electivo; **electoral campaign** campaña electoral
electric eléctrico; **electric outlet** enchufe (m)
electrician electricista (m/f)
elegant elegante
elevator ascensor (m)
eleven once
embassy embajada
embrace abrazar
emerald esmeralda
emphasize enfatizar
employ emplear
employee empleado(-a)
employment empleo; **employment agency** agencia de empleos
empty adj vacío; v vaciar
encourage dar ánimo
encyclopedia enciclopedia
end n fin (m); v poner fin; **weekend** fin (m) de semana
energetic enérgico
engaged: become engaged to comprometerse con; **engaged couple** los novios
engagement compromiso; esponsales (m); **engagement period** noviazgo; **engagement ring** anillo de compromiso
engineer ingeniero(-a)
engineering ingeniería
English inglés (m)
enjoy disfrutar de, gozar de; **enjoy oneself** divertirse (ie, i), pasarlo bien
enjoyable gozoso
enough bastante; ¡Basta!
enrich enriquecer
enroll in inscribirse
enter entrar, ingresar
enthusiastic entusiasmado
entire entero
entity entidad (f)
entrance entrada; **entrance exam** examen (m) de ingreso
entrée entrada (E), plato principal
environment ambiente (m)
equal igual
equipment equipo
errand diligencia; **run errands** hacer diligencias
error error
escape escaparse
establish establecerse, fundar
ethnic étnico
European europeo
even aun, hasta; **even when** aun cuando; **not even** ni siquiera
evening noche (f); **in the evening** por la noche

event acontecimiento, evento
every cada, todo; **every day** todos los días; **every other day** cada dos días; **everywhere** todas partes
evident evidente
evil mal (before *ms* noun); malo (with *ser*)
evoke evocar
exact exacto; **exactly (telling time)** en punto
exam *n* examen (*m*); *v* examinar; **pass an exam** aprobar (ue); **take an exam** tomar un examen; **examination period** temporada de exámenes
example ejemplo; **for example** por ejemplo
excel sobresalir
except menos
exchange *n* intercambio; *v* intercambiar; **exchange money** cambiar dinero; **exchange student** estudiante (*m/f*) de intercambio
exclude excluir
excuse *n* excusa; *v* disculpar
execute cumplir, ejecutar
executive ejecutivo(-a)
exercise *n* ejercicio; *v* hacer ejercicios; ejercer; **aerobic exercise** ejercicio aeróbico; **warm-up exercise** ejercicio de calentamiento
exhausted exhausto
exhibit exposición (*f*); *v* exhibir
exist existir
exit salida
exotic exótico
expensive caro; **expensive store** tienda de lujo
experience *n* experiencia; *v* experimentar
explain explicar
export exportar; **export trade** comercio de exportación
express expresar
extend ampliar
extensive amplio
external externo
eye ojo; **eye shadow** sombra de ojos; **eyeglasses** anteojos, gafas, lentes

F

fabric tela; **printed fabric** estampado
fabulous fabuloso
face *n* cara; *v* dar a, enfrentarse
fact dato; **as a matter of fact** en realidad
factory fábrica
faculty profesorado
fail salir mal
faint desmayarse
fair justo
fall caer; **fall asleep** dormirse (ue); **fall in love** enamorarse de
false falso
familiar conocido
family *n* familia; *adj* familiar
famous célebre, famoso
fan aficionado(-a)
fantastic fantástico
fantasy fantasía

far *adv* lejos; **as far as** hasta; **far from** lejos de
fare pasaje (*m*) **(A)**, tarifa **(E)**
farewell despedida
fascinate fascinar
fasten abrocharse
fat *adj* gordo; **get fat** engordar
father padre (*m*)
father-in-law suegro
faucet grifo
favor favor (*m*); **do the favor of** hacer el favor de
favorite favorito
fax machine máquina de fax
fear temer; **fearful** temeroso
feature seña
February febrero
feed oneself alimentarse
feel sentirse (ie, i); **feel at ease** sentirse a gusto; **feel dizzy** marearse; **feel like (doing something)** tener ganas de + *inf;* **feel pain** (*emotional or physical*) doler (ue)
Ferris wheel gran rueda
fertile fértil
festival feria
fever fiebre (*f*)
few poco; **a few** algún, alguna(-s), alguno(-s), unas, unos
fiancé(e) novio(-a)
field campo; **field of study** campo de estudio; **playing field** cancha
fifteen quince
fifth quinto
fifty cincuenta
fight pelear
figure figura
file *n* documento; *v* archivar; **file cabinet** archivo; **file folder** carpeta
fill cumplir; llenar; ejecutar; **fill out** llenar
film película
final final
finally finalmente, por fin, por último, posteriormente
finance finanzas; **financial** financiero; **financial advice** consejo financiero; **financier** financista (*m/f*)
find encontrar (ue); **find out about** enterarse de
fine *adj* fino; **fine arts** bellas artes
finger dedo
fingernail uña
finish acabar, terminar
fire fuego, incendio; **fire fighter** bombero(-a); **fire someone** despedir (i, i); **fire station** estación (*f*) de bomberos
fireworks fuegos artificiales
first primer, primero; **first class** de lujo; **first name** nombre (*m*); **first course** entrada **(A)**
fish *n* pescado (*food*), pez (*m*); *v* pescar; **fishing** pesca; **fishing rod** caña de pescar
fit caber, quedar
five cinco; **five hundred** quinientos
fixed fijo

flashy vistoso

flavor sabor (*m*)

flexible flexible

flight vuelo;   **flight attendant** aeromozo(-a) **(A)**, azafata **(E)**, camarero(-a)

flirt *n* coqueta, *v* coquetear

flirtatious coqueta

flood inundación (*f*)

floor piso;   **floor show** espectáculo

flour harina

flower flor (*f*);   **flowered** de flores;   **throw flowers and rice** echarles flores y arroz

flu gripe (*f*)

fly volar (ue)

fog neblina

folkloric folklórico

follow seguir (i, i);   **follow someone in a post** suceder

following siguiente, a continuación

fond of tener cariño a

food alimento, comida, comestibles;   **fast food** comida rápida;   **foodstuffs** comestibles;   **unprepared food** comestibles

foot pie (*m*);   **on foot** a pie

for (by, in, through) por;   **for** (in order to) para;   **for example** por ejemplo

force *n* fuerza;   *v* forzar (ue)

forecast pronóstico

foreign extranjero;   **foreign language** idioma (*m*) extranjero

foreigner extranjero(-a)

forest bosque (*m*)

forget olvidar

fork tenedor (*m*)

form forma, formulario;   **registration form** tarjeta de recepción

former aquél, aquélla, aquéllas, aquéllos;   antiguo

forty cuarenta

forward adelante

found *v* fundar

fountain fuente (*f*)

four cuatro;   **four hundred** cuatrocientos

fourteen catorce

fourth cuarto

fracture fracturarse

frankly francamente

freckle peca

free gratis, libre;   **free time** ratos libres

freedom libertad (*f*)

French francés (*m*)

frequent asiduo;   **frequency** frecuencia;   **frequently** frecuentemente

Friday viernes (*m*)

fried *pp* frito

friend amigo(-a);   **be a close friend** ser amigo de confianza

friendly amigable

fringe benefit beneficio social

from de, desde;   **from dawn to dusk** del amanecer al anochecer;   **from time to time** de vez en cuando

front: in front of delante de, enfrente de

fruit fruta;   **fruit in season** fruta del tiempo

fulfill cumplir

full completo, lleno;   **full time** tiempo completo

fun *adj* divertido;   **have fun** divertirse (ie, i)

function funcionar

funny cómico; chistoso, gracioso

fur piel (*f*)

furious furioso

furnish amoblar, amueblar

furniture muebles (*m*);   **piece of furniture** mueble (*m*)

furthermore además

G

gain alcanzar;   **gain weight** engordar

Galician gallego

gallery galería

game juego, partido;   **game of chance** juego de suerte;   **game show** programa (*m*) de concursos

garbage basura;   **take out garbage** sacar la basura

garage taller (*m*)

garnet granate (*m*)

gas station estación (*f*) de servicio;   gasolinera

gasoline gasolina

gate puerta

generally generalmente, por lo general

gentleman caballero; señor

geographical geográfico

geography geografía

German alemán

get conseguir (i, i), sacar;   **get along with** llevarse bien, caerle bien;   **get into shape** ponerse en forma;   **get off** bajar, desembarcar;   **get together** reunirse;   **get up** levantarse;   **get up early** madrugar

gift regalo;   **gift shop** tienda de regalos;   **wedding gift** regalo de bodas

ghost fantasma

girl chica, muchacha

girlfriend novia

give dar;   **give a present** regalar;   **give a shot** poner una inyección;   **give advice** aconsejar, dar consejos;   **give birth** dar a luz;   **give up** darse por vencido, rendirse (i, i)

glacier glaciar (*m*)

glass vaso;   (*material*) vidrio

glasses anteojos, gafas;   **sunglasses** gafas de sol

gloves guantes

go ir;   **go away** irse;   **go out with** salir con;   **go shopping** ir de compras;   **go straight** seguir derecho;   **go up** subir

goal meta

goblet copa

godchild ahijado(-a)

godfather padrino

godmother madrina

godparents padrinos

gold oro;   **gold chain** cadena de oro

golf golf (*m*);   **golf club** palo de golf;   **golf course** campo de golf

good   bueno;   **Good afternoon.** Buenas tardes;
  Good evening. Buenas noches;   **Good luck.**
  Buena suerte;   **Good morning.** Buenos días;
  the good thing lo bueno
good-bye   adiós, chau, hasta luego, hasta pronto;
  say good-bye despedirse (i, i)
gossip   *n* chisme *(m)*;   *v* chismear
government   gobierno
grade   nota;   **get grades** sacar notas
graduate   *n* graduado;   *v* graduarse, licenciarse;
  postgraduate posgraduado
graduation   graduación *(f)*
grandchild   nieto(-a)
grandfather   abuelo
grandmother   abuela
grandparents   abuelos
grape   uva
grass   césped *(m)*;   **grassy plain** pampa
gray   gris;   **gray hair** *adj* canoso
great   gran *(before s n)*, grande;   **greater part** la
  mayor parte
great-grandchild   bisnieto;   **great-great-
  grandchild** tataranieto
great-grandfather   bisabuelo;   **great-great-
  grandfather** tatarabuelo
great-grandmother   bisabuelo;   **great-great-
  grandmother** tatarabuela
great-grandparents   bisabuelos;   **great-great-
  grandparents** tatarabuelos
green   verde
greet   saludar
greeting   saludo
grocery store   tienda de comestibles
groom   novio
group   grupo;   **in a group** en grupo;   **musical
  group** conjunto
grow   crecer;   **grow plants** cultivar
guess   adivinar
guest   huésped *(m/f)*;   invitado(-a);   **stay as a guest**
  hospedarse
guide   guía *(m/f)*;   **TV guide** guía *(f)* de televisión
guilty   culpable
guitar   guitarra
gymnasium   gimnasio
gymnastics   gimnasia;   **do gymnastics** practicar la
  gimnasia
gypsy   gitano(-a)

H
hatchet   hacha
hair   pelo;   **gray hair** canoso   **hair dryer** secador
  (m);   **hair spray** laca;   **red-haired** pelirrojo
half   mitad *(f)*;   **half hour** media hora;   **half-time**
  medio tiempo
ham   jamón *(m)*
hand   mano *(f)*;   **hand in** entregar;   **on the other
  hand** en cambio, por otro lado
handle   tratar de
handsome   guapo
hang   colgar (ue);   **hang up** colgar (ue);   **to be
  hanging** estar pendiente

hanger   gancho de colgar **(A)**, percha de colgar **(E)**
happen   pasar, suceder
happiness   alegría
happy   alegre, contento, feliz;   **be happy** alegrarse
hard   duro;   **hard sausage** chorizo
hard-working   trabajador
hardly   apenas
hardware   hardware *(m)*
harm   hacer daño
hat   sombrero
have   tener;   haber *(auxiliary verb)*;   **have a good
  time** divertirse, pasarlo bien;   **have a tendency to**
  tender (ie) a + *inf*;   **have an opinion** opinar;
  have just acabar de + *inf*;   **have to** (do
  something) deber, tener que + *inf*
he   *subj pron* él
head   cabeza
headline   titular *(m)*
healer   curandero(-a)
health   salud *(f)*;   **healthy** saludable
hear   oír
heart   corazón *(m)*
heat   *n* calefacción *(f)*;   calor *(m)*;   *v* calentar (ie)
heavy   pesado;   **heavy sleeper** dormilón(-ona)
heel   tacón *(m)*;   **high heels** zapatos de tacón;
  low-heel shoes zapatos bajos
height   estatura;   **at the height of** en pleno apogeo;
  of average height de talla media
helmet   casco
help   *n* ayuda;   *v* ayudar
her   *dir obj pron* la;   *indir obj pron* (to, for) le;   *poss
  adj* su, suyo;   *prep pron* ella
here   acá, aquí
hers   *poss pron* suyo
herself   *refl pron* se
Hi.   Hola.
high   alto
high school   colegio, escuela secundaria, liceo,
  instituto;   **high-school diploma** bachillerato
highway   autopista, carretera;   **information
  superhighway** autopista de la información
hijack   secuestrar
hill   colina
him   *dir obj pron* lo;   *indir obj pron* (to, for) le;   *prep
  pron* él
himself   *refl pron* se
hip   cadera
hire   contratar, emplear
his   *poss adj* su;   *poss adj and pron* suyo
hiss   chiflar
historic   histórico;   **historic government-run inn**
  parador *(m)*
history   historia
hit   golpear;   **hit oneself** golpearse
hobby   diversión *(f)*
hockey   hockey *(m)*;   **hockey puck** disco;   **hockey
  stick** palo de hockey
holiday   día *(m)* feriado, feria
home   a casa, casa, residencia;   **at home** en casa;
  Home Page página base
homework   tarea;   **do homework** hacer la tarea

honeymoon luna de miel
honorable honrado
hope *n* esperanza; *v* esperar; **I hope that** ojalá (que)
hors d'œuvre entremés (*m*)
horse caballo; **ride horseback** montar a caballo
hose manguera
hospital hospital (*m*); **private hospital** clínica
host (hostess) anfitrión(-ona); **show host** presentador(-a)
hostel albergue (*m*)
hot caliente; **be hot** tener calor; **It's hot.** Hace calor.; **hot chocolate** chocolate (*m*)
hotel hotel (*m*); **stay in a hotel** alojarse
hour hora; **half hour** media hora; **rush hour** horas punta
house casa; **dollhouse** casa de muñecas ; **house of horrors** casa de fantasmas; **house of mirrors** casa de espejos
housewife ama de casa
housework quehaceres (*m*) domésticos
how como, ¿cómo?; **How . . .!** ¡Qué…! **How are things?** ¿Qué hay?, ¿Qué tal?; **how many?** ¿cuántos?; **how much?** ¿cuánto?; **know how to** saber + *inf;* **somehow** de algún modo
however sin embargo
hug *n* abrazo; *v* abrazar
humid húmedo
humidity humedad (*f*)
hundred cien, ciento
hunger hambre (*f*); **be hungry** tener hambre; **be starving** morirse de hambre
hurry apurarse; **in a hurry** apurado
hunt cazar
hurt herir (ie, i), lastimar; **get hurt** herirse (ie, i), lastimarse
husband esposo, marido
hustle-bustle algarabía

I

I yo
I.D. card tarjeta de identidad
ice hielo; **ice cream** helado; **ice skates** patines (*m*) de hielo
idea idea, ocurrencia; **What a great idea!** ¡Qué ocurrencia!
ideal ideal
identify identificar
identity identidad (*f*)
if si
illness enfermedad (*f*)
illustrate ilustrar
imagination imaginación (*f*)
imagine imaginarse
immediate inmediato
impatient impaciente
impede impedir (i, i)
implore rogar (ue)
impolite descortés
import importar; **import trade** comercio de importación
important importante; **be important** importar

impossible imposible
impression impresión (*f*)
improve mejorar, mejorarse
in dentro de, en; **in a group** en grupo; **in advance** con anticipación; **in back of** detrás de; **in case that** en caso que; **in charge of** encargado de; **in front of** delante de, enfrente de; **in pairs** en parejas; **in search of** en busca de; **in spite of** a pesar de que; **in the beginning** al principio; **in the name of** en nombre de; **in this way** así; **inside of** dentro de
include incluir
income ingreso, renta
incredible de película, increíble
independence independencia
Indian indio(-a)
indicate indicar, señalar
indifference indiferencia
indifferent indiferente
indigenous indígena
individual individuo
industry industria
inexpensive barato, económico
infer inferir (ie, i)
inferior inferior
inflation inflación (*f*)
influence *n* influencia; *v* influir
inform avisar, informar
information información (*f*); **a piece of information** dato; **information superhighway** autopista de información; **information technology** informática
informercial telepromoción (*f*)
inhabitant habitante (*m/f*)
initial inicial
initiative iniciativa
injection inyección (*f*)
injure hacer daño, lastimar
injury herida
injustice injusticia
in-laws parientes (*m*) políticos
inn parador
innocence inocencia
inside adentro; **inside of** dentro de
insist on insistir en
insomnia insomnio
install instalar
installment plazo
instance vez (*f*)
instead of en vez de
instruct instruir
insure asegurar
interaction interacción (*f*)
interest *n* interés (*m*); *v* interesar; **interest rate** tasa de interés
interesting interesante; **be interesting** interesar
internal interno
international internacional, multinacional
Internet Internet (*used without an article*), red (*f*); **person using Internet** cibernauta (*m/f*); **surf the Internet** navegar la red

interrupt interrumpir
intersection bocacalle (f), cruce (m)
interview n entrevista;   v entrevistar
intimate íntimo
intolerable insoportable
introduce presentar
inventory inventario
invest invertir (ie, i)
invitation invitación (f)
invite invitar
Irish irlandés (m)
iron n plancha;   v planchar;   **ironing board** tabla
   de planchar
island isla
isolated aislado
isolation aislamiento
it *dir obj pron* la, lo;   *indir obj pron (to, for)* le;   *prep
   pron* él, ella
Italian italiano
item artículo
its *poss adj* su;   *poss adj and poss pron* suyo
itself *refl pron* se

J
jacket chaqueta
jail cárcel (f)
January enero
Japanese japonés (m)
jazz música jazz
jealousy celos (m);   **be jealous** tener celos
jewel joya;   **costume jewelry** joyas de fantasía;
   jewelry joyas;   **jewelry shop** joyería
job empleo, profesión, puesto, trabajo;   **job
   application** solicitud (f)
jog hacer jogging;   **jogging suit** calentador (m) **(A)**,
   chandal (m) **(E)**
joint bank account cuenta mancomunada
joke n chiste (m);   v bromear
journalism periodismo
journalist periodista (m/f)
judge n juez(-a);   v juzgar
juice jugo **(A)**, zumo **(E)**
July julio
jump saltar
June junio
jungle selva
just justo
justify justificar

K
keep conservar, guardar;   **keep for oneself**
   quedarse con
key llave (f), tecla
keyboard teclado
kick n patada;   v dar una patada, patear
kid chamaco, chaval(-a), chico
kidnap secuestrar
kind *adj* amable, gentil;   n tipo;   **be so kind as to
   (do something)** tener la bondad de + *inf*
kindness amabilidad (f), gentileza
king rey (m);   **king and queen** reyes

kiss besar
kitchen cocina
knee rodilla
knife cuchillo
knock tocar (la puerta)
know conocer, saber;   **know how** saber + *inf;*
   well-known conocido
knowledge conocimiento

L
label etiqueta
laboratory laboratorio;   **language lab** laboratorio
   de lenguas
lace encaje (m)
lack n falta;   v carecer, faltar
lady señora;   **lady** (*title of respect*) doña;   **young
   lady, unmarried lady** señorita
lake lago
lamb cordero
lamp lámpara
land n tierra;   v aterrizar;   **landing** aterrizaje (m)
language lengua, idioma (m);   **specialized
   language** lenguaje (m)
large grande
last *adj* pasado, último;   v durar;   **last name**
   apellido;   **last night** anoche;   **lastly** por último
late tarde;   **arrive late** llegar tarde;   **be late**
   atrasarse
later después, más tarde, luego
latter éste, ésta, éstos, éstas
laugh reír (i, i)
laughter risa
launch lancha
laundry room lavandería
laundry service servicio de lavandería
law ley (f);   **law** (*course of study*) derecho
lawn césped (m);   **lawn rake** rastrillo
lawnmower cortacésped (m);   **power lawnmower**
   cortacésped de motor ;   **riding lawnmower** carro
   cortacésped
lawyer abogado(-a)
lax flojo
lazy perezoso
lead plomo
learn aprender
least menos;   **at least** por lo menos
leather cuero
leave irse; partir, salir;   **leave something** dejar
lecture conferencia;   **give a lecture** dar una
   conferencia, dictar una conferencia
left izquierda;   **be left** quedar;   **to (on) the left** a
   la izquierda
leg pierna
legal legal
leisure-time activity pasatiempo
lemon limón (m)
lemonade limonada
lend prestar
less menos
lesson lección (f)
let dejar

letter carta; **letter of recommendation** carta de recomendación
lettuce lechuga
liberal arts filosofía y letras
library biblioteca
license: driver's permiso de conducir
lie *n* mentira; *v* mentir (ie, i)
life vida; **lead a happy life** llevar una vida feliz
lift alzar, levantar; **lift weights** levantar pesas
light *adj* liviano; *n* luz (*f*); *v* encender (ie); **light in color** claro; **light in consistency** suelto; **light in weight** ligero; **light meal** comida ligera; **traffic light** semáforo
like *adv* como; *v* gustar
line cola, línea; **airline** línea aérea; **stand in line** hacer cola
linen lino
linguistics lingüística s
link enlace (*m*)
lip labio
lipstick lápiz (*m*) de labios
liquid líquido
liquor licor (*m*)
list lista
listen to escuchar; oír
listener oyente (*m/f*)
literacy alfabetización (*f*)
literary work obra
little pequeño, poco; **a little bit of** un poco de
live vivir
lively vivo (with *ser*)
living room sala
loan préstamo
lobby salón (*m*) de entrada, vestíbulo
lobster langosta
local local
locate ubicar; **be located** quedar
logical lógico
loin lomo
long largo
longing gana
look after cuidar; **look at** mirar; **look for** buscar; **look like** parecerse a
loose flojo; **loose change** sencillo, suelto
lose perder (ie)
lost perdido; **get lost** perderse (ie)
lot mucho
lotion loción (*f*); **sunscreen lotion** loción solar
lottery lotería
loudspeaker altavoz (*m*)
love *n* amor (*m*); *v* amar, encantar, querer; **fall in love with** enamorarse de
lovely precioso
lower bajar, rebajar
luck suerte (*f*); **be lucky** tener suerte; **good (bad) luck** buena (mala) suerte
luggage equipaje (*m*); **carry-on luggage** equipaje de mano; **luggage claim area** sala de reclamación de equipaje; **luggage claim check** talón (*m*); **luggage tag** etiqueta; **bring down the luggage** bajar el equipaje; **bring up the luggage** subir el equipaje; **check luggage** facturar el equipaje; **claim luggage** reclamar el equipaje
lunch almuerzo; **have lunch** almorzar (ue)
luxurious de lujo
luxury lujo

M

machine máquina
machinery maquinaria; **machinery part** recambio
made *pp* hecho
magazine revista
maid criada; **maid of honor** madrina
mail *n* correo, correspondencia; *v* enviar, mandar; **e-mail** correo electrónico; **mail a letter** echar una carta
main course plato principal
main dish entrada
main square plaza mayor
maintain mantener
major *n* especialización; *v* especializarse
make hacer; **make a reservation** hacer una reservación; **make an attempt** intentar, tratar de; **make an effort** esforzarse (ue); **make the bed** hacer la cama
makeup maquillaje; **put on makeup** maquillarse
mall centro comercial
man hombre (*m*); **businessman** hombre de negocios; **best man** padrino
management administración (*f*); **business and management** administración de empresas
manager gerente (*m/f*); **sales manager** jefe(-a) de ventas
manner manera, modo; **bad mannered** maleducado
manufacturing fabricación (*f*)
many mucho; **how many?** ¿cuánto?; **so many, as many** tantos(-as)
map mapa (*m*), plano
March marzo
marine marítimo
marital status estado civil
maritime marítimo
market mercado; **stock market** bolsa (de acciones)
marketing mercadeo
marriage proposal petición (*f*) de mano
married casado; **get married** casarse; **married couple** matrimonio
marry casarse con
marvelous maravilloso
mascara rimel (*m*)
mass misa
master's degree maestría
match *n* partido; *v* combinar, hacer juego con
material tela; **raw material** materia prima; **subject material** materia
maternal maternal
mathematics matemáticas
mattress: air colchón (*m*) neumático

mature maduro
May mayo
Mayan maya
maybe acaso, quizás, tal vez
mayor alcalde (*m*)
me *dir obj pron* me; *indir obj pron* (*to, for*) me; *prep pron* mí
meal comida; **complete meal** comida completa ; **Enjoy your meal.** Buen provecho; **light meal** comida ligera; **main meal** comida; **native regional meal** comida criolla; **typical meal** comida típica
mean *v* querer decir
meaning significado
measure medir (i, i)
meat carne (*f*)
meatball albóndiga
medicine remedio; **medicine** (*course of study*) medicina
meet conocer, encontrar (ue); **meet accidentally** encontrarse con
meeting reunión (*f*)
melting pot crisol
member miembro
memorize aprender de memoria
memory memoria
mention mencionar
menu menú (*m*); **special menu of the day** menú del día; **tourist menu** menú turístico
merchandise mercancía
merit merecer
message encargo, mensaje (*m*), recado
messenger mensajero(-a)
metal metal (*m*)
Mexican mexicano
Mexican-American chicano
microchip chip (*m*)
microwave oven microondas (*m*)
middle medio
midnight medianoche (*f*)
milk leche (*f*); milk shake batido
million millón
mine *poss pron* mío
mineral mineral; **mineral water** agua mineral
minimal *adj* mínimo
minimum *n* mínimo
mining *adj* minero
minute minuto
miracle milagro
mirror espejo; **house of mirrors** casa de espejos
mischievous travieso
miss faltar; **miss someone** echar de menos; **miss someone, something, or someplace** extrañar; **miss something** faltar a, perder
Miss señorita, *abb* Srta.
mistake error (*m*)
mistaken equivocado; **be mistaken** equivocarse
mixed mixto
moderate moderado, templado
modern moderno

monarchy monarquía
Monday lunes (*m*)
money dinero; **collect money** cobrar; **money order** giro postal; **money returned as change** vuelto; **save money** ahorrar; **spend money** gastar; **withdraw money** retirar dinero
monitor monitor (*m*)
monotonous monótono
month mes (*m*)
monthly mensual; **monthly payment** pago mensual
mop *n* fregona, trapeador; *v* pasarle la fregona al suelo, trapear el suelo
more más; **more or less** más o menos
morning mañana; **A.M.** de la mañana; **in the morning** por la mañana
mortgage hipoteca
most la mayor parte
motel motel (*m*)
mother madre (*f*); **mother-in-law** suegra; **stepmother** madrastra
motorboat lancha
motorcycle moto (*f*), motocicleta
mountain montaña; **mountain range** cordillera, sierra
mountainous montañoso
mouse ratón (*m*)
moustache bigote (*m*)
mouth boca
move mover (ue), mudarse (change residence)
movement movimiento
movie película; **action movie** película de acción; **documentary** película documental; **horror movie** película de terror; **movie theater** cine (*m*); **western** película de vaqueros
Mr. señor; *abb* Sr.
Mrs. señora; *abb* Sra.
much mucho; **as much, so much** tanto(-a); **how much?** ¿cuánto?; **not much** poco; **too much** demasiado
multimedia *adj* multimedia (*m/f*)
murder *n* asesinato; *v* asesinar
murderer asesino
muscular ache dolor (*m*) muscular
museum museo
music música
musical musical; **musical group** conjunto
musician músico
mussel mejillón
must deber, hay que
my *poss adj* mi, mío
myself *refl pron* me
mystery policíaco

N

nail-polish remover acetona
name *n* nombre (*m*); *v* nombrar; **first name** nombre (*m*); **last name** apellido
nap siesta; **take a nap** echar una siesta
napkin servilleta

narrate   narrar
narration   narración *(f)*
narrow   angosto, estrecho
national   nacional
nationality   nacionalidad *(f)*
natural science   ciencias exactas
naughty   travieso
near   *prep* acerca de, cerca de;   *adj* cercano
necessary   necesario, preciso;   **it is necessary** hay que + *inf*
neck   cuello
necklace   collar *(m)*
need   faltar, necesitar;   **be in need of** carecer de
neighbor   vecino(-a)
neighborhood   barrio
neither   tampoco;   **neither … nor** ni … ni
nephew   sobrino
nervous   nervioso
net   red *(f)*
network   cadena; red *(f)*
never   jamás, nunca
new   nuevo;   **New Year's Eve** Nochevieja;   **What's new?** ¿Qué hay de nuevo?
newlyweds   recién casados
news   noticias;   **news item** noticia;   **news program** noticiero
newspaper   periódico
newsstand   quiosco
next   próximo;   **next to** al lado de, cerca de
nice   amable, bonito, gentil, lindo, simpático
niece   sobrina
night   noche *(f)*;   **at night** por la noche;   **last night** anoche;   **P.M.** de la noche;   **tonight** esta noche
nightclub   club *(m)* nocturno
nightgown   camisa de noche
nighttime   nocturno
nine   nueve;   **nine hundred** novecientos
nineteen   diecinueve
ninety   noventa
ninth   noveno
no   no
no one   nadie, ninguno, ningún, ninguna
no way   de ninguna manera, de ningún modo, ¡qué va!
nobody   nadie
nocturnal   *adj* nocturno
noise   ruido
noisy   ruidoso
none   ninguno, ningún, ninguna
noodle   fideo
noon   mediodía *(m)*
nor   ni
north   norte *(m)*
northeast   noreste *(m)*
northwest   noroeste *(m)*
nose   nariz;   **blow one's nose** sonarse (ue) la nariz
nostalgia   nostalgia
not   no;   **not any more** ya no;   **not … either** tampoco;   **not even** ni siquiera;   **not much** poco;   **not yet** todavía no

note   apunte *(m)*; nota;   **take notes** tomar apuntes
notebook   cuaderno
nothing   nada
notice   *n* aviso;   *v* fijarse en
nourishment   alimento
novel   novela
novelty   novedad *(f)*
November   noviembre *(m)*
now   ahora
nowadays   actualmente, hoy (en) día
nuisance   molestia
number   número
numerous   numeroso
nurse   enfermero(-a)
nut   nuez *(f)*

O

obey   obedecer
object   objeto
obligation   obligación *(f)*
obligatory   obligatorio
oblige   obligar
observe   observar
obstruct   impedir (i, i)
obtain   alcanzar, conseguir (i, i), lograr, obtener
occasion   ocasión *(f)*, vez *(f)*
occupation   ocupación *(f)*
occupy   ocupar
occur   ocurrir
occurrence   ocurrencia
ocean   océano
October   octubre *(m)*
octopus   pulpo
of   de;   **of average height** de talla media;   **of course** claro, cómo no, por supuesto;   **of good quality** fino
offend   lastimar, ofender
offense   delito
offer   *n* oferta;   *v* ofrecer
office   consultorio, oficina;   **administrative office** oficina administrativa;   **business office** oficina comercial;   **office worker** oficinista *(m/f)*
official   *n* funcionario
often   a menudo, muchas veces, seguido
Oh!   ¡Uy!
oil   aceite *(m)*, petróleo
old   viejo;   **to be … years old** tener … años
older   mayor
olive   aceituna
on   en;   **on board** a bordo;   **on sale** en rebaja, estar en liquidación;   **on the dot** en punto;   **on the other hand** en cambio, por otro lado;   **on time** a tiempo;   **on top of** encima de, sobre
once   una vez
one   un(-a), uno
onion   cebolla
only   *adj* único;   *adv* sólo
opal   ópalo
open   *v* abrir;   *pp* abierto
opera   ópera

operate funcionar; **operate on someone** operarle
a uno
or o, u (replaces **o** in words beginning with **o-** or **ho-**)
orange *adj* anaranjado; *n* naranja
orchestra orquesta
orchid orquídea
order *n* orden (*command*) (*f*); orden (*chronological*)
(*m*); pedido; *v* ordenar, pedir (i, i)
organize organizar
other otro
our *poss adj* nuestro
ours *poss pron* nuestro
ourselves *refl pron* nos
out loud en voz alta
out of the ordinary de película
outdoor café café (*m*) al aire libre
outing excursión (*f*), paseo
outside afuera; **outside of** fuera de
outskirts afueras (*f pl*)
outstanding sobresaliente
over encima de; sobre
overcoat sobretodo
overtime horas extra
own poseer
owner dueño(-a)

P
P.M. de la noche, de la tarde
pack hacer las maletas
package paquete (*m*)
page página; **Home Page** página base
pain dolor (*m*); **feel pain** doler (ue)
painting cuadro, pintura
pair par (*m*); **in pairs** en parejas
pajamas pijama (*m s*)
palace palacio
pants pantalones (*m pl*)
paper papel (*m*); sheet of paper hoja de papel;
toilet paper papel (*m*) higiénico
parade *n* desfile (*m*)
paragraph párrafo
paraphrase parafrasear
parents padres (*m pl*)
park *n* parque (*m*); *v* aparcar; **amusement park**
parque de atracciones
parking estacionamiento
part parte (*f*); **play the part** hacer el papel
part-time medio tiempo
participate participar; **participate in sports**
practicar los deportes
particular particular
pass (an exam) aprobar (ue)
passenger pasajero(-a)
passport pasaporte (*m*)
past pasado
pastime pasatiempo
pastry pastel (*m*)
paternal paterno
patience paciencia
patient *adj and n* paciente (*m/f*)

patio patio
patron saint santo patrón (*m*)
patriotic patriótico
pay abonar, pagar; **pay attention** prestar atención;
pay attention to fijarse en; **pay in cash** pagar al
contado; **pay in installments** abonar, pagar a
plazos
payment pago; **balance of payments** balanza de
pagos; **down payment** pago inicial; **monthly
payment** pago mensual
peace paz (*f*)
peak apogeo
pearl perla
pedestrian peatón(-ona)
pen bolígrafo
pencil lápiz (*m*); **pencil sharpener** sacapuntas (*m*)
penicillin penicilina
peninsula península
people gente (*f*)
pepper chile (*m*), pimienta; **pepper shaker**
pimentero; **stuffed peppers** chiles rellenos
percent por ciento
perfume: put on perfume perfumarse
perhaps acaso, quizás, tal vez
period of time temporada, tiempo
permission permiso
permit permitir
persecution persecución (*f*)
person persona
personal personal; **personal effects** efectos
personales
personality personalidad (*f*)
personnel personal (*m*)
pharmacist farmacéutico(-a)
pharmacy farmacia
photocopy *n* fotocopia; *v* fotocopiar; **copy
machine** (foto)copiadora
photograph fotografía; foto (*f*); **take photos** sacar
fotos
physical físico
physics física
pick up recoger
picnic picnic (*m*); **go on a picnic** hacer un picnic
piece pedazo, pieza
pig cerdo; **roast suckling pig** lechón (*m*) asado
pill píldora
pillow almohada
pinch apretar (ie)
pineapple piña
pink rosado
pity lástima; **That's a pity!** ¡Qué lástima!
place *n* local (*m*), lugar (*m*), sitio; *v* colocar, meter,
poner, situar; **placed** *pp* puesto
place setting cubierto
plaid a cuadros
plain *adj* sencillo; *n* llano, pampa
plan *n* plan, proyecto; *v* pensar + *inf*, planificar,
planear
planning planificación (*f*)
plant plantar

plate plato

plateau altiplano

play a musical instrument tocar; **play a sport** jugar (ue); **play cops and robbers** jugar a ladrones y policías; **play hide and seek** jugar al escondite; **play house** jugar a la casita, jugar a la mamá; **play the part** hacer el papel; **playing area** cancha; **playing cards** cartas (A), naipes (m)

pleasant agradable

please por favor; v complacer

pleasure agrado, gusto, placer (m); **take pleasure** complacerse

plumber plomero(-a)

pneumonia pulmonía

point punto

police officer policía (m/f); **police station** cuartel (m) de policía, comisaría; **police woman** mujer (f) policía

polite cortés

politeness cortesía

political science ciencias políticas pl

politician político(-a)

politics política s

polka dot de lunares

pollution contaminación (f); **air pollution** contaminación (f) del aire

pool piscina

poor pobre

popcorn palomitas

population población (f)

pork carne (f) de cerdo

porter maletero

portrait retrato

position puesto

possess poseer

possible posible

post office correo, oficina de correos

postcard tarjeta postal

poster cartel (m)

postgraduate posgraduado

poverty pobreza

power poder (m)

practice practicar

pray rezar

precious precioso; **precious stone** piedra preciosa

predict predecir

prefer preferir (ie, i)

preferable preferible

preference preferencia

pregnant embarazada

preoccupied preocupado

preparation preparativo

prepare preparar; **prepare oneself** prepararse

prescribe recetar

prescription receta

present adj presente; n regalo; v presentar, tratar; **present-day** actual; **at the present time** actualmente, hoy (en) día

presentation presentación (f)

preserve conservar

president presidente (m/f)

presidential presidencial

pretend fingir, pretender

pretext pretexto

pretty bonito, hermoso, lindo

previous previo

price precio

priest cura (m), padre (m)

printed (fabric) estampado

printer impresora

private hospital clínica

prize premio

problem problema (m); **No problem!** ¡Ningún problema!

produce producir

product producto

profession profesión (f)

professor catedrático(-a); profesor(-a)

program programa (m)

programmer programador(-a)

progress progreso

prohibit prohibir

project proyecto

promise prometer

promotion ascenso

property propiedad (f)

propose proponer

protect proteger

protest protestar

proud orgulloso

prove probar (ue)

provided that con tal que

psychological sicológico

psychologist sicólogo(-a)

psychology sicología

public público; **public relations** relaciones (f) públicas

puck disco

Puerto Rican puertorriqueño(-a)

purchase n compra; v hacer compras

purple morado

purse bolsa (E), cartera (A)

pursue perseguir (i, i), seguir (i, i)

put poner; **put a cast on** enyesar; **put away** guardar, recoger; **put on** ponerse; **put on makeup** maquillarse; **put on perfume** perfumarse

Q

qualification calificación (f)

quality calidad (f), cualidad (f); **of good quality** fino

quantity cantidad (f)

quarrel reñir (i, i)

quarter cuarto, trimestre (m); **quarters** local (m)

queen reina

question n pregunta; v hacer preguntas, preguntar

quiet callado; **be quiet** callarse

quiz prueba

R

race carrera, raza
racquet raqueta
radio (sound from) radio (*f*); (*set*) radio (*m*)
rag trapo
rain *n* lluvia; *v* llover (ue)
raincoat impermeable (*m*)
raise *n* aumento; *v* alzar, levantar; **raise animals** criar
rapid rápido
rate tasa; **at any rate** de todas maneras, de todos modos; **interest rate** tasa de interés; **rate of exchange** tasa de cambio
rather bastante
raw materials materias primas
reach *n* alcance (*m*); **be within reach** estar al alcance
react reaccionar
reaction reacción (*f*)
read leer
reader lector(-a)
reading lectura
ready listo (with *estar*); **get ready** arreglarse
real real, verdadero
reality realidad (*f*); **virtual reality** realidad virtual
realize darse cuenta
reason razón (*f*); **for that reason** por eso
receipt factura
receive recibir; **receive a degree** licenciarse
recently recién, recientemente
reception recepción (*f*); **wedding reception** cena
receptionist recepcionista (*m/f*)
recognize conocer, reconocer
recommend recomendar (ie)
recommendation recomendación (*f*)
record disco; **record player** tocadiscos (*m*)
recount *n* recuento; *v* recontar
recreation diversión (*f*)
red rojo; **red-haired** pelirrojo; **red wine** vino tinto; **reddish** rojizo
reduce rebajar
reduction in price rebaja
refer referirse (ie, i)
referee árbitro(-a)
reform reforma; **tax reform** reforma fiscal
region región (*f*)
register *v* matricularse
registration inscripción (*f*); **registration desk** recepción (*f*); **registration form** tarjeta de recepción
regret sentir (ie, i)
regulation reglamento
reimburse reintegrar
relation relación (*f*), trato; **public relations** relaciones públicas
relationship relación (*f*)
relative pariente (*m/f*)
relax descansar; **relaxed** *pp* relajado
relief alivio
religious religioso

remain quedar; **be remaining** quedarle a uno(-a)
remedy remedio
remember acordarse (ue) de, recordar (ue)
rent *n* alquiler (*m*); *v* alquilar
repair *n* arreglo; *v* arreglar, reparar
repeat repetir (i, i)
repent arrepentirse (ie, i)
report *n* informe, parte (*m*); *v* reportar
reporter reportero(-a)
representative diputado(-a), representante (*m/f*); **sales representative** representante de ventas
republic república
request pedir (i, i)
require requerir (ie, i)
requirement requisito
rescue rescatar; **rescue someone or something** salvar
research investigación (*f*)
reservation reserva (**E**), reservación (*f*) (**A**)
reserve reservar
residence domicilio; lugar (*m*) de residencia
resolve resolver (ue); **resolved** *pp* resuelto
resort complejo turístico
resource recurso
respect respetar
respectful respetuoso
respond responder
responsibility responsabilidad (*f*)
responsible responsable
rest demás (*m*), resto; *v* descansar
restaurant restaurante (*m*)
result resultado
resume currículum (*m*) vitae
return *adj* de regreso; *n* devolución (*f*); *v* regresar, volver (ue); **return something** devolver (ue); **returned** *pp* vuelto
review repasar
rice arroz (*m*); **throw flowers and rice** echarles flores y arroz
rich rico
riddle adivinanza
ride montar; **ride a bicycle** montar (en) bicicleta; **ride a horse** montar a caballo; **amusement park ride** atracción (*f*)
ridiculous ridículo
right *adj* derecho, correcto, cierto; *n* derecha; **all right** bueno, regular; **be right** tener razón; **right?** ¿verdad? **to (on) the right** a la derecha
ring anillo, sortija; **engagement ring** anillo de compromiso; **wedding ring** anillo de bodas
river río
road camino
roast *adj and n* asado
rob robar
robbery robo
robe bata
robot robot (*m*)
rock roca
role papel (*m*); **play the role** hacer el papel
roller coaster montaña rusa

romantic romántico

room cuarto, habitación (f); **double room** habitación doble; **large room** salón (m); **living room** sala; **room service** servicio de habitación; **single room** habitación sencilla

roommate compañero(-a) de cuarto

rose rosa

rough áspero; **rough draft** borrador (m)

round redondo

round-trip ticket billete (m) de ida y vuelta, boleto de ida y vuelta

route ruta

routine rutina

row fila

ruby rubí (m)

rug alfombra

ruins ruinas

rum ron (m)

run correr; **run away** huir; irse; **run errands** hacer diligencias; **run out of** acabar

runway pista

rural area campo

rural person campesino(-a)

Russian ruso

S

sad triste

sadness tristeza

safety deposit box caja de seguridad

said *pp* dicho

sail navegar; **sailboat** velero

saint santo; **patron saint** santo patrón (m)

salad ensalada; **salad oil** aceite (m); **tossed salad** ensalada mixta

salami salchichón (m)

salary sueldo

sale liquidación (f), rebaja, venta; **be on sale** estar en liquidación, estar en oferta; **sales representative** representante (m/f) de ventas; **sales zone** zona de ventas; **salesclerk** dependiente(-a), vendedor(-a)

salt sal (f); **salt shaker** salero; **salty** salado

same mismo; **the same thing** lo mismo

sand arena

sandals sandalias

sandwich bocadillo **(E)**, sándwich (m)

sapphire zafiro

satisfied *pp* satisfecho

satisfy satisfacer

Saturday sábado

sauce salsa

saucer platillo

sausage salchicha; **hard sausage** chorizo

save guardar; **save money** ahorrar

savings ahorros; **savings account** cuenta de ahorros; **savings book** libreta

say decir; **say good-bye** despedirse (i, i)

scanner escáner (m)

scar cicatriz (f)

scarce escaso

scare dar miedo a; **scared** asustado; **be scared of** tener miedo de; **easily scared** asustadizo; **get scared** asustarse

scarf bufanda

scene escena

schedule horario

scholarship beca

school escuela; **elementary school** escuela primaria; **high school** colegio, escuela secundaria, liceo; **school (university)** facultad (f)

science ciencia; **computer science** informática; **natural science** ciencias exactas; **political science** ciencias políticas; **social sciences** ciencias sociales

scientist científico(-a)

scold regañar

score puntaje (m)

scoreboard marcador (m)

scorn desdén (m)

Scotch escocés

screen pantalla

scrub fregar (ie)

sea mar (m)

seafood mariscos; **marinated seafood and fish** ceviche (m); **seafood cocktail** cóctel (m) de mariscos

seasick: get seasick marearse

season estación (f), temporada; **rainy season** época de lluvia

seat asiento

seatbelt cinturón (m) de seguridad; **fasten the seatbelt** abrocharse el cinturón de seguridad; **unfasten the seatbelt** desabrocharse el cinturón de seguridad

second segundo

secondary secundario

secretary secretario(-a)

section sección (f)

security seguridad (f); **security check** control (m) de seguridad

see ver; **see someone off** despedir (i, i)

seem parecer

seen *pp* visto

seize coger

self-portrait autorretrato

selfish egoísta

sell vender

semester semestre (m)

send enviar, mandar

sense sentido; **make sense** tener sentido; **sense of humor** sentido de humor

sentence frase (f), oración (f)

separate separar

September se(p)tiembre (m)

series serie (f)

serious serio

serve servir (i, i)

service servicio; **laundry service** servicio de lavandería; **room service** servicio de habitación

set off partir; **set the alarm** poner el despertador; **set the table** poner la mesa

seven siete; **seven hundred** setecientos

seventeen diecisiete
seventh séptimo
seventy setenta
several unos(-as)
shame pena
shampoo champú *(m)*
share compartir
shave afeitarse; **shaver** afeitadora; **shaving cream** crema de afeitar
she *subj pron* ella
shell concha
shelter refugio
shine brillar
shirt camisa; **tee-shirt** camiseta
shock choque *(m)*
shoe zapato; **athletic shoes** zapatos deportivos; **high-heeled shoes** zapatos de tacón; **low-heeled shoes** zapatos bajos; **shoe store** zapatería; **tennis shoes** zapatos de tenis; **wear shoes** calzar
shop *n* tienda; *v* hacer compras; **shopper** comprador(-a); **shopping** de compras; **go shopping** ir de compras; **shopping center** centro comercial; **shopping mall** centro comercial
short bajo, corto; **short time** rato
shorten acortar
shot inyección *(f)*; **give a shot** poner una inyección
shoulder hombro
shout gritar
show *n* espectáculo; *v* enseñar, mostrar; **game show** programa *(m)* de concursos
shower *n* ducha; *v* ducharse; **heavy rain shower** aguacero
shrimp camarones *(m)* **(A),** gambas **(E);** **shrimp cocktail** cóctel *(m)* de camarones
shy tímido
sick enfermo, malo (with *estar*); **feel sick** estar mal, sentirse (ie, i) mal; **get sick** enfermarse; **sickly** enfermizo
side lado
sidewalk acera
sign *n* aviso, cartel *(m)*, letrero, rótulo; *v* firmar
silk seda
silver plata
similar parecido, semejante, similar
similarity semejanza
simple sencillo
simplified simplificado
since como, desde, puesto que
sing cantar
singer cantante *(m/f)*
singular singular
sink fregadero; lavabo
sir don *(title of respect)*; señor
sirloin solomillo
sister hermana
sister-in-law cuñada
sit sentarse (ie)
situation situación *(f)*
six seis; **six hundred** seiscientos
sixteen dieciséis

sixth sexto
sixty sesenta
size número, talla; **wear size...** usar talla...
skate *n* patín *(m)*; *v* patinar; **ice skates** patines de hielo; **skating** patinaje *(m)*
sketch dibujo
ski *n* esquí *(m)*; *v* esquiar
skill aptitud *(f)*, destreza, habilidad *(f)*
skinny flaco
skirt falda
skyscraper rascacielos *(m)*
sleep *n* sueño; *v* dormir (ue, u); **be sleepy** tener sueño; **fall asleep** dormirse (ue, u); **heavy sleeper** dormilón(-ona)
slender delgado, esbelto
slight poco
slipper pantufla
slogan lema *(m)*
slowly despacio
small chico, pequeño
smart listo (with *ser*)
smell oler (ue)
smile sonreír (i, i)
smiling sonriente
smoke *v* fumar
smooth liso, suave
snack *n* merienda; *v* picar
snail caracol *(m)*
sneeze estornudar
snow *n* nieve *(f)*; *v* nevar (ie)
so tan; **so many** tantos(-as); **so much** tanto; **so-so** regular; **so that** de manera que, de modo que, para que
soap jabón *(m)*
soap opera telenovela
soccer fútbol *(m)*
sociable sociable
social sciences ciencias sociales
social worker asistente social *(m/f)*
sociology sociología
sock calcetín *(m)*
soft blando; débil *(sound)*; **soft drink** refresco; **software** software *(m)*
sole lenguado *(fish)*
solution solución *(f)*
solve solucionar; **solve crossword puzzles** hacer crucigramas
some algún, alguna, algunas, alguno, algunos; unas, unos
somehow de algún modo, de alguna manera
someone alguien, algún, alguna, alguno
something algo
sometimes a veces, algunas veces
son hijo
son-in-law yerno
soon pronto; **as soon as** así que, en cuanto, luego que, tan pronto como
sorry lamentar, sentir (ie, i)
sound sonar (ue)
soup caldo, sopa; **chilled vegetable soup** gazpacho; **soup spoon** cuchara

sour agrio
south sur (*m*)
space espacio
Spain España
Spanish castellano, español
special especial; **today's special** especialidad (*f*) del día; **specialized language** lenguaje (*m*)
specialist especialista (*m/f*)
specialty especialidad (*f*); **restaurant specialty** especialidad de la casa
specific específico
speech discurso
spend money gastar; **spend time** pasar
spicy condimentado, picante
splendid formidable
spoiled mimado
sponge esponja
sport *n* deporte (*m*); *adj* deportivo; **sports equipment** equipo deportivo; **sports field** campo deportivo
sprain torcerse (ue)
spring primavera
spy *v* espiar
square cuadrado; **main square** plaza mayor
squid calamar (*m*)
stadium estadio
stain mancha
stamp estampilla (**A**), sello (**E**)
stand *n* puesto; *v* estar de pie; **stand in line** hacer cola; **stand out** destacar
staple grapa; **staple remover** quitagrapas (*m*); **stapler** engrapadora, grapadora
starve morirse (ue, u) de hambre
state estado
station estación (*f*); **gas station** estación (*f*) de servicio, gasolinera; **police station** comisaría, cuartel (*m*) de policía
stay *n* estadía, estancia; *v* quedarse; **stay in a hotel** alojarse
steak bistec (*m*)
steel acero
stepbrother hermanastro
stepdaughter hijastra
stepfather padrastro
stepmother madrastra
stepsister hemanastra
stepson hijastro
steward aeromozo (**A**), camarero
stewardess aeromoza (**A**), azafata (**E**), camarera
stick palo; **hockey stick** palo de hockey
still aún, todavía
stitch *n* punto; *v* dar puntos
stock acción (*f*); **stock market** bolsa (de acciones)
stockbroker accionista (*m/f*)
stocking media
stomach estómago
stone piedra; **precious stone** piedra preciosa
stop parar
stopover escala; **make a stopover** hacer escala
store tienda; **store window** escaparate (*m*) (**A**), vitrina (**E**)

storm tormenta
story cuento
straight derecho; **go straight** seguir derecho; **straighten** arreglar
strange raro
strawberry fresa
street calle (*f*); **street block** cuadra (**A**), manzana (**E**)
strict estricto
strike huelga; **be on strike** estar de huelga
striped a rayas
strong fuerte
student *n* alumno(-a), estudiante (*m/f*); *adj* estudiantil; **exchange student** estudiante de intercambio; **student center** centro estudiantil; **student I.D. card** carnet (*m*) estudiantil
studious aplicado, estudioso
study *n* estudio; *v* estudiar
style moda; **be in style** estar de moda; **out of style** pasado de moda
subject asignatura, asunto, materia, sujeto
subscribe suscribirse
substitute sustituir
suburbs afueras (*f pl*)
subway metro
success éxito
such tal
suddenly de repente
suede ante (*m*)
suffer padecer, sufrir
sugar azúcar (*m*)
suggest sugerir (ie, i)
suggestion sugerencia
suit *n* traje (*m*); *v* caer bien; **bathing suit** traje de baño; **bullfighter's suit** traje de luces; **jogging suit** calentador (*m*) (**A**), chandal (*m*) (**E**)
suitable: be suitable convenir, caer bien
suitcase maleta; **pack a suitcase** hacer las maletas
summary resumen (*m*)
summer verano
sun sol (*m*); **It's sunny.** Hace sol; **sunbathe** tomar el sol; **sunglasses** gafas de sol; **suntan** bronceado
Sunday domingo
supermarket supermercado
supervisor supervisor(-a)
suppose suponer; **supposed** *pp* supuesto
sure seguro
surf the Internet navegar la red
surprise *n* milagro; sorpresa; *v* sorprender
surprising sorprendente
surround rodear
suspect sospechoso(-a)
sweat sudar
sweater suéter (*m*)
sweatsuit calentador (*m*) (**A**), chandal (*m*) (**E**)
sweep barrer
sweet dulce
sweetshop confitería
swim nadar; **swimming** natación (*f*); **swimming pool** piscina
swollen hinchado

sword espada
symbol símbolo
symptom síntoma (*m*)
syrup jarabe (*m*)

T

table mesa; **table place setting** cubierto
tablet pastilla
take agarrar, coger, llevar, tomar; **take a trip** hacer
un viaje; **take advantage** aprovechar; **take care**
of (oneself) cuidar(se), atender (ie); **take off** *v*
despegar; **take off (clothing)** desvestirse (i, i),
quitarse; **take out** sacar; **take time** tardar;
take a walk dar un paseo, pasearse; **takeoff** *n*
despegue (*m*)
tale cuento
talent talento
talk hablar
talkative hablador
tall alto
tan broncearse; **suntan** bronceado
tank tanque (*m*)
tape cinta; **utility tape** cinta adhesiva
tardy tarde; **be tardy** llegar tarde
task quehacer (*m*), tarea
taste *n* sabor (*m*); *v* probar (ue), saber; **in good**
(bad) taste de buen (mal) gusto
tax impuesto; **duty taxes** derechos de aduana;
tax evasion evasión (*f*) fiscal; **tax reform**
reforma fiscal
taxi taxi (*m*); **taxi stand** estación (*f*) de taxis
tea té (*m*); **tea shop** confitería; **have a tea party**
jugar a las visitas
teach enseñar
teacher maestro(-a), profesor(-a)
teaching enseñanza
team equipo
teaspoon cucharita
technical técnico
technological tecnológico
technology tecnología
tee-shirt camiseta
telegram telegrama (*m*)
telephone *adj* telefónico; *n* teléfono; **cellular**
telephone teléfono celular; **dial a telephone**
discar; **telephone operator** telefonista (*m/f*)
television televisión (*f*); **television set** televisor (*m*)
tell decir, contar (ue), recontar
temperature temperatura
temporary provisional
tempt provocar
ten diez
tennis tenis (*m*); **tennis court** cancha de tenis;
tennis shoes zapatos de tenis
tenth décimo
terminal terminal (*f*)
terrace terraza
terrific estupendo, formidable
territory territorio
test *n* prueba; *v* examinar, probar (ue)
textbook libro de texto, texto

thank *v* agradecer; **thank goodness** menos mal;
thank you gracias
that *adj* aquel, aquella, esa, ese; *pron* **that (one)**
aquél, aquélla, ésa, ése; *neuter pron* aquello, eso; *rel*
pron que; **that which** lo que
the el, los, la, las; *neuter def art* lo
theater teatro
their *poss adj* su, suyo
theirs *poss pron* suyo
them *dir obj pron* las, los; *indir obj pron* (*to, for*) les;
prep pron ellas, ellos
theme tema (*m*)
themselves *refl pron* se
then entonces, luego
there ahí, allá, allí; **there is (are)** hay; **there was**
(were) hubo, había
therefore por eso
thermometer termómetro
they *subj pron* ellas, ellos
these *adj* estas, estos; *pron* **these (ones)** éstas, éstos
thief ladrón(-ona)
thin delgado
thing cosa; **How are things?** ¿Qué tal?
think pensar (ie); **think of, about** pensar (ie) de,
pensar (ie) en
third tercer, tercero
thirst sed (*f*); **be thirsty** tener sed
thirteen trece
thirty treinta
this *adj* esta, este; *pron* **this (one)** ésta, éste;
neuter pron esto
those *adj* aquellas, aquellos, esas, esos; *pron* **those**
(ones) aquéllas, aquéllos, ésas, ésos
thousand mil
three tres; **three hundred** trescientos
throat garganta
through a través de, por, por medio de
throw lanzar, tirar
Thursday jueves (*m*)
thus así
ticket billete (*m*), boleto, entrada; **round-trip ticket**
billete de ida y vuelta, boleto de ida y vuelta;
ticket office boletería; **ticket window** taquilla,
ventanilla
tie *n* corbata; *v* atar
tight apretado; **be tight** apretar (ie)
time (in a series) vez (*f*); tiempo; **at the present**
time actualmente, hoy (en) día; **at times** a veces;
free time ratos libres; **from time to time** de vez
en cuando; **full-time** tiempo completo; **have a**
good time divertirse (ie, i), pasarlo bien; **on time**
a tiempo; **overtime** horas extra; **short time**
rato; **time of day** hora
timid tímido
tired cansado
to a
today hoy
toe dedo del pie
together junto; **get together** reunirse
toilet inodoro; **toilet paper** papel (*m*) higiénico
tolerate soportar

tomato tomate (*m*)
tomorrow mañana (*m*); **day after tomorrow** pasado mañana
tongue lengua
tonight esta noche
too también; **too much** demasiado
tooth diente (*m*); **toothbrush** cepillo de dientes; **toothpaste** pasta de dientes (**A**), pasta dentífrica (**E**)
topaz topacio
topic tema (*m*)
torn *pp* roto
torture torturar
tossed mixto
touch tocar
tourism turismo
tourist *adj* turístico; *n* turista (*m/f*); **tourist bureau** oficina de turismo; **tourist resort** complejo turístico
toward a
towel toalla
town pueblo
toy juguete (*m*)
track pista
trade comercio; **export trade** comercio de exportación; **import trade** comercio de importación
traffic tráfico; **traffic jam** embotellamiento; **traffic light** semáforo; **traffic report** parte (*m*) de las carreteras; **traffic sign** señal (*f*) de tráfico
train *n* tren (*m*); *v* entrenar, entrenarse; **train station** estación (*f*) de trenes
transaction negocio
translate traducir
transmit transmitir
trash basura
travel viajar; **travel agency** agencia de viajes; **traveler** *adj and n* viajero; **traveler's check** cheque (*m*) de viajero
treat tratar
treatment trato
tree árbol (*m*)
trip viaje (*m*); **take a trip** hacer un viaje
tripe soup menudo
triumph triunfar
trolley tranvía
truck camión (*m*)
true real, verdadero; **true?** ¿verdad?
trust *n* confianza; *v* confiar en
truth verdad (*f*)
try intentar, probar (ue), tratar de; **try on** probarse (ue)
Tuesday martes (*m*)
tuition matrícula
tuna atún (*m*)
turn doblar; **be the turn of** tocar; **turn around** dar vueltas; **turn on the television** poner la televisión; **turn out to be** salir; **turn... years old** cumplir... años
turnover empanada
turquoise turquesa
TV tele (*f*); **TV guide** guía de televisión

twelve doce
twenty veinte
twice dos veces
twins gemelos(-as)
two dos; **two hundred** doscientos
type *n* tipo; *v* escribir a máquina
typewriter máquina de escribir
typical típico

U
ugly feo
umbrella paraguas (*m*); **beach umbrella** sombrilla
umpire árbitro
uncle tío; **uncle and aunt** tíos
uncomfortable incómodo
under debajo de
underdevelopment subdesarrollo
undergo experimentar
underneath debajo de
understand comprender, entender (ie)
understanding *adj* comprensivo
uneasy intranquilo
unemployment desempleo
unexpected inesperado
unfasten desabrocharse
unforgettable inolvidable
unfortunate desafortunado, pobre
unfortunately por desgracia
unhappy infeliz
united unido
United States Estados Unidos; **USA** EE.UU.
unique único
university *adj* universitario; *n* universidad (*f*); **university professor** catedrático(-a)
unknown desconocido
unless a menos que
unmarried soltero
unoccupied desocupado
unorganized desorganizado
unpleasant desagradable
unsatisfied insatisfecho
untie desatar
until *prep* hasta; *conj* hasta que
upon al + *inf*
upper class clase (*f*) alta
us *dir obj pron* nos; *indir obj pron* (*to, for*) nos; *prep pron* nosotros(-as)
use *n* uso; *v* usar, utilizar
useful útil
useless inútil
usual de costumbre
utility tape cinta adhesiva

V
vacate desocupar
vacation vacaciones (*f pl*); **be on vacation** estar de vacaciones
vacuum pasar la aspiradora; **vacuum cleaner** aspiradora
valley valle (*m*)

value valor (m)
variation variación (f)
varied variado
variety variedad (f); **variety show** espectáculo de variedades
various varios
vary variar
VCR videocasetera
veal ternera
vegetable legumbre (f), vegetal (m); **vegetables** verduras
vehicle vehículo
veil velo
Venezuelan venezolano; **Venezuelan currency** bolívar (m)
verify averiguar, verificar
very muy, bien; –ísimo
vest chaleco
victory victoria
videotape videocinta
violence violencia
violent violento
violin violín (m)
visit visitar, llegar de visita
vitamin vitamina
vocabulary vocabulario
voice voz (f)
volleyball vólibol (m)
voltage voltaje (m)
volume volumen (m)
vomit v vomitar

W

wait for esperar
waiter, waitress camarero(-a) **(E)**; mesonero(-a) **(A)**
wake up despertarse (ie)
walk n paseo; v andar, caminar; **take a walk** dar un paseo, pasearse
wallet billetera, cartera
want desear, querer (ie)
war guerra
warm cálido
warn advertir (ie, i)
wash lavar; **wash one's hair** lavarse el pelo; **wash oneself** lavarse; **washing machine** lavadora
waste perder (ie)
wastebasket papelera
watch n reloj (m); **wristwatch** reloj de pulsera; v mirar
water n agua; v regar (ie); **mineral water** agua mineral, gaseosa; **waterproof** impermeable
waterfall catarata
waterski practicar el esquí acuático
waterskiing esquí (m) acuático
wave ola
wavy ondulado
way manera, modo, trayecto; **in this way** así; **no way** de ninguna manera, de ningún modo, ¡Qué va!; **some way** de alguna manera, de algún modo
we subj pron nosotros(-as)

weak débil, flojo
wear llevar, lucir; **wear shoes** calzar; **wear size …** usar talla…
weather tiempo; **What is the weather like?** ¿Qué tiempo hace?
wedding boda; **newlyweds** recién casados; **wedding cake** torta de bodas; **wedding ceremony** ceremonia de enlace; **wedding day** día (m) de la boda; **wedding gift** regalo de bodas; **wedding gown** traje (m) de novia; **wedding reception** cena; **wedding ring** anillo de bodas
Wednesday miércoles (m)
week semana
weekend fin (m) de semana
weigh pesar
weight n pesa; peso; v pesar; **gain weight** engordar; **lift weights** levantar pesas
welcome bienvenido; **You are welcome.** De nada., No hay de qué.
well bien, bueno; **well…** pues; **well-known** conocido
west oeste (m)
what lo que, ¿qué?, ¿cuál?; **¡What (a)… !** ¡Qué… !
wheat trigo
when cuando, ¿cuándo?; **even when** aun cuando
where donde, ¿dónde?, ¿adónde? (used with verbs of motion)
which que, ¿qué?; **that which** lo que; **which one(-s)?** ¿cuál(-es)?
while mientras; **a while** rato
white blanco
who que, ¿quién(-es)?
whose cuyo
why? ¿por qué?
wide ancho
widow viuda
widower viudo; **be widowed** quedar viudo(-a)
wife esposa
win ganar, triunfar
wind viento; **It's windy.** Hace viento.
window ventana; **small window** ventanilla; **store window** escaparate (m) **(E),** vitrina **(A)**; **ticket window** ventanilla
windsurfing windsurf (m); **windsurfing board** tabla de windsurf
wine vino; **wine list** lista de vinos; **wine punch** sangría; **red wine** vino tinto; **white wine** vino blanco
winter invierno
wish n gana; v querer (ie)
witch bruja
with con; **with me** conmigo; **with you** contigo
withdraw retirar, sacar
without prep sin, conj sin que
witness testigo (m/f)
witty: be witty tener gracia
woman mujer (f); **businesswoman** mujer de negocios
wonderful chévere, macanudo, magnífico, maravilloso
wood madera; **woods** bosque (m)
wool lana

word   palabra

word processor   procesador (*m*) de textos

work   *n* obra (*literary, artistic, or charitable*), labor (*f*),
  trabajo;   *v* funcionar, trabajar;   **day's work** jornal
  (*m*);   **hard-working** trabajador;   **work as** estar
  de + *profession*;   **work day** jornada;   **work of art**
  obra de arte

worker   obrero(-a);   **office worker** oficinista (*m/f*);
  social worker asistente (*m/f*) social

world-wide   mundial

World Wide Web   telaraña (**E**);   **surf the Web**
  navegar la red

worry (about)   preocuparse (de)

worse   peor;   **become worse** empeorar;   **the worst
  thing** lo peor

worth   valor (*m*);   **be worth** valer

wound   herida;   **wounded** herido

wrap   envolver (ue);   *pp* envuelto

wrestle   practicar la lucha libre

wrestling   lucha libre

wrinkled   arrugado

wrist   muñeca

wristwatch   reloj (*m*) de pulsera

write   escribir, redactar

written   *pp* escrito

Y

yacht   yate (*m*)

yard   jardín (*m*)

year   año;   **to be... years old** tener... años

yellow   amarillo

yes   sí

yesterday   ayer

yet   aún, todavía   **not yet** todavía no

you   *dir obj pron* la, lo (*form s*), las, los (*fam and form pl*),
  os (*fam pl* **E**), te (*fam s*);   *indir obj pron* (*to, for*) le (*form
  s*), les (*fam and form pl*), os (*fam pl* **E**), te (*fam s*);   *prep
  pron* ti (*fam s*), usted (*form s*) *abb* Ud., ustedes (*fam and
  form pl*) *abb* Uds., vosotros (*fam pl* **E**);   *subj pron* tú
  (*fam s*), usted (*form s*) *abb* Ud., ustedes (*fam and form
  pl*) *abb* Uds., vos (*fam s in Argentina, Uruguay, and parts
  of Hispanic America*), vosotros (*fam pl* **E**)

young   joven, pequeño

younger   menor

youngster   chaval(-a)

your   *poss adj* su (*form s, fam and form pl*), suyo (*form s,
  fam and form pl*), tu (*fam s*), tuyo (*fam s*), vuestro (*fam
  pl* **E**)

yours   *poss pron* suyo (*form s, fam and form pl*), tuyo
  (*fam s*), vuestro (*fam pl* **E**)

yourself   *refl pron* os, se, te

yourselves   *refl pron* os, se

youth   juventud (*f*);   **youth hostel** albergue (*m*)
  juvenil

Yugoslav   yugoslavo

Z

zero   cero

zip code   código postal, distrito postal

zoo   jardín (*m*) zoológico